CROSS OVER THE RIVER

D1160725

CROSS OVER THE RIVER

LIVES OF STONEWALL JACKSON

BRUCE WEIR BENIDT

iUniverse, Inc.
New York Lincoln Shanghai

NEW PORT RICHEY PUBLIC LIBRARY

Cross Over the River
Lives of Stonewall Jackson

All Rights Reserved © 2004 by Bruce Weir Benidt

No part of this book may be reproduced or transmitted in any form or by any means, graphic, electronic, or mechanical, including photocopying, recording, taping, or by any information storage retrieval system, without the written permission of the publisher.

iUniverse, Inc.

For information address:
iUniverse, Inc.
2021 Pine Lake Road, Suite 100
Lincoln, NE 68512
www.iuniverse.com

ISBN: 0-595-31756-1 (Pbk)
ISBN: 0-595-66420-2 (Cloth)

Printed in the United States of America

How has he, the most unromantic of great men,
become the hero of a living romance?

—Rev. Robert L. Dabney, Jackson's chief of staff

Dead is the Man whose Cause is dead,
Vainly he died and set his seal—
Stonewall!
Earnest in error, as we feel;
True to the thing he deemed was due,
True as John Brown or steel.

—Herman Melville

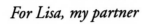

For Lisa, my partner

CONTENTS

Part One   *The Hill* 1

Part Two   *The Valley* 13

Part Three *The Wilderness* 203

Part Four   *The Return* 345

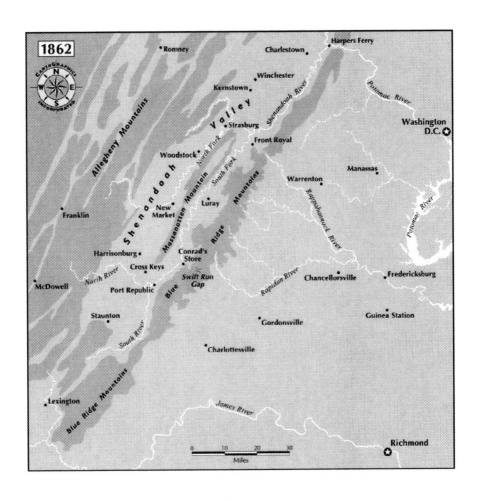

CARTOGRAPHICS INCORPORATED

1862

Romney • Charlestown • Harpers Ferry •

Winchester •

Kernstown •

Shenandoah River

Allegheny Mountains

Shenandoah Strasburg •

Woodstock • Front Royal •

North Fork

Valley

Warrenton • Manassas •

Washington D.C. ◉

Potomac River

Franklin • New Market • *Massanutten Mountain* Luray • *South Fork* *Blue Ridge Mountains* *Rappahannock River*

Harrisonburg • Conrad's Store •

Cross Keys • *North River* Swift Run Gap

McDowell • Port Republic • *Blue* Chancellorsville • Fredericksburg •

Rapidan River

Staunton • *South River* Gordonsville • Guinea Station •

Charlottesville •

Potomac River

James River

Lexington •

Richmond ◉

0   10   20   30
Miles

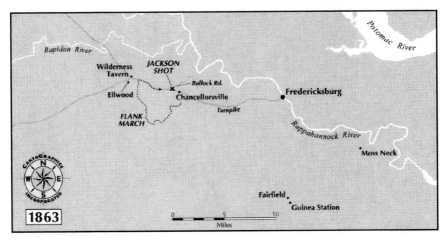

CARTOGRAPHICS INCORPORATED

Potomac River

Rapidan River

Wilderness Tavern • *JACKSON SHOT*

Ellwood • *Bullock Rd.*
✗ Chancellorsville • Fredericksburg ●

FLANK MARCH *Turnpike*

Rappahannock River

Moss Neck •

Fairfield •
Guinea Station •

1863

0   5   10
Miles

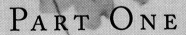

PART ONE

THE HILL

"There stands Jackson like a stone wall. Rally around the Virginians."

—General Barnard Bee

Manassas, July 21, 1861—Confederate Army

In a little stretch of woods above Bull Run, birds chittered brightly. In Holkum's Branch, a tiny rill of water that ran down through the woods to Bull Run, frogs called to one another in high trills, the incessant push of biology bulging to reproduce itself. The bell of a cow clinked, and the distant bleating of sheep floated in from pastureland behind the woods at Lewis Ford. It was warm this July day, and fat sluggish breezes only now and then stirred the poplar and beech leaves and swished through the occasional tall pine.

Morning's first light fell through the trees, broken into fragments by the branches. Leaves hit by the sun were an iridescent yellow-green, those in the shade a soft rich emerald. You could see maybe fifty yards, but your sight was scattered by the thousands of small thin tree trunks. You couldn't run a straight line here if all the Yankees in the north were chasing you. But a little trace ran through the woods from the Lewis farm to the high open fields of Henry Hill near Manassas. From the trace you could see the fallen trees off to the side, some leaning against trees still living, others broken on the ground. Grey squirrels used the fallen trunks for highways, racing along, sending out their clicking screech at any movement in the woods.

It was a beautiful place. Peaceful for only a few moments longer.

From the northeast, a sound came that fit with nothing in the woods. A squirrel stood up on its hind legs, tucked its front paws to its breast, and stopped breathing. The frogs went silent.

A cannon thumped. A few rifles crackled, without pattern. Yelling voices could be barely heard.

Federal troops were pushing across a stone bridge over Bull Run. A battle— the battle—long awaited, might now be coming.

But the patch of woods between the Lewis and Henry places felt no human tread yet. As an hour, then two passed, the sound of firing faded. Birds began to bounce again among the branches. Locusts sawed away high in the trees. Dogs barked down by the Lewis farm. The sunlight poured through the trees at a straighter angle, illuminating the brush on the forest floor. The business of the woods—young plants pushing through the mast of leaves and twigs on the ground, mushrooms spreading on dead wood, small blue flowers opening to the light, beetles rooting into fallen bark—went on. Trees sucked water from the earth and pulled it up their trunks to feed the leaves fluttering in the sun.

Then, this time from the northwest, the tha-rump tha-rump of cannon came again.

The noise started small, a few intrusions into the steady hum and chatter of the woods. Rippling water in Holkum's Branch could still be heard.

But the noise grew. The sound of the sharp reports of individual rifles winged between the trees like single raindrops when the rain is not quite here. Then, in a little time, the single shots flowed together into a stronger sound. It was now like a freshening wind at the edge of a storm starting to push against the trees.

Blasts of cannon began, both fairly close to the woods and farther away across the hills. In minutes, the shots rolled together into a rough-edged thunder. Rifle fire was now coming in waves. The sheets of sound gathered into a mass that heaved into the woods like a solid front of storm clouds sweeping the ground. The normal morning sounds of the forest were swept away before this rising storm.

The woods and its creatures seemed to crouch against the pressure. The sound was a gushing force now, hitting the animals' ears and slamming against their nerves. It sailed through the woods like the darkness of an eclipse, overwhelming hundreds of trees each rushing second.

The sound was now a howling gale, and the woods went under.

On the wagon track from Lewis Ford, men were now moving among the tree trunks, toward the noise. The marchers leaned forward as they trudged, the bitter torrents of sound pushing at them. They were sent to plug the wavering lines of Confederates being ripped apart on Henry Hill.

The men kept coming, climbing steadily up the wooded hill, sheltered still from the battle itself but not from its fearful din. The noise slammed at their hearts, pumping up the speed of their breathing, making the sweat flow under their grey wool.

Months of bluster, endless talk, drilling in peaceful meadows, and now it had come to this. They were going in. Into the storm.

The trees thinned ahead. The marchers could see men moving in a haze of smoke. Some were running, riders were galloping among them, cannon were bucking back, digging their tails into the sod with their recoil. The men in the woods kept moving, urged now to a trot by their officers. Swords flashed in the sun. Bayonets sparked in the light.

A few more steps, driven through fear by obedience, and the troops of Thomas Jonathan Jackson came out from the woods and walked into the fire, into their fate, into their fame.

Port Republic, July 21, 1861

Far up the Shenandoah Valley of Virginia from Manassas, William Sutton felt his life coming apart. His wife, Martha, had died a month ago, fast, of a fever that knocked her down and burned her away. That beautiful dark hair, once lush as summer fields, knotted and soaked around her tossing head, her face sunken onto the bones of her skull, her eyes rolling from side to side, trying to find something beyond the pain and the falling, the fading.

Since burying Martha, he'd worked the fields of his small farm near Port Republic in the Shenandoah Valley of Virginia, but with no reason, no spirit. He plodded through the days like a mule, sunk into his bed at dark until consciousness disappeared, rose in the morning because he could think of nothing else to do.

And now a war. Unthinkable. In his own country. In his own state. Not a hundred miles to the north.

The United States of America had lasted only 85 years. A bright, powerful idea, now guttering like a candle stub.

This voluntary union had been fraying for two decades. Over slavery, most said, and territorial expansion, states' rights. Seemed to Sutton to be mostly over the national government telling the states of the South how to live, how to work and sell goods, and how to govern.

And now the break had come. Troops of the Federal government had dragged their iron-wheeled cannon into the soft rolling hills of Virginia. And there would be years of horror and tumult like no one had never known. Sutton had heard boasters at the mill in town say the South would beat the Yankees in one good battle. He didn't think so. Sutton felt a weight inside him, filling his limbs, his chest, with lead. It had settled on him when Martha fell ill, and had only gotten heavier.

After the Southern states seceded one by one, there'd been some shooting along the Potomac, the border between Virginia and Maryland, between North and South. Sutton had read about troops and civilians killed in Baltimore riots as Northern soldiers tried to pass through that town to protect Washington City. Fort Sumter had fallen, nearly buried in Southern cannon balls. Minor skirmishes had occurred here and there, killing numbers small enough to remember.

Now, this hot July, the Federal army of 33,000 men was camped about 30 miles southwest of Washington, on the plains of Manassas by a creek called Bull Run. An invasion, Sutton's neighbors called it. And the South was rising. And Sutton feared for everything he'd ever known.

Coiled, unsure, frightened and excited, the two armies at Manassas flowed slowly over the green hills, searching for the right position from which to strike. From which to start this war in earnest, and with a killing blow end it.

But it wouldn't end. Somehow Sutton was sure. This war would empty saddles and tablesides and farms and stores and swings on sweet summer front porches from Florida to Maine and through Texas and Minnesota to the Pacific.

It was all coming apart. The first grand, awful battle was beginning.

Long before the shooting started at Manassas, Sutton had heard about Thomas Jackson. The son of one of Sutton's neighbors was a student of Jackson's, before the war, at the Virginia Military Institute in Lexington, farther up the Valley southwest of Sutton's farm.

Jackson, a Mexican War veteran and a rigid Presbyterian, was not a very good teacher, from what the neighbor said. He lectured from memory, with little spontaneity, as if he could drive knowledge into students like a drover with a stick. He was socially clumsy and stiff. In the quiet town of Lexington he was an oddity, but an earnest man who liked to garden and serve his church.

But three months ago this professor of natural and experimental philosophy had seen his VMI cadets ready to shoot fellow townspeople dead in a fight over which flag, United States or Confederate States, would fly over the courthouse. The students were eager and ready—thought they were ready—for war.

Jackson, so Sutton read in the newspaper, had quieted the cadets by doing something very rare for him—standing in a crowd and making a speech. It was short.

"Soldiers, when they make speeches, should say few words and speak them to the point. And as for me, I am no hand at making speeches anyhow," Jackson had said.

"The time for war has not yet come, but it will come and that soon. And when it does come," he'd continued in a penetrating voice that held each cadet it touched with its intense determination, "my advice is to draw the sword and throw away the scabbard." The boys had cheered.

And now Jackson had taken his West Point training and his Mexican War experience and some of those boys to Manassas to fight the Yankees.

"Dear God," William Sutton said aloud as he stood in his field, behind the small, two-room house with a sloping porch across the front. He had started for the tool shed, then walked past it, stopped, and looked north to the ragged end of the Massanutten Mountain that split the Shenandoah Valley lengthwise. He was thinking again of the battle near at hand.

Sutton was a tall, thin man of 30 with sandy hair and a narrow, fine-featured face. He had almost no eyebrows, the hair was so pale, and his eyes were a silvery blue that made his gaze a light touch on another person. He listened a lot, rather than talking much, but he always kept his eyes trained on the person talking. His shoulders were generally rolled forward from so much labor near the earth, and while his legs were thin his forearms were taut with muscle and his hands were large and nicked from years of repairing tools and machinery. His hair swept up in two arcs from the middle of his forehead and fell carelessly before his eyes, and he'd flick it aside with a flip of his head.

He raised corn, wheat and sorghum and kept some pigs, chickens and two cows. He'd loved working his farm, when he'd had a wife to share the work and the peaceful moments. This place was so pretty, where meandering streams came together amid pastures and forests to form the South Fork of the Shenandoah River.

But now he didn't know why he was here. There seemed no purpose. He and Martha had lived a quiet life, had some good friends down the road and a few in town. They'd played cards of an evening in another couple's kitchen, gone to church most Sundays and to Bible study some Wednesdays. They'd loved the peaceful Valley, welcomed each season's changes, and hoped for children that hadn't come. But they hadn't really minded. Their life had been calm and full. After a light midday lunch, they'd often sit on the little porch and read to one another, from the Bible, a newspaper, a book. Often they'd nap, sometimes stretched out next to each other right there on the porch floor.

Sutton looked at the wooded slopes of the mountain, slipped his eyes over the treeline by the river, over the fields around him, and rested his gaze on the empty house.

The war was near. Some day it might come here, hard as that was to imagine. The leaden feeling throughout his whole body made it seem impossible to live, to move, as he always had.

He would go to the war. He would join Jackson's troops. He hadn't enlisted at the beginning, when his wife was still here. But his old life was over, lost. If he couldn't find a new life in the war, at least he could stop staring at the ruins of what was. He knew he should accept what God sent for good or ill, but he'd rather do it where he didn't have to think or feel so much. He felt a faint sense of duty, a stronger desire to defend Virginia, but he also just felt empty.

He walked back to the house to gather a few things, a little food, to take along. He would see what this Thomas Jackson was like, and he would cast his lot with him.

They would become linked, Jackson and Sutton, by a gravity, a magnetism. This farmer turned footsoldier and this teacher turned general would change the course of history. Across muddy roads and burgeoning fields ripped to silage by bullets and cannon balls, and through a troubled peace after war, these two would be linked even beyond death.

Manassas, July 21, 1861—Confederate Army

James Sparrow sat in the shattered field and tried to get his right knee to bend. It had been hit with a scrap from an exploding cannon ball—the flat side, thank God, not the jagged edge, or he might be bleeding to death.

He was on top of Henry Hill at Manassas. He had helped turn back the Federals. He had seen Jackson make his stand. He'd made it with Jackson, been part of the "stone wall" of men that would give Jackson the most famous nickname in the war, in the world.

And now Sparrow couldn't stand. He let go of his leg and leaned back on his elbows, his hefty midsection a mound under his shirt, his tangled beard spilling over his collar. He stank, of sweat soaking his cotton shirt and woolen jacket, of unwashed hair and body, of spittle and snot in his beard. The smell was smooth because it was always there, and sharp when his nose came close to his armpit or pants, but he'd gotten used to it. His elbows rested in raw dirt, the earth torn open by a Federal shell. Sparrow's face was broad, his cheeks full above the dark beard, his eyes a warm brown, his dark hair starting to recede. He thought a little rest would help his leg.

The battle had been ferocious. Jackson, in command of 2,600 troops, had been called in from the Shenandoah Valley to help General Pierre Beauregard and his 22,000 men take the attack of General Irwin McDowell's Federal army. Jackson's troops had marched from the Confederate right all the way to the left when Federals almost flanked the line. The Confederates had been blown off Matthews Hill and up Henry Hill, where Jackson aligned his troops behind three Virginia cannon with only one shell left each.

Sparrow had been down on his belly breathing hard and waiting for the next Federal wave when an officer came to Jackson and said, "General, the day is going against us." Jackson, on his horse a few paces behind Sparrow and the front line, calmly looked down and said, "If you think so, sir, you had better not say anything about it." That had scared the hell out of Sparrow, but then he'd looked at Jackson and seen the man's steady resolve. Sparrow saw no fear in Jackson's expression, only an eager watchfulness. Sparrow didn't understand how the general could be so calm, sit in his saddle so still; but he wanted to be near the man. Maybe borrow some of Jackson's steel.

And steel was the order from Jackson. Another officer, as the Federals flooded up Henry Hill, called out, "General, they are beating us back," and Jackson replied through thinned tight lips, "Sir, we'll give them the bayonet." Jackson had placed Sparrow and his other few hundred troops just behind the crest of the hill, where the Federals couldn't see them and where the cannon, their ammunition now replenished, could fire from the crest and be reloaded after their recoil below the ridge in the shelter of the hill. Sparrow saw that Jackson's quick eye measured each inch of ground, each angle. In the flying chaos of the fight, with the noises of running feet and grunting men and yelling officers and the constant pap-pap-pap of gunfire and the faah-hroooom of exploding shells and the air ripping open as metal flew overhead, Sparrow had always wanted to know where Jackson was, had always wanted to be close enough to know the commander was still alive and beaming his will against those Federals trying to push up the hill.

In the middle of it all, Sparrow, his ramrod half out of his musket barrel, dirt flying around him, noise pounding down on him, had stopped on his knees and looked at Jackson. Mounted, only a few feet behind his infantry line, Jackson was exposed to the Federal fire.

He sat quietly. All alone amid the men and the turmoil. His back straight. His head turning slowly, gaze flaring out like a lighthouse beam. His horse backed a step, Jackson's wrist flicked the rein and the horse stopped. The skin was drawn tight around his eyes—pale grey-blue eyes that seemed kindled with light. His lips formed a straight line, his jaw thrust forward, his dark beard curled off his jaw line and down his neck. His face was absolutely calm. Only through the eyes, when they swept the line where Sparrow knelt, could Sparrow see the sparks, the living fire that drove this man. Intelligence, alertness like a wolf's, rock-hard conviction and some molten, pressured rising could all be glimpsed behind those eyes.

A shell burst behind Jackson, cascading dirt on the infantry line, whistling fragments of shrapnel zipping through the air. A sudden cry of pain to Sparrow's right. "Steady, men, steady. All's well." The words, strong and clear, in the middle range high-pitched enough to carry but not so high as to show fear, were thrust into the air by Jackson. And though every man could see right in front of him that nothing at all was well, the words reached and soothed dozens of them up and down the line.

Sparrow kept looking for another moment. Jackson's blue uniform jacket made him look incongruously like a Federal. It was the uniform of the VMI, which Jackson had worn on the artillery field there in gunnery practice. Although the jacket was spotted dark with sweat from the heat and the hard ride to the battlefield, Jackson showed no more agitation now than he might have in Lexington on a sunny afternoon of maneuvers with cadets. Still. Firm. Determined as fate. A cap was pulled down on his broad forehead but Sparrow could see his eyebrows lift and pinch together slightly as another man up the line shrieked when part of the ambient metal storm tore into him. The only emotion Sparrow had seen from Jackson, this quick moment of sympathetic pain, then the brows lowered again and the eyes focused front.

Jackson bent forward at the waist and the horse took short steps ahead. Jackson leaned out of the saddle, looking down, to make sure he didn't trample any prone soldier on the line. His left hand was wrapped in a kerchief stained bright red, a finger hit by a bullet when he'd earlier raised the hand into the air, perhaps in prayer. His eye touched Sparrow's for a moment, stopped, locked, and passed amid the furor a simple message of duty, of what must be. Sparrow nodded and turned toward the firing again. To his side, Jackson raised himself in his stirrups, looked ahead, then to both sides and behind, then turned his horse to the right and moved up the line toward the trees beside the field, saying, "Steady, men, we'll give them the bayonet when they come." And he rode slowly, steady himself, a rock for his men to build a wall with.

At the height of the battle, as the Federal waves crashed up the hill, South Carolina General Barnard Bee had cried out to his men, "There stands Jackson like a stone wall. Let us determine to die here, and we will conquer."

The determination did it. Jackson's perfect placement of his men did it. The surprise that ripped through the Federals as men rose out of the cropped field in front of them and slammed fire and screaming metal balls in their faces did it. The will that Thomas Jackson telegraphed through the roiled air to his men did it. And the Federals fell back down Henry Hill.

General Bee was shot and killed shortly after naming Jackson for all eternity.

At least an hour had passed, and now Sparrow, still on the ground, untied the white strip of cloth Jackson had had all his soldiers tie around their arms or hats so they could identify each other in the maelstrom. The men had thought it strange, like a secret society, but when the fighting broke open it was indeed hard to tell who was friend and who was foe. Shooting one's comrades was a horror that stayed with the men of what was now called the Stonewall Brigade.

The Federals had skedaddled, running in ragged groups all the way back to Washington. The Confederate troops chased them a ways, but victory had disorganized them almost as badly as defeat had unraveled the Union army, and the pursuit flagged. The battle was over. The war far from it.

Sparrow, lying on his back, stretched his head and looked, upside down, through the wheels of a Confederate cannon. Quiet now, the cannon barrel still radiated heat, bending the air around it in ripples. The metal looked so hard, the surface dark and pocked. It was such a simple machine, Sparrow thought. Just a huge gun barrel on wheels. Its round mouth, maybe three inches across, empty now. Not long ago it spouted flame and metal. My God how could anyone stand before that? But now all was peaceful—through the spokes of the cannon's wheel Sparrow saw the sky a light blue, clouds flowing across, a hot beautiful summer day.

He closed his eyes. Rest would help his knee. It was swollen, but he could feel his kneecap was still whole. Nothing broken. Rest. That was it.

He would need his strength.

Jackson's brigade stayed on Henry Hill that evening as a light rain came with the darkness. Jackson himself rode to a field hospital in the rear to have his bleeding hand looked after. The first doctors he saw said the wounded middle finger would have to be cut off, but Dr. Hunter McGuire, the brigade surgeon, said he could save it with a splint and a sling. "Do what you think best," Jackson told him. The next time McGuire would tend a wound on Jackson, things wouldn't go so easy.

Confederate President Jefferson Davis, having ridden to the battlefield, unable to stay away as the fate of the new country was decided, found Jackson in the hospital tent that evening. Davis commiserated with Jackson on his wound. Jackson immediately offered to pursue the fleeing Federals and take Washington with 10,000 men. But there would be no pursuit.

Jackson's instinct was always to hit the enemy and keep hitting. He knew those blustering Southerners safe in their homes who thought one battle would end the war were fools. Assault the enemy where they're weakest or where they don't expect an assault, and don't let up. That was Jackson's battle plan, always. "We must give them no time to think," he'd told his wife, Anna. "We must bewilder them and keep them bewildered. Our fighting must be sharp, impetuous, continuous. We cannot stand a long war."

Jackson knew. He'd fought in Mexico 15 years before. Avid for glory, he'd shown almost foolhardy courage and been promoted to major. He knew about war to the hilt. He'd tasted the cannon smoke, seen the torn bodies, flies on dead eyes. He'd seen blood-soaked clothing and ground enough for a lifetime.

He would see more.

Throughout the coming hard years of war, Jackson would be called everything from a genius to a fool. The views people would have of this man, from the marching ranks to the command tents on both Federal and Confederate sides, would form a kaleidoscope of contradictions.

He was a hard man to know. Few got close to him. He would craft brilliant successes on the battlefields and stumbling failures. No commander would draw more complaining, and more loyalty, from his troops. And no one would have a greater military and psychological impact on this bloody and terrible contest.

He was an unmovable force, yet the swiftest-moving of all. Cruel, passionate, unbending, kind. Who he was exactly—what demons drove him, what angels— was difficult to pin down. A man of few and terse words, his deeds spoke with the resounding echoes of cannon thunder. His shadow, his reputation, seen in quickly shifting forms, would sweep with a force far stronger than his armies over every corner of this heartbreaking war.

On this gentle hilltop near Manassas, lit up this day for all history by fate or chance or his own fires within, Thomas "Stonewall" Jackson became a legend. In two years, he would become almost a saint.

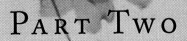

PART TWO

THE VALLEY

"Daughter of the Stars"

—Native American name for the Shenandoah Valley

Richmond, Feb. 3, 1862

"He's resigned."

"WHAT?"

"Resigned. Executed the order, prompt as can be, pulled Loring in from the mountains, and then he resigned. R E S I G N E D."

"He's mad," said Captain Rathburne.

"Well, he's clearly angry, is that the same thing?" Alexander Boteler had come to know Thomas Jackson only in the last few months. From what he'd seen, he thought Jackson could do righteous indignation better than just about anyone. And do a fine job on proud, and stubborn, and maybe cross into petulant on not so rare occasion. This occasion.

"What happened?" Michael Rathburne asked, holding a crystal glass of sherry a few inches from his open mouth.

"Oh, Judah Benjamin sent him an order, told him to get Loring out of Romney because the Federals looked like they were heading for him. Jackson says that's exactly why he put Loring there, of course, to stop the Federals from taking northwest Virginia. He worked like hell to get Loring's troops up there through the snow and ice, and Benjamin in his comfortable Richmond office said bring him back." Boteler was worried. Losing Jackson, the hero of Manassas, the Stonewall on Henry Hill, would be a disaster to public morale. The Confederacy needed a hero, now they had one, and now because of the secretary of war's order, the hero wanted to go back to the Virginia Military Institute and be a mediocre teacher again, boring young men to death instead of leading them into enemy fire.

"How can we have such a mess so early in this war?" Boteler said as he dropped into a chair by the empty fireplace in his office in Richmond. It was a chilly February evening, but Boteler didn't have the patience to build a fire.

Boteler was a colonel, but he was also a representative from the Shenandoah Valley in the Confederate Congress. He had represented Virginia in the Federal Congress before his state seceded. Now he had before him as delicate a matter of diplomacy and politics as anything he'd faced in the legislature. He had to handle the same forces that always got in the way of doing something useful—pride, arrogance, ignorance, certitude.

After Manassas, Jackson had been given command of the Shenandoah Valley District, and General William W. Loring's force had been assigned to augment his brigade of Valley men. Jackson had marched the army up into the mountains northwest of Winchester. Loring's men had hated it as they floundered in the winter mud and ice. They called Jackson "that crazy general." They hissed and swore at him as he rode by, prompting fistfights with men of the Stonewall Brigade who reserved to themselves the right to curse their general. Jackson became furious with Loring for not marching his men hard enough and fast enough, couldn't understand why he was letting them rest so much.

Jackson had grown up in this rugged mountainous country northwest of the head of the Shenandoah Valley, and he wanted to protect it. The people of the Valley had been reassured when one of their own was assigned to defend their homes. But Jackson also saw the strategic value of this countryside, as George Washington had during the French and Indian War. If the Federals held it, they could sweep down into the Shenandoah Valley and hold the transportation routes that led deep into Virginia. They could also keep the Valley from providing the food and forage the Confederate armies would need the following summer. Jackson wanted to protect the Valley from the western side, from the passes in the rugged Allegheny Mountains, again as Washington had done. It didn't matter to him how hard it might be; it had to be done, and he would do it.

But Jackson saw more when he looked at northwest Virginia. He saw the possibility of cutting off the railroads and canals that brought coal and food and supplies from Pennsylvania and Ohio and the west through Maryland and Virginia to the Federal armies threatening his home state. And, always aggressive, he also saw a staging platform for an invasion of the North. He'd wanted to cross the Potomac and march on Washington after the fight at Bull Run, and he hadn't given up the idea. This time he was thinking of pushing north and destroying some of the industrial might of Pennsylvania. And from the perspective of the nervous politicians and generals in Washington, D.C., trying to hold the country together as they'd known it, the Shenandoah Valley looked like a dagger aimed at the Federal capital and the Union's survival. Running from the southwest to the northeast, the Valley led straight to Washington's flank and rear. The specter of Confederate troops moving down the Valley toward Washington brought fear beyond reason to the Union men.

But the Romney expedition had been a reprise of Napoleon's campaign for Moscow. Men froze, horses slipped and shattered their legs, wagons tumbled and broke. More than two thousand men fell ill in the harsh winter weather; hundreds died of pneumonia. Loring's men had been close to open mutiny. When the

Federals withdrew without a battle, Jackson ordered his own Stonewall Brigade back to the relative comfort of Winchester in the Valley, while leaving Loring's men in the frozen mountains, and that had been more than enough for Loring and his officers. They sent a petition to the Confederate War department to bring them in from what they considered worse than a fool's errand. Wires were pulled, letters were sent, and the secretary of war, Judah Benjamin, ordered Jackson to bring Loring out of the mountains. Jackson complied, then immediately resigned over the second-guessing.

"What did Jackson say to Benjamin?" Rathburne asked. Boteler reached over to a table, grabbed a stack of papers, and read, "'With such interference in my command I cannot expect to be of much service in the field.'" Boteler dropped the hand holding the paper into his lap. "Jackson never was one to mince words. Direct, I'd say. His point is damned clear. I doubt Benjamin's used to that." He put his left hand to his face, rubbing his eyebrows. "He asks to be reassigned to the VMI, and if that can't be done, he wants to resign."

Boteler riffled through the papers in his lap, lifting a letter to him from Jackson, a reply to one of Boteler's asking him to reconsider. "Here's what he wrote to me—'I don't see how I can be of any service in the field, so long as that principle which has been applied to me—of undoing in the War Department, what has been done in the field—is adhered to.'" Boteler looked around the room, an elegant office of dark wood and flowered Parisian wallpaper. It seemed battles were being fought in rooms like this as much as in the mountains and fields beyond Richmond.

"If Jackson's talking about principle, he won't move. How can I untangle this one?" he asked the dark room.

Rathburne stood, went to the basket by the fireplace and started piling wood on the andirons. He said as he worked the logs into place, "Go talk to him. He'll listen to reason. We can't lose Jackson, you've got to make him see that. What does Benjamin say?"

"He doesn't know what to do. He's asked Governor Letcher to get Jackson back in line. I don't know if that will help. I think Jackson only listens to his inner voice of rectitude."

"That's a pretty strong voice, from what I hear. Touchy, isn't he?"

"I wouldn't say touchy," Boteler said, standing, walking, thinking as he spoke. "He's not a hothead. He's just damned sure of himself. And sure a civilian hundreds of miles away, and a lawyer like Benjamin at that, shouldn't be making command decisions." The congressman shook his head. "Jackson believes he has to make a point. Not just to get Benjamin and Davis off his back, but to keep them from interfering with any general's command decisions. He's doing this as a protest, says there's no better way he can serve his country. That means it's bigger than him." He made a fist of his left hand, then opened it, waved it at nothing, then let it drop. "And that means he won't back down. Damn, damn."

The congressman had met Jackson in the fall, when the general took over the Valley command. He'd called on Jackson in his Winchester headquarters, not far from Boteler's farm near Shepherdstown. They talked about the defense of the Valley they both loved, about the strategic importance of northwest Virginia. Boteler was worried about the border, about his Valley, and he wanted to know the man who would defend it.

He had seen Jackson arrest men for sneaking out of camp to visit their families. He had seen the steel, the unbending rectitude. It wasn't Boteler's own style, and it surely didn't warm you to the man. But Boteler had seen this forcefulness change ragged militia into men who now took their job seriously and showed some measure of skill at it. Boteler had been intrigued, saw promise in Jackson, and became his advocate in pressing Richmond for reinforcements.

"You don't think he's just blown his stack, and he'll cool down and do what he's told?"

"Jackson doesn't lose his temper. I have a letter here from Rev. James Graham, the minister Jackson and his wife have been staying with in his winter quarters in Winchester. Said Jackson got to his headquarters in the morning, found the dispatch from Benjamin, obeyed it, quit, and came back for breakfast calm as can be. No steam, no vituperation, that's not Jackson's style. Just said he and Mrs. Jackson would be returning to Lexington. Calm as asking for toast." Boteler had to smile, had really to admire as a politician this almost unnatural composure of Jackson's. It was so powerful. "Explained the point of principle to Graham in a perfectly even voice. Graham says the troops are exasperated, the whole town is in a ferment, but Jackson is the only man in Winchester right now who's perfectly self-collected and serene. The only man in Virginia, I'd say."

Boteler shook his head. "No, this isn't pique. Jackson, he's, he's…a strange mix of ice and passion, that man. He doesn't run his mouth, although I hear he tamed the VMI cadets who got all exercised and wanted to charge into the field before Virginia seceded by speaking just a few calm words in an assembly. He said wait for the right moment, and then draw your swords and never put them back in the scabbards until the fight is over. He calculates his times and places very fine, I'd say. He sees beyond the immediate moves, and wants to let the whole thing play out." The colonel came over to the fire Rathburne had gotten to catch. "His trouble, major, is he doesn't let people know his plans, so they don't see what he's aiming at, only the immediate move. He doesn't bring people in, get them on his side."

"You like Jackson, don't you?" Rathburne said, looking up. "I mean you feel for him, you respect him, don't you?"

"I don't know him that well. He's a very unusual man, Michael. He doesn't trust many people, and that's a failing in this business."

"It helps him keep secrecy, that's damn valuable," Rathburne said. "Most of our generals' plans show up in the *New York Tribune* before the first boot hits the trail."

"Yes, that's a fact. But look at Sidney Johnston, Joe Johnston, Beauregard. They put their trust in lieutenants like Jackson, and it leaves them free to be effective. Jackson benefits from that, but I don't think he understands how it works, he doesn't give the same trust to his own men."

"Well, perhaps he doesn't have a Jackson under him like Joe Johnston does," Rathburne said.

Boteler swung his gaze to the captain, paused as if measuring what he said, and nodded his head. "True. That's true. But there aren't many like him. None, I'd say, at least in the South.

"I don't know if I like him, Michael, and I don't think that matters, really," Boteler said, picking up the earlier question. "But he's…compelling. He's honest. He doesn't play for glory. He doesn't spend all his time telling Lee and Davis in Richmond about his qualities and successes. He just goes about his job and gets it done. You know, he's humble in a funny way. Sure of himself as if he were marching with God, but he doesn't seem to puff himself up. He seldom talks about himself at all, in my experience. He'll talk about his men, he'll talk strategy and pull the lessons from old campaigns and wars all night, but he doesn't put himself on the stage."

"It sounds, sir, like we can't spare a man like that. Go see him. He can't go back to the VMI and sit out the war."

"No," Boteler said, "and we can't lose the war in Richmond. Every officer in this army has friends at the capital, and they'll all be telegraphing somebody and petitioning somebody to get their way, to get this man put aside or that man promoted. They'll be too busy pulling strings and whining to higher authority to ever fight, and that's what will do us in. Good God, politics and backbiting and currying favor. Everybody thinks they know better than everybody else what to do. Can't we just all face north and finish this thing? But we've got to do this damned fighting among ourselves." He tossed a fingernail he'd been worrying off his thumb into the fire and shook his head, dejected.

"Pride, colonel." Rathburne looked at him. He continued softly. "Some say it's what got us into this war."

"Yes, and it's what will lose it for us. Damn this stubbornness. They're both wrong, Benjamin and Jackson. And so's Loring. Dammit, can't they sort this out and get on with it? What will the public think, if Richmond chases the hero of Manassas back to tend to damn boys at the VMI?"

Boteler kneeled by the fire, holding his hands out. One by one he put the papers with Jackson's words into the flames. "You're right, major. I've got to go see him. We can't let him go. We've got a hell of a lot of Yankees to keep out of Virginia, and Jackson knows how to press them."

He watched the flames grow.

Virginia, he thought. You are sorely tried, and you deserve better.

He looked at Rathburne through the flickering light and nodded his head.

The next day he went to Jackson in Winchester, and made promises no one could keep, that Jackson wouldn't be interfered with again. He appealed to his patriotism, told him no one else could do what he could to beat the Yankees and secure the Confederacy's independence. He talked about duty, over and over. He said Governor Letcher and Jefferson Davis and Judah Benjamin all said he must stay with the army, that he was needed. Virginia needed him. His country. His Valley. Boteler talked and talked.

He came back to Richmond and told Benjamin delicately that he had to back off, that Jackson was a proud man and the best soldier other than Albert Sidney Johnston in the army. He told Benjamin that Jackson would help him win the war. He talked to President Davis and appealed to his military experience. Reminded him commanders in the field had to make their calls as they saw them, that the war couldn't be waged from the drawing rooms of Richmond.

It was a delicate thing, dealing with so many people who were wrong but sure that they were right. But Boteler had negotiated these thickets for years, knew when to press and when to lay low, knew how to put an idea in someone's head and then praise it when it came out that person's mouth. He knew how important this was for his struggling new country, for his Old Dominion, and he used every wile and arm-twist he had. And he won one of the most important engagements of the war. By going from tent to office to parlor, talking, and listening, and nodding, and assuring everybody they were right and things would work out, he got everyone to stand down. To sheathe their swords and pride to be brought forth another day, against the common enemy. He exhausted himself and surprised himself, and he won.

Jackson stayed.

And Boteler found a growing admiration for the strange man who would put principle before his own career. Who knew enough about himself to stand up against the leaders of the country because he knew if he operated by their rules he couldn't be effective. And he couldn't help his country.

Boteler got a glimpse beyond what, to the outside, looked like hot-headed arrogance. He saw a man who was so single-minded that he just might be able to help overcome the fearful odds the United States would be able to throw against the Confederacy.

He wasn't sure he liked Jackson—he was indeed a hard man to get close to. And he seemed so stiff. But Boteler liked the man's decisiveness. His clarity. Boteler hadn't seen much of that in politics.

Jackson had a gravity. It pulled Boteler in.

Cedar Creek, March 18, 1862—Union Army

Jackson had given up Winchester without a fight.

"Stonewall my ass," said John Nichols, staring from the Federal camp across the creek to see where the Rebel cavalrymen were picketing their horses.

"He didn't do nothing up around Romney and the Potomac. Scared our commanders, sure enough, but that was just cuz they don't want to get bloody. They're scared of Jackson's shadow. There wasn't anything to it, he didn't come up there to fight."

"Some people say that when General Bee called Jackson 'Stonewall,' it was because Bee thought Jackson moved too damn slow. It wasn't exactly a compliment, Bee was exasperated," said Emerson Grady. Grady and Nichols and half a dozen others were jabbing sticks into the fire, trying to get enough heat to boil some coffee. Both men were short, wiry, but with thick biceps and bulky shoulders. Grady was already balding, Nichols had long dark hair that fell in his eyes. Their cheeks were lean, darkened with a stubble of beard and dirt from the march. Like all soldiers, they talked endlessly over what had happened in previous days as they marched into Virginia's Shenandoah Valley, invading the South and hoping to end the war while it was young and they were still alive.

"That's how legends are puffed up," Nichols replied. "Take a little bit of truth, twist it around and make a big story you can tell around the campfire to make yourselves feel better. That Jackson ain't much, in my book."

"Don't you think he did well at Bull Run? Was he brave or slow, I surely don't know. But the rebs say, and the newspapers, that he turned the tide and won the battle."

"Luck," Nichols scoffed. "He got a few cannon aimed at us and blew us back down the hill. Dumb luck, I say."

The Federals had been chased back down Henry Hill in that first big fight of the war, across Bull Run creek and halfway to Washington. Society folk had brought chicken and table cloths to watch the battle from their carriages, and they got churned up in the retreat as the Federal lines collapsed. Fools, to think war was an occasion for a picnic and wine.

Now Jackson had an independent command in the Shenandoah Valley, his home and the home of most of his troops. He'd taken his forces down the Valley toward the Potomac and Washington, then veered northwest into the mountains. There he separated his command, and mostly they had wandered around, with little apparent coordination.

"He did nothing in his big push north," Nichols said. "This general's a windbag." Nichols' eyes were bright in the firelight. He was shaking his head. "Why are our commanders so scared of him?" There hadn't been a battle, up in the snowy ranks of worn old mountains. More Federal troops came out from the Washington area, and Jackson moved south, away from them. "When we got enough of our boys up there, the man just ran away with his army. His headquarters up there in Winchester, he just up and left. We walked into the town without even a fistfight or a rock thrown. Push him and he folds."

Nichols and Grady were two mechanics from Ohio, part of the command of James Shields, serving under Nathaniel Banks, a political general of very little military skill from Massachusetts. Banks' job was to push Jackson up the Valley away from Washington and get him out of the way, freeing up troops to join General George McClellan for his invasion of Virginia by way of Norfolk and Fortress Monroe down on the coast. McClellan had floated his men down the Potomac and Chesapeake Bay and was going to come up on Richmond from the sea, and he wanted all the men with him he could get. This chase in the Valley was a sideshow, a holding action.

Shields pushed southwest, up the Valley, and Jackson faded away before him. Shields' men were cocky, ready to fight. ("Up the Valley" was southwest, toward Lexington, Jackson's home. "Down the Valley" was northeast, the direction of the Shenandoah River's flow, toward Harper's Ferry, the Potomac River and Washington.)

"One look at our Union steel and he's finding better things to do up the Valley," Nichols said with a laugh.

"Maybe he's going home to his wife," Grady said, laughing too. "He's a school teacher, you know. Maybe he got in over his head at Bull Run and doesn't want to be in the middle of all that lead again."

"Teaching spoiled brats from Virginia's rich families how to play at war. That doesn't make him a general."

"He was in the Mexican war, though," Grady reminded Nichols.

"So were a lot of army clerks. That was a little toy war. Facing Mexicans. Not Western troops. He won't stand up to us boys from Ohio and Michigan and Pennsylvania. He's going home."

Grady wasn't so sure. He hoped Nichols was right. He liked hearing Nichols bluster. Half of war was talk, from what he'd seen so far. Talk of what you'd do, talk of how the other side would run, talk after of how well you'd done, whether it was true or not. He liked the talk. Better than the shooting. He'd always liked sitting by Nichols in the saloons of Cincinnati as his friend talked a blue streak. Grady would pitch in, but just throwing enough fuel in to keep Nichols' fire going. Nichols was the great talker. Grady hoped that would make him a great soldier too. Or at least an alive one.

Now here they were south of Winchester, Virginia, in the Shenandoah Valley. Supposed to be a pretty place, from what he'd heard. A few hills, nice enough, but nothing like the majesty of the Ohio Valley. Couldn't get a decent steamboat up the Potomac where they'd crossed above Harper's Ferry, and the Shenandoah didn't look like much more than a quiet fishing river. Now here they were at something called Cedar Creek. Clear shallow water riffling over cracked sheets of limestone. You could almost jump across. But the army was stopped.

The rebels had burned the bridge.

"That fellow Ashby, now he's a fighter. He's going to give us some trouble, you watch," Nichols said.

"Some of the boys said they saw him across the creek, sitting on his horse like it was just any day, paying no mind to the shots coming from our side," Grady said. Turner Ashby was Jackson's cavalry commander, a man with a strong face buried in a good six inches of black beard. He'd been the rear guard as Jackson's army faded south. He harried the Federals, slowing them to a crawl. Ashby was making a name for himself, north and south, as a dashing cavalry leader. He was a fourth-generation warrior, and carried himself like it. His great-grandfather fought in the French and Indian War, his grandfather was wounded with Washington in the Revolution, and his father served with distinction in the War of 1812.

Now Ashby was on the other side of this shallow creek, and it looked like he wasn't leaving. Looked like he hardly knew there was a war on. He had a few light cannon pulled by horses and several hundred troopers. He liked this fighting, it seemed, and he was good at it. But no one knew where Jackson was. This great rebel commander, Stonewall, disappeared without a trace when things got hot. When real troops pushed into Virginia to put an end to this insurrection.

The fire was sputtering out, and the men were too tired from marching to scrounge more wood. They walked up the creek a little where they saw a brighter light. The night was cold, crisp. No leaves were on the trees yet in this March in Virginia. It was foreign country to them, and they didn't want to be here. There was work to do at home, but, they were told, more important work here first. Stop the uprising. Put the Union back together.

Grady looked across at the campfires on the southern bank. Wondered about the men there. What they were thinking. What they wanted. Despite all the hue and cry of the abolitionists, he'd heard most Southerners weren't slaveholders. Maybe they were farmers and mechanics just like him, just trying to get along. But they were doing something wrong. You can't tear apart the Union because you don't like who got elected. That's what you sent people to Congress for, to argue and figure things out. You don't just pull out if you don't like the way things are going. You stay and work it out. You stay in the Union.

"Ashby might be tough, but they say he can't handle his men. Just a bunch of rabble on horses," Grady said. "They don't have discipline."

"Cavalry never has to do any hard work," Nichols said, already steeped in the infantryman's scorn of horsemen. "They just ride, stir up dust for us to eat, and show off. Still, Ashby's stopped us. If Jackson had Ashby's grit we might have something to worry about."

"We may have plenty to worry about, Johnnie. I'm not eager to face cavalry, they seem to have plenty of spirit—and ammunition."

"Well, tomorrow we'll rebuild this bridge and then the ball will open. And then we'll see."

"You're too damn eager, Johnnie. Don't be such a hotspur. You really ready to get shot at?"

"I'm ready to catch them that's running from us. Means they're more scared than we are."

Up ahead, they could see flames. At a little curve of the creek, there were burning timbers where the bridge had been. The rebels had spread tar on the bridge and lit it on fire after they crossed to keep the Federals from following. It still burned. The platform and railings of the bridge were gone, but the stringers and pilings still smoldered and glowed. Stubs of wood stuck out of the water, capped with a molten glow. Yellow flickered in the rippling silver of the creek. Smoke drifted on the wind toward them.

As what he was looking at came clear, Grady stopped, shocked. He could see, on his side of the bank, men from a Pennsylvania regiment kneeling near the flames. Grady looked closer. They were setting their coffee cans on the embers of the bridge.

To Grady, it was like something from a painting of hell. The fire of war turned to everyday use. Men standing by the glow and heat of the burning bridge as if it was a normal thing. Boiling their coffee over the flash of death. Like warming your cold hands on the hot barrel of your smoking gun, not even thinking about what had made the barrel hot, where the bullets might have gone, what they'd done.

He looked away, strangely shaken. Had war become so commonplace in such a short time? Weren't other men horrified at what they were in?

Nichols walked ahead to ask the Pennsylvanians for some warm coffee. Grady stayed behind, looking again now at the reflection of the burning bridge. Shadows hung in the trees like dark wings above the men leaning over their coffee pots. It made Grady shiver.

What was happening here in this once-peaceful valley? What did Ashby have in mind? Was Jackson really running?

Did that coffee taste as good as it smelled? Could he drink from that cup?

Kernstown, March 23, 1862—Union Army

Five days later Grady and Nichols came out of the woods south of Winchester and had the breath sucked out of them by the howling noise of massed rifle and cannon fire. The cup was trembling now, spilling.

The armies hadn't fought south of Cedar Creek. After building a new bridge on the stumps of the old, Shields' troops had crossed and exchanged a few artillery shells with Ashby. Ashby's cavalry and Jackson's foot soldiers drew farther south, and Shields pulled his men back north towards Winchester. He, too, felt he had nothing to fear from Jackson. There'd be no fight here. Shields would protect the Upper Valley just by chasing Jackson away. Shields would stop in Winchester and send more of his troops east to join McClellan's drive to Richmond. And the Union would end the war there.

But Shields was wrong. Ashby came after him. And so did Jackson.

As Shields moved north, Jackson shadowing him in unknown numbers, an artillery shell burst near Shields, a wobbling but arrow-fast fragment breaking his left arm above the elbow and knocking him out of the battle to come.

Now he lay in bed in Winchester, sheltered and hurting in a two-story brick house, ready to make up lies about a battle with Jackson that he hadn't seen coming.

And Grady and Nichols were about to be immersed in it.

The fight had started east of the Valley Turnpike, the main road up and down the Shenandoah, with Ashby bashing away at infantry skirmishers. Now it had spread to two hills west of the Turnpike, south of a little place called Kernstown. Pritchard's Hill held the Union guns, and Sandy Ridge held the Confederates'. To stop the Federal guns from pounding his infantry, Jackson had sent troops and artillery to Sandy Ridge, west of Pritchard's hill. To stop the Confederate cannon from pounding his own guns and infantry, Union Col. Nathan Kimball sent infantry, including Grady and Nichols' Ohio unit, up Sandy Ridge.

It was terrifying. Already, they heard, most of a Pennsylvania regiment had run screaming in blood and dishonor from the Rebel fire.

They could see why.

As they stepped from the woods, a big man in front of them was torn nearly in half by a sharp flash of canister fire. This was a can full of iron balls and scrap metal shoved down the muzzle of a cannon and blasted forward like a monstrous shotgun shell. As the metal hit him, the man's breath was ripped out through his mouth and his shredded chest, he bent way backwards from the hips as his spine turned to mush, and he folded in an impossible angle until the back of his head touched the back of his heels. His eyes were huge, then they blinked off and he tipped sideways. A mist of red hung where he'd stood.

The two Ohio mechanics couldn't move.

This was the first serious battle in the main theater of the war since Bull Run—called Manassas by the South—the autumn before. Only men who'd been in the thick of the Manassas fight had any idea what war was like. Grady and Nichols' regiment hadn't seen the elephant at Bull Run. Now that thundering, bleeding monster was trampling and roaring in front of them. They were stunned.

The explosion of a cannon shot jolted Grady's heart and every nerve in his body at the same instant it made the ground beneath him jump. The ball whipped past with a whuffling rip of air, eeeeee-hyooo. He'd never felt or heard anything like it.

Ahead, a clearing to a stone wall. To the left, less than a hundred yards, two wheeled guns aimed right at them. To the right, a melee of blue troops pushing against the weight and speed of concentrated rifle fire, men being torn back from ragged lines as Minie balls ripped their faces, their shoulders, their arms, their chests.

Between the Ohioans and the wall, men were strewn like autumn leaves. Nichols and Grady couldn't hear the wounded in the din of explosions and the zipping of bullets, but they could see them yelling and trying to move. Ahead of them, a horse had fallen, and four or five riflemen were sheltered on their stomachs behind it, trailing away from the direction of the shooting like snow drifted behind a hillock on an Ohio winter field.

Wafting over the stone wall was thick grey smoke flashing with red. The red was the muzzle flashes of hundreds of muskets and rifles. The bullets, they came to understand, were aimed in a general way at them.

It all moved so fast. You couldn't breathe. No one was in charge. It was chaos.

They were pounded by sound. The trees behind them were crackling, shedding leaves and sticks from the rifle fire. The ripping gunfire was a pressure stabbing their ears. Men were yelling so loud no one could hear. There was a metal clatter of rebel bullets hitting Federal gunbarrels, belt buckles, buttons and cap insignia. Bullets hitting wool cloth sounded to Grady like a swatter hitting carpets hung outside on cleaning day.

Grady fell to his knees and Nichols thought he was hit. But he just couldn't stand.

Nichols reached his left hand down, touched Grady's shoulder. Grady's mouth was open, but unable to catch air. His gaze drifted past Nichols, then came back. The muscles bunched below his eyes, quivered, and tears came. "What," he choked out. "What?"

"It's a fight," Nichols yelled against the din. "It's what we came here for. The Union."

Nothing more showed in Grady's eyes. Just the question again. Then a puff of dust as a bullet ripped through Grady's coat, missing his body. Dirt hit Nichols' cap from a shell exploding. Branches fell behind. A body hit the ground close enough to hear.

"Nah, that's not it," Nichols yelled. "We came here to stay alive. Those boys are trying to kill us," he said, swinging his head toward the Virginians pushing ramrods into barrels in the smoke by the fenceline and at the blackened men swabbing cannons. "We've got to knock them out, Emerson, we've got to get those goddamn guns. They're killing us."

Nichols picked up Grady's gun, pushed it into his hands. He grabbed him under the left arm and pulled. "Come on, Emmy, we've got to go." A group of men rushing by knocked Nichols into Grady, and Grady stood to keep them both from falling. They were both sideways to the firing now, looking at each other, Grady confused, Nichols firm.

"Come on Emmy, we've got to go."

Then Nichols' jaw was gone, his hanging tongue drooling blood into the hollow at the base of his neck. Shock tore over his face. Next his eyes burst, as a second bullet plowed his head from temple to temple. Wetness rained on Grady. Nichols fell sideways, toward the woods.

Grady looked down as Nichols shuddered on the ground. As Nichols lay on his side, another bullet hit him just above his belt, opening his guts. Grady stared, astonished. He prayed Nichols was dead. He crouched, suddenly able to move his muscles again. He felt his friend's chest. No motion. It was over.

It had taken no time at all.

All that long way from Ohio. The training camps, the mindless drills. The marches. The waiting. The bluster around the campfire. Days and days of terrible food. Cold sleep, hard ground. All that distance, all that time. And now in a flicker he was gone.

Grady knelt, stared at the slick gore where Nichols' face had been. Then he stood with a gasp, a cry, and trudged toward the guns. He came back in a second, leaned down to pick up the rifle he'd forgotten, and walked again toward the stone fence and the cannon.

Grady fired his gun, he had no idea at what. He ripped a cartridge with his teeth, loaded and fired again, kneeling on one knee in the pasture. He stayed there for what seemed hours, between the woods and the stone fence, firing at the rebels. Sometimes other men were beside him, sometimes not. Men ran both ways, but Grady stayed. All he could taste was bitter powder; he didn't think he'd breathed since coming out of the woods. He couldn't hear anything anymore. He just shot until his cartridge case was empty. Then he reached over to a dead man next to him and got more bullets. He kept firing.

The pasture filled with bodies.

Then the Virginians were drifting away. Horses pulled at the cannon, one dead in the traces, men cutting at the leather. Rebels fell, but the guns got away.

Grady and the men around him kept firing. Then they stopped, because there was nothing to shoot at.

The clearing settled, smoke blowing off. And, to Grady's great surprise, it was over. This corner of the world, this little clearing between woods and stone fences, had been torn apart. And now it was quiet. Grady's head was too heavy for his neck and shoulders, and it sank. His arms had no muscle.

He breathed. He sobbed. His chest felt like torn bellows.

It was over.

A sergeant yelled to chase the Virginians, to hit them while they were on the run. But Grady couldn't move.

It was over. For a time.

The Union regiments that fought the Virginians at the series of stone walls surrounding the farm house on Sandy Ridge were too tired and disorganized by two hours of constant shooting to pursue the Confederates. And too many of them were dead.

After a period of time—who knew how long—motion resumed. Grady slowly stood. He looked at the fenceline where the shooting had come from, just staring. His face was grimed with powder and dirt. His eyes squinted, as in a wind. His gaze was empty.

Men groaned by the stone wall. The stones were chipped. Rifles with bent barrels and splintered stocks leaned tipping off the wall.

Rebels called for water, for help, for God or a stranger to end their misery. Grady walked away from them. He didn't want to see the people who'd killed Johnnie Nichols.

He helped bury Nichols and dozens of others. He moved slowly through the maudlin work, as did those around him. Little was said, and that quietly. Each man was trying to recover his wits, his equilibrium. His sense that this day, and more days, could go on.

Grady stared for a moment at the ground piled over Nichols, over what had been his walking and laughing friend. All he could do was stare, then turn away.

Wounded were carried away, many in agony, to fill every church and public building in Winchester. There, Virginia women tended northerners and southerners alike.

Jackson pulled away to the south.

Grady sat in a cold camp that night. They were ordered not to build fires because the officers feared Jackson might return and attack again in the dark. The temperature fell to the forties, and the ground seemed to give off a smoke from all the cartridges and bags of cannon powder that had exploded during the battle.

Grady's shoulder was battered and sore from the recoil of his rifle. His muscles hurt from clenching, and he couldn't relax his jaw. When he wasn't thinking about it, his jaw muscles would tighten and grind his teeth together. The constant tightness of battle wouldn't leave his body. He shivered, from what he'd seen as well as from the chill of night. The shivering further weakened him. The man next to him, wrapped on the ground in a greatcoat, wanted to talk, but Grady only grunted. His mind was dull. He'd occasionally see before him Nichols' eyes, just before they were shot out, brightening in terror as the first bullet hit his face. There was a quick realization behind those eyes that something impossible had happened. And then more things that had no place in a human being's life happened. Grady's mind shut down to stop the memory.

Damn that Stonewall Jackson. Where had he come from? The men had been told the rebels were running south. Nobody expected a battle here. Now Nichols was gone, tucked under a few inches of sandy ground in a place he'd never heard of.

He and Nichols had known each other for 15 years. They worked together in a boiler factory in Cincinnati, ending each day covered in grease and laughing together as they walked home. Often they'd stop at a saloon to drink a pail of beer and tell stories. They hunted together in the river bottoms, owned a rowboat together so they could go out for ducks. Sometimes they'd take Grady's son with them, and Nichols always joshed the boy about girlfriends. Always told him he had something wonderful to look forward to. Grady was married but Nichols wasn't, and he always had an eye for the girls. He kept trying to get Grady in trouble, picking out factory women for him to talk to, trying to get Grady to join him and several women for a night on the town. Once or twice Grady had. Johnnie loved to laugh, loved to hold the women on his lap and tell them jokes. Johnnie lived life fast and hard.

Not any more.

Now what was Grady going to do? To get through this war, and once he got home?

Sounds drifted by, muted. Cries of wounded still awaiting rescue, the jingle and creak of harness on horses pulling guns, wagons and bleeding men. A low murmur of talk as survivors told each other about what they'd just experienced.

Grady leaned against his knapsack propped against a tree stump. He cupped his chin in both hands, his fingers rubbed his eyes. The morning seemed far away, and it would be empty when it came.

"We beat the hell out of Stonewall," the man next to him said. "Made him run like a dog."

"Maybe," Grady said. But Jackson had beaten us, too, Grady thought.

It wasn't like how he'd heard about battles. One side victorious, wrapped in glory, the other trudging away in anger and despair. Both sides bleed. Both leave drifts of broken men on the ground. Both sides are shattered, men searching in the dark for their friends, their units, for the way things were before the shooting started. Both sides must be terrified, as he was, that the shooting would start again, that that feeling of everything being torn out of anyone's control would come smashing back and grip each man's chest so tight he couldn't breathe.

"Were you hit?" the man on the ground asked. "I was, by Jesus. My cartridge box and my belt stopped the ball. Otherwise my hip would be in pieces. Can you believe it? Lucky. Providence, maybe."

"Go to sleep."

"I can't."

"No."

"Were you scared?"

"Still am."

"Yeah, I know."

The man coughed. "Did you think of runnin'? Those Pennsylvania boys sure ran."

"I didn't think."

"Did you think it would be like this?"

"Go to sleep."

"What happened out there…" the man said, jerking his hand a few inches toward the pasture and the walls, then pulling it quickly back.

"Leave it be."

"There's blood still pooled, I bet." The man breathed in and out a burst of air. "It was, it was purely awful."

"Stop." And Grady closed his eyes, dropped his head between the dirty knees of his pants and tried to shut his mind down again. He said nothing more, as the man muttered on in the dark.

A few miles ahead of them rose the northern end of Massanutten Mountain, a black shape in the night. Stars winked above it, and a flickering light shone on its summit. A Confederate observation party there watched the Federals' movements. The majestic long narrow mountain split the Valley of Virginia, with the two forks of the Shendandoah River flowing on each side. The head of the mountain swept up from the plain at Front Royal, south of Kernstown, in a gradual and graceful slope rising to a subtle, rounded knob. The promontory looked like the pilothouse atop the armored prow of a huge ship sailing toward the Potomac, toward the North.

Grady didn't know it yet, but 40 miles to the south, the Massanutten range ended in an almost identical shape—a turreted summit dropping through a wooded slope to the plain just north of a little town called Port Republic.

Less than three months later, Grady would be looking up at the southern battlement of Massanutten from another bloody field. The war would take no rest.

Behind Grady, from Winchester, an inaccurate picture of the battle and the forces engaged worked its way to Washington.

Shields reported that he'd planned the battle and knew what he was getting into, but he'd had no idea. He reported that Jackson had more than 11,000 soldiers in the battle, and that they were still out there, ready to march again. He didn't have his staff interview the wounded and captured Confederates, or he'd have known there weren't enough southern units at Kernstown to come to a fourth of that number. Jackson had no more ability to move north now than the mountains did. But the time would come.

The exaggeration of Jackson's strength that would accompany him, and aid him, throughout the war was under way. The ferocity and tenacity of Jackson's attack amplified his numbers and his impact. Soon he would seem to be everywhere, with menacing numbers and frightening speed. Jackson had lost this battle, but won the psychological war. Suddenly the lower Valley, and even Washington itself, seemed unsafe.

The alarm spread. Jackson was coming. Marching on Washington, maybe beyond. The governors of Pennsylvania, Ohio and Massachusetts put out stirring but frightened calls to raise yet more soldiers to meet the invasion that must be coming. Jackson, weeks before thought bottled up in the Valley by Banks, was rising in the tales of two nations, casting a huge shadow northward.

That shadow would grow and multiply with bewildering rapidity in the months ahead.

Before Winchester, Jackson had called a council of war, asking his brigade commanders what they thought should be done. They said leave Winchester to the Federals and pull back to the south. Jackson did. But he wished he hadn't, and he never held another such meeting. Ever. Never asked the advice of a committee again. He would take his own counsel. And he would fight.

The stumbling defeat at Kernstown was the beginning of a whirlwind of long marches, surprises, nasty little fights and slicing battles that would stun the North and buoy the South. The Shenandoah Valley, its mountains and passes, rivers and roads, would be the stage setting for a swirling drama that wrapped legend around history and would be remembered for generations.

Jackson's Valley Campaign had opened.

Narrow Passage, March 26, 1862—Confederate Army

William Sutton was damned glad General Richard Garnett had gotten the Confederate forces off Sandy Ridge, although he'd heard that Jackson was angry with Garnett for withdrawing. They'd marched up the Valley for three days now, in retreat. The Federals had won the battle, Sutton's first.

By the time they'd backed off the hill under the relentless Federal attack, Sutton's ammunition had been gone. And, frankly, so had his nerve.

Walking south today, he'd noticed the men around him were becoming more lively. After the fight at Kernstown, they'd been sullen. Or shocked. This was the first time this army had fought together in the Valley, and they hadn't expected to be pushed so hard by the Yankees. Hadn't expected to run.

Sutton had joined up with Jackson's little army after Manassas, and Kernstown had been his first fight. He was still stunned. A few months before he'd been at his own farm up the Valley, staring at his fields and no longer knowing what they were for or how his life connected with them, knowing only that the world had changed. A few days ago he'd been in someone else's field, crouched behind a stone fence, and had watched the world explode.

Sutton had kept mostly to himself in the months he'd been in the army. He hadn't said much at all to anyone at the beginning, just did what he was supposed to do and was quiet on the marches and in camp. He wasn't entirely sure why he was in the army, except that there was no reason to say at home, with his wife gone. And he felt it was wrong that the Northerners had invaded Virginia. But he didn't care much about politics, and didn't own any slaves. The war was abstract, or had been until Kernstown. He supposed he was trying to find something, marching with these hundreds of men. Maybe find a reason to keep going. He hadn't found much yet, except bad food and lice and wet blankets. And sore feet. His already thin frame had gotten leaner, tighter, from all the marching.

As much as anything, he was there because there was a war in his state and he didn't know what to do about it except be in it. It was hard to believe, so much killing in his own state, the place that had always been so peaceful, at least since the British were chased away generations ago. Now they had to chase away the Yankees. And Sutton thought this Stonewall Jackson might have the best shot at getting that accomplished. And he wanted to be close to Jackson when he did it. Help him do it. Follow him as long as he was going somewhere.

And he'd followed Jackson to Kernstown. And my God, he thought, the fighting had been awful.

He'd fidgeted behind the stone wall up on Sandy Ridge, waiting for it to start, opening up his cartridge case over and over, moving his blanket role from beside him, to behind him, to beside him on the other side. Nervous, he'd talked to the man next to him who'd been at Manassas. "Aim low," the man had said several times.

"Aim low? Can you see them, do they get that close?"

"Oh, you can see them, friend, like they're in your parlor, coming for pie," the man had said. He was a big man, with a long thin beard and a worn hat that he set low over his eyebrows. He hadn't seemed nervous, so Sutton had asked him how he remained calm.

"I ain't calm, I'm just not dwelling on it. There's nothing you can do. You can't run, they'd just come after us farther down the line," the man had said.

Sutton had walked back several times to the trees to relieve himself, and each time he'd turned back to the stone wall and the field in front of it he'd expected to see lines of Union troops coming out of the woods. But they hadn't come. He'd heard plenty of firing off to the right, and cannon shots closer, to the right and front of where his Virginia regiment waited. At first the sounds had made him jump, but then they just became part of the day.

The man had gotten out a set of dominoes and asked Sutton if he wanted to play. He'd tried, but he couldn't concentrate and lost quickly. "I've got jacks, that's easier," the man had said, and tossed down the little spiky metal jacks and a ball on his rain slicker.

"How can you play now?" Sutton had asked him.

"What else are we going to do? It eases you." But the ball didn't bounce well on the slicker, and Sutton gave it up. He'd looked at the men down the line to his left. Some were talking, some were staring. Some leaned their backs against the stone wall and wrote on scraps of paper. Some faced forward, with their muskets resting on the top of the wall, ready. Pipe smoke rose from a few. An officer had walked by, telling the men to stay up close to the wall. "When it happens, it will happen fast," he'd said, "and you'll want to be ready."

The big man next to him had offered Sutton a piece of sausage, but just looking at it had turned his stomach. The man had shrugged and chewed the meat, slowly concentrating on every bite.

"I make sausage, do you?" the man had said. The man had talked about his smokehouse, where it set beside a little run that only had water in the springtime. He'd talked about the spices he used, and how he liked to put a little rice in the mix, to spread it out. "You've got to fool yourself a little to make it last. That's true of a lot of things, ain't it?" he'd said.

The man said this sausage wasn't as good as his own, but he was glad to have it. "Tell me about your place, friend. Talking makes the waiting easier. What's it look like?"

Sutton hadn't wanted to talk, but he'd tried. His home—was it still home?—seemed so far away now. He'd said his farm was small, the house just two rooms and a porch. But he liked the views. He'd described the peak at the end of the Massanutten mountain, how it lifted to a graceful point, and how you could see the Allegheny ridge to the west.

The man had asked him about plowing, and when he'd plant his corn. The man had said he hated to plow, would do almost any other work first. He'd put his son on the plow as soon as the boy got tall and heavy enough to hold the handles and the reins. "It's just boring, walking behind that plow," he'd said. "I feel like I ain't getting nowhere, just going over that little patch of ground again and again." He'd said he talked to the mule, but the animal wasn't much for conversation. Just wanted to shake off the harness and stand in the pasture. Lazy as a lizard, he'd said.

"If you're good at handling mules, I think that would make you an officer in this army," the man had said, and laughed.

Sutton had risen to his knees, arching his back and rotating his shoulders to loosen his muscles. He'd sat back on his haunches and scratched at his arms.

"There's chiggers in this pasture, plenty of 'em," the man had said. "That's the worst thing about being in the field, there's bugs all over you. You got to boil your clothes whenever you have a chance, I'm telling you, or at least beat them on a rock in a creek if you can get to one. Can't let them take over. They're always ready, they're a good little army, they are."

Then came a sudden ripple of noise along the stone wall—metal rattling, leather cartridge boxes hitting gunstocks, shoes creaking, knees popping, urgent sharp whispers.

A tense silence followed, and voices could be heard clearly from the woods across the field. "Spread out," "Jamie, get on over here," "We're coming to them now," "Stay low," "Easy, boys, slow and easy." "Aim low, now, aim low."

Then they could see shapes. Then quickly a sound came that shocked Sutton, froze his body and ripped his mind open. A few whuffling pops that rose in an instant to a blast of noise like a hundred dogs barking at once right in his ear. And smoke and men in blue came out of the woods and into the clearing.

All around Sutton the air exploded as the Confederate rifles cracked and kicked. Time leaped, and swept Sutton into battle without a thought. Only reaction and muscle and instinct. To stop the men shooting at him.

The big man next to Sutton had been shot in the first volley from the woods. Sutton hadn't seen anything happen, just noticed when he turned to reload that the man was slumped against the wall, huge and still, his rifle tipped forward over the wall, the jacks spilled down a little rise of dirt the man's knee had plowed in the ground.

Two hours later, with the Federals finally breaking through to the wall off to the right, Sutton and about half the men by the wall had pulled back. Every part of Sutton's body hurt, as if he had been stretched over a wheel and whipped. He moved like a cripple.

They'd walked south, moving fast in frightened clumps, hearing cavalry shooting at stragglers, capturing prisoners.

Finally they'd gotten beyond the Federals, and their walking slowed. Sutton had found others from his regiment, from the Stonewall Brigade that hadn't held the ground in this fight, and plodded through the night.

Now, three days later, walking through a place where the North Mountain that was the first of the Alleghenies pushed up against the North Fork of the Shenandoah River and the Massanutten Mountain beyond, making a narrow spot in the Valley, he thought again about the fight. There had been so many gunshots that he had no idea how he was still alive.

What the big man, now dead, had told him was true. Something took over in battle, and you just kept at your work. Loading, firing, loading, firing. He'd wanted to just duck behind the stone wall and never look above it, but he hadn't. He'd stayed there, shooting over the wall. At first he'd shot at nothing, just aiming in the general direction of the enemy. Then he'd slowed down, just before firing, long enough to pick a target. That had seemed more terrifying, shooting at a face. But he could see it was more effective.

He remembered some of the Yankee faces. Some were yelling in anger. Some were white with fear. Some looked dazed. Others, perhaps the bravest, were set with determination. Some stayed where they were, unable to move, it seemed. Some turned like a waning moon and fled. Some came toward him until the faces fell to the ground.

All looked like people he'd see on the streets of Harrisonburg near his own little farm.

He wished he couldn't remember the faces.

He'd hated the shooting, but apparently he was good at it. He hadn't run. And he was alive.

"You doin' all right?"

A voice to Sutton's side, a tall, bulky man was suddenly walking next to him. Beard, kepi pushed back on his head, a smile.

"I'm here, is all," Sutton said.

"James Sparrow," the man said, nodding at Sutton. Sutton nodded back, told Sparrow his name.

"You'll get used to it," Sparrow said, with a light slap to Sutton's dusty blouse.

"I don't think so."

"No, you're probably right. But you'll keep on."

Sutton turned his head as he walked to look at Sparrow. The man was looking ahead now, just striding along.

"How do you know?" Sutton asked.

Sparrow looked over, the skin around the eyes above his beard crinkling with the edge of another smile, his gaze firm, but his brown eyes soft. Sutton felt a steadiness in the man, and liked it.

"We follow Old Jack," Sparrow said, his head turning forward again, bobbing a little as he walked. "We go where he goes." Another step or two. "And he goes where it's hot."

"Sure as hell seems so," Sutton said.

"Yep," Sparrow said, walking, walking. "We'll be all right, though."

Sutton didn't believe the man, but he wanted to.

Sparrow told him he was a sergeant, and part of his job was keeping the boys in line. Tending to their troubles. Help them not to worry. Make sure their gear was in order. Make them laugh sometimes. From the way Sparrow talked to the men around them, calling out nicknames, joshing them about worn-out shoes and dirty rifles, knocking off a hat now and then with the tip of his bayonet, Sutton could see Sparrow was popular with the men. He'd occasionally throw an arm around a soldier's shoulder and ask him if he'd heard from home, or ask another if his bum leg felt any better. He talked a lot, but he wasn't a windbag. Just a man with a lot of energy who kept things lively around him. His talking and joking helped men pass the time, helped them think not just about guns and wounds and sickness.

Sutton thought about the man who'd died beside him at the stone wall back at Kernstown. He'd been easy to talk to, too. Helped Sutton keep calm, or as calm as he'd be. That man was also big—had been big. Maybe these big men, barrel chests and round guts and thick arms and wrists, had a sort of stability that attracted people to them. Felt solid. Almost sheltering.

Sutton liked marching near Sparrow. He seemed to know what to do, with all these men, with all this gear. Maybe he'd know what to do with this war.

Sparrow looked over to Sutton, smiled, and said, "It's a long way, wherever we're going."

Sutton nodded.

They walked on, side by side, eyes ahead, the only noise for awhile the shuffling of their shoes, and of hundreds of others.

Near Rude's Hill, April 1, 1862—Confederate Army

Richard Garnett thought Thomas Jackson a sanctimonious bastard. Had since the horrid frozen march up toward Romney near the north end of the Shenandoah Valley in January. Garnett now commanded the Stonewall Brigade, had inherited it when Jackson was promoted after Manassas to command the Valley army. Then Jackson asked for reinforcements, and got his old brigade back, with Garnett at its head.

The march to Romney in the Allegheny mountains west of the Shendandoah had been icy and ill-organized and crippling to men and horses. General William Loring's army had joined Jackson's and had marched like snails. Everything had been a mess. Starting out from Winchester, they'd stumbled for two days northwest in temperatures that fell below freezing. Men and wagons slipped off the narrow roads. Bleeding icicles dripped off horses' knees from constant stumbling and falling. Supply wagons couldn't keep up, and men went without overcoats or food. On the third day, after leaving a little settlement called Unger's Store, Garnett had halted his men to let them cook rations when the wagons finally caught up, and Jackson had ridden over and asked him why he'd stopped. To feed the men, Garnett had said, wondering if Jackson was daft or just a monster.

"There is no time for that," Jackson had told Garnett. Garnett, barely holding his anger, had said it was impossible for his men to march farther without food. Jackson had glared at him—that goddam Presbyterian deacon's Old Testament rectitude—and repeated his orders to move out. Nobody knew to where, of course, or why in such an inhumane hurry, because the man apparently shared his plans only with God, never told his generals what was in his crack-brained head.

Then the bastard Jackson had growled out his deep nasty insult. "*I* never found anything impossible with this brigade." He'd pulled on the reins and turned his horse north, leaving Garnett hot and tight with fury.

But that fury was a Sunday afternoon argument over lemonade compared to what was pushing like scalding steam against the straining rivets of Garnett's temper now.

"That's preposterous," Garnett said, bending forward at the waist as if to get closer and re-hear what he must have heard wrong just a second ago.

Sandie Pendleton, Jackson's assistant adjutant general, stayed quiet. He knew Garnett had heard him.

Garnett's narrow face was turning from sun-brown to a deep violet. It was quivering. "No, lieutenant, not preposterous, it's totally mad! My God, man. *My God!!*" He shook his head, waved a hand in front of his face as if trying to sweep a bug away. He kept staring at Pendleton, squinting his eyes, shaking his head again. When he saw no different message on Pendleton's face than he'd heard from the words, he slammed his open right palm onto the camp table, knocking pens and field glasses and a mug to the ground, and turned his back.

Pendleton, in Jackson's name, had just arrested Garnett and relieved him of his command—the Stonewall Brigade—for neglect of duty. At Kernstown, the week before.

Garnett took several deep breaths, trying to stop shaking. "What are the charges, what does he charge me with, what is this neglect of duty?"

"Not being at the head of your troops, not supporting Col. Fulkerson at Pritchard's Hill, ordering your brigade to fall back off Sandy Ridge against your orders to hold your position. General Jackson hasn't formally completed the charges, sir. But he has ordered you relieved, as I said." Pendleton did not like this assignment. He was the son of a West Point-educated general who had left the army to become an Episcopal rector but came back into uniform when the war started and would become Robert E. Lee's chief of artillery. His father's son, Sandie Pendleton understood about discipline, about carrying out orders, and was used to delivering messages, leading men, doing whatever needed doing for Jackson.

But this he didn't like. The battle at Kernstown had been such a jumble. Nothing had been clear. From the beginning everything was off, including Jackson's estimate of how many Federals they faced. With Garnett coming under fire from two directions, Jackson had sent Pendleton to a high spot to see what they were up against, and Pendleton had reported seeing twice as many troops as Jackson had originally been told were even in the area. The news was a shock, and clearly the Valley army was in trouble. "Say nothing about it, we are in for it," Jackson had told Pendleton.

Pendleton had been one of the staff aides sent to find Garnett as the pressure of Federal cannon and massed rifle fire pushed Jackson's men farther to the left than they had planned to go. He'd never found Garnett, although he knew the man wasn't shirking. It was Garnett's bad luck to not be visible when Jackson was looking for him, but then to be very visible turning around reinforcements that Jackson had sent once the retreat had begun.

"You know those charges aren't true, Pendleton. Dammit, that's calumny."

"General Garnett, I regret being the bearer of these orders, but they are orders and we must both obey them."

"Oh, yes, yes, I'm sure you do regret…Oh, Sandie, I know you don't want to do this, and I don't want to take this out on you. But it's absolute rubbish! It's nonsense. It's bloody tyranny. My boys were shot up on Sandy Ridge, and they had nothing but spilled powder and sand left in their cartridge boxes, man! It would have been suicide—murder—to keep them there."

"But a brigade commander can't unilaterally withdraw once he's been posted…"

"What, we were supposed to throw rocks at them? I know, I know, the vaunted Stonewall said we'll give them the bayonet when he made his famous stand on Henry Hill. But he didn't have to, did he? He had plenty of ammunition there, didn't he? Bayonet, what pock-brained romantic claptrap."

Garnett turned away from Pendleton, cooling the heat of his argument. He looked down at the small cot in his tent, picked up the coffee cup from the ground, slapped it into his palm, dropped it. He spoke more softly, back still to Pendleton: "He tried to relieve Loring, too, after that idiot march in the mountains last winter, and it didn't stick. Richmond knows he's a lunatic."

He arched his neck, lifted his face toward the tent ceiling, rubbed on his brows with his hands, then spun around. "Pendleton, the whole thing was busted up before it began. Jackson never told any of us what he was doing, what he wanted. We had no idea of the plan, the strategy. He gave us no written orders, just mumbled a few words to an aide, 'Support Fulkerson.' He never even came to me in person to tell me what to do! Didn't say with what troops, so I sent one small regiment. Then we headed for the high ground of Sandy Ridge, but he never told us what to take, or what to do when we got there. Does he expect us to divine his plan, to witch it out of the ether?"

He looked Jackson's aide square in his long, thin, boyish face, and fever returned to his voice. "He doesn't tell us because he doesn't know, or he doesn't want to take responsibility if it all goes up in smoke. Then when he's beaten," he paused, lowered his voice to a sonorous, pulpit tone, "he looks for a scapegoat."

He slapped the knuckles of one hand into the palm of the other. "I won't be that," he pushed the words between his teeth.

"General, maybe this will all become clear in time," Pendleton said. "But for now I must relieve you and place you under arrest. Let's not make this worse than it is."

"Oh, it will come clear, all right, lieutenant. We'll have a hearing, all right, and then the world will see what a mess Jackson made of Kernstown. I'll make damn sure of that!" He paused, and his voice became softer, but still acid. "What will the drawing-room ladies and armchair generals at Richmond say about their heroic Jackson when they hear that he didn't even come to the front, Sandie? He directed this battle from the rear, never even came close to the fire to find out what was going on. What does this say about his bravery, eh?"

"General Garnett," Pendleton said, his own voice now sharpening, "be careful of your words. Don't say something you'll regret."

"Why should I be careful? Jackson never cares how his words wound."

"General Jackson is your commanding officer, and you must show him respect, sir," Pendleton said in strong, slow, staccato words.

"He doesn't show his officers respect, I'll tell you that. Sir."

They stared at each other. Garnett's face was red, Pendleton's miserable. He had no desire to fight with Garnett.

"What will President Davis think of Jackson when he finds Jackson didn't even talk to Turner Ashby when he came up to the battlefield?" Garnett asked. "Ashby had been there for hours, fighting Shields, and he knew what we were up against, even though he had had no idea at the start how many Federals were out there. Jackson didn't take the trouble, the normal precaution, the intelligent step any responsible commander would take of consulting with the man who had been fighting on the field. Jackson would have learned the situation then, but no, he apparently had no interest in finding out the facts of the matter. He just came in with his decisions made in his rock-hard head and told us all what to do. And he had it wrong, sir, and he nearly sent us all up the spout. He had no damned idea of what it was like up there on Sandy Ridge. They were pressing us like demons, and then they got around our right flank. With no ammunition left, Sandie, what in hell was I supposed to do? Let my men die because our saintly general didn't know what was happening?"

Garnett pulled the chair back with a snap of his hand and sat down heavily. "Sandie, this is madness. This is patently unfair. He can't do this."

"He has, general."

Garnett looked up at Pendleton, his own face now matching Pendleton's for misery. "Sandie, I didn't even know what Fulkerson's orders were. Jackson sent him up on that hill, to flank around the federal cannon, it seems, but I had no idea what his specific charge was. Don't you think that if my purpose was to support Fulkerson I should have been told what his orders were? I wasn't. Jackson kept us all in the dark." He looked searchingly at Pendleton. "Is that any way to run a battle? Shouldn't we know as much as we can?"

Pendleton was uncomfortable with the question. That was not Jackson's way. Other subordinates had complained of the same thing. To Pendleton, the question seemed fair.

"The general prosecutes his battles in his own way, General Garnett, and it's our job to follow his orders to our best ability," Pendleton said with no great conviction.

"Pishhh," was Garnett's response. He shook his head and looked down at his hands. "You know better." Silence followed.

"What does he mean, not being at the head of my troops?" Garnett then said quickly, looking up as he thought back on Pendleton's litany of charges.

Pendleton faltered for a moment, then said quietly, "When the general sent me to find you, sir, I could not."

"What do you mean, could not? I was in the thick of the fight."

"I could not find you, sir."

Garnett's lips became a thin tight line. "Perhaps you didn't look hard enough, lieutenant. I was mounted at the head of my troops. Hard to miss. The Yankees had no trouble seeing me, from the volume of fire they directed my way, sir."

Taking up the metal coffee cup again and tapping it in an irritating tattoo on the table, Garnett said, "Why can I not stay in command of the brigade? What does Jackson say about me?"

Pendleton remained silent. He looked at Garnett like a man seeing a firing squad assembling.

"What does he say?"

"That your incompetence, rather than building up the brigade, would make it deteriorate under your command," Pendleton said, his eyes on Garnett's.

Garnett's face lit like a flash of gunpowder. "This is an attempt to blast my character, as a soldier and a man. I won't stand for it."

The two men faced each other, anger mixed with deep regret. There was no more to say.

Garnett rose. "You've done your duty, lieutenant. You've delivered your message. I shall of course comply. But we've not heard the last of this, by God."

Pendleton turned to the tent flap, turned back again quickly and saluted, then ducked his head and shouldered his way out of the tent, exhaling heavily as he passed outside.

Garnett stared blankly at the canvas as it fell back in place. He shook his head, closed his eyes, growled a long sigh. The battle, the men falling, the young lives snuffed out, the retreat, it had all been more than bad enough. Why this, on top of such misery? Was Jackson so small he had to cover up his own mistakes by heaping infamy on the very generals who had given their all to try to win the day? Garnett hadn't thought so, but now he'd seen Jackson's worst side.

Garnett swore softly. He sat again, and lit a lamp. He couldn't let this go. He heard again the sound of bullets thunking into his men's jackets, cutting into tree bark, snapping off of canteens and belt buckles. "Have you got any cartridges" he heard men calling. Jackson hadn't sent any ammunition wagons up on Sandy Ridge to resupply his men and Fulkerson's. Garnett had faced an agonizing decision. He knew he had to hold the hill. He knew that an order to hold a place must be obeyed. He knew that subordinate commanders couldn't make their own decisions if a battle plan was sound. The general in charge had a larger view and moved his troops where he knew they were needed. If unit commanders acted on their own, there would be chaos. He also knew that Jackson liked it well enough if brigade commanders acted on their own initiative to start a voluntary charge that pushed back the bluecoats. *If* it worked, of course, *if* it succeeded.

But Garnett's men were being slaughtered on the hill. A charge was impossible without ammunition. He had to get them off that hill. It had been a terrible decision, but one that was very clear to him. He had had no choice.

And now he was being skewered for it.

After awhile, after Garnett had stared at his table for perhaps another half hour, a major came in and told the general he and the troops were shocked by what they had already heard about Garnett being relieved. "If our cause were not too sacred to jeopardize, we would make a considerable commotion, sir," the major had said.

Garnett had thanked him with a nod, and the major had left.

Our cause is sacred indeed, Garnett thought. I wonder if it will survive this man Jackson.

Perhaps, with Jackson's action, other generals will think twice before retreating, Garnett thought.

And then there will be more men dead and captured. And no one to fight on the next hill.

Near Fisher's Hill, April 16, 1862—Confederate Army

It was a lovely day for a ride and beautiful country. Trees coming into bud, softening the hills. Sun bright, sky blue, breeze brisk and dancing. But the rider was having trouble enjoying the scenery. He knew at any moment the perfection of the day could shatter. He could be captured, or killed, in a flash. What had seemed like a good idea back at camp now seemed rash, bordering on idiotic.

He was behind enemy lines, riding not on a scouting mission, but just to see his family.

He suddenly felt as if he were surrounded, although he could see no one in the woods. Danger, self-imposed, seemed everywhere.

Patterson Neff, a lieutenant in Turner Ashby's cavalry, which was Jackson's cavalry, kept riding, staying in the woods beside the Valley Pike so he wouldn't be seen. Even if he made it back to camp, he realized, he might be arrested by his own general. That would be a wonderful way to boost his glorious career, he thought, shaking his head. What had he gotten himself into?

Neff knew General Jackson had thrown Roger Preston Chew, a gunner, out of the army once for leaving without permission. Chew and his gallant battery just last month had helped hold off the Federals for hours at Kernstown, and it was hard now to imagine Jackson once having been incensed at Chew. But the summer before, Chew had been assigned to help Jackson drill recruits in Richmond as troops gathered to fight the coming war. Chew had been one of Jackson's students at the VMI, and his class had been declared graduated a year early as South Carolina seceded and it became clear that years of harsh words between North and South would turn into years of hard war. After the boredom of drilling, Jackson, then a colonel, and his cadets were reassigned to the strategic post of Harper's Ferry, where the Shenandoah flowed into the Potomac.

Chew and several classmates were delighted to be sprung from Richmond and sent back to the Valley, so close to their homes. They pictured heroic evenings on front porches with local girls dazzled by their uniforms. They looked forward to dances, seeing family, eating good meals at home.

But Jackson said no.

To Jackson, being on duty meant being at your post. He had left the VMI and his home in Lexington on April 21, 1861 to take his cadets to Richmond, and after that he would never go home, not through two years of war. He set an example. War was a hard business, and the only thing it had to do with the comforts of home was to protect them. He wanted his men to stay with the army, always ready to move and to fight. No victory would be won from a porch swing. He would do himself what he required of his men. Even if they were only 18 years old, like Chew. The cadets should set examples for the recruits, Jackson said.

Chew and a friend, larking before any bullets flew, went home anyway, thinking Jackson was unfair and had no memory of what it was like to be young. When they returned to headquarters at Harper's Ferry, Jackson quickly and coldly sent them back to the VMI. Soldiers were soldiers; cadets who went home to frolic weren't soldiers, so back to school they went. Humiliated.

Unfortunately for the Yankees, Chew didn't stay in Lexington. After several weeks with their tails between their legs, Chew and a friend hooked up with Turner Ashby, commander then of irregular cavalry, and told him they wanted to form a battery. Ashby was game, but said they had to get permission from the commander of the Shenandoah district, their former professor, Tom Fool Jackson. Chagrined, they asked. Jackson thought about it for a few days, then assented, and Chew went on to blow holes in the Northern ranks. But a lesson was taught to all Jackson's command.

And now Neff, who reported to Ashby, who reported to Jackson, was off bushwhacking. Behind the lines. With no permission. To see his sister. Good Lord.

He came to a clearing in the forest, reined in his horse and peered through the trees. The clearing ran alongside a road, following the weaving line of Tumbling Run up from the North Fork of the Shenandoah and the Valley Pike. He was getting close now. He could see the little creek slipping over great slabs of granite as it fell down the valley. Trees hung over the rushing water, and across the run the land rose again, rough and heavily wooded. He could hear birds singing, see them dart from branch to branch. He could hear the swishing trill of the water. He was getting close to home, and he knew every turn of this creek, every boulder it brushed past. He could feel his breath quicken, not from the tension this time, but from expectation. What was his mother doing right now? It was past lunchtime, she'd be washing dishes, maybe starting on a pie for supper. Or out working in the fields.

This was home for Neff. The little side valley made by Tumbling Run that cut through the hills, falling down to the Shenandoah. He had gone to school here, until he was about 16. Ridden everywhere, always on a horse, since the first pony his father got him when he was eight years old. Always running somewhere, on a succession of small horses. Patty, as his mother never stopped calling him, only grew to about five and a half feet tall. But he had strong legs, able to grip the sides of a horse, and balance that kept him in the saddle no matter what turns and dips and jumps his horses took. He didn't much care for the work of the Neff farm, hated cutting and stacking hay, hated the chaff that cut up his arms and crawled inside his sweaty shirt. He was better at figuring, and from about age 14 kept the books for his father, recording supplies bought, the few horses and pigs sold, and the small income from the crops. He'd joined the militia three years ago, at age 20, and seemed made for the drills and reviews on horseback. Seriously as all the neighborhood boys had taken the drills, he knew now they were games. He'd seen a great deal of shooting at Kernstown and in the retreat up the Valley. Seen too many—one was too many—shockingly fast collisions between silent flying bullets and soft flesh and not-hard-enough bone.

Still, he was thrilled by the war. He loved the camaraderie of Ashby's cavalry. He was excited by how unruly it was, after the militia drilling, how independent each rider was, and yet how enough pulled together to chase away an enemy patrol or defend a friend who got too close to the Yankees. Riding up the side of a Yankee column, off in the trees or on a side road, put his heart in his throat, and then all the nerves and emotion came howling out as they cut through the startled marching men or rode down a plodding squad of Yankee cavalry.

He didn't feel invulnerable—the danger was surely part of the thrill. But he felt confident. In himself, his horse, his fellow riders, and in Ashby. Jackson he didn't know much about, except what people said. And they said you didn't want to come before him as a deserter, even though Old Jack mostly kept his hands off Ashby's cavalry, as long as they kept after the Yankees.

Neff stood in his stirrups. Pulled off his hat and ran his hand through his thick chestnut hair. Stroked his thin chin beard. Should he continue? No, he shouldn't.

He was miles north of Jackson's headquarters down at Rude's Hill. Way beyond the normal range of patrolling to find where the enemy was and where he was moving.

But he had to keep going. His sister was supposed to be married soon. The presence of the Yankees in the lower Valley had turned everything on its head, including the wedding. Life was defined now by where the Yankees were, and how they behaved. Most left civilians alone, but the army did take food and supplies when they could get at them. And houses were taken over for headquarters, their peace and quiet shattered by muddy boots, cigar butts and garbage that ruined carpets and chased the rightful inhabitants away. But as soon as the Yankees left the Valley for good, Neff and a fellow trooper, Robert Hazlewood, would ride up in these hills and Hazlewood would marry Elena. For a day, maybe two, the war would recede, and hope would come back to the Neff home on Tumbling Run.

Their father was infirm, and Neff needed to help get things ready for even the small celebration the war would allow. And the farm wasn't doing well without him, his mother had written. There was so much to do. He wanted to help where he could. But his main reason for coming was just to help them see some light. See reasons to not give in to despair. So many places in the neighborhood were missing men and so had work left undone. Crops would be smaller because less ground would be planted, animals would be tended less well. As the battles and skirmishes and nasty ambushes down in the Valley continued, many farms would have work that would never get done as men young and old fell to the ground with Federal metal inside them. Neff wanted to ride in and brighten his home with the energy and hope he felt riding with Ashby. The war *would* end, they *would* chase the Federals away. Virginia would prevail, and peace would return to the Valley. Things would be right again. Things would be fine. It was part of the cavalry's job, he'd come to realize, to be dashing and carefree, to bring liveliness and noise and hope, to represent the speed and the daring and youth that would save Virginia.

He wanted his sister, 17 and just beginning to open to the world, to feel there was still a future. The people who stayed home as the rumors flew and the armies marched had no idea what the next day would bring. If the Confederate army moved away and the Federal army came in, would it be that way forever? Would the Neff home be occupied territory, ruled by the despot in Washington crushing his boot on what once was the cradle of freedom? Would his mother and sister have to work for years, afraid that the bread and crops and animals they raised would be taken to feed the invader? Or would the cannon raise their muted rumble from the Valley floor again and signify the return of General Jackson and the routing of the Yankees? Would the farm be freed, in a day, in a week? The people at home could never know. And they could do nothing to affect their fate. They were simply tossed back and forth by the waves of war. At least Neff himself could feel he was doing something, was laboring to bring the world back to normal. His frustrations and fears could be channeled into the bursting speed of a charge, the quick snapping blast of a pistol shot, the shrill vibration of a yell as he rode to push the Yankees away.

His sister could do nothing, and he didn't want her to be crushed with the weight of uncertainty. He didn't want her to look forward and see only grey days and fear. He wanted to bring the lilt of life back to her, if only for a few stolen hours.

So he nudged his horse and she slipped down the stony hillside to the road by the run. On the road, she shook her head, blew spittle from her lips, pricked up her ears and listened. So did Neff. They both heard horseshoes clattering on rocks in the road down the hill to Neff's right. Coming up from the Valley Pike. Coming toward Neff.

He quickly turned Sylvan, the big roan, back into the woods. They rode about a hundred yards, then he dismounted. He stood by Sylvan's head, whispering to her, quieting her, wrapping an arm around her nose. He drew his pistol.

Don't let it end this way, he thought. Way out of bounds, way out of line. If he was captured, the Yankees would think him a deserter. And so might his own men. Everyone wanted to go home when they were this close, he knew. Some did. Some snuck out, saw family or sweethearts, and came back with no one knowing. A few had been captured, both on regular patrols and on free-lance errands like Neff's. It was ignominious, dishonoring. A Confederate trooper should be able to outrun any cloddish Yankees on their plowhorses. Nobody should get caught. But what do you do if there's a bunch of them, aiming their pistols at you? And then there would be the Yankee prisons. Exchanges were running slow—he might be imprisoned for months.

Neff crouched, pulled Sylvan's head down. Her nostrils were opening and closing rapidly, tasting the air, smelling the other horses. A sharp tripping fear shot through Neff. He eased back the hammer of his pistol. I won't be taken, he thought. But God, I don't want to be shot here in the woods a mile from home.

He heard horses and voices, then saw shapes through the woods. It looked like four Federals. They were leading a string of horses. "Let's get a few more and get out of here," he heard one man say, making the "more" a "mowah" sound and the "here" a "heeyah." The uncouth accent of Boston or Maine, Neff thought. They talk funny. What louts. Don't let me be taken by Yankee dullards.

"Let's see if we can get ourselves some more of them hams, too, Brad," another said. Then came laughter, and someone said, "Oh, I'm sure these Virginny ladies would be proud to have us enjoy some of their vittles."

The horses trotted on, up the road. Up the road that Neff wanted to travel.

He exhaled, let Sylvan's reins go, patted her long forehead as she jerked her head up and twisted her ears to pick up the receding sounds. She whickered lightly and backed away from Neff.

"Good girl, Sylvie, good girl. Let it go, just take it easy, now." He walked her slowly to the edge of the woods. The Yankees were gone. He decided to push back into the trees and wait a few minutes to make sure they weren't coming right back. There were homes and farms strung all along Tumbling Run up toward Fisher's Hill, where Neff's home was. The Yankees could be stopping at any one of them, or all of them.

Neff nibbled on some dried apples a farmer had given him back near Woodstock, gave Sylvan a few pieces. After 15 minutes or so, he mounted again, crossed the road, waded across the rocky bottom of Tumbling Run, and climbed the opposite bank. He'd ride on the north side of the run, stay in the woods, circle in to his neighborhood from behind. It would take longer, but he was less likely to run into the Federal patrol again.

He had ridden like this all the way from Rude's Hill. Staying off the Valley Pike, staying up against North Mountain, the Allegheny edge of the Shenandoah Valley. He hated riding like a fugitive, hiding, swiveling his head to look all around him. He understood a little of what it must be like to live under the Federal occupation. Always wondering where the Yankees were, what they might do next. Never feeling at home in your home. At least with the army, they had the freedom to range on their side of the lines, even if those lines were always changing, and always could be penetrated. This was his country, his home, and he felt ashamed riding through it so tentatively. He felt displaced, as he knew his neighbors still at home must feel. Many had become refugees, although they didn't like that term. They preferred to be called displaced, or even prisoners of war, as they left their occupied homes, bundled up a few possessions and went off to impose on relatives or friends. There they slept too many to a room, got on each other's nerves, longed for Jackson to come back and sweep the invaders into the Potomac.

He was eager for the day when that would happen. He got angrier as he rode through the trees, branches plucking at his hat and coat. He wanted to ride screaming at the head of Ashby's cavalry and slash at the Yankees with his sword.

That sword caught on a small maple and slapped his thigh as he rode. He looked down, saw the dent in the scabbard where a Yankee bullet had struck it. The scabbard had saved his leg. He was fond of the dent; it showed he'd been in the thick of the fight, up at Kernstown. And many skirmishes since then.

When would his luck run out? When would a Minie ball from someone he'd never see find his heart or his head? Would it be today? When he wasn't part of a fight? When he was skulking here in the woods, slouching in his saddle, trying to steal a few hours of peace?

He came out of the woods at a small crossroads, where a bridge crossed Tumbling Run and took the little north-south road to an intersection with the road next to the creek. A three-story house clung to the north bank of the run, with porches on all three levels overlooking the water and the shallow valley. His friends the Buckmans lived there, at least what was left of them. The father killed at a little fight near Winchester, the son captured. Across the road was a barn right next to the run, and next to it a two-story house with the first story surrounded by a broad shady gallery—the Ewings' place. Next to it a feed store, and across the road a post office. On a hill a few hundred yards from the bridge a tall white house with columns, where James Simington, a retired judge, lived with his servants and the best cook in the northern Valley, Neff thought. What he'd give now for some of her red-eye gravy and sweet potato pie. And the fragrant lamb stew she made on Sundays. Neff felt sad to see this little neighborhood so quiet now. Usually there were children running along the road, pushing hoops with sticks. Neighbors leaning over gateposts or easing into a seat on the Ewings' front porch, gratefully taking a glass of lemonade. A wagon or a buggy would come down the dusty road and always stop so the people riding could chat with the people in the yards.

But now no one was moving. People stayed inside when they heard horses, peering nervously out windows, wondering what was going to happen to their lives.

Neff nudged Sylvan and she walked out onto the road. Neff stopped, stood in his stirrups, and looked up and down both roads. Nothing moving. Just beyond Judge Simington's place was his own house, over the crest of the hill. "C'mon, Sylvie, let's go home," he said to the empty road and the closed houses.

He rode, alone, between his neighbors' houses. He refused to slink along here, in front of his home folks. They needed to see a grey rider sitting tall in the saddle. Needed to be reminded they weren't alone. Hadn't been abandoned. Neff didn't care if he made a good target for any Federal lurking nearby. He'd be damned if he'd sneak down this road. His road.

A noise on his left, and he twisted in the saddle, his right hand reaching across his waist for his pistol. A door was opening at the Ewings', and a form in a long dress stood in the doorway.

"Pat, is that you? Pat Neff?" It was Jane Ewing. A woman he'd known all his life. About 50, she looked older. Her curly blond hair was piled on top, many strands escaping. Her dress was a bit ragged, and she held a dish towel in her hands. She smiled, surprised, through her weariness, and Neff thought it was the most beautiful sight in the world.

She leaned toward him, tripped lightly down the steps and ran to his horse's side.

"Pat, what are you doing here? There's Yankees here, they just went down the road," and she lifted her arm to show the way, on the dirt track that led away south from Tumbling Run. "They're after horses, and Lord knows what else. Are you alone, are there more of you coming?"

"I'm alone, Mrs. Ewing. I've just come to see my family."

He could see her shoulders drop a little. She'd hoped for a long line of troopers who could restore her home to the Confederacy. "But we'll be coming back, Mrs. Ewing, with the whole army. We will, soon. How are you doing?"

"Oh, Pat, nobody's doing well." She looked up at him, shading her eyes with her left arm. "We're not getting any field work done. I'm not so good at repairing machinery, you know. It's all I can do just to cut the wood and keep a few chickens and pigs here. Just to keep us going."

"I know. You keep up your spirits," Neff said. "This won't last long." His anger came back. "We have to get these Yankees out of here. You folks just have to hold on."

"We will, we're trying." She dropped her head, wiped her brow with the towel. The lines around her eyes were deep, and she looked tired. She looked up again, and smiled. "Your mother will be mighty glad to see you, Pat. You go on up there, and watch out for those bluecoats. Oh, wait, let me get you some corn muffins, Just took them from the oven."

As she turned to the house, Neff said, "You keep them, Mrs. Ewing, but thank you just the same. Mother will feed me. You folks enjoy the muffins. But, you hear, you hide them from the Yankees if they come."

"I will do that," she said with a small laugh. "I'll give them a pan to the head if they come into my kitchen."

"I'll bet you would. I'd like to see it, too."

Jane Ewing stopped in her front yard, turning back to Neff. "How long do you think it will be, Pat?"

"I don't know, ma'am. General Jackson doesn't tell us much. But he's the very devil to those Yankees, and he won't let them stay here. We'll come up here pretty soon and chase them back to Washington for you." He smiled, hoping he believed this. "You just hang on here. Stay strong, and keep that muffin recipe handy for when we come back. We'll be hungry."

"I'll pray for you, Pat, and I'll pray for your return. Soon, and with a brigade, all right?"

"Thank you ma'am." Neff raised his right hand to his hat, slapped the reins on Sylvan, and cantered up the road.

At the Simington place he crested the hill and could see the creek and pastures and sloping hill leading to his home.

It wasn't the prettiest spot in the Valley, this Shenandoah country that was so crowded with pretty spots. But it had a fullness, a roundness, a richness, a soft understated roll to it that filled his eyes with pleasure and made his breath pull in sharp little tugs. Off to the left was an old weathered shed, with weeds growing up tall and raggedy next to it, where he'd hidden to smoke corn-silk cigars with Bruce Buckman when they were kids. Nearby a marshy meadow where they'd caught frogs, just to hold them cold and slimy in their hands. The land rose into a wooded hill beyond, graceful, quiet, the boundary of his vision to the southeast from his bedroom window. He'd watched the light die in those trees many nights, wishing he didn't have to be in bed, wanting to be out where the animals were making strange frightening noises in the underbrush.

The fields now were bulging, some with crops, some with weeds and grasses.

He kept riding, and ahead on his left rose the gradual slope of Fisher's Hill. It was a low hill, not very exciting to the eye. But it had been a playground for him, a land of wonders, a place where imagination flowed through the trees and over the rocks and into distant lands and scenes of pirates and caravans and pioneers and battles. It was his hill, he'd felt. As a boy.

So calm here. He hoped no battle would ever come here. Hoped no Ohio or New Jersey men would ever march here, up from the Valley Pike, dragging their cannon and their dirtiness and their noise. Their oppression. Their killing.

But it could happen. It was just a little winding country road that reached up here from the river. Only trees and breezes defended the way. Into his home. A short ride on a northern mount, an easy march up the grade. And battle and dying and terror and the feeling that everything was out of control could sweep around his family's trim little house and blast the peace to chaos. And displacement. And despair.

But he was here, not with an army to defend this place of his, but with a smile and an empty stomach to try to dispel the fear for a few hours with his family.

He pushed back his hat with his left hand, drew his right down his long face, stretching his jaw down as he pressed on the muscles that had been so tight since he'd left Rude's Hill. Whose fear was he trying to dispel? His mother's and sister's, or his own? They must not be so different, he realized now as he was steps from his home. They all feared the loss of their lives. Not the loss of the breath and the heartbeats. But the choices, the freedom to move on a whim, to stop a chore and stare at the hill and follow a bird's flight or a deer's bounding run with eyes not afraid of what they might see coming at them through the trees. The easy walk to the neighbor's, the talk over hollyhocks and pansies, the feel of a fat loaf of still-warm bread carried to a friend who was sick, the bread lightening your own steps on the crumbly dirt road as you walked to lift the spirits of a good person you'd known for years and years. The life of days that go by as the days have before, held gently by the hills and woods of Virginia, sheltered by the whole idea of America, a place where your grandparents had escaped the fist of the old world's tyranny.

What had happened?

As he rode, he looked with a tight yearning at the woods and hills, the greens and rich tawny golds of the world he had known. Before the cavalry. Before the need for cavalry.

He hadn't come here to see his sister. To make his mother laugh. To take a hand to a horse or a cow or a broken hoe.

He'd come to touch his life. He'd come to ground himself. He'd come to stand in the wind off the hill and feel his home. This land he was so tied to, rooted to. He'd come to find home again, and see what he was fighting for.

The tears came before he even saw his mother open the front door and step, hesitantly, onto the small porch. He touched Sylvan's side lightly with his cavalry boot and they moved forward, faster. His mother put her hand to her mouth, the other to her breast.

A mile away, the Federal troopers swung south, taking another road back down to the river, unknowingly leaving Neff in peace. For half a day.

The Peak, Massanutten Mountain, April 30, 1862— Confederate Army

Dawn was coming in, wet. From the craggy summit at the south end of Massanutten Mountain, the world below was a swirl of rivers and soggy roads. The wet roads would hurt Jackson's speed, and he would greatly need speed now.

Jedediah Hotchkiss was looking for Federals. As the land fell away from Hotchkiss to the west, leveling into the broad, fresh green valley of the North Fork of the Shenandoah River, Hotchkiss could just begin to see the camps of Nathaniel Banks. This was the army that had chased Jackson south since Kernstown. It was big, maybe 20,000 men or more. And this was the army that Jackson now wanted to slip past with his 8,000 men so he could attack the vanguard of Charles Fremont's army farther west, beyond Harrisonburg in the Allegheny Mountains.

Once again, Hotchkiss was thrilled, and frightened, by Jackson's audacity. Jackson had been playing cat-and-mouse with Banks' army, falling back, turning and slashing, then falling back again. For the last several days Jackson had tucked his army up into the Blue Ridge hills east of where Hotchkiss now stood, waiting for a move to come clear. There was a growing Federal army under Irwin

McDowell behind Jackson, across the Blue Ridge near Fredericksburg, and Banks' army in front of him. One might look at the map and say Jackson was trapped, or at least penned in, by these two armies. But, Hotchkiss knew, Jackson saw opportunity in the situation, not danger.

And now he was going to hit an army—Fremont's—that was farther away. Fremont was marching south through the Alleghenies to the west of the Shenandoah Valley. In this Federal move Jackson saw the greatest danger to the Valley and the Confederacy. If Fremont got beyond Jackson and took Staunton, south of Harrisonburg, he would take control of the upper Valley and could join with Banks to form a host large enough to hold it all. Then the grain and cattle of the Shenandoah Valley, Jackson's home, would be denied to the hungry Confederacy. And another front against Richmond could be opened.

So Jackson was going to march west, right past Banks and hit the first units of Fremont's army, under General Robert Milroy, before the rest of Fremont's troops could join Milroy and before Fremont could join Banks.

From his lofty promontory, Hotchkiss could see with his eyes the land below emerging from the haze, and with his mind he could almost see the bold moves Jackson was contemplating. It was all very clear in both views, for Hotchkiss was a mapmaker.

Jedediah Hotchkiss was 33, a tall man who loved books and travel. A thick black beard fell from his face, he had dark, full hair, ears that stuck out a little and a long straight nose. He looked serious, but approachable. Born in New York, he had come to Virginia as a young man to teach, and had stayed, returning north only to marry a Pennsylvania woman. Virginia was now his home, and he was learning every inch of the Valley as Stonewall Jackson's topographical engineer. Many thought Jackson lacked plans, but Hotchkiss knew that was just because Jackson never shared them with anyone. Jackson had asked Hotchkiss to make a map of the entire Valley, and called on him for detailed maps of every part of the Valley they passed through. Because he captured the land on paper for Jackson, Hotchkiss knew how carefully indeed the general thought out every movement.

The theater of operations in Hotchkiss' mind—and Jackson's—was expansive. It stretched to the Potomac and Washington City, to the Atlantic and the transport boats that had brought McClellan's 100,000 Union men to the peninsula below Richmond, to the Alleghenies where John Charles Fremont, the Pathfinder who had trekked to California in 1848, was winding south with his army, and to a little settlement called McDowell west of Harrisonburg where Milroy faced a small force under Confederate General Edward Johnson. The linked movements of all these forces were complicated. Part of Banks' army, under General Shields, was moving through Manassas to join McDowell near Fredericksburg where the combined Federal force would open a second front against Richmond, descending from the north while McClellan worked his way toward the Confederate capital from the east. General Joseph Johnston was shielding Richmond from McClellan with an army less than half the size of McClellan's. A small Confederate force, again much outnumbered, was guarding Fredericksburg.

The only Southern army in Virginia that could move right now was Jackson's. Only he could disrupt the tightening Federal grip around Richmond, and he was going to do it by marching away from the capital, into the mountains, and fighting a small Federal detachment under Milroy. This, he thought, could break up the plans of the Federal commanders and make them fear the one Confederate army whose moves couldn't be predicted. Was it the right strategy? It seemed so off track. It seemed this Valley campaign was already a sideshow to the main action around Richmond, and now this little scene would take place even further off-stage. Could hitting Milroy make enough strings tremble to pull on the main Federal armies so distant? It had worked at Kernstown, Hotchkiss reflected, but that was many days' march closer to Washington and the nervous Lincoln. Would anybody care if Milroy's army were defeated, assuming Jackson could get past Banks to get at Milroy? Was Jackson truly crack-brained, like so many of his own officers said? Was this the right risk to take?

Hotchkiss' head was light, thinking of all these places and armies. He felt he was moving through the air, turning inside his skin, as he stood on the high peak of the mountain. As the clouds rolled above him, the mountain itself seemed to be moving, like the bow of a huge ship. He wavered on his feet, rubbed the heels of his hands into his eyes, pressing weariness away. He was tired. In the past few days he had ridden to see General Edward Johnson, to scout Milroy's situation, and to assess the conditions of the roads toward the Alleghenies from Swift Run Gap in the Blue Ridge where Jackson awaited developments. He had returned to tell Jackson what he'd found, and Jackson had immediately ordered him to climb the Massanutten and watch what Banks would do. Hotchkiss had ridden through the night, ascending the graceful slope of the mountain, reaching the top at 5 a.m. in time to watch the darkness fade away. Now he was close to exhaustion, breathless, and apprehensive.

But there would be no rest. It wasn't in Jackson's nature to wait and watch very long. It was now time to move. He would take his force right past Banks, hoping the North River, which flowed into the South Fork of the Shenandoah, would keep Banks off his flank. Rivers and mountains were always part of Jackson's plans—he used them like armies to block his opponents, and he moved around them like wind. The plan was risky, but it would work if it was done quickly, with the shock of surprise. That was Jackson.

And it was Hotchkiss' job to watch Banks and signal to the valley below if the northern general moved to strike Jackson on his march or to reinforce Milroy.

The mapmaker looked out over the Valley, trying to calm his nervousness. The rough shoulders of the Alleghenies to the west were just becoming visible, as were the soft hazy slopes of the Blue Ridge to the east. He relaxed his engineer's mind and saw the sharpening shapes as touches of beauty brushstroked on the emerging day, as backdrops to homes and common lives, to slapping the flanks of cows while milking, to scattering feed to scuttling chickens, to stretching the kinks out of backs after chores, to neighborly helloes from porches and in town squares.

How had these armies come with their blight to such a peaceful place, he thought. How could anyone rise on such a morning to kill?

Below, he saw the first stirrings in the Federal camps. Men from the North, his birthplace. He knew men just like them. Wouldn't they rather fish today on the curving Shenandoah? Wouldn't they rather walk up this mountainside, blow out hot breath at the top and sit with him and talk of the places they'd seen? Couldn't they just be together and take in the sweep of this Valley, laugh a little with one another and all go home?

No. They'll level rifles and roll out cannon and blow each other apart. Tear arms from their sockets. Rip jaws off with lead. Drop gouts of blood on rich rolling ground. That's what they'll do. Just hours from now.

My God, he thought. Can't I just stay here? Above the crashing surf of metal that will pound the soft bodies. Of his neighbors from the North and his neighbors from the South.

He touched the flank of rock that broke like a breaching whale through the green rise of the Massanutten. Leaned against it. Felt its ancient solidity.

This high refuge, he thought. What if I could just stay here? I'm not truly a soldier. I'm an explorer, a wanderer, a drawer of maps. I walk, I look, I measure, I draw. I'll just draw shapes and lines on paper, trace the sweep of rushing water, catch hillsides in bending lines. Then I'll put what I've drawn in my pouch. Won't let anyone see it. Won't let Jackson turn the hills and creeks into battlefields.

Just stay here.

He saw motion to the south, the light now swelling with dawn. His breath quickened, his shoulders tensed, his calves tightened inside his boots as he leaned forward. He saw Jackson's men moving, well beyond the Federal pickets.

He peered down at Banks' army. Watched for men packing their cooking gear, forming in columns. But so far, nothing like that.

And no one was moving toward the river to fish.

Not this day. Not, maybe, for years.

"They're stirring, sir." The voice came from behind him, and he jumped. "Sorry, didn't mean to scare you. I guess you saw them moving, so I didn't need to tell you what you're seeing."

It was the lean, brown-haired cavalryman who'd been sent along to accompany Hotchkiss up the mountain. One of Ashby's men. Neff, Hotchkiss thought he remembered.

"It's fine, I'd just slipped into thinking, I guess. Neff, is that your name? I'm sorry." The man nodded. "What's your rank?"

"Oh, Ashby calls me a lieutenant, but we don't go much by titles in his little parade."

"No?" Hotchkiss remembered hearing some grumbling on Jackson's staff about Ashby being lax. "Is Ashby a good commander, Neff?"

"Oh, yes sir. He gives us plenty of room to maneuver. Doesn't tell us what to do all the time. Trusts us to do what's needed. That's a good way to run cavalry, especially, I think."

"I suppose, as long as the rest of you boys know what you're doing," Hotchkiss said.

"We know our way around horses all right, and we're learning to fight. Ashby shows us, from out in front."

Hotchkiss liked the point, and found he liked listening to this brisk soldier. He looked over at Neff, wanted to keep him talking, wanted Neff's energy to help him stay awake. "I hear Ashby's brave, even foolhardy sometimes. Sits still, right in the open, under enemy fire."

"Oh, he's brave. Crazy sometimes, it seems to me," Neff said. "I don't have much of a hankering myself to be in the middle of flying metal, but he doesn't mind. Setting us an example, I suspect. Up north, a few days ago, he was protecting the rear with another trooper, Banks coming up behind, and the trooper's horse got shot out from under him. Ashby sat there calm as could be, bullets whipping all over, told the man to take the saddle off the shot-up horse, and then they just walked out of there."

Hotchkiss shook his head, said, "hmm, that's cool under pressure." He knew horse soldiers loved to talk about their exploits, something that made them tiresome to infantry.

"And he can ride," Neff continued. "We were burning the bridge over the North Fork, up past Rude's Hill, but the Yankees got across the bridge and stopped the fire before the bridge fell. Came boiling across, chasing us, and Ashby's horse was shot through the lungs. Ashby stood his ground, took out a couple of Yankees, then rode that horse back like a runaway train into our infantry lines. Horse dropped like a rock when he made our lines, Ashby put him down with a shot. Who else could ride a dying horse like that? The men were awed, I'll tell you."

"You cavalrymen like the fighting, do you? Seems you like that prancing and rushing around."

Neff laughed a little. "I guess we'd rather be hunting game than Yankees, but if it's got to be done we'd a damn sight rather do it from a horse, that's for certain. There was one boy up at Kernstown, right in the middle of the fight, scared up a fox that ran between the lines. The boy, named Thad Thrasher—honest that's his name—chased that fox right up to the Federal line, and those boys over there stopped their shooting and cheered him."

"He'll remember that chase the rest of his life, won't he?" Hotchkiss said.

"He would have, but he was killed later that day driving at the Federal left. Had some fun, though, before he went, you can give him that."

Neff half-whistled out a breath, dipped his head and looked at the ground. "War is damned strange," he said. "The most exciting thing there is, and the most tragic. All in the same moment."

Hotchkiss nodded, and the two men looked down into the Valley. Neff slapped his gloves on his thighs, Hotchkiss scratched his neck under his beard. The soldiers below kept moving, tiny in the distance. After a quiet couple of minutes, Neff said, "I think they're just making breakfast down there. See those cookfires starting?" He pointed with his gloves.

"I hope that's the case," Hotchkiss said, rubbing his eyes again. He put his right hand to the small of his back, pressed, arched his shoulders back, twisted at the hips, trying to loosen up.

"What's Jackson going to do, move on Banks?"

Hotchkiss smiled. "Jackson doesn't tell anybody his plans, don't you know that by now, Neff?"

"Yeah, I hear that's what General Garnett said is the man's problem. Should let his officers know what he's planning. Sir."

"I've heard that complaint. Might be something to it. But he doesn't want the Yankees knowing his moves before he starts."

Neff looked at Hotchkiss, then looked out over the fields again, the gleaming muddy roads. "You're scouting for him, aren't you? What do you think he's going to do?"

Hotchkiss smiled again, looked at Neff. "Well, since he's already doing it, by what we see down there toward Port Republic, those troops moving, I'd say he's going to try to get past Banks and go up in the Alleghenies and go after Milroy."

Neff's face showed surprise. "Why?" Neff tried to put it together in his head. Here was an army right below them, that had chased them south up the Valley, and Jackson was skipping it. "I know Banks' army is a lot bigger than ours, is that why Jackson won't fight him?"

Hotchkiss shook his head once, face bent toward the scene below. "Not just because Banks is big, I don't think. Seems to me Jackson likes to put his forces against the enemy where the enemy is weakest, generally. And he sees maneuvering as just as powerful a tool as a battle, sometimes better. He marches his men to the bone sometimes to save them from being shot."

"I'm not trying to push this," Neff said, "but I'm trying to learn how the strategy of this works. We talk a lot about it in camp, as you can imagine, and I'd like to know how things fit together. I don't want Old Jack shooting me as a spy, though, I'll tell you that." Neff laughed and glanced a little nervously at Hotchkiss.

"I'm glad you're interested. I try to put it together, too, as I watch and listen around General Jackson. He's a close one, but he's damn smart about this."

Neff wondered. He hadn't seen a lot of brilliance in Jackson. The mountain marches up by Romney hadn't yielded much more than a lot of complaints and frozen men. Kernstown was a loss, almost a rout. And they'd mostly retreated since then. Manassas showed the man was brave, but it hadn't taken much strategy to push his men into the Federal rush, just raw guts.

"What good is fighting Milroy?"

"I don't think he wants the Federals to take Staunton or Harrisonburg, to control the Valley," Hotchkiss said. "And Fremont's coming up behind Milroy. I think General Jackson wants to knock out Milroy before Fremont gets here, then go after Banks. Maybe knocking Milroy back will upset Fremont's plans, even Banks'. Hit them one place and they'll tremble in others, maybe even withdraw. A victorious battle, even a small one, can make your army seem bigger than it is and put a scare into other armies. Maybe that's what he's thinking. I don't know, he hasn't said anything, but he's been studying the ground all around here, looking for the best places to fight and maneuver, I'd guess."

"And we're trying to keep Banks from reinforcing McClellan, right? Fight him here, keep him busy?"

"Yes, for now." It had worked at Kernstown, hitting the Federals there and keeping a nervous Lincoln from reinforcing McClellan with troops from the Valley. But Hotchkiss thought of times he'd heard Jackson talk about the Federals in the Valley. Talk about how to trap them, keep harrying and pushing them until they make a mistake, then descend on them and destroy them. "He doesn't want to just parry, lieutenant. Not this man." Hotchkiss nodded, looking out over the expanse of hills and riverbottom. "He wants to kill."

And not just here in the Valley. Hotchkiss didn't tell Neff how Jackson had been looking at the maps of the lower Valley, the Potomac end, the approaches to Washington. Hotchkiss suspected Jackson had farther targets in his sights. He didn't tell Neff how Jackson had questioned Hotchkiss about the coalfields of Pennsylvania, which Hotchkiss had surveyed as a young man. Hotchkiss shivered a little when he thought of what Jackson might have in mind. But he wouldn't talk about that with this cavalryman. Jackson wanted to keep his cards close, and Hotchkiss wouldn't be part of showing them. He'd wait and see what came.

He found it exciting being around Jackson. He felt a sense of pent-up energy in the man, almost fury sometimes. A desire for big, sweeping deeds. Crushing blows. Famous campaigns. The man had ambition, but seemed to try to suppress it. He was a tense blend of piety, humility, imperiousness and stubborn, single-minded drive. While keeping many possibilities and options in mind, he'd bore in on one course and push it to the end, but still keep, somehow, the flexibility to change course in an instant if he saw a quicker way to his goal. He'd look at one of Hotchkiss' maps and take it all in, and hold it in his mind, locked in place, ready to be retrieved in an instant when he needed to weigh options and find the best course. Hotchkiss knew terrain, had studied it all his life. Jackson apprehended information from a map, and then a sweep of his eyes across the features around him, faster than anyone Hotchkiss had ever known. The man had a genius for knowing ground, feeling possibilities, envisioning what might unfold. Hotchkiss found it intoxicating to be pulled along by the sweep of this man's mind.

He looked again with Neff at the rivers and roads, the moving men, the men not moving. He could feel the day accelerating, he could feel the pieces in play. His nerves buzzed.

"This man, this general, has something big in mind here, lieutenant. We're his eyes up here. Let's help him keep track of these invaders. Let's help him send them home, or what will be left of them."

"You're confident of Jackson? You think he can beat these people?"

"I do, lieutenant. I do. The man is a hawk. A spinning, whirling hawk, watching everything that moves, picking out the place he'll dive and pounce.

"You just watch, Neff. Just watch."

Neff scuffed at the earth of the mountain peak with his boot, adjusted his sword at his hip, and looked out over the Valley. He caught Hotchkiss' sense that something was building up out there. He hoped the engineer was right, and he began to suspect that he was. Neff's brief visit home had shown him again how oppressed the people of Virginia felt by the presence of the Federal armies on their soil. Nothing was normal, life was in tatters, fear and uncertainty filled every day. He wanted to believe Jackson could evict the Federals.

Neff caught a movement barely noticeable, and looked up. There was a hawk flying above them, off toward the west a little, drafting on the air that flowed up the mountain. He tapped Hotchkiss on the shoulder, gestured with his head and his hat upward. Hotchkiss looked up, saw, and grinned. The hawk tilted its wings, slipped sideways, soared in an arc, cut back, shot close over Hotchkiss and Neff, then wheeled and sailed out over broad Valley and the Federal camp. Watching everything below.

The sun broke over the Blue Ridge behind the men, flooding the Valley with golden light. The hawk's wings caught the glow, and lifted.

The War Department, Washington May 9, 1862

"The Tycoon wants to know where this man Jackson really is," said John Hay, one of President Abraham Lincoln's secretaries, with a laugh that had a frustrated edge to it.

"He's—everywhere." Fred Campion, the telegraph clerk, tossed himself against the rungs of his straight-backed chair and tilted it on its back legs. He looked at Hay, shook his head and spread his hands wide in the air.

"Now, you know, he just can't be everywhere. Let's find out what's real in all this bleating," Hay said, waving at the pile of telegraph slips that carried the alarms of several Union generals.

"Here, sir," Campion said, picking up several sheets. "He's reported hiding in Swift Run Gap in the Blue Ridge, lurking at Harrisonburg in the Valley, marching toward McDowell west of there, and here are two saying he's on his way to Warrenton and Gordonsville, and those are both outside the Valley altogether.

"And yesterday, we heard he was coming north toward Harper's Ferry again, where we almost caught him last month.

"You take your pick, Mr. Hay. He's everywhere."

Hay sat down. He was tired. Everybody around the President was tired.

"The boss doesn't want to be as flumoxed as his generals. He's got to see this straight. He's not a man patient with bad information, my friend."

"No sir," said Campion, looking frightened.

"He likes to look straight at the facts, when he can find them, and then logic it out." Hay paused. "Along with being a lawyer who arranges facts to his advantage, he thinks he's a military man. He fought in the Blackhawk War, for about 15 minutes, and he's read a substantial pile of books. He thinks he can reason this war to an end." Hay tilted back in his chair too, loosened his coat.

"What can we believe from these generals? Do they know what's going on out there?" Hay asked, tipping his head at the telegraph officer, inviting candor with his look and his soft voice. "We need to sort this out, Freddy."

"Well, Mr. Hay, they're not always on the mark. Remember in March, when General Banks sent telegram after telegram saying that Jackson had left the Valley? And all the time Jackson was right there, quietly creeping up on him."

"He made mincemeat of Banks," Hay said, laughing, easing the tension.

"With your permission sir, he made a fool of Banks."

"No, no, Banks made a fool of himself," Hay corrected, laughing more. "Didn't need much help, either. You know what they're calling Banks over at the Willard bar, Freddy?"

"Yes, I do, although I don't stop at that bar, Mr. Hay. He's known as 'Commissary Banks' now."

"Because he's provided so many wagonloads of supplies to be captured by this Jackson. I think that's funny, in a morbid sort of way," the President's secretary said.

Hay relished humor. Fortunately, the White House was alive with playful and wry humor, even in these grim days. Lincoln set the tone, with an anecdote ever ready to take the frustrating edge off events. Many of the men in Congress were put off by his stories and japes, thinking him not serious or smart enough to deal with the national emergency. But Hay knew the President's love of laughter kept him afloat. And, he thought, the man was smarter than any dozen of his generals and any score of his critics. He and his fellow secretary, John Nicolay, joked often about the President, calling him The Tycoon, His Excellency and other names when talking about him. Everybody joked about their bosses, of course, but this was more collegial and even respectful, said from inside the influence of the President's personality and conviction. Nicolay and Hay knew how strong the President's conviction was, and could see every day how heavy his burden was. They shared his conviction, and wished to lighten his burden. Keeping a light attitude thinned the heavy atmosphere, in themselves and around the troubled Lincoln.

A large shadow appeared in the doorframe. The smile dropped off Campion's face. "Mr. Secretary," he said loudly, standing quickly.

"Commissary Banks, is it? I don't believe we need to waste time berating our own generals. Their failings are obvious enough to the country, to the whole world." Secretary of War Edwin Stanton stepped through the door, seeming to fill the small telegraph office. He was a big man, big in stature, big in voice, big in presence.

Stanton, and Lincoln himself, came often to the telegraph office in the War Department. It was just across the lawn from the White House, and Lincoln seemed to find it an escape from the press of his official duties, from those seeking favors and—worse—answers. As often as the President or the Secretary had dropped in on Campion, he still felt a trip in his heart when a high official of the government came through his door.

"We were just trying to find Jackson here, Mr. Secretary," Hay said, gesturing to the pile of message slips. "And we were recalling how inaccurate some of General Banks' reports about Jackson's whereabouts were in March."

Stanton stepped toward the table, touched a slip or two, then sagged into a chair. It creaked.

Stanton took off his little wire glasses, rubbed his florid face, combed his long frizzy beard with his fingers. "Banks got worse than he deserved, although he thought he knew more than he did. I do recall him wiring, after he thought Jackson had gone, that he would 'grieve not to be involved in the military operations of the summer.' He got involved, all right, indeed he did."

"Perhaps," Hay replied, "General Banks should have stayed in politics, where he seems more suited, rather than dabble in war."

"War *is* politics, Hay, as well as the other way around," Stanton all but hollered. "Haven't you learned anything in Washington?"

Hay remained silent. He had to concede the point.

"So where is our General Jackson now?" Stanton asked, his voice dropping to a low grumble.

Before Hay could say something arch and set Stanton off again, Campion spoke up. "We have conflicting reports, sir."

"I dare say. This man has the wrong name. 'Stonewall' is for someone who stays put. This man never does. So where do the reports say he is?"

Campion told him, listing off the names of several Virginia towns a few days march from where they sat.

"And at the Robin's Nest at Willards," Hay added, deadpan. Willard's was the hulking hotel near the White House where every officer visiting Washington seemed to stay and join with politicians in the circular Robin's Nest bar to fight battles with whiskey and rum.

Stanton perched his tiny glasses back on his nose, looked over them at Hay, and snorted. "No doubt. And tea in the East Room next." He laughed a few strong, releasing notes, then stopped.

"I wish our generals could march in a month as far as Jackson does in a few days." Stanton stood to look at the map of Maryland and Virginia spread on the wall.

"You know we've held troops back from McClellan because of Jackson's attack at Kernstown?" he said.

"Yes, the President is very concerned about Washington," Hay said, "which I admit I'm rather glad about as a resident here now."

Campion, in a careful voice, said, "I thought we beat Jackson at Kernstown. It was a victory, wasn't it? Jackson left the field."

Hay sat down across from Campion. "Just the fact that Jackson fought there, so close to Washington, against such a strong Federal army under General Shields, showed the President how vulnerable the capital is. And what audacity Jackson has. With General McClellan and our main army down on the other side of Richmond, coming up from the sea, the President feels a bit skittish these days in the White House."

Stanton grumbled. He wasn't going to tell these boys, but he felt boxed in. The President had demanded McClellan move against the rebels after the general had taken nine long months to drill and outfit the troops. At one point Lincoln even said to McClellan, 'if you're not going to use the army, I'd like to borrow it.' Stanton had to smile at that. The President had gall. So finally McClellan devised this scheme to float the army down the Potomac and come up on Richmond from the backside. Unorthodox, but McClellan was supposed to be a great strategist. So far he'd only shown himself to be great on the review field, and a dashing presence in Washington salons.

Lincoln had agreed to the Potomac operation, but insisted McClellan leave enough troops behind to protect Washington, as McClellan was taking his army off of the direct line from Richmond to Washington, away from Confederate General Joe Johnston's army. McClellan had assured the President he'd leave more than enough men behind to guard the capital, but Stanton figured McClellan had counted in all the War Department clerks, the wounded, and the drunken slouchers in Washington hell-holes to come up with a big enough number. Lincoln had caught on, and, with Jackson lurking in the Shenandoah, the President detached a force under the loser of Bull Run, General McDowell, to stay behind and guard Washington.

Then Little Mac got down on the peninsula between Virginia's York and James rivers, ran up against a few Rebel cannon and began crying for reinforcements. With most of the Federal chips bet on McClellan, Stanton and Lincoln had agreed to send him some of Banks' men from the Valley.

But now that Jackson had slammed into Shields at Kernstown, Lincoln had the vapors again. He stopped the reinforcements. That was just what Bobby Lee had in mind, Stanton was sure. Robert E. Lee was the military advisor to Jefferson Davis, and no smarter man wore a uniform. Lee had been offered command of all Union forces when South Carolina seceded and it was clear war was coming. He'd still worn a U.S. uniform then, because Virginia hadn't gone out, but he refused the offer and went home, saying he'd never raise his sword again save in defense of his native state. Lee would cause them no end of trouble if he ever got a field command again. In the meantime he was directing strategy from Richmond. And doing damn well at it.

Stanton was sure Jackson didn't pose as big a threat as Lincoln feared. Jackson was making noise just to keep the Federal armies from uniting against Richmond. And it was working. He couldn't have that many troops, Stanton believed. There were three major Federal armies in and around the Shenandoah Valley, and any one of them was bigger than Jackson's forces, Stanton thought. If the Union armies joined forces, they could annihilate him. But Jackson had already stymied Shields, and that set Banks back on his heels.

Lee and Jackson were playing the Union leaders like chess masters, Stanton thought.

If only his generals would move.

If only they knew where Jackson was.

"How can so many people see him where he isn't?" Stanton turned. "And the larger question. How can he actually get to wherever he is so fast? This man isn't a magician, he isn't a sorcerer, he doesn't move his men by balloons. What does he do that our generals don't?"

"He makes decisions. And he moves." Hay wondered if he'd spoken too forthrightly, if he was out of place. He was only the President's secretary, not a military man. But he saw all of what was happening from the perspective of the center, at the White House. And he saw all of what wasn't happening.

"Hmmmph," Stanton grunted. "Decisions. But you must have decent intelligence to make good decisions. Why does he have it and we don't?"

"We're marching and fighting in his country, sir," Campion said.

"It's *our* country, boy." Stanton barked this at Campion. "When will people learn that it's *all* our country. They don't have a country, it's all the United States of America and we're trying at way too dear a cost to keep it that way."

There was silence. Hay had heard Lincoln say these words many times as well. Lincoln refused to recognize, even in his speech and his thought, the Southern states as a separate country. Those who did, in the President's view, had lost half the battle before starting—the logic of it, the emotional, even spiritual part of what made the United States of America. Lincoln sent men by the thousands to their deaths to hold onto what the patriots of the century before had crafted bright and shining from the corruption of failed old-world tyrannies. Those who gave the southern oath-breakers standing against this ideal drove Lincoln to explosion.

"Of course, Mr. Secretary. There's no other way to look at it. What Campion meant, quite rightly, is that the populace works for Jackson and against us. So he has eyes everywhere."

"But even *his* eyes got it wrong at Kernstown," Stanton said. "He and Ashby thought Shields had left Winchester, left the Valley. They didn't expect to hit regular troops as they moved north, and we bloodied him. So even his intelligence is off sometimes.

"Still, I'll give you the point, of course, Campion, that overall he gets better information. He knows more about us than we do about him. But that's not all of it."

"As Mr. Hay said. He *decides*, sir, and he moves," Campion said.

"That's it, Mr. Secretary. He does gather information, as good as he can get. But he doesn't wait for every detail, for every 't' to be crossed. He's willing to make a decision and take the responsibility. It's decisiveness our generals lack."

Stanton responded. "Maybe he doesn't have as many Congressmen looking over his shoulder, waiting to pounce on his mistakes."

"I don't think he cares who's looking over his shoulder," Hay said. "He doesn't give a fig for what they think. Even when his own superiors and a few fat men in the War Department in Richmond countermanded his orders in the Valley this spring, he resigned. Just like that. Said he wouldn't take such interference. Richmond put him back in command in a hurry."

"That's hubris. I'd cashier him," Stanton said.

"I don't think so, sir, with all due respect. I think you'd love to have someone who made decisions and stuck to his guns. And moved," Hay replied.

Stanton smiled just a little. "I'd give 10 of our generals for Jackson."

"What do *you* see in him, Mr. Secretary," Campion asked. "What do you think makes him what he is?"

"Asking me to answer my own question, Campion? You've got a future in Washington."

Stanton moved to the window. "I see a man who's willing to take chances, and who's a zealot. Dangerous, that zealotry, when linked with talent.

"Yes, most of all, I see a man who's willing to take grave chances. He knows the odds. We outnumber the South more than two to one. A few counties in New York have more industrial strength than all the Confederacy. They will always have less of everything than we do. Our armies could overwhelm him, if they'd only move," Stanton said.

"He doesn't care how much he's outnumbered, as long as he knows our commanders will sit in their tents and wait for reinforcements," Hay said, his voice rising with long-felt impatience. "They'll dally, they'll dither, and they'll wait for a better chance."

"And Jackson knows there will be no better chance. He's willing to throw in whatever he has." Stanton slapped his open hand on the desk, hard, twice. "He'll take the risk. And he's paralyzing us because we don't know how to."

Stanton had heard from a spy that, before Kernstown, when Jackson was still in Winchester, he knew two Federal armies were nearby, each of which greatly outnumbered him. But instead of quailing at the prospect, Jackson blithely told Richmond he'd take each one on separately. That kind of aggressiveness could frighten the North enough to win the war, despite the numbers.

"And, Mr. Secretary, he doesn't see thousands of our troops where there are only hundreds. He isn't scared by ghosts, the way our generals are, by armies that don't exist. He isn't overwhelmed by a blizzard of blather like this," Hay said, ruffling the telegrams on the desk.

Campion mustered the courage to come back to his point. "We are invading his country, sir. I know it's our country, but he was there first. His family was there first, came there from Scotland I think. He's fighting for his neighbors."

"And for his God," Stanton said with a contemptuousness that shocked Campion. "As if God wants to see so many killed. As if God can be enlisted for one army and not the other. As if God cares about tariffs and howling in the Senate."

"God cares about injustice, Jackson would say," Hay responded. "Jackson stood there and watched John Brown hang. He heard Brown's last words read, that he'd written in the Charlestown jail. That the sins of this country can only be washed away with blood. He seems to believe that, Mr. Secretary, and with a passion. He thinks Brown got it wrong, I'm sure, but we've crossed the line, the Mason-Dixon line, and now Jackson's going to supply the blood."

"Religious zealotry. It's ripped apart nations all through history. It's a terrible force," Stanton said harshly. "Jackson thinks he's an avenging angel now. The only way to extinguish that kind of self-righteousness is to kill him."

Stanton looked at the map again, as if it could show him an answer. Jackson had looked at the same map, he knew, and it *had* shown him answers.

"This is his ground, Campion, you're right about that. He knows it. Born up here in northwestern Virginia, lives in Lexington, moved up and down the Valley all his life," Stanton said. "He knows how to hide here, how to lose himself and then appear where we don't expect him.

"Look at this, the Massanutten Mountain chain that cuts the Valley in two lengthways. Jackson can be on one side pressing one of our armies, then in a matter of hours cut through this pass at New Market and be on the other side. And we'd never know, if he leaves a little force behind threatening our spooked generals."

Stanton poked the map again. "And look here, didn't you say one report had him going to Gordonsville? He can cut through Swift Run Gap in the Blue Ridge and be gone from the Valley, then march up the side and drop back into the Valley through another pass and come in behind our forces. This is a game board for him, and he knows all the moves."

"And he knows that speed is a weapon," Hay added, "especially against those who can't imagine speed. That's the combination he's found, sir. He's decisive, he takes chances, and he moves like the wind."

"Ummhmm, an ill wind," Stanton said softly, sitting down, weary.

The ding and clatter of the telegraph startled them.

"It's from General Milroy," Campion called excitedly, reading the message as it came across. "At McDowell."

"Where's that?" Stanton asked, quickly lifting his bulk from the chair and crossing to the map again.

"West of Staunton in the mountains, 30 miles up the Valley from Harrisonburg."

"Banks just retreated from Harrisonburg," Hay said. "Reported Jackson had been joined by Ewell and they outnumbered him."

"Pfff, Banks thinks a church choir outnumbers him. What's happening?" Stanton demanded.

"Milroy reports a battle, at McDowell," Campion said, sweating in the cool night as he read. "Said he attacked General Edward Johnson's forces there, but found Jackson had joined him. Milroy said they fought a good battle, and he's moving toward Franklin now to join with General Fremont."

"North!? He's retreating," Stanton said, slamming his foot down so hard it jangled the coffee cups on the table. "How the devil did Jackson get at Milroy if he's also chasing Banks down the Valley?"

The clicking telegraph echoed the crickets outside the window.

"*Where's   Jackson   now?*" Stanton roared.

"Pursuing. Milroy says he's firing the woods to provide cover so Jackson can't close on him."

The telegraph stopped. The three men were silent. Each was thinking about what Jackson was doing. And how in hell he could be doing it.

Hay pictured a forest burning. A nation burning.

Swift Run Gap, May 8, 1862—Confederate Army

Across the Valley from McDowell, at Swift Run Gap up the side of the Blue Ridge, General Richard Ewell's staff could see a little smudge of blue beyond Staunton. They couldn't tell if it was smoke or just the haze that always draped the mountains. In fact, it was the woods burning behind Milroy's retreat.

Ewell was providing smoke of his own.

"I've never seen Old Baldy so mad," said Parker Long, one of Ewell's scouts. "And that's saying something. Ewell makes mad an art. That man can cuss."

"He just wants to know where Jackson is," said Campbell Brown. "We're supposed to join up with him so we can fight, and here we are just sitting on our rears."

"I don't mind the rear, it keeps mine safe," Long said, whittling at a stick of pine.

"The general minds it, plenty. He wants to get at them, and so do I, Parker. Staying safe won't get you anywhere in this war." Brown and Long sat in a pass in the eastern range that defined the Shenandoah Valley. The view across the spring-green valley was stunning, but nobody had come there for the view. Least of all Ewell, in command of 6,500 Confederates and looking for a fight.

Richard S. Ewell was a Virginian whose family home, Stony Lonesome, just west of Manassas, was behind Federal lines. He wanted to fight Yankees, and get them out of Virginia. Ewell had been an Indian fighter in the old army, posted in New Mexico Territory. He'd chased Apaches, seldom getting them to turn and fight in the dry, hot hills of the Southwest. He'd risen slowly in rank through that hard duty, and also contracted diseases that had wasted him down to a wiry 140 pounds—malaria, yellow fever, dysentery, neuralgia. He was the definition of dyspeptic, with a stomach that writhed inside him and gave him a sour reputation. But Campbell Brown, the son of Ewell's first cousin and an aide on Ewell's staff, knew him also to be a kind and honest man with a soft side. Especially soft for Brown's mother, Lizinka. Born in St. Petersburg where her father served as U.S. minister, she was nicknamed after the Russian Empress. She and Ewell had been playmates in Virginia, and now, a widow, she lived in Tennessee. She had great wealth in land holdings, but Ewell seemed to love her for herself, not her land.

Brown, thrilled to answer Ewell's invitation to take a staff position, was uncomfortable hearing the other men call his uncle "Old Baldy" and joke about his rages. But he didn't want to seem too much of a goody-goody by defending Ewell all the time. Men like Long aimed to get a rise out of him by talking rough about the general, but Brown tried not to mind.

His uncle had been the first Confederate field officer wounded in the war when a Union cavalry patrol nicked him on the shoulder as he stood in a road in his nightshirt trying to rally green troops surprised by a 3 a.m. raid on Fairfax Court House. A month later, he commanded a regiment at Manassas, but was on the Confederate right and missed most of the action. There was a controversy about whether General Beauregard had ordered Ewell to cross Bull Run and hit the Federals as they pulled back toward Centreville. Ewell said he never got such an order, and Beauregard agreed that the order must have gone astray. But many critics said if Ewell had pushed across the Union Mills ford he could have decimated the retreating Yankee army after their lines broke in front of Jackson on Henry Hill. A Georgia newspaper wrote that Ewell was guilty of treason for not pursuing the Yankees. In fact, Ewell had suggested chasing the Federals, but Beauregard then sent him back to head off a rumored counterattack that never materialized. Ewell felt his reputation had been unjustly sullied, and he was eager to clear his record with a victory against his former comrades in the old army. He knew reputations were made by fighting and winning, and that's what he was hungry to do.

Since Manassas, mostly Ewell had marched. Confederate General Joseph Johnston had pulled the Army of Northern Virginia back from Manassas to the Rappahannock River, and Ewell set up a base at Brandy Station. When Johnston took most of the army to Richmond to face McClellan, Ewell was left minding only a small Federal force across the Rappahannock. Ewell, wanting to get into it, asked that Thomas Jackson's force in the Shenandoah Valley come down and join him to hit the Federals. Instead, Johnston sent Ewell to the Shenandoah to join Jackson.

Jackson ranked Ewell, so he was in charge. Ewell didn't much mind where he fought, so long as he fought. But under whom was the question. He respected and had enjoyed reporting to Johnston. Jackson he was not sure of. The man had a bad reputation. Since Manassas he hadn't done much. Now he'd apparently retreated up the Valley and was over somewhere near the town of McDowell.

Ewell had no idea what Jackson was up to. If anything.

"The man never tells his subordinates anything," Ewell had fumed to Brown. "How are we supposed to know his plans? *If* he has any."

Jackson was famous—or infamous—for keeping his cards close to his vest. When he'd occupied Harper's Ferry early in the war, a committee from the Maryland legislature had asked him how many men he had. Wanting neither to lie nor to divulge his strength to anyone, he said only, "I'd be glad if Lincoln thought I had 15,000." Asked earlier in the Valley Campaign by a civic leader what his next move would be, Jackson asked the man, "Can you keep a secret?" "Yes," the man said. "So can I," Jackson replied.

Ewell had paced by the campfire the night before in Swift Run Gap, kicking at the dirt with his boots, swishing at the flames with a long tree branch. "I understand the need for security. We can't tell everyone where we're going. But dammit he could tell a general. I always let my officers know what I had planned when we were in Indian country. They need to know enough to make good decisions. *I need to know.*" The last words he'd almost hollered into the night.

Ewell was frustrated. McClellan had a hundred thousand men coming up the peninsula at Richmond. Johnston was there facing him. The capital was in peril. All the chips were on the table there. That's where the war was. That's where the action was. This was just a backwater. He hadn't seen any real fighting yet in this war. And now all he was seeing was trees.

As he headed toward McDowell across the Valley, Jackson had sent Ewell a message asking if Ewell could bring any forage, because Jackson had trouble finding it. "*Forage*, can you believe it?" Ewell had been volcanic. "Am I to be his quartermaster now? Next he'll ask me for a flock of shit-assed sheep," he had yelled. He was so mad he nearly ate that message.

To add to his frustration, Ewell had been getting messages from Robert E. Lee, President Davis' military advisor. Lee said that if Jackson didn't need him, Ewell should take his force and head out of the Valley to Gordonsville or beyond and get ready to fight the Federals there to take pressure off Richmond. Ewell didn't know whom to listen to. Then came a message from Jackson saying "I desire you to stay in the Valley as long as Banks does, at least until I return."

"And when might that be? The fool doesn't say a thing, gives me no idea what may happen next. Just seems to want us hanging around, watching his goddam back," Ewell had said.

The next dispatch had been from Johnston, saying that if Banks leaves the Valley, Ewell should join with Jackson and they should both move to Fredericksburg. "How many different directions can we go in this war at once? Does anyone know what's going on?" Ewell had spat.

"I think the general's going to explode," Brown said now to Long. "He's being told to go here and there and then to stay. It's driving him plumb crazy."

"Well, then he'll be a matched pair with Old Jack," Long said, adjusting his blanket as a pad against the outcropping of rock he was leaning on.

"He's under Jackson's command and he can't move until Jackson tells him to," Brown said. "But Jackson tells him nothing, and we just sit up here in the mountains watching the birds and listening to occasional cannon fire to remind us we're not on a holiday trip. I can see why he's angry."

"Why are you in such a rush to get in a fight?" Long asked. "You ain't seen it yet, have you? Ain't been in it. Once you hear those bullets sing around your head you'll treasure a time like this, boy. It's good for your health up here. War ain't."

"I want to see it. I know it will probably scare the devil out of me, but I came here to see the war. I want to help save my country, don't you?"

"Sure," Long said. His home was near Warrenton, surrounded now by Yankees. "I want to send them home. But there will be plenty of time for fighting. We'll all have our fill of it, those who live." He looked at Brown. "I know a lot who've gone under already, and more will follow. You'll see your war, boy. You'll see a great plenty."

Long looked out over the Valley. "This Virginia's a big place, and it's lousy with Yankees right now. Our job is to find the ones we can beat. Find them where they're isolated. Find them where we can cut them up." He tossed a stone down the hill below them. "There's plenty of our boys behind us, back toward Richmond. Our job is to keep Banks and his troops from leaving here and adding their weight to the push on Richmond. Everybody's got their part to play. This one's ours right now."

"How heroic. Moves and feints," Brown said. "That's not real war."

"Success in war happens in the heads of smart generals first," Long replied. "Johnston's smart, Lee's smart. And they say this Jackson's smart."

"Well, you couldn't prove it by General Ewell," Brown said. "I'm tired to death of waiting too. Jackson better show his face soon, or I believe we'll march out of this valley and go find the war."

That night, Brown was with Ewell at Conrad's Store, a little Valley settlement tucked up against the Blue Ridge at the foot of Swift Run Gap. Ewell stayed here, waiting for word, with his men stretched from the top of the mountain to the bottom.

"Crazy. A god-damned fanatic," Ewell barked at Brown. "He thinks this valley is the center of the world just because he lives here, and he'd keep me pinned here like a god-damned bug while Richmond itself fell. And here we are doing nothing. At least a god-damned mother dog knows to try to bite the fucking foot that's trying to kick it. Armies all around us, but do we move? Not a blessed inch, by damn." Ewell's speech was marred by a lisp, and it added a comical dimension to his cursing, although nobody laughed. Ewell's anger just blew his words right through the lisp, and he seemed unconcerned about how he sounded.

And the general was now in a serious rage. A complex rage, with levels and channels and tributaries rolling into a singeing torrent. His dyspepsia was chewing at his guts and his neuralgia was pick-axing through his balding skull.

"This man Jackson is a *crazy fool,*" he yelled into the air, kicking at a log with the left leg which would disappear four months later, shot through the knee at Second Manassas and cut off by the same surgeon who would a year later take Jackson's arm. "An IDIOT. That rotting log has more brains than this wretched spawn of rankest hell, and moves just as fast. Dammit." He tried not to show the pain in the foot he'd kicked with.

"Every whore's son in the Federal Army is marching toward Richmond, those reeking shit-smeared motherless Dutchman mercenaries trampling down my home and devastating thousands of good Southern people. Shields is marching his vagrant bastard hordes right out of this valley to pounce on Lee and we sit with our thumbs up our righteous asses. By Christ it's a bleeding crime! I can't stand it."

Ewell was a professional swearer. West Point's cadet corps and the regular army nurtured the art, but Ewell had reached a post-graduate level years ago. A preacher who knew him said, "he did not confine himself to the dull neutralities of undecorated speech." A private in his corps called it straighter, saying Ewell was the most "violently and elaborately profane man" he'd met. Ewell's profanity "was ingeniously wrought into whole sentences. It was profanity which might be parsed, and seemed the result of careful study and long practice."

This fulminating didn't set well with some of Ewell's subordinates. He was likely to snap at someone who asked what Ewell thought was a stupid question, and lashed out often at men who weren't coming up to his standard of bravery and commitment. One of Ewell's brigade commanders, Arnold Elzey, had told Brown he thought Ewell was the crazy one. Ewell did not have an easy way with his men, Brown had to concede. Crazy was a word that was being kicked around quite a lot in the Valley just then.

Brown had to admit—if only to himself—that his uncle wasn't being quite fair about Jackson, even though Brown too was frustrated by the lack of movement. Jackson had told Ewell he was going off to Staunton, and then likely would go after Milroy in the Alleghenies. It was Jackson's lack of detailed information, his mysteriousness, that aggravated Ewell.

"Do you recall, Campbell, a few days ago when that fool sent wagons all the way up into the Blue Ridge gaps, to make Banks think we were leaving the Valley? Then that night he had us haul the fucking wagons back down the damned mountains? Damnable foolishness, I say. Let's square off against the bastard invaders and get on with it."

Brown only grunted, not wanting to say anything. Deception was clearly a weapon in Jackson's arsenal, and one he liked quite well. Mystery was the key to success, men quoted Jackson as saying. Brown thought it might be effective, if it wasn't overdone.

"Crazy as a March hare, and that's the goddam truth," Ewell spat.

They heard voices down the road, and someone calling, "I think the general's over by the store. I saw him walking on the porch, and they had a fire built nearby."

"Thank you," said another, deeper voice, and Brown could hear hooves clattering toward them. A rider pulled up.

His face was rugged and swarthy, his hair and thick beard black, his eyes a clear grey. He was strained with exhaustion, breathing as heavily as his mount. This man was small and thin, and sat gracefully in the saddle, as if he'd grown up on horseback, which he had.

It was Turner Ashby, Jackson's hard-to-control cavalry commander. Ashby had come to the defense of his native Virginia early in the war, had helped capture Harper's Ferry the first time, in 1861. His brother, Capt. Richard Ashby, had been killed shortly after, while trying to surrender, by some accounts. Over Richard's body Turner Ashby raised his sword and vowed to free his country and to kill the assassins who'd taken this tender life. The death and the vow both darkened Ashby and freed him. He was gentler and more generous with his men, but he also felt his life was already sacrificed to the cause. He became more daring, even reckless in pursuit of his foe. The name "Ashby" carried a fearful force of its own as it rippled through the ranks of the Federals he chased.

Ashby always moved with a speed that pleased Jackson, a speed that seemed internal to Ashby, a part of how he was, how he lived. He led his men from the front, not the rear, with his spirit, not with discipline. The loose rein Ashby kept on his cavalrymen was sometimes a source of aggravation to Jackson.

"General Ewell, how are you sir?" Ashby said, rubbing his face with his forearm, then swinging down from the saddle.

"I've been in hell, Ashby, hell for three days, hearing absolutely nothing and as useless as a tit on a goddam bull. What news do you have? Where is Jackson?"

Ashby's boots scuffed onto the pebbles in the road, his legs sagged at the knees, weary from the long ride. He steadied himself with a hand on the rifle case strapped to his saddle, then looked at Ewell. "He's beaten Milroy, and he's chasing him. Wants to bag his wagon train, wants to destroy him."

"Wagons, heaven's great fool, what does he want with wagons when Banks' whole blessed army is here in the Valley?"

"He'll come for Banks, general. He wants to put Milroy down, knock him back on Fremont, keep them out of the Valley."

"And what does your hairbrained general plan to do in this Valley, anything?" Ewell was thoroughly exasperated. Ashby had heard of Ewell's temper, but this was the first time he'd felt it up close.

"Sir, with all respect, this is the smartest man I've served with. You'll see what he'll do. He'll clear this Valley, push them all out of here and chase them back to Washington. Those that can still run." Ashby heaved for breath, slapped his hat on his trousers, raising dust.

"Colonel Ashby, we have some coffee here, or water if you like," Brown said quickly, stepping forward. "Can I take your horse, sir? Sit over by the fire."

Ashby handed Brown the reins of his tall white horse. "Thank you, Mr. Brown, I could use a bite if you have anything to eat." He moved off with Ewell toward the fire. "Are your men ready, General Ewell?"

Brown could hear his uncle snort, saw his bald head rear back. "Ready?" he yelled. "Ready? We're nothing but ready, by holy weeping Christ. We've just been playing checkers and chasing frogs in the creeks. We're ready for a blasted tea party, that's all we've got to do."

"We'll be moving north soon, general. Going after Banks or Shields. Is Shields still in the Valley?"

The two men sat by a fire giving off the heavy, sharp smell of oak. Daylight was dwindling. Brown brought a chunk of ham and some bread to Ashby, and a steaming cup of coffee. Ewell sat down hard in a canvas camp chair, Ashby pulled around a sawed-off tree stump and sat on it, his knees sticking up to the side, the leather of his high cavalry boots shining in the firelight. Ewell said he thought Shields was moving out of the Valley to go to Richmond, that they may already have missed the chance to hit him. But Banks was still on the west side of the Massanutten, moving north.

"When will Jackson come?" he asked eagerly. "We can't wait much longer. Johnston and Lee wanted to pull me out of here, and I haven't had a goddam idea of what I'm supposed to do."

"It will take him a few days. I don't think he'll catch Milroy, to be honest. The coward set the woods on fire so we couldn't follow him close. General Jackson should be here in a few days, and then we'll have a turkey shoot with old Banks."

Ewell pushed out of his chair, smacking his hands together. "Ashby, this is the best goddam thing I've heard. I've been positively stir crazy here. The war's been passing us by, and there's plenty of Yankees that need killing all around us. It's time we get at it, by the righteous God of all that's true. Let's get at it."

Brown saw Ewell smile for the first time in days. The thick muttonchop whiskers that swept down his cheeks into his mustache and chin beard creased upward with the smile, and he looked like a large weathered version of a boy just told he could go out after dinner to play. Brown allowed himself a little smile. Now he would see, now he would have his chance to find out what this war was all about.

The three sat by the fire talking until it was dark. Ewell made no more verbal attacks on Jackson. He'd suspend his fire, see what the hero of Manassas did in the next few days. Ashby went off to catch a few hours' sleep before riding back to Jackson, and Ewell and Brown went back up the Blue Ridge to tell their officers to get ready to move more men down to Conrad's Store in the morning.

But the calm didn't last. It took two more weeks for Jackson to come out from McDowell and bring his troops back into the Valley. Ewell was apoplectic, feeling slighted again with not enough messages from Jackson. But finally word came that Jackson was marching up through Harrisonburg to New Market on the west side of the Massanutten, then swinging right up the slope of the mountain to cross over the pass to the east side, where Ewell was to meet him. Ashby's cavalry was sent north from New Market, up the main part of the Valley, to shield the move across the Massanutten from the Federal's view. Jackson was in stride again now, using the topography of the Valley to make his army disappear.

The New Market gap was the only place an army could cross over the Massanutten. It was a lofty place of stunning views. From the pass the soldiers could look down on the small town of New Market and see fields of green rolling gently toward the Allegheny ridge, a view of 30 miles or more. A few minutes later they looked down on the Luray Valley on the other side of the pass, the long road winding down among the mountain crags to the bridge over the South Fork of the Shenandoah, then more swells of new crops, and the town of Luray beyond. The sight was breathtakingly beautiful, for those not too weary from the march and the climb to take notice. The Blue Ridge rose beyond the town, smaller foothills raising one's gaze to the darker, misty range that made the Valley's eastern border. An old settler in a cabin at the pass called to the men as they trudged by, "Look at this view, boys, this is our country. Nothing like it in the world. This is what you're fighting for, boys, and God bless you for doing it."

A few waved at him, most just kept on walking. They just wanted to get down the mountain, follow Jackson to find another Federal army, beat them and go home. Everyone had thought the war would be over after Manassas, but it had gone on. More Federal armies had invaded Virginia, and now the task before them was much harder. They were beginning to realize this wouldn't be settled easily. The North wouldn't leave them alone, let them depart from the Union in peace. The men's faith that Jackson could handle the Federals had grown with the victory at McDowell, and although they didn't quite know where they were going, they were sure they'd find action soon. And they were afraid it wouldn't be the last. But they were ready.

They crossed a bridge over a creek that ran through Luray, then turned left, north. This road would take them in several marches to Front Royal, the town at the head of the Massanutten mountain where the two branches of the Shenandoah came together. And where another Federal army guarded the Blue Ridge passes out to the plains of Manassas and the road north to Harper's Ferry.

Finally, here in Luray, on May 21 Jackson's troops met those of Ewell. The balding general was sprung from purgatory. Since their first meeting on April 28, when Jackson had marched toward McDowell and left Ewell stuck at Swift Run Gap, he'd only seen Jackson once. He'd ridden to meet his commander on May 18, but still hadn't learned much except that they were going after more Yankees. Now they were marching north together, Ewell not entirely certain what he had gotten himself into, but ecstatic about being on the move at last.

Shields had indeed left the Valley by this time, and under some of the conflicting orders and suggestions Ewell had received from Lee and Johnston, this fact gave Ewell permission to leave the Valley and try to get between Shields and Richmond. He could shed himself of Jackson, this strange and taciturn man whose tactics—and sanity—he questioned. But Ewell wanted to fight, and Banks was still in the Valley. Jackson now provided Ewell's best and most immediate opportunity to get into battle. Jackson, he was learning, could always find a Federal army to lay into. Ewell asked Jackson to take responsibility with Johnston and Lee for keeping him in the Valley, which Jackson did immediately, in writing. Jackson had no qualms about making decisions, especially ones that led to chasing Yankees. Ewell, satisfied, and impressed with Jackson's decisiveness, at least temporarily stopped his harangues about Jackson and fell in line, a strong partner for the hard days to come.

Two days later, Ewell heard a familiar voice calling to him as he rode next to his marching men. He turned and saw first the black beard, then the rest of Turner Ashby as the cavalry commander cantered up the line.

"General Ewell, hello. Glad to be moving?"

"As glad as a man who's been thoroughly constipated for a week and finally gets to run for the outhouse," Ewell said, with both an edge and a light lift in his voice.

"Nicely put, general, and a lovely image. Your men might agree that the prospect of battle opens things up for them," Ashby said, happy to hear a little levity from Ewell.

"Well, I've seen plenty with their guts sloshing just from being in camp too long," Ewell said, the lightness falling from his voice. "We lost half a dozen men to camp sickness just last week. A most ignoble way to die. What can I tell the parents of those poor bastards, that their sons died gloriously, shitting their guts out on the ground for our sacred cause?"

"That's too awful. The worst part of war, this crowding and poor eating that makes so many sick. I'm sorry to hear, general."

They rode for awhile, looking at the tired men around them. Some were barefoot, too many. A few looked up, and one tall thin man in ragged brown homespun hollered out the infantryman's favorite jibe, "Say, I see you there inside your hat, cavalry boy, I see your legs hanging down. Come on out of there and walk with us, see what real marching is like."

Ashby doffed his hat at the man and grinned. "I'd give you my horse, soldier, but she's quite attached to me and would be broken-hearted to have another man spread his legs around her." Both laughed, and the thin man cocked his hand at Ashby in a mock salute.

Ashby turned again to Ewell, saying, "What do you think of General Jackson now, General Ewell?

"I'm remaining agnostic, sir," he said, his lisp slipping across the words. "I've thrown in with him now, because he seems to be heading for Banks. If he takes us to the Federals, then I'm his man. But if he pulls more goddam tricks hiding us in the fucking mountains, I'm going to run my men all the way to Johnston at Richmond, find a proper battle for my boys. They need to be blooded, by God."

"We'll find the Federals, all right. Jackson's on the scent. And you'll see enough fighting to hold you for awhile, I'll wager."

Ashby touched his right hand to his hat, said a brief "good luck," spurred his horse so it bunched its prodigious muscles beneath him and cantered away toward the head of the column. Ewell waved.

The men rode and marched north, the Massanutten on their left and the Blue Ridge on their right. The South fork of the Shenandoah rolled beside them, shallow, peaceful, rippling over stone shelves in the riverbed. The green around them was lush with the push of life renewed.

As Ewell rode in the midst of this beauty, he saw little of it. He thought about Jackson. He'd thought about not much else for weeks. How can you fight a war by hiding and sitting, he wondered? How can you win by anything other than facing the enemy and shooting him down? Yes, Ewell had studied strategy and tactics at West Point, had read about the great campaigns. He had argued all night with friends like George Thomas and Cump Sherman—on the other side now, even Thomas, a Virginian—about the choices made in historic battles. But that was 20-some years ago, and Ewell had little taste for theory. What he wanted was fighting.

What did Jackson want? Ewell didn't know, but he wished to hell the general would tell him. Even General Richard Taylor, another of Jackson's commanders, had been horrified when he heard that Ewell hadn't been told Jackson's plans. But that was like Jackson—tell nothing to nobody. "If silence is golden, Old Jack is a bonanza," Taylor said.

It was better now that Jackson and his Stonewall Brigade were with Ewell's troops. But not much. Ewell still didn't know the plan. If there was one. But at least they were moving. Ewell knew the overall idea, to keep Shields and Banks in the Valley so they didn't join with McDowell and McClellan around Richmond. He'd had enough telegrams to let him know a dozen strategies, and he was tired of it all. He'd heard too much or too little from too many generals in charge, and all he wanted to do now was put some Yankees in front of his guns.

His fate was tied to Jackson's now, and he'd just have to see.

Front Royal, May 23, 1862

The most beautiful view in the world was once again clear. The blue stain had withdrawn.

Just west of Front Royal, Adam and Eulah Stiles had, every evening for 47 years, stepped onto their narrow front porch and together watched the light disappear from paradise.

Eulah had trouble walking now, and she couldn't see much through the milky white cataracts that had reached darkening hands across her corneas. Adam held her firmly with his left palm under her right elbow, talking quietly. "Step down, now, Eulah, that's right." She was so slender now, where once she had been heavy. Her feet in the past would have hit the boards of the porch hard; now they whispered down, her slippers kissing the worn oak. "We'll go a little left, here, my dear. Your rocking chair is just where it always is. Lucy is in it, of course." A calico cat lay tangled in Eulah's knitting. Adam reached down with his right hand, lifted the cat just behind her forelegs and hoisted her to his left shoulder. He guided his wife to her chair, she sat down with a grace and a sigh that still pleased him immensely, and he lowered Lucy to her lap. Eulah's thin, knotted, spotted fingers twined into the cat's golden, black and white fur, and a rich, elegant purr rose from the little cat and wouldn't stop until she fell asleep again on the woman's withered thighs.

"They're gone, are they?"

"Yes, dear, they are gone. Jackson's here, and they've run."

"Bless him."

Beyond the porch, the hillside on which the little house sat fell away into a flat valley. Through trees at the base of the hill Adam could see the last sparkle of the South Fork of the Shenandoah River. Then a farther border of trees gave onto a level terrain of farm fields until his eye met another rank of tall trees that marked the bank of the Shenandoah's North Fork To the right, hidden by more trees, the two rivers came together into one and flowed toward Harper's Ferry, the Potomac and the sea.

The prospect was lit from the left, the west, by the falling sun. The new green of May was losing its full lush glow as evening slipped across the Valley. No matter what had happened during the day, this sight centered Adam, calmed him, drew together the scattered tired parts of his being the demanding day had pulled from him.

When it rained, the two sat here and listened to the water wash the leaves and patter on the roof. When it snowed, they stood for only a few minutes, holding each other against the cold, shivering while they took the white benediction of evening. On fine nights like this, they'd sit for a long time, talking only a little of what the day had brought, breathing in the peace of the Valley.

Behind them and to the west, the powerful sentinel of the Massanutten Mountain lifted to its rocky summit.

This day had brought the angry grumble of cannon from south of the town behind them, the harsh yells of men in danger, the keening of men in pain. The quiet had been ripped by rifle fire, and the aged couple thanked God they were on their hill, above. Many people in the area had left when the Yankees came, become refugees, gone south to crowd into the houses of friends and relations. The Stileses had stayed. Too old, they'd seen too much, lived too long on their hill to go.

But today General Ewell had fallen on the Federal troops with pent-up fury, and the road north out of Front Royal had been crowded with wagons of wounded, cannon, horses and marching men as the defeated Federals fled north toward Winchester.

Adam, back from tending his modest grove of apple trees, had stepped up on the porch and looked north just in time to see the last of the blue column disappear. He'd gone inside, eaten the barley soup Eulah had prepared, then brought her out for their evening time together. He hoped he'd never see another soldier, dressed in blue or grey. He was glad to see his Valley clear of Yankees, and hoped Ewell and Jackson would push them out of Virginia altogether. Then all the men could take off their uniforms and return to their farms and shops and schools.

"How will Ellis' family fare if the Yankees go to Winchester?" Eulah asked. Ellis, their nephew and a teacher in Winchester, was in Jackson's army, along with his 20-year-old son. His family had stayed in Winchester as it was taken over by the Federals. Now as the Union troops moved back toward Winchester, and the Confederates were no doubt preparing to follow, Eulah worried about Ellis' wife and the four children still at home.

"They'll be fine, Eulah, don't worry. They've been through this before. Those people in Winchester know how to handle the armies. It'll be fine, fine." He suspected it wasn't right of him, but he truly felt no worry. This beautiful evening, with the quiet heightened by contrast to the day of war, he felt only release. The opening of the land to let the rain puddles seep in following the raging storm. That's what he felt like, just lying down and soaking it in. This tranquil view, this blessing of an evening.

They sat side by side. Eulah rocked and stroked the cat. Adam lit his pipe, blue smoke slipping through the porch rails.

"It's getting darker, isn't it?" she said, her head tilted up to catch the change.
"Yes."
"It's lovely, isn't it?"
"Yes, it is, again."
She smiled. It was quiet. The cat had fallen asleep.
Behind them, Ewell's troops arose and began the march toward Winchester.

Middletown, May 24, 1862—Confederate Army

Smoke. From an overturned wagon. Its front wheels blown away by a cannon shot. Its bed splintered and afire. Tumbled broken boxes of food smoldering.

From under the wagon, legs. Blue pants. On fire.

A black horse's left foreleg, torn from its body, the strong-muscled shoulder attached to nothing now.

A man on his back, left leg under his horse, on its side, red and yellow guts trailing behind. The man's right leg back among the entrails.

Behind, a tangle. Hard to tell men from horses in the pile. All tipped sideways, reaped by metal, speed turned instantly to pain and darkness.

Sitting against the low stone wall on the west side of the pike, a man in blue. Trying to hold his bleeding left breast in place against his white ribs.

A dog, short-legged, tail up and beating, white except for its muzzle, red from nosing into carrion.

Flies everywhere. Already.

Henry Kyd Douglas stared. Couldn't turn away.

Jackson and Ewell, with speed and shocking surprise, had burst out of the hidden trails of the Valley and fallen on the Federals. Jackson's cavalry and artillery had cut into Banks' supply train from the east at Middletown as it retreated north from Front Royal to Winchester. A turkey shoot.

Federal cavalry had charged, trying to break through. Douglas, 23, on Jackson's staff, had directed a line of Confederates to the stone wall that lined the road. Stapleton Crutchfield had sent two cannon wheeling down to the field by the road. The rifles and the cannon erupted into the faces of the Federals.

"Murder," Douglas had said. He remembered now what Jackson, standing beside him for a moment, had said. "Let them alone."

Quiet, appallingly firm. Let them keep shooting. Let the killing go on.

Of course, Douglas thought to himself. His own home just a day's march north was now in Federal control. Kill them, or they'll take it all.

He saw again one blue rider coming apart in his saddle as a canister shot from the cannon ripped through his belly, red slashing out his back, shards of vertebrae flying, his chest and shoulders lifting while his hips stayed tight to the saddle.

The Confederates at the stone wall had stood and cheered, jabbing their rifles into the air.

I don't have the coldness. I don't have the heat, Douglas thought. But they have to be stopped. These invaders.

Thank God there are men who like this.

Jackson had left minutes ago, with the rest, racing for Winchester to cut off Banks again, to try to capture the whole lot.

Douglas had to follow.

The man at the stone wall tipped sideways. His chest fell open.

Douglas, seared empty, turned his horse north.

The War Department, Washington, May 25, 1862

"Up, Campion, another telegram for Little Mac." John Hay, Lincoln's secretary, slapped Fred Campion on the soles of his boots, which rested on the desk while Campion napped, head hung over the back of his chair, nose up, mouth open. The telegraph clerk snorted awake and lifted his balding head so fast, eyes opening on the way, that the little hair circling the crown fluttered.

"What is it?"

"It's the Tycoon giving Mac a lecture. Here, put this across, make it scorch."

The telegrapher took the sheets from Hay, cleared space on the desk by pushing bread, dirty glasses and papers aside. "Jackson's movement is a general and concerted one," Campion tapped on his key. The next words from the president told General McClellan that the time had come to either move with dispatch on Richmond or come home and defend the Federal capital, threatened now by Stonewall Jackson.

"Take their king or defend your own, but don't get caught in between," Hay said. "That's where McClellan has gone wrong, he's too slow. He's given the Tycoon too much time to think."

The president's message told McClellan that Washington had been "stripped bare" of troops. Lincoln himself, and Secretary of War Stanton, had sent some of those troops toward the Valley to try to stop Jackson. But the president's bigger worry was Washington itself. Campion tapped away: "If McDowell's force was now beyond our reach, we should be utterly helpless. Apprehension of something like this, and no unwillingness to sustain you, has always been my reason for withholding McDowell's forces from you."

"McDowell's not happy with this, Mr. Hay," Campion said when he'd finished keying in the message and grabbed a bottle of water.

"I know. No one's happy with this, except maybe that damned Jackson. He's stirred everybody up with his barefoot army. I wonder if he knows?"

From the telegraph room across the lawn from the White House, Hay in the last few days had seen a flurry of reports fly through about Jackson. Always about Jackson. Lincoln had come there often, shuffling the telegraph slips, consuming the maps, ruffling his always-ruffled hair. As usual, the reports about Jackson were many and contradictory. They'd read alarms from Federal General John Geary, east of the Blue Ridge near Manassas, that Jackson had crossed out of the Valley and was surrounding him, probably on his way to Washington. But Banks reported that Jackson was still south of Banks' fortifications at Strasburg in the Valley. Confused reports from Front Royal showed Jackson pushing Maryland Union troops north toward Winchester. Then came word from Banks that he had been attacked by Jackson at Winchester. Other messages had Jackson going to Fredericksburg to battle McDowell, or to Richmond to reinforce Johnston.

From this little room where nobody had slept more than a catnap for days, where electric messages had drawn pictures of confusing movement, but always movement, Hay had watched the war turn. They had been so close, the Union armies. Everything was in place, at last, after more than a year of frustrating, faltering fits and starts. McClellan was closing on Richmond. The president had finally agreed to send McDowell's force from south of Washington on to Richmond, confident that Banks was holding Jackson far from the capital up the Valley around Harrisonburg. And McDowell was a day or two from joining with McClellan's right wing to squeeze and seize the rebel capital. Reinforcements for McDowell were coming from Banks in the Valley to ensure a strong enough push to secure the victory that would stop this hated war.

And then those forces flowing all in one concerted movement were disrupted. The armies hesitated, quivered, and now some had started moving in reverse direction, away from concentration, away from effectiveness. Ice floes that had been coming together to form a solid mass were now breaking apart, with nothing firm enough to stand on.

Because of Jackson.

After going for Milroy in what had seemed a wild goose chase, he'd pushed Fremont into the mountains, then chased Banks down the Valley with such speed no accurate reports could track him. He was, again, everywhere. He roared through Front Royal, slammed into Banks at Winchester; one report talked of an unstoppable and breathtaking infantry charge by Taylor's Louisianans. Banks had fled north, and seemed now to be crossing the Potomac, running out of Virginia altogether to hide.

Shields had been moving toward McDowell, McDowell toward McClellan. Now, Shields was coming back, McDowell was coming back, all to pursue this Jackson. McDowell said it was a waste of time, Jackson would retreat up the Valley before McDowell got close. McClellan wired that depriving him of McDowell could cost him success before Richmond. Everybody was angry as the focus of the war shifted from east of Richmond to west of Washington.

"He's busting up all our plans, isn't he, Mr. Hay? Jackson, I mean."

"Oh, I thought you meant Lincoln, and if so I was going to have to pretend I hadn't heard or severely reprimand you." Hay sat down by Campion's desk, twisting his moustache, looking over at the telegrapher with exaggerated seriousness. Then he explained, in a schoolteacher voice, "Mr. Lincoln, perfectly dissatisfied with almost every general he has, is now acting as commander in chief, and is moving around all his armies. Our Little Mac thought that was his job, but the Chief disabused him of that notion rather smartly. He's in charge, now, the President, and he may be making a muddle of it, or he may finally have found a man of action—himself. But you didn't hear that from me, Campion."

"He's just trying to protect Washington, right?"

"Precisely, and McClellan says *he's* trying to win the war, and needs McDowell and every other soldier drawing breath to do so. You can protect, or you can push forward to win. I've got to say that if Little Mac had done a more convincing job of pushing, instead of drilling and parading for months, and now tiptoeing up the peninsula, he'd have firmer ground to stand on now with the president. The chief thinks Mac bamboozled him, not leaving behind enough troops to protect this swampy little town that Mr. Lincoln still wants to be the center of the Union that Mr. Lincoln still wants to put back together."

Campion was quiet. Hay looked out the window, half expecting to see Lincoln striding over from the Executive Mansion to try to pull some clarity from telegraph reports that provided anything but. All was quiet, though, on the lawn—the only place Stonewall Jackson hadn't been reported in recent days.

"Has Stanton been here recently?" Hay asked, looking back over his shoulder at Campion.

"Yes he has, just a while ago. Mighty agitated, he was."

"He seems to believe all the reports about Jackson."

"What do you believe, Mr. Hay?"

Hay started to answer, then stopped. He turned toward Campion, thought a moment, and said in a tone that no longer carried a trace of jocularity, "I don't know. After being beaten at Kernstown and retreating almost to his lecture hall at VMI, he seems to have been reinvigorated. If we can believe half these reports, he's blasted down the Valley in record time and shattered Banks. He's a major problem. He may in fact be a very good soldier, and that would be disastrous for us."

"He certainly seems to push, like you said McClellan should."

"He does that." Hay fell quiet.

"Will he come after us, here, in Washington?"

"Well, we're beginning to learn you can't tell what this man will do. I'd say he doesn't have a big enough army to come against our fortifications. But if he knew we had secretaries and invalids manning those fortifications, he might come indeed."

"Can we stop him, do you think?"

"Yes. We have the capability, at least on paper." Hay kicked out a little wry laugh. "Although on paper we have a lot more troops guarding Washington than it turns out are really here. But we need some guiding force to bring the soldiers together, to go after Jackson."

"McClellan? Should he come back and take command here?"

Hay shook his head, slowly. Then he spoke, deliberately, stray thoughts and observations falling into a pattern. "I don't think it's Little Mac. I think it's the man in that big ugly house over there. Lincoln."

He put both hands on Campion's desk and leaned forward. "The man is smart, Campion. Lincoln's been studying this war. Not just the tactics and the geography, but the men. He's learning how generals work. He's learning from McClellan, often what *not* to do, and I think he's learning something from this Professor Jackson of Lexington, Virginia."

Hay paused, reflecting. "I think Lincoln is learning about speed and about bringing many parts together. In the last day or two he's been pulling troops away from McDowell, others out of Baltimore, out of the ranks here in the city, and pushing them toward Jackson. I think he's learning about initiative, and risk." He tapped the first and second fingers of each hand slowly, deliberately, on the desk while he talked to the telegrapher, a man older than he, but just as much a novice at war. "I do believe, Campion, that he's learning from Professor Jackson how to move small pieces with a speed that magnifies their impact. An apple someone tosses at you doesn't hurt if you miss and it hits you. But that same apple dropped from a four-story building would hurt you a great deal, right? That may be Jackson's great lesson. And Lincoln is learning, I hope, how to push at strategic spots—soft spots—that make other forces in distant places react." Hay raised his eyebrows, pulled his lower lip between his teeth, and nodded at Campion. "Another Jackson specialty, we're seeing."

Campion nodded. Hay continued, pointing at the wall map. "The president is going to try to catch Jackson, it seems, up here in the northern part of the Valley. And if he's learned enough in this fast, bloody little course he's taking, and if he can find some generals who will move, he just might have a chance."

Campion had listened intently. Hay made things very clear. Campion hoped it all added up to something. "Is the president frightened, Mr. Hay?"

"Hmm?" Hay's thoughts had been elsewhere, but he found the question intriguing. "He's not frightened for himself. He was pretty sure he'd be shot on his way from Illinois to take the oath here, you know, and he didn't hide. He is afraid, I'd say, that his generals won't match up to Jefferson Davis' generals. And he's terrified of letting the Union break up. He's—what?—monomaniacal about that. He won't let it happen. I think Lincoln agonizes, but he's not afraid."

"Secretary Stanton seemed afraid, if I can say that, only to you," Campion said in a low voice.

"Hard to picture that big bull of a man afraid. What did he say?"

"It's what he did. Wired all the governors that Jackson was marching on Washington, asked them—well, almost ordered them—to send their militia here. And he wired the heads of all the railroads, taking control of them to move the troops. He was in a spin, you know how he gets. Only moreso," Campion said, softly still so his voice didn't carry beyond Hay.

"Look at this, Mr. Hay. Governor Andrew of Massachusetts' wire back to Stanton. He called the militia to assemble on Boston Common, said 'a wily and barbarous horde' was descending on Washington. That Jackson has stirred up a hornet's nest."

Hay only grunted. He was surprised at Stanton's reaction, but his attention was pulled in by another telegram he'd found while tapping his fingers on the desk. It was from McDowell, arguing against being called back from so near to Richmond, the target he'd sworn he'd reach in '61 when the war had just started and he was in command.

McDowell was saying he shouldn't be sent after Jackson, shouldn't be pulled back from the powerful combination he was about to make with McClellan in front of the rebel capital. "If the enemy can succeed so readily in disconcerting all our plans by alarming us first at one point, then at another, he will paralyze a large force with a very small one," McDowell's message read.

Hay was troubled by that language. "Paralyze a large force with a very small one." It seemed so terribly accurate.

Was Lincoln overreacting, playing to Jackson's hand? Had Jackson already won the battle to rescue Richmond? From mountains off to the west? By pushing a small force fast enough to knock the breath out of the Union offensive from a hundred miles away? Had Jackson already won?

Hay looked at the ceiling, seeing cracks, spider webs. Was Lincoln too far behind the game? Would he not learn what he needed to know in time?

"Well, Campion, you look tired," he said, putting McDowell's wire down on the table, pushing it away, then drawing it back. "Don't you have some relief? You need some sleep. We all do."

"No, Mr. Hay, I want to be right here. I'm not going. I want to see what happens. It's a crisis, and my post is here."

"The crisis seems close enough, it may find us all," Hay said, wondering if it had already passed for Jefferson Davis because of this nettlesome, zealous professor from Lexington.

Charlestown, May 30, 1862—Confederate Army

This pretty little town between Harper's Ferry and Winchester was surveyed by George Washington's brother. A small stone building still standing not far from the courthouse had been Charles Washington's office. In the courthouse itself, three years earlier, John Brown had been tried for his abortive raid on Harper's

Ferry aimed at inciting a slave rebellion. On a nearby hill, Brown had been hanged in front of a crowd that included Professor Thomas J. Jackson and his VMI cadets and an actor named John Wilkes Booth.

Jackson's army was now strung along the Valley from Winchester to the Ferry. He had snuck up the Luray Valley, as the Shenandoah Valley on the east side of Massanutten Mountain is called, and blown the small Federal force out of Front Royal where the two branches of the Shenandoah River come together. Then he'd pressed on quickly and retaken Winchester in a tough but fast fight, and the citizens of that town, which was to change hands 72 times between North and South during the war, were celebrating. Jackson had sent troops on toward Harper's Ferry, and there had been skirmishing at Halltown. Ewell's staff members, armed with new Merrill carbine rifles they were eager to put in play, went after five Federal snipers who'd been picking off Confederates. They killed a few of the snipers, got an infantry barrage from two regiments in return, and sent back artillery fire in response. Not much else was happening, and most of the Valley Army was relaxing, although watchful. The army of General Nathaniel Banks, defeated and nearly captured at Winchester, had done its fastest marching of the war to escape north of the Potomac River. But there were rumors that Banks was being reinforced. And behind Jackson's army, and to the west, the Union forces of General John Charles Fremont lurked in the Allegheny mountains where they'd marched after Jackson chased them away from the battle at McDowell. And Union General James Shields had an army behind Jackson and to the east, outside the Valley. In effect, Jackson had pushed so far north so quickly that he was now surrounded.

But the northern generals and politicians had been knocked back on the defensive. The audacity of Jackson's punches had Federal forces quivering from Washington to Fredericksburg. By joining with Ewell and sweeping north down the Valley, Jackson had once again magnified with speed and daring the impact of his little army.

Banks, breathless but safe on the north bank of the Potomac, had wired the War Department that he had executed a deliberately planned move, fighting Jackson wherever he found him. But Lincoln would have none of it. He knew what Jackson had done, and feared what might come next, with the bold fighter so close now to Washington. But Lincoln had more grit than any general he'd found to put into the field, and he also saw a rare opportunity to checkmate Jackson and remove his threat.

Lincoln stopped Shields from marching to Fredericksburg where he would have combined with McDowell. He also stopped McDowell from pushing on toward Richmond until the situation in the Valley was resolved. This kept 40,000 troops from joining McClellan, and clearly would make it harder to take

Richmond, which McClellan seemed too timid to go after on his own. But the payoff could be bagging Jackson, who'd now come far enough north out of his protective mountain shell to be vulnerable.

Fremont had 15,000 men and Shields 10,000. Banks had 7,000 and another 7,000 were gathering at Harper's Ferry under General Rufus Saxton. Another 20,000 Federals could move in from the Fredericksburg area to join the hunt. Jackson's Valley Army numbered 15,000 men. Tired men, who'd marched from the southern end of the Massanutten Mountain almost to the Potomac, fighting as they went.

If it could be seen from above, it was like gathering weather patterns swirling over Virginia. Huge lowering clouds were moiling over Richmond, darkening the hopes of the fresh nation. But now lightning was flashing in the northern Valley, with thunderous forces drawing the power away from the rebel capital. The centrifugal force generated by the drive of one man and his ragged legions was sucking the attention and fears of the North into the tumbling hills and rivers of the Shenandoah Valley.

In a field north of Charlestown, as the sun burned through thinning grey layers of cloud, men were drying their blankets, knapsacks, clothes and tents. Spring flowers were everywhere, bright pinks, reds and yellows.

"Tom Fool got soaked last night, did you hear?" Colton Ramsey said gleefully, shaking wet bugs and straw from his blanket.

"Wouldn't stay in town with his fancy friends after supper, and the rain made a river through his tent, swept his stuff out on the grass."

"Guess he knows how we feel this morning," said Givens Woods, spreading a tattered shirt on the grass. "Get him a taste of what real sojerin' is like."

These men—boys really—were from Rockbridge County, around Lexington, Jackson's home. Some in their regiment had been students of Jackson's at the Virginia Military Institute, and others had recently left the halls of Washington College, next to the VMI on a lovely Lexington hill.

"He's had plenty of a taste of it, and shared it around, hasn't he, Cole," Albert Paxton said. "The man doesn't pamper himself."

"Wish I could have the suppers he has in those big houses, not pampering himself," Woods replied.

"Let him have a warm meal and a rocking chair by the fire now and again, Givey, he's an old man," Paxton said, tugging at his pants.

"Old man hell, he ain't 40 yet," Woods said.

"Don't swear, Givens," Paxton said, quietly. "We need the Lord to stay on our side, don't you chase Him away with your iniquities."

"Oh, in-iq-ui-ties, is it? I wish I had the opportunity for iniquities, I tell you," Woods said with mock sadness. "Hey, Pax, your hind end is hanging out of your pants. Is that an in-iq-ui-ty?"

It was true, the seat of Paxton's pants was out, and the rags of his underwear were showing. His pleas for new clothes from home had not yet been answered. "I'll trade you my pants for your shoes," Woods said. "I don't walk on my hind end, but my feet surely are sore." His square-toed brogans were about shot, the soles, riddled with holes, tied on with leather straps that kept breaking on the march.

The young men all looked physically tired, but also energized. The war was trying, but an adventure. They didn't exactly enjoy it, but they were enlivened by it. Woods, the strongest personality, was thin and rangy, with balding blond hair and a long, equine face. Paxton was small, whey-skinned, but with powerful arms and chest built up by mill work. Ramsey was starting on portly, although the marching was whittling him down, and his lightly pocked face seldom showed a smile beyond a student's wry grimace. They liked being in each other's company, talked and argued at the slightest provocation, tried to stay close on the march and under fire.

William Sutton was walking, slowly, past the men. His unit was camped north, almost to Harper's Ferry. He'd been separated on the fast march, so broken down he'd had to rest—almost pass out—for a few hours. Now he was trying to catch up. Passing by these young Rockbridge men from another regiment in the Stonewall Brigade, he heard Ramsey, Woods and Paxton talking about Jackson, and he stopped.

He stood nearby, listening. After hesitating several moments, he asked, "You boys know Old Jack?"

"Old Square Box? We might, what's it to you?" Ramsey said.

"I'm fighting with him, friend, but I don't know him. I'm from down near Port Republic, haven't seen him like you college boys have. People say so many different things about him, and I wondered," Sutton told them.

"Square box, we call him, on account of his big feet. And he's got an ego to match," Ramsey said. "Sit down, we'll fill you up."

"He most certainly does not have a big ego," Paxton said, turning his rear away from Sutton. "He's a humble man who gives God the credit for his victories."

"It's us should get the credit," Woods said with a snort. "We give him the victories."

"He prays to God to put him, and us, in the line of fire so he can be a big man," Ramsey said. "Look at Mexico. Begged to be put out front, handled a cannon single-handed in front of the Mex palace so everyone would see him. It's the ones under fire get the promotions. He's hungry, that man."

The three men had almost forgotten Sutton was there as they jumped eagerly back into a debate that clearly they'd engaged in many times, over many miles. Sutton listened.

"He feels he's God's instrument, and it would be a waste to sit in the rear not fighting," Paxton said.

Ramsey responded with heat, "I fear a man who thinks he's the instrument of God. That's arrogance, or worse, madness. John Brown thought he was an instrument of God, and he'd have turned the slaves on us in our beds. Who's got a direct telegraph line to God, then, Brown or Jackson?"

Ramsey and Paxton were leaning towards each other, eyebrows high on their foreheads, hands moving fast as they talked, voices climbing.

"You can't mean that, Cole. There's only one right. Don't you think this whole army is an instrument of God, Cole?" Paxton asked. "The Yankees have broken the covenant of the Constitution, and now they're in our country ravaging our homes. They are the forces of the devil, and God has raised a great army against them. And great armies need great commanders, and that's General Jackson."

"I think he's self-righteous, Pax. Sure, we have to beat the Yankees, and yes they're wrong. We'd never march on them in their country if they'd leave us alone. But Jackson stands up all pious and points loudly to what he's achieved and says the glory is God's. It'd be more seemly if he just kept quiet."

Sutton, sitting now, saw he'd hit a deep vein by asking these young men about Jackson. The general stirred passions. Sutton pushed for more. "Why do you fight for him then?" Sutton asked Ramsey.

"I don't fight for him," Ramsey said, spitting the words. "I fight for my home, this Valley." He looked for a moment at the green rising hills. "And Jackson gives us victories. He beats on the Yankees mercilessly, and that's what it's going to take. Look here, he's nearly chased three armies out of the Valley. He gets results, but I think he's pompous. I don't like him, but I'll fight with him because he wins."

The men were silent for a time, turning their blankets over, picking at the last of the food sent in a box from Woods' family back home.

"Do you want some cheese?" Woods asked, holding a greasy paper out to Sutton. "It's about gone bad, the box was held up because of the Winchester fight. We've got to eat it now."

They talked a little of the recent battle, told Sutton what little they knew about where his regiment was, speculated on where they'd go next. Maybe join the vanguard at Harper's Ferry, keep going to Washington. There were rumors of Federal armies coming in behind them, higher up the Valley. They weren't eager for another fight soon.

The talk turned to Winchester, and the women in the town. Jackson from the beginning of his time commanding in the Valley had forbidden his men to go into Winchester, a singularly unpopular decision as so many of the soldiers had relatives, friends and sweethearts there. But these young men had always seemed to find a way to slip through the guards. "Tell Sutton how you do it, Cole," Woods prompted. "Go on, it's genius."

"Nothin' to it, really," Ramsey said, clearly pleased to be asked. "There's a lot of ways for a resourceful old country boy. Sometimes I find a spot between two guards and march along it until some officer comes up from the town, and I challenge him for the password. He gives it to me, and as soon as he passes through I light out now that I've got that day's key to returning."

Woods laughed. "You're a peach, Cole. That's pure smart."

"Well, then other times I've slipped in between two guards, march along the perimeter with my rifle, come up to one and say I've forgotten the password will you tell me? They always do, and off we go once they turn away on their rounds. Once I used chalk to put some—what do you call them, epy-lets?—on my shoulders so they'd think I'm an officer. Easy as snatching pie coolin' in a window, I tell you."

"You'll do fine in this war, Cole. Half of what you have to learn is how to get around the enemy, flank 'em, sneak past and get in their rear. That's a victory every time," Woods said. The men all laughed, picking at little bits of straw on the ground, nodding at Woods.

"And oh, it's worth it," Ramsey said. "The dances, the lemonade on the porch, those ladies are sure nice to us poor soldiers. Makes me glad I signed up."

"You going to slip in when we go back through Winchester again?" Woods asked.

"Does Old Blue Light Jackson have a beard? You bet, and I hope I'm going to slip in, yes sir I do." Ramsey waggled his eyebrows and cackled a laugh.

Paxton pretended not to be listening, although he'd gone in with Woods and Ramsey one night, and had enjoyed the respite from camp life.

They got back to Jackson, as men in the Stonewall Brigade always did, on the march or in camp.

"Harvey Hill says the man's nervous as a cat," Ramsey said of Daniel Harvey Hill, a commander under Jackson, and his brother-in-law. "Boys over there say Hill wants to get away from him. Doesn't trust him to bring off a fight because he wants it too much. He'll run in headlong and not know what to do."

"Powell Hill said Jackson's an explosion waiting to happen. Wrapped too tight," Woods said, of Ambrose Powell Hill, a colonel under Joe Johnston.

"Oh chicken feathers, Hill hardly knows Jackson," Paxton said.

"They went to West Point together, and Hill was up around Romney," Woods said. "Someday those two will cross swords, I'll wager with you."

"He's crossed plenty of swords already," Ramsey observed, standing up and stretching, looking over the shallow hillsides around them. "Loring and his boys hate Jackson for that stupid freezing march up around Bath and Romney, and Garnett is pushing every day for his court martial to be held so he can rip Old Jack apart on the witness stand, prove Jackson's orders were muddled at Kernstown and that he doesn't let his commanders know what's going on."

"Seems Old Jack doesn't get enough fighting on the battlefield, he's got to fight his own generals," Woods said, shaking his head. "Me, I wish they'd just figure it out so we don't pay the butcher's bill for their incompetence."

Sutton listened. All men in camp talked about their officers. The commanders had their men's lives in their hands, so how they behaved was a vital matter to the men in the ranks. And people liked to gossip. The commanders were the "big bugs," always visible, and men talked about every aspect of their lives like they did about politicians and rich people back home. Around campfires, some men picked apart what the officers did, said they could do better themselves. Others, needing to believe they were in good hands, inflated their commanders' talents and made idols of them.

He couldn't get a bead on Jackson still. What he'd heard about Jackson was so contradictory, and the opinions about the man were so strong. He wanted to get closer to what this general was made of, what he'd done, what he might do. And what he might do that would affect Sutton, a common soldier in Jackson's ranks. "Before, down in Lexington, what was he like?" Sutton asked.

"Terrible as a teacher, I can tell you that much," Woods said. "He just read the text books to us. I think he'd memorize his lectures the night before. Ask him a question, he'd just back up and repeat what he'd said. Tried to beat knowledge into us."

"Didn't work with you, did it?" Paxton said immediately and got a clod of dirt thrown at him in reply, amid laughter from the others.

"He's got a voice dull as farmwork," Woods said. As the only one who'd had a class from Jackson, he was the authority.

"My daddy says that down at Charlottesville, at the University where he went for law, they have lecturers so good they fill the halls with people not even in their class. They can spin stories that teach you, there," Ramsey said.

"Jackson would die there. Nobody would come to his lectures. Rather have their teeth pulled," said Woods, starting to put things back in his knapsack, poking through the last of the box from home.

"They have a talking society in Lexington," Ramsey told them, "where people get up and lecture each other. Jackson was terrible at it, remember the stories? Would mutter and get stuck, just stop dead. But then later he'd get up again and have another go, get stuck just the same."

"I think that's admirable," Paxton said.

"That's arrogance. He should have sat down and stopped torturing those people." Woods laughed and bobbed his head on his long thin neck.

"No, it shows fortitude," Paxton insisted. "You have to keep trying to get good at something. I learned that at Washington College, trying to get mathematics into my head. Jackson says you can accomplish anything you will yourself to do. And he shows it's true. And, he's making it true for us."

"If we live through it," said Woods.

Sutton knew he should be finding his own unit, but he liked this talk. He wanted to figure out why the men liked Jackson so much, or why even the ones who didn't like him still felt such a strong connection to him. As if he were theirs, or they were his.

"I hear he has strange habits," Sutton said. He said he'd heard from some men that he held one arm in the air.

"He's praying," Paxton said. "On the battlefield, with that hand up, calling on God's blessing for his troops."

"He's hoping to pull lightning down, probably," Woods said, shifting on the ground to find a drier spot. "Some say he's holding up the hand that got shot at Manassas, to ease the pain," he added. "He's a weird one about health. I've heard he believes that holding up one arm helps his circulation. He thinks one arm is heavier than the other, and holding it up will even things out. The man's a hypochondriac supreme." Woods shook his head and rolled his eyes.

"I think it just shows he's crazy," Ramsey said. "Hardly ever says anything to his troops, just looks at us as we march by. Arm in the air, face grim as a preacher at a funeral. That's hardly inspiring leadership, I'd say."

Sutton scuffed at the ground with his boots, the heavy ones he'd used for farm work. Like those of most of the troops, his boots were starting to fall apart from hard wear. "Down where I come from, we hold up one arm to keep the gnats off our heads. When the weather gets dry, they're fearsome. They chew away at your temples. A woman at the post office in Harrisonburg told me one time that they go for the highest part of you, and that if you hold one hand over your head, they'll fly up there and leave your face alone. I tried it, and it's true. Maybe that's what Jackson's doing."

Ramsey laughed a short, sharp burst and said, "Wouldn't that be lovely. Here people are thinking he's so all-fired religious that he's praying all the time, and what he's doing is keeping the bugs off his forehead."

"And he's got plenty of forehead," Woods said, laughing too. "That's what makes him so religious."

"Do you really think he's crazy, Mr. Woods?" Sutton asked.

"Oh, hell, call me Givey, everybody does. I don't know if he's crazy, but he's damn sure peculiar. Won't mail a letter on Friday because he doesn't want it traveling on a Sunday, because that's the Lord's day, and nobody should work, including mailmen."

"He thinks a moving letter is an insult to God," Ramsey said. "Strange view of God. And letters."

"He won't even read a letter that comes on a Sunday, even a special delivery that is coming on Sunday because it's urgent," Woods said. "Back in Lexington, he told us a story of going to church on Sunday with a friend, who wanted to stop by the post office to see if there was a letter from a relative who was sick. Jackson persuaded him to leave the letter and the relative in God's hands. On Monday the man went to the post office, and found a letter from the relative saying he had gotten worse and wanted the man to come to him. But there was also a later letter that said the man had gotten much better, and the man didn't need to come. Jackson said that proved his point."

"And once that man thinks he's right, good luck shaking him from that view," Ramsey said. "He's got that straight line, he has."

"But he's honest, and he's modest," Paxton jumped in to defend the man he so admired.

"Oh, here it comes, let it fly. You looking for a promotion, Pax?" Woods poked at him. Paxton tried to ignore him.

"Back in Lexington, in conversation, if someone referred to an author or scientist or someone and assumed Jackson knew who he was talking about, Jackson would come right out and say he wasn't familiar with the person's work. The rest of us would just nod and try to look smart," Paxton said. "And if someone was talking about something Jackson knew much better, like military science, Jackson would never let on because he didn't want to embarrass the person. I think that makes him a big man."

"And a boring one. I'm sure he was a delight at parties," Woods said. "He's a maniac about food. Won't eat sugar, doesn't smoke or drink tea, doesn't drink coffee, wine or spirits." His voice was sing-song, like one child tattling on another, rattling off a list of transgressions. "And he'd never eat anything after his meager supper. At a party he'd refuse all food after supper." Givens shook his head and looked up at the others with a 'can you believe it' look on his face. "When a friend told him to just take the food and push it around on his plate so he wouldn't offend his hostess, Old Jack said that would be dishonest and he couldn't do it. And when his bedtime came, boom, he was out the door. The man doesn't know how to have any fun, that's what I think."

"Oh, he can have fun, Givey," Paxton said. "I've seen him laugh like a kid. His smile is huge and his eyes light up and he's just gleeful, just laughs and laughs."

"Well then you've seen something I've never seen," Woods said.

"You should see it, Givey, you'd think differently about the man. He's a human being like the rest of us. He's just so serious now because he's got a war to win, and he's got people like you to keep in line."

"That's no easy task, at least I hope not. I like to kick up my heels, and I could show him how to have some fun if he'd loosen up."

The picture of Jackson loosening up was one Woods couldn't construct, even though Paxton told him Jackson had loved to dance with the senoritas down in Mexico once the war was won and the U.S. troops were on occupation duty. Jackson's sober, dull reputation as a teacher and a church deacon had overwhelmed any lighter view of him as a younger man.

Paxton was set on giving Sutton a good impression of Jackson. "He's kind, too, when he has the chance," he said. "On the march up here a woman stopped him and asked where her son was, she had some socks and food for him, you remember that, Givey? Jackson said he didn't know her son among all the men in the army. The woman was surprised, said he must know her son, he'd been with Jackson for a year. The staff started to laugh, but the general stopped them cold and sent Sandie Pendleton to find the boy and bring him to his mother. Took an hour, but they found him. That's a good heart."

"He was probably just scared of the old woman, didn't think he had a choice. Couldn't flank her," Woods said, to more laughter.

"You know, Sutton, the man's got the imagination of a rock. When John Brown was caught and going to be hanged at Charlestown, Colonel Smith, the superintendent of the VMI, called in Jackson to tell him to prepare the cadets because the governor might want them up there as guards. Smith had to leave the room and told Jackson to remain as he was until further orders. Smith forgot about Old Jack until the next morning, when he went back into the room where he'd talked with Jackson and there the crazy old fool still was, sitting on a camp stool." Woods looked at Sutton, waiting to see if he got the point. But then he had to finish it, it was so good. "Smith asked him what he was still doing there, and Old Jack said, 'You ordered me to remain as I was last night, and I've done so.' Can you fancy that? Orders, that's his only passion. Can't think on his own. Wore his heavy wool uniform into the summer at the VMI because, he said, nobody ordered him to change. And this is the man who's in charge of our tender hides."

Woods blew his nose into the weeds, his final word. Even Paxton had nothing to say.

"So, have we given you a picture of this zealot?" Ramsey asked Sutton. "What do you think of your general now? Still want to follow him?"

"I reckon I don't have much choice. He's in charge. And like you say, he wins battles. If we can keep pushing the Yankees north, I'll be pleased to stay with him. Keep those fellows from my home and he's a hero."

"Where'd you say you were from?" Ramsey asked.

"Near Harrisonburg, between a little place called Cross Keys and Port Republic. Maybe you'll get down there sometime." Sutton thought for a moment. "It's as pretty a place as there is." At least, he used to think so. Pretty didn't seem to mean much anymore, to Sutton, with this war being fought so ugly in so many pretty places.

"We must have been close when we went after Milroy," Woods said. "Could be there again tomorrow the way Old Jack moves."

Sutton stood now, ready to go find his regiment. The moisture was rising from the ground, making the air thick. A faint breeze stirred, faltered. He hesitated. He enjoyed hearing these men talk. The hardships of the marches, the wet sleepless camps, the swift, irreversible terror of battle—it starts and everything pitches forward and down and you can't turn around—tended to draw men together. These boys were in another regiment of the Stonewall Brigade, so he knew he'd probably see them again. If they were spared bullets, and sickness, and breakdown from hard marching.

He looked at them for a moment. Ramsey throwing little pebbles, Woods sprawled on his back, his elbows behind him and his legs splayed, Paxton sitting cross-legged, looking at a letter from home that he'd read already many times. They were all quiet now. Sutton couldn't quite pull away. It had been a long series of marches and fights. He'd gotten to know several of the men in his regiment, a couple were from the part of the Valley he lived in, but he hadn't really reached out to anyone to the point where he'd call him a friend. Except for James Sparrow, the sergeant who was so gregarious and lively he immediately made Sutton feel close to him. But he hadn't seen Sparrow for several days, as troops were so mixed up on the march. Now Sutton felt a connection with these men who were so free with their opinions about the unusual man who was leading them. No one knew where they were going, or what they were after, but they knew they preferred going in the company of men who knew how to handle themselves on the march and the battlefield. Relationships were formed quickly, and as quickly torn apart.

"I don't look forward to more battles," Woods said as if in the middle of a conversation with himself, his voice low and slow. "People who say they're eager to fight the Yankees haven't been out here."

All four men stopped their small random motions, focused quickly on what Woods said.

"That's right. That's twaddle, as my sister would say. Used that word in a letter," Paxton said, touching his pocket where he kept several other letters, reminders of home.

More moments with no talking.

"Do you remember when you first came under fire?" Ramsey asked them.

A heartbeat or two, then, "I remember more the moment just before," Paxton said. "When a line of Yankee skirmishers came up over a hill, walking towards us. It was like they rose up slowly out of the ground, their caps, their beards, their shoulders, their guns. Walking right at us, and you knew they had no idea of stopping. I couldn't breathe, you know?"

"Yep. My heart, it was so tight it hurt," Ramsey said. "Thought it would rip out of my chest. I remember, Pax."

Paxton looked at them, his young face sheepish. "The moment came so fast. I knew it would come sometime, but *not now*, I thought. We were walking, then from nowhere, there they were. And it was on us. There it was. Smack into a day like any other out in the countryside. War. And everything changed in an instant. 'We're just kids,' I thought. 'Take it back.'

"I knew I couldn't, but I wanted to yell out, 'Hey, boys, how you doing? Where y'all from?' A thought zipped through my head, 'Let's talk about this, boys.'" He paused, smiling at himself, looking at the others. They didn't say anything, but listened like they understood. "I wanted it to stop. I thought, 'This can't be happening.' Maybe they were hunting deer, and we could join them, show them the best places we knew. But time was racing, you couldn't stop it, couldn't call for a pause. Couldn't say, 'We didn't mean it.' Because we did. But I didn't know it would be like this. Men like us, men we didn't know but they looked pretty much like us, coming at us. They hadn't even raised their rifles, and I just about wet myself, I swear.

"They rose up out of that swell, in a pale green wheatfield, and I thought I'd die."

They were all quiet for a while.

"You might still get that opportunity, my poetic friend," Ramsey said. More brightly he added, "And we'll write some heroic verse about you, won't we boys?"

The men were lightened by this diversion. Woods said, "Absolutely. Publish it in the *Lexington Gazette*. Nice black border. People will cry every time they see one of us after the war." He pushed one hand flat against his breast, flung the other out wide. "Women will throw themselves at us grieving heroes."

"Yes indeed, we'll tell your sad story to the young ladies of Lexington and they'll console us with their soft round favors, and that'll make us feel a little better about our grievous loss," Ramsey told Paxton, wiping an imagined tear from his cheek. "Say, can I have that nice new cartridge box you got if you're shot?"

"I don't want his clothes, that's for sure," Woods said.

"Yeah, I got my own lice, a full assortment," Ramsey said.

"Greybacks on parade," Woods said, holding out his shirttail.

An officer on a tall chestnut horse cantered up to a knot of men just beyond Woods, Ramsey, Sutton and Paxton. A sergeant stood and listened to the officer, then swung around to the men nearby. "Pack it up," they heard him yell. "Pack it up, boys, we're moving. Move sharp, let's get going, there's more Yanks to take care of."

Men rose, began rolling up blankets, ran to their tents and gathered cook pots and guns. "Christ, more marching," Ramsey said, and Paxton didn't even chastise him for his language. Sutton looked at the three men as they all rose, saying, "I better find my unit. Thanks, boys, I'll see you down the road."

"We'll do some fast marching now," Paxton said.

"Yep, I'll give Old Jack one thing, he can make us march faster than we ever thought we could," Ramsey said.

"Faster than we want to," Woods added. "He marches us out of our damned shoes. Hey, if you see any extra shoes down the line, Sutton, snatch them up for us."

"We'll see you in the next fight, Sutton. If you're beside us, stand firm for the Old Dominion," Ramsey said.

"Hell," Woods said, "stand firm to protect our butts. The Old Dominion can take care of itself."

They all laughed as Sutton moved off and the three picked up their clothes and blankets, snapped the grass, dirt and bugs off them and moved toward their sagging tent halves. Sutton picked up his pace to a trot.

Around them, the aged shoulders of the Blue Ridge and Allegheny mountains rose into the brightening sun. The mountains were part of this war, draped with mystery, hiding movements of columns of men, setting the boundaries of a stage on which were mixed speed and fear, uncertainty and decisiveness, risk and horror and glory.

Jackson was willing to make a run for his country's freedom. No one knew what would happen. Would the halting Federal forces, bewildered by the daring aggressiveness of the quiet professor, be able to catch up with him and hammer a sundering nation back together?

Fremont was about 40 miles west of Strasburg, Shields 32 miles east. Jackson's army was 40 miles north, exposed. In Washington, a day's march away, Lincoln looked at the map and thought he saw opportunity as much as danger. Depended on what side of the thing you looked at. And depended on what you did. If the

Union generals summoned their courage and moved—*moved* for a change—they could swing the door shut behind Jackson and make this valley of his a trap.

It was now, in the words of the prairie lawyer from Illinois grabbing anxiously at dispatches in the White House, "a question of legs."

Front Royal, June 1, 1862—Union Army

Emerson Grady had thought he was shut of this damned valley. He looked up at the north peak of Massanutten mountain with disgust and tired impatience. Back again.

His Ohio regiment, with Shields, had crossed Thoroughfare Gap a few days ago to head for Fredericksburg and Richmond. And maybe the end of the war.

Then they'd stopped, out beyond the foothills of the Blue Ridge, in a land of woods and fields patrolled by the dangerous and irritating Virginia partisan rangers. He and the other boys had sat in camp, kept their heads down, waiting for the little hit-and-run attacks that this time didn't come.

Then orders arrived. And they marched. Countermarched. Back over the gap. Into the Shenandoah Valley again. Would this never end, he'd thought.

At first they'd all been angry, thought their generals and the politicians in Washington all fools. Then had come word that Jackson had raced down the Valley again, smashed up Banks and headed for the Potomac. Now, it seemed, they were on their way to catch him. Close up behind him and press him against the river.

They'd had a brisk little fight, pushing the rebels out of Front Royal with surprising ease. Now they'd go after Jackson, slam up his rear and pound him to death. Make him pay for the death of Grady's friend John Nichols, maybe.

But, then they'd sat. Here in this hilly little town where the rivers came together. They'd gone nowhere. The game was out there and they'd done nothing.

And Grady had sunk into himself again. Staring at the prow of the mountain. It looked like a ship sailing north through the floating clouds. Hawks glided down the blanket of air that flowed over the dark trees of the low hills that rose up to the mountain's flanks.

An older man lowered himself to the ground beside Grady, his thick thighs stretching the cloth of his pants as he squatted. Otis Opperman. He'd marched with Grady, they'd talked together about what the hell might be going on. Opperman had walked into the town earlier, to see what he could find, and now he had half a roasted chicken wrapped in a dirty rag and a few potatoes. He held this out to Grady, who took a potato and held it cupped in his hand. Opperman lifted his battered canteen, drank, wiped the dribble off his bristly chin.

"Couldn't find no whiskey, Grady. I bet Stonewall's boys took it all."

"Shame. We got nothing else to do here but drink. We could have used it."

Grady looked toward the road heading north out of Front Royal. Nothing moved.

"Hear anything?" he asked Opperman.

"Yah, and you don't want to hear it."

Grady looked at him. Opperman was shaking his balding head.

"He got away, didn't he?"

"Yah, that's what happened. Skinned south, clean out of our trap. We missed him. Ran like a fox."

Grady let his head fall forward, looked at the seams of his pants, wondered idly how many lice were rooting in there.

"Was there a fight?" he asked.

"Little one. Fremont tried to hit him from the west, over toward Strasburg, but seems he didn't try too hard. Ewell brushed him back and Jackson slipped through clean as a wet hog. Banks didn't come up to help."

Grady looked up to the sky, shushed air through his pursed lips. "And we just sat here on our skinny butts."

The breeze lifted Grady's hair, he waved a "no" to the chicken in Opperman's offering hand.

"Shields musta thought he couldn't catch him out there," Opperman said, gesturing with the chicken to the land north of the Massanutten's crest.

"I don't think anyone who's in charge of this little shivaree thinks much." Grady hawked and spit on the ground.

"Well, they say Jackson's running south on the other side of that ol' mountain, and we're gonna chase after him down this side," Opperman said, his tone matter-of-fact like he didn't share Grady's view that nobody knew what was going on. "Maybe cross over at Luray and fight him on the other side while Fremont gets him from behind."

"We'll never catch him, Otis. He doesn't intend to be caught, and we move too damned slow, like we don't want to catch him." He picked at the ground, pulled up a weed, rolled the roots and dirt in his fingers. "We're just going to keep slipping around in this godforsaken valley, getting shot at and getting nowhere."

"What are you so het up about? Least we didn't get shot at today or yesterday."

"We will. They got plenty of shooting left in them. We'll just have to march forever to get in front of their goddam guns again."

"I don't mind not being in no fight, I'll tell you that."

"I don't like being here," Grady said. "I just hate it." He tossed the weed. "I hate this country. Let them have it."

"We can't. It ain't theirs. It's ours."

"I don't want it."

Grady stood, bit into the potato, said thanks through his chewing.

"Guess we'll be marching soon, from what they say," Opperman said.

"We been marching forever. Lotta good it does."

Grady watched the shadow of a cloud roll up the mountain. He shook his head at the scene, at the mountain, at the wind that blew always, at the valley that felt like the edge of Purgatory to him.

Woodstock, June 2, 1862—Confederate Army

Cold, wet, tired, and a goddam captive.

Clifton Byrne was up to his shins in mud. Just standing in it. The light was fading from the sky, the hills to the west and east rose dark and sullen, penning in the march, closing down his spirit.

He bent his head back on his shoulders, let the rain fall on his face. His arms hung straight down, water dripping off his fingertips. Around him, murmurs, curses, coughing. A splash as a man hit the wet ground, exhausted.

They'd been marching for three straight days, long hours and hard going. You couldn't really call it marching. The Valley Pike was supposed to be a good road, hard surfaced all the way down to Harrisonburg. When he'd marched it with Banks in May it had been better, occasional rain but the road had been firm. There had been no battle down there for Banks' troops, but after McDowell where Jackson beat Milroy, Banks had retreated back down the Valley. Then Jackson's foot cavalry had caught Banks at Winchester and drubbed him. But before that fight Byrne had been captured by Jackson's troops between Strasburg and Winchester. A few cavalry had come by and shot the wagon drivers, then infantry came up. A short fight, because the Union troops were so packed together. Three of his friends had been shot—he had no idea how bad. There was nothing for it but to surrender. He hadn't hated it as much as he'd thought; he'd just been disgusted. At being caught in the open like that, when there was nothing they could do. He'd been frightened at first, because he'd heard partisan rangers were killing prisoners. But there'd been nothing like that. He'd been kept with hundreds of others, herded back to the south as Jackson slipped past the Federal armies sent to catch him. Then the Federals had reawakened and given chase to Jackson. And everybody started moving south in as much of a hurry as mud and flooding rivers and creeks would allow.

Byrne's boots were full of silty mud, and the skin of his feet was rubbing raw. His pants were ripped, his shirt was filthy. His beard grew down his neck and he spent a lot of his time scratching at it. His hair was matted, and the top of his head where the black hair was disappearing was cold and slick. He was miserable and he was angry. He didn't know if he was angry at Jackson for capturing him and so many of his fellow soldiers and teamsters, or at Banks for letting him get captured. He thought mostly he was mad because of the damned march. Mad because of the damned war. Whatever it was, he was mad enough for everybody.

He'd spent much of the day with his shoulder pressed against the bed of a wagon. A captured Union wagon. Heavy with food and tents and cooking gear, it stuck in the deep mud every few yards. Byrne and the other prisoners were detailed to push the wagon, to lift it out of the mud, to keep it going so his fellow Northern soldiers didn't take it back where it belonged.

Bad enough to have the wagon captured in the first place. Bad enough to have to walk beside it, deeper with every step into the barbarous land of the Rebels. But to have to push the damned thing, to have to strain like a dray horse to make sure the Rebels got to keep the food and supplies they didn't deserve made him spitting mad. It was depressing. The constant rain, the stupid accents of the cloddish men guarding him, the gloating over what they'd stolen from "Commissary Banks," the surging hot pain in his shoulders from pushing, it all added up to a crushing gloom for Byrne.

He envied the men who'd been wounded and now lay in churches or homes in Winchester. At least they were only a good day's march from Harper's Ferry, the Potomac, Maryland, civilization. He was going deeper into Virginia. Farther and farther away from home, from what was left of the United States. He was surrounded by people who'd had the gall to break the law of the land by seceding from the Union, then by taking arms against the government. They were fanatics. They were rebels. They were defending something that was indefensible, and so in Byrne's mind they were simply mad. Barbarians. Capable of anything. He might never see freedom again. Might never feel the brisk wind off Green Bay, taste the apples and cherries of the peninsula that stuck into Lake Michigan and had been his home before this madness started.

The air stunk. It was thick and hot and rank, like a sweaty fat man at hog-killing. Sour sweat, soaked wool, oily dirty hair, piss and human shit, horse droppings ground into your shoes, and the grabbing mud that smelled like a rotting swamp in August. It all wrapped around Byrne and made him shudder.

"All right you Northern bravos, push that wagon for me now. Lean into it, let me see some *conviction* from you." The Rebel sergeant was a pain in the ass, thought himself a comic as he drove the prisoners like cattle. "This poor Pennsylvania team, they're probably Quakers now, don't like this war, so you've got to help these tender nags do their work. Go, and NOW, I mean it, push!"

Byrne pulled his feet from the glop, splashed over to the wagon, bumped into two other Union soldiers, growled and leaned against the wagon again. The horses' hooves slipped and stamped to get some purchase in the muck. One went down on its forward knees, a Southern teamster whipped it up. The wagon jerked to the right, lurched for three feet then a horse went down again, the wagon stopped sharp and Byrne's right shoulder was slammed against the ribs of the wagon bed.

"Damn, ah hell," he cried at the pain in his shoulder.

"Settle down, boys, we didn't invite you here, you hear me? Mind your manners and let's get this rig out of Mr. Fremont's grasp. Push now, and keep your whinin' to yourselves." The sergeant, James Sparrow, a big man from near Harper's Ferry, leaned out of the dripping evening, knocked his right shoulder into Byrne's left as he leaned close to Byrne's ear. "Just do your work and keep your mouth shut, soldier. Show a little character, and don't be pitchin' no fits here. We won you fair and square, so take your medicine like a good boy."

Byrne turned on him, his dripping eyebrows raised, his face showing consternation along with anger, his hands clenched at his sides.

"What do you take me for, a slave?" He spat the words at the sergeant.

"No, you're no slave, you haven't got the backbone." Sparrow was taller than Byrne, maybe six feet, and outweighed him, judging from the belly, by a good 40 or 50 pounds. He stepped up close to Byrne, his jaw almost touching Byrne's forehead. "But you're my prisoner, lad, and that means I own your hide while we're marching, and I'll either have it leaning into that wagon there or I'll be peeling it off you. You make your choice, but make it fast, because we ain't got time for stragglin'. We've got to get these vittles to safety where we can have us a nice feed, compliments of you and your skinny ape of a president."

Sparrow's words were firm, but there was a bit of a wry smile in their delivery, as if he was playing a role. He was aggravating, but so was everything right now. The sergeant, done talking, pushed Byrne with a strong hand toward the wagon. Byrne looked over his shoulder, started back for the smartass rebel, was grabbed by the man next to him, who'd been marching and shoving quietly next to Byrne all day. "Come on, let it be, let's get this wagon going. Ignore that hick," the man said quietly, close to Byrne's ear. "We'll have our time again, it's just not now. We'll have a chance to make these boys bleed again," the man whispered hoarsely, his breath hot and smelly on Byrne's face.

Byrne shook off the man, spat toward Sparrow, who'd turned away to tend the wheel horse that had fallen again.

Byrne was surprised, and disgusted, that he was still in captivity. After the rebels had descended on Banks' train and taken dozens of wagons and hundreds of men, Byrne had expected to be paroled, let go on the promise not to fight again. But he and his comrades had been pushed south. He knew from cavalry that had passed through just before the capture that Fremont was coming in from the west and Shields was closing on Front Royal. It looked as though Jackson would be caught having gone too far north, pinched off by the convergence of Fremont and Shields behind him while he chased after Banks toward Harper's Ferry. Then the Union prisoners taken on the Strasburg-Winchester road would be freed and returned to their own army, and it would be these damned insolent rebels who would be marching under guard.

But that hadn't happened, and it looked like it wasn't going to. Where was Fremont? Where was Shields? These rebels didn't look strong enough to hold off a good charge by a picnic of his friends back home. But there was nobody here to push them over. The Union plans didn't seem to come to anything, again. This valley was a disaster. A muddy filthy trap.

Byrne tried to swipe the mud off his face with his dirty hand. He saw men around him pointing ahead, to the wagon stuck in front of the one Byrne was leaning against. There was a man up there, in the midst of the rebels, with a bushy beard and a battered forage cap, shoving against the wheels with the rest of them.

"That's Stonewall," a rebel said as he slopped by in the mud, gesturing to the group at the wagon in front. "It is, Sparrow, you look at him," he said to the sergeant who'd been shoving at Byrne. "Look at him, up there right in with the rest of the boys. What do you think of that?"

Sparrow straightened up, rubbed his sleeve over his beard, turned and said, "I think he's trying to get us the hell out of here, and we can use his shoulder." The two of them laughed, and the first rebel slapped the sergeant on his shoulder. "Damn," the rebel said, a big dumb smile on his face, "he's just right in there with the boys."

Byrne looked. The man, Jackson if that was indeed him, was in a cluster of men on the left rear of the wagon, all of them grabbing the spokes of the wagon wheel, pushing them ahead one by one, moving the wagon through the sucking mud a few inches with each shove. In the mass of shoulders and arms and slipping legs and bobbing heads, nobody was paying the general any special attention. Once or twice a man would take a quick glimpse over his shoulder to look at the general, as if to see if it was really him. But the work was too hard to take more than a second or two away, and they'd turn their heads back forward to strain with every muscle of shoulders, neck and back.

"He's not even talking to his men," Byrne said, scowling, to the prisoner who had calmed him down a few moments ago.

"What, you expect a speech, in this mess?" the man answered, looking at Byrne with a fragment of a damp grin.

"Nah, not that. But a general moving among the men, you know, he could buck them up a little, give them a few words to encourage them. He doesn't even look at them," Byrne said, still watching the wagon and the men in front of him.

Sparrow leaned his shoulder and face toward the two prisoners. "He don't say much, that's not Old Jack. He leaves all that bluster and parlor speechifying to your big bugs." Sparrow nodded his head at the Yankees as he said that, his bushy moustache spreading to emphasize his smile. The smile, the nod, the words, weren't angry this time, or sour, but more like joshing in a way that seemed to bring Byrne inside the joke rather than jab him away.

Byrne looked at Sparrow, thought about saying some more, then did, almost invited by Sparrow's smile.

"Well, then, if he doesn't give speeches to you boys, what does he do for you?" he said in a low voice, testing this little connection with the rebel.

"He beats you," Sparrow said, holding Byrne's eyes with his own, bright under rising eyebrows. "That's all he does for us."

Byrne looked back at Sparrow, steady, considering.

"Not right now he's not," Byrne said, a touch of a lilt on the "now." "He's running from two of our armies."

Sparrow nodded again, looking content, as if with a more full knowledge of what was to unfold. "Yes, for now, it looks that way. But Old Jack marches us like the devil when he thinks we'll get too mauled up going at you head on, then looks for a soft spot in you all where we can stab you so it hurts. So you'll remember." He cocked his head at Byrne again. "Remember that you're in the wrong here, in our state. And at the right time, in the place he chooses, Old Jack will hit you so hard you'll remember it still when you're an old man gumming your soup by the fire, boy."

Sparrow gave off a jovial feel, even in this trudging, tiring nightmare. Byrne found the man engaging, even though he didn't want to, even though they'd hollered at each other a few wagonlengths back. The big bluff man would slam them and hammer them with insults to keep them moving, but it felt to Byrne now that he didn't seem to hold any personal grudge against them. He didn't seem to patronize them. He treated them, sometimes, almost like fellow soldiers caught in something beyond their control. The talk wasn't far off from that Byrne and his comrades slung around their evening fires, critiquing their own generals' talents and failings.

"You'll see, Billy Yank. Stick close by, and you'll see what that old gunnery professor can do. He'll be doing it to your puffed-up generals, your Pathfinder, your politician Banks," Sparrow said, his light tones given heft by the barrel chest they came from.

"You might eat those words when they trap you from two sides in this back alley Shenandoah of yours," Byrne said, turning forward to start walking again.

"Might could. But we'll see who eats what here in a mighty few days. Right now, boy, we're eating your feed. And much obliged. Now git." Sparrow jerked his head up, the motion flipping his cap bill forward like a command. He put two fingers of his right hand to the cap, then snapped them toward Byrne in a salute and a signal. Byrne nodded back, and walked, or slipped, ahead.

It wasn't like other wars Byrne had read about, when the men you were fighting didn't speak your language, were from another country, probably hated you. Here he was with a straining mass of men and they were all like him, at least in some ways. He shoved at the wagon box again, grunting and pushing and swearing under his breath.

Virginia looked a little like Wisconsin, he'd had to admit as they'd marched in the Valley. The hills were taller, but the forests were dark and thick like around his home, and the rolling meadows and fields were lush and green and pretty in the sunlight, like those around his place. He'd expected big plantations, but the houses he'd seen were mostly modest, some of them ramshackle and low and small like places his neighbors lived in.

He thought of Wisconsin as he walked through this dripping country. He tried to picture his home. Tucked in among trees near the big water of Green Bay. Tall trees, pines that went straight up 10 or 20 feet before shooting out branches that waved in the wind from the lake and sheltered his two-room house. With a little porch that faced the lake. Got to fix that north corner that's falling down, he thought. A woodchuck's been digging in under there, helping the rot of the wet weather take the wood down. A bit more forest behind him, thick with berry brambles. Then across a little country dirt road were his fields. Wheat, corn, stretching in flat golden bounty to the tumbled granite cliffs that lifted the land up to a stunning view of the water. He didn't climb up there as much as he would like, he reminded himself. Too much work to do, always. But wouldn't he love to go up there now, watch the sun set golden behind the far shore, watch the water dance in the day's last light. If he ever got back home, he promised himself, he'd go up there every day. Take Wilhelmina and the little boy with him. Make sure they have a chance to feel the peace of it, every day. Every day.

They had the wagons going better now. Jackson had moved on, mounted his horse without saying a word and ridden ahead. Keeping things moving, Byrne guessed. Keeping the rebels running. He hoped like hell Fremont would fall on them soon, and get him out of here. But he wasn't holding his breath for it.

These southern boys hadn't been too bad to him, except for riding him about how sorry the northern generals were. And they weren't far wrong on that score. None of the rebels had hit him or the others, they hadn't hurt anyone, even though they'd shot a batch of hot lead at them during the capture and for the weeks before. Once he and the others had been captured, some of the rebels had talked to them. Taunting sometimes, but just as often one or two had asked them about their homes, about what they did back home, about what they thought of the war. The talk had been wary, and some of his fellow prisoners had been sullen and wouldn't say much. But some of the men talked quite a bit together as they slogged along. They'd complained together, of the mud and the exhaustion of the march. One rebel had asked Byrne how many men the Federals lost to straggling. When Byrne said not many, the rebel said it must be because they weren't in their own country, that the Federals must be afraid to be caught alone in Virginia. The rebel had said they were losing a lot of men, some just dropping from being played out, some fading away to go home.

The fear had left Byrne after the first day. But he had this sense of being unfairly treated—by fate, not by the rebels. If he was out of the war, he shouldn't have to work so hard, walk so long and so fast, shove this damned wagon down this endless road in Virginia.

To the left of the soggy track, he saw a man crumpled on the ground. He was tumbled on his left side, his arms curled up over his head, everything about him soaked and muddy. His legs, bent a little at the knee, were just barely out of the way of the wagons and marching men. If a horse veered a little, the man's ankles would be crushed by wagon wheels. His musket lay beside him, his canteen and cartridge box and blanket roll spilled around him. He looked like he'd just fallen. He was a rebel, it looked like from his clothes. His head flopped back a little from his shoulders, so the rain caught him about three-quarters full in the face. His mouth was open, his muddy beard was wet, his crushed hat partly under his head. It looked like he was breathing. It looked like he'd fallen while he walked, and just hadn't gotten up. Fallen asleep, or passed out from exhaustion. Hadn't tried—maybe hadn't been able—to drag himself away from the danger of the passing column. How could he sleep, with all this swearing and grunting and whinnying and slapping and yelling, Byrne wondered. But he realized he himself was tired enough to fall over and sleep, even in this thick stomped-up swamp of a roadside. Some of the rebels said they'd learned to sleep while they walked, and Byrne wasn't sure it wasn't true. He'd have to pick up that skill or end up like the man in the mud.

Byrne thought of the sergeant, Sparrow. Big in body and presence, he was the kind of man Byrne might actually get along with, given time, might enjoy if he met him back home. A little heavy on the balderdash, but that went with the style and swagger of the man. Byrne allowed as how he might be fun to sit with in the saloon. At least for a night.

But Byrne knew he'd never find out if that was true.

Sparrow sloshed on up the line, and Byrne trudged on next to the wagon. The brief lift of energy the exchange with the sergeant had given him quickly drained away in cold spatters of rain, and exhaustion settled back down on his shoulders like a wet heavy cape. Dense and rank smelling and so old it made you weary to your bones.

New Market, June 3, 1862—Confederate Army

"So what's he like up close?"

"Well, he's—he's damn serious," James Sparrow said.

"Serious?"

"Yeah, like his mind is always spinning. Doesn't seem much to pay attention to what people say. There were officers with him, giving reports, telling him what they'd heard from scouts. Didn't look like Old Jack was listening, not paying any attention at all. But he sure was. One fellow said 'he's asleep' and Jack spun around and 'bout bayoneted him with a stare, that's the only way you could tell the fellow was wrong because until then it almost looked like he was right. That ol' boy near 'bout sank into his boots, I tell you."

William Sutton laughed, and Sparrow smiled at the laughter. Sparrow, just back from taking a message to Jackson's headquarters tent, had stopped by where Sutton sat next to a small fire. Sparrow liked what he saw of Sutton, on the battlefield, where Sutton didn't waver, and on the road, where Sutton moved smart and didn't complain. Sparrow wanted to get to know Sutton a little better. Encourage him, maybe; he was the kind of soldier that could win this war if there were enough of them. And Sparrow was always happy to talk about Jackson, and more than pleased to know something somebody else wanted to know. And more, Sparrow just liked to talk. It had turned into a long war and a lot of long wearying marches, and talking helped ease the slowness of it, the boredom. He liked being close to the troops, too—part of his job. Get to know them, know how they work, move them along and get them through. There was a lot to get through.

"You haven't seen him yet?" Sparrow asked.

"Not close. Just riding by."

Sparrow thought a moment, running his thumbs inside the suspenders that curved over his belly. "He's got a look to his face that's stern. Most of the time. Like a preacher, Old Testament type. His nose is kind of fine, sharp, big ridges over his eyes, makes him look like a hawk. Beard hanging down on his collar, thick, wiry. Thin lips, what you can see. Like he's tight. Pulled tight. His voice is high, surprising, really, from such an imposing man, you'd think it'd be deeper."

Sparrow nodded his head, squinted a little, trying to see Jackson again in his memory. "His eyes are deep set, blue or grey, I can't tell. They look at you and they go right through. Clean through."

Sparrow stopped, threw his hands out, open, like he couldn't find something. "He's...striking, I'd say. Not really good looking, with all that forehead where he's losing his hair. But he's..." the hands again, "...you don't forget him once you've seen him. He's tall, about six feet, and all business. He looks around like he's just sucking in information from the men around him, just bits and pieces, not like he's paying attention to anyone for more than a few seconds, he skips from one to another, turns his head or his back in the middle of a sentence someone's saying to him. But he's listening, faster than the men are talking, and he's taking it all in and rolling it around in his mind and thinking ahead. The men are still talking and it looks like Jackson's left them behind, he's put the pieces together and he's off somewhere else, moving on to the next thing, days ahead. He's moving faster than his officers. It's like they're all bunched up on the road talking about what's around them and behind them and he's passed them by, he's off the road and across country and somewhere else before they know he's not there anymore."

"Sounds like he moves at a different speed."

"Yeah, slow like he's asleep, and then before you notice he's up and gone. Like a lion, crouching, then up and in an instant running full speed."

Sparrow pointed at the battered pot at the side of the fire. "What you got there?"

"Coffee. That's what it's called, but it's damn thin. You want some."

"I'd be pleased to." He pulled a cup from his belt and handed it to Sutton.

"Is he...good to the men around him?" Sutton asked. "I mean, does he try to inspire them, talk to them, make them feel part of what he's doing?"

Sparrow snorted. "Nope. He's clumsy, kind of, he's stiff. Silent. Brooding, a lot of the time. He's nothing for conversation. Breaks off in the middle of a sentence. He's not easy to be around."

"Not a speech maker."

"No, not at all. Not even much for just talking with people, one on one or a group of us. He doesn't draw people along with what he says. He drags us along with what he does."

Sutton touched a spot on his right forefinger with his thumb. At Kernstown, when he had fought behind the stone wall, shooting for what seemed like an hour at the Federals coming out of the woods, he'd burned the finger on his musket barrel. He hadn't known how hot the barrel would get, and he'd touched the metal near the breach while reloading. It was as if a knife point had been jabbed into his finger tip, the pain was so sharp. The skin had instantly turned white, like ash, then dark days later. Now it was a hard little pad on the tip of his finger, and as he absently rubbed it with his thumb he thought of the roar of that battle. It made him shiver. There hadn't been a big fight like that since, that he'd been part of. But he knew more were coming. Jackson was taking them to more.

A strange commander, Sutton thought. Not much of a leader, from what Sparrow said and what those three boys up at Charlestown told him—Ramsey, Paxton and Woods. Not a handsome man, not a stirring speaker, not a man with personality who moved among the troops and made them love him. But a man with weight, somehow. With the heft to get things done and the vision to see where the army should go. Maybe he'll be all right, Sutton thought. Maybe we'll be all right.

Sparrow had continued talking, Sutton realized, hearing the voice rolling on through his thoughts. "He doesn't have to say much, because of how he acts. There was one morning, up in the mountains when he dragged us through the snow and ice on that damned Romney expedition. The boys in his own brigade woke up covered in snow, and they started in cussing Old Jack, saying he was a crazy fool, like they do when he pushes so hard. Then this pile of snow nearby rustled and up sat Jackson, brushed off the snow, said good morning to them and walked away." Sparrow laughed at his own story, one he'd told many times. "He'd been right there with them, sharing that pain-in-the-ass march and that damned freezing weather, and he just walked off pretty as you please. They still thought he was crazy, but at least they knew he was with them."

Sparrow looked around them. "This suits a sight better than that snow. Seems like a long time ago," he said. Around Sutton's campfire, others sat on the ground amid the scattered trees. It was a warm evening, mild and soothing. The rain had finally stopped, and Sutton heard laughter from groups around other fires. A hundred yards away, the woods stopped and a field, lush green, rolled to another copse of trees. Sparrow said, "The boys seem to be doing fine. Cooking pretty well, smells like. That bunch over there's making pretty lively music." One tall thin man had a small fiddle up to his chin and the others around him were clattering on pots and clicking spoons to the tune.

"You still doing all right?" Sparrow asked him.

Sutton heard the change in Sparrow's voice. This wasn't story telling now. This was one man quietly asking another about something true, something close to the soul that got so tattered in the war. "Tolerable. I'd rather be home by my own cookfire," Sutton said, and as Sparrow replied, "Wouldn't we all," Sutton realized it wasn't true. There was nothing much at home anymore. Life now, in the army, was full—of aching muscles, painful blisters, bugs chewing on every part of you, marches day and night, men everywhere crowding against you, horses and wagons and sounds, iron wheels and huge cannon tubes rolling by, packs and rifle pulling on your tired shoulders, and every now and then the chaotic rush of shooting and the chill of fear jumping along your spine. The emptiness wasn't so noticeable in all that.

"And how about you?" Sutton asked, also quietly.

Sparrow leaned toward the fire. "I hate this, and I kind of love it." Sutton nodded, to show he was listening. "I feel like I've got a purpose here, you know?" Sparrow said. "Nothing about the Yankees, but taking care of these boys. Trying to get them through. I like that part." He brushed off a cinder that had popped out of the fire onto his pants. He looked at the hole it had burned, shook his head. "The fighting, that's exciting until it's over and then it's horrible." He shook his head. "But it's the part with these men that lasts. It's being with them, when things are so intense in the fights, and then the easy times like this. It makes us into something bigger than just ourselves, I guess that's what I mean. Even though it's a bad thing, it's ours. Makes me feel part of something. Don't know how to say it. But I feel it, nights like these."

"You're doing well, Sparrow."

The big man looked up, pleased. "You're a good soldier, Sutton."

"Hmm. I'm not sure it's something I want to be good at."

"I know. But it's what we need to be doing."

"Yeah."

Sutton liked this big man. He talked a lot, so Sutton didn't have to, much. Sparrow was jolly, but not a buffoon. Thoughtful. Kind. A good comrade in all this mess of war.

"What do you think of the men?" Sparrow asked, gesturing around them.

Sutton looked too. Shapes, by fires, some stretched on the ground. "They're good. Seem to look out for one another. This brings them together, like you said, like a hunting trip. Only moreso."

Sparrow chuckled. "Yes, just a bit more."

"A lot of them seem to be having a good time, laughing and carrying on. Like at a barn raising or something," Sutton said.

"Yes, some of the boys are on a lark, and that's good. Keeps the morale up. But quite a few of them aren't making it so well. The marching is breaking some down, the fear's getting others. And there's a lot sick."

"We're losing some, aren't we? Deserting?"

"Yep, quite a lot. Fewer in camp every night. This is hard."

Sutton nodded. "It'll get harder."

"Yes." Sparrow looked at Sutton, his eyes focusing on Sutton's thin face. He held Sutton's gaze for a few heartbeats, serious himself now. Then he smiled, and the smile lightened Sutton.

"Thanks for the coffee. You owe me a real cup when this is all over. I'll come find you for it." Sparrow stood.

"It's yours, any time."

"You watch out for yourself, now," Sparrow said. "I'll see you tomorrow, we'll find us some Yankees."

Sutton waved his open hand in a little informal salute, and Sparrow walked off toward the Valley Pike, the road that ran from the fights they'd had to the north all the way up the Valley to Sutton's home. The fiddle music and the men's ragged singing filled the evening air. Sutton looked down, pushed a stick into the fire, wondered how long the road would be, how long the march. How long the war. And what would happen after.

North of Luray, June 4, 1862

The South Fork of the Shenandoah was shallow here. The water was colorless, all light as it rippled over the gravel beds and flat shelves of rocks. Across the river, by a stagehouse that served the people who used this ford a little north of Luray, a young girl was fishing. Or trying to. She was casting with a pole that was too long, and more often than not the bait and hook snagged in tree branches above her head instead of landing in the river. She didn't seem to mind; she kept casting and casting. Every now and then she'd give a little petulant stamp when the tree snatched her hook, but then she'd lean down and talk to the grey cat that was patrolling the shallows near her, laugh, retrieve the line, and try again.

"Johnnie, you can't stay here. You've got to go back."

"No. I'm not going to. I can't do it any more. It's too hard being away. It's just too hard all ways."

John Williamson Wharton and his younger brother Andrew sat on the river bank across from the stagehouse, watching the young girl fish. And talking about what John had done. He'd left the Second Virginia. He'd deserted.

John stretched his legs on the grassy slope, leaned back on his elbows and looked at the blue summer sky. "Andy, this is the first time I've felt like a man in months. I've been worked like a draft horse, like a mule. I'm done."

Wharton had been with the Stonewall Brigade since it earned its name on Henry Hill at Manassas. He'd marched all over the Valley. He'd frozen his feet in the Romney campaign. He'd marched all the way down past Staunton to go after Milroy in the Alleghenies, but hadn't gotten into the fight. He'd chased Milroy with the brigade, then marched all the way back down the Valley almost to Harper's Ferry and nearly been nabbed as the Federals closed in behind Jackson's troops. A piece of shell had slammed into his leg near Strasburg, mashing his pants into the muscle of his thigh and making such a thick clotted bruise that he couldn't bend the leg for a week. He'd had to ride on a caisson, each jolt of the wheel sending needles toward his bone.

He'd seen boys he'd grown up with be killed and maimed in such a variety of ugly ways that he could hardly sleep at night for the images that flitted through his churning mind.

"John, it's a disgrace, isn't it? You can't leave the army. You can't disgrace the family." Andrew looked down at the bent grass around them. "What would father say?"

"He's dead. 'Sides, you never know. He might cheer me for trying to stay alive." Their father had died of yellow fever in 1855, when they were both little boys. Andrew revered their father, and he was shocked at John's harsh words.

"Johnnie, don't be so hard. Father would want you to do the honorable thing."

"Father's dead, Andy, and I don't want to be. I want to be home, with you and mother. And the dogs. I want to have a life, Andy. I want to stay alive and live." Their father had worked making saddles and harness in a little shop in Luray. The business had passed to a neighbor, and the boys' mother was having trouble getting by on the little food she could raise at their cottage just outside of town. Andy did odd jobs for people in the neighborhood, working their gardens, painting, fixing things, to add a little cash or bartered food to the family's scant economy.

When Virginia seceded, John had answered the call. His mother had worried about how she and Andy would make do, but she didn't say a word. Women weren't supposed to. They were supposed to square their shoulders and proudly send their men to war, telling them not to worry about the home front. But John had been able to see the concern, the fear, something close to desperation darting in his mother's eyes when he'd gone off. Despite what he saw, he went and joined what became the Second Virginia. He felt he had to. And he wanted to. It was war. It would be glorious to chase the Yankees clear back to New York and come home a hero.

"You can't quit. It isn't right. And besides, they'll arrest you." Andy looked up at his big brother, squinting against the sun. "They'll shoot you, won't they?" Andy was 13, five years younger than John. He could too easily imagine rough soldiers coming up the road to their home, pushing in the gate, grabbing John from around behind the house and dragging him up to a tree and shooting him for desertion. He looked down, his face saddening, then over again at his brother, saw John's head bent, his eyes drifting over the water of the Shenandoah. "That's not going to keep you alive, Johnnie."

John looked over at him, saw a young kid who only knew the stories about war, the way it was supposed to be. John didn't blame him for it. The war that was fought in living rooms and stores through people's endless talk was different than what he'd seen out there with the Stonewall Brigade. People at home pictured a clean war, ranks of soldiers marching under bright banners in the sun. And when someone was shot, they only saw a name on the roles of the dead and wounded printed in the papers. They didn't see the guts ripped out, the brains leaking, the face shot away, the legs and arms sent spinning through the air. They didn't hear the sick kids groaning and whimpering as they vomited out their lives in cold and rainy camps.

To be truthful, war wasn't what he'd thought it would be, either. It wasn't just the horror of guns and bullets and cannon. He hadn't known he'd be so homesick. He didn't know he'd want so much to do just normal things, like fishing, eating at a table, sleeping in a bed, laughing with his mother while he snitched a finger of cake batter, even going to school. He so missed the little things of daily life. He missed his retriever, Ben, with his shaggy golden coat and his wet nose and tongue. He missed pretending to be asleep on Sunday morning, hoping his mother wouldn't get him up for church.

He missed sitting by a river, just watching it go. Not burning a bridge so people who wanted to kill you couldn't get across it.

John grabbed a stone and winged it into the river. "Andy, you'd be surprised how many of the boys have left. Through this whole mess I bet half of my regiment has deserted at one time or another. Just gone home. Just given up. Some come back, but a lot never do."

It had surprised him, how easy it was, and how few men were caught and punished. The Stonewall Brigade was supposed to be one of the finest fighting units in the army, and General Jackson was supposed to be such a firm disciplinarian. But day after day, men just drifted away. And nothing happened. On rare occasion a man would be punished. He'd once seen a man he knew, who used to run a boarding house in Luray, made to stand on a barrel in camp all day in the hot sun because he'd deserted and been caught. He'd heard of men being bucked and gagged in other units—hands tied around their ankles, a rifle or stick shoved behind their knees so they can't stand up, and a gag tied around their mouths—but he'd never seen it. He knew there'd been a shooting or two of deserters, but he hadn't seen that either, or known anyone himself who'd been shot. That was the threat, and their officers said discipline had to be maintained or the Yankees would roll up the Valley and burn all their houses. Men had to have the threat of something awful behind them if they ran, because what they could see right in front of them was so much more unspeakably awful.

Still, with all these threats, not much really happened, and men just kept leaving. John didn't really understand it. Early on, he didn't think he could do it. It had come into his mind many times, strongest right after Manassas. He'd stood firm on Henry Hill, although he'd wet his pants as they marched out of the woods and into the fields and into the flying hell of metal and noise. In the fighting, he had been too scared to waver even when he saw men right by him hit by bullets, bright blood looping in the air as they fell. But afterwards, when he could breathe again, when he saw what had happened, when he saw so many men torn apart, dragging themselves and pieces of their bodies through the stubble and dirt, he didn't think he could ever go through this again. He thought of running. But he didn't know how to start. And then there was such a pride that grew in the regiment and in the whole brigade. Throughout the South, the Stonewall Brigade and their tall strong general were famous. He couldn't leave that. It was a brotherhood, tempered in fire. All these men he'd never seen before were suddenly part of something beyond themselves. He'd lived through it with them, and maybe he could live through more. So he stayed.

But the months had worn him down. The marches. The rain. The bad food, if there was food. The clothes and shoes falling apart. The lice and chiggers and gnats. The gunfire. The boom and thwack of cannon balls. The splatter and whiz of exploding shells and metal in the air. The loneliness in the middle of all these men. The officers who told you what to do all the time. The thinning ranks, men dying or walking away.

Why not walk away? Why stay? The pride of the fighting unit had been eroded by the miles and nights and deaths. You couldn't live on newspaper clippings, on the reactions of the people back home. Because you weren't home to see it. To feel their admiration. Their thanks for what you were doing. Yes, you got letters. Mother telling you that you were doing a good thing, saving your country's freedom. That stirred a little pride, but it was just handwriting on a page, after all. And those letters also brought the details of home life you missed so much. People back home told of the regular things that happened each day. But they weren't happening to you any more. All you did was march and hurt and eat wretched food and get shot at. Or the letters told of what was not getting done at home because the men were gone, of the misery and hunger and homelessness that had replaced the life you knew.

"Aw, little brother, they're not going to shoot me. There's enough Yankees doing that."

"But isn't General Jackson tough, mean? He'll get you, won't he?"

John laughed, twisted a little where he sat, poked his brother's side, making Andy squirm away. "Quit that, I mean it. He'll get you."

"No, Old Jack won't get me. He's hard enough, all right, and a strange one. But he's let a lot of other men skedaddle and not done a damn thing about it. For all his big push about discipline, we're pretty much a ragged lot and we get away with it." He stretched again, as if his body had months of recovery to do. He swept his hand in front of his eyes, trying to push away the gnats that swarmed up from the river. He thought about Jackson, this man with the big reputation, this man who pushed his troops so hard on the march that they became dull unthinking animals that just trudged along to get to a place where they could rest in blind exhaustion. Until they were prodded to their feet again and shoved more miles down the endless road. Roads they'd walked in the opposite direction just days or weeks before. Over and over again, the push, the march, the falling forward, the deadening miles and miles.

Jackson. Tough. Hard. A stern master. And yet his army was falling apart, wasting away. And he just let it happen.

So finally John had let it happen to him.

He'd stopped. He'd quit. And Jackson couldn't do a damn thing about it. Or wouldn't. John was certain. He hoped he was right. He wanted a pie, a nap, a swim, a laugh. Two days in a row with just plain nothing to do. He wanted his life back. That's what he wanted. Why couldn't he have it? Why should he stay in the ranks when so many others had just lit out? It wasn't his war alone. He didn't have to carry the whole stinking thing on his tired shoulders. Why was it up to him? Let someone else do it for awhile. He'd had enough. Plenty. Stop.

"Are we going to lose the war?" John started; he'd almost forgotten his little brother was there.

"What do you mean, lose the war?" John hadn't thought lately of losing, or winning. He'd just trudged along, hoping to live through each day, waiting to be able to rest.

"Well, if you leave, and all those other men leave, there won't be anybody to fight the Yankees, will there? They'll get us, won't they?"

"Nah, they're a pretty sorry lot. And the men say their generals are idiots. Thank God for that."

"Mom won't let you stay, you think? She'll be awful mad, I bet," Andrew said, quietly. He dug at a mosquito bite on his elbow, making it bleed. John looked at him, thinking about his mother. She'd cut her finger yesterday, chopping vegetables for soup. He'd liked the sight of the blood, although he knew it was a strange reaction. It seemed like blood honestly come by, blood given for daily life, not blood torn by metal from someone who didn't want to give it up. The blood on his little brother's arm, just a little oozing drop, seemed so innocent, so much a part of being a kid, that it almost made him cry with yearning.

"Mom will want me alive, Andrew. Besides, she can't tell me what to do so much anymore. I'm a soldier."

"You're not anymore. You said so." This even more quietly.

"Jeez, you're like a bedbug, Andrew. You just gnaw away, don't you?" John looked across the water at the stagehouse, two stories, porches off both floors, an inviting place embraced by trees and the river. He'd liked coming over here as a kid, listening to the people talk on the porch. They were from Charlottesville, Richmond, Harper's Ferry or even Baltimore or New York. They'd talk of places outside the Valley, places he'd wanted to see. They told stories, smoked, laughed. It was a gathering spot. He'd learned more about Virginia history there than he'd ever learned in school. Heard about Jefferson and Monroe, Washington, Patrick Henry and Light Horse Harry Lee. People were proud of what Virginians had done, and never stopped talking about it. He heard about the planters, men who served in the Assembly and made the laws. Men who decided Virginia couldn't stay in the Union anymore. He hadn't paid clear attention to all the reasons, but from what everybody said about these men he was sure they'd made the right decisions. Now he wondered how many of those men had gone into the army, had ripped their feet up on the Valley Pike like he had. Not many, he was sure.

"What ever happened to the big hound they had over there, Andrew? I don't see him around."

"He died. Drowned, I think."

"Drowned? I never heard of a dog who drowned."

"He was old."

"How's Molly doing? She looked sick." Molly was their second dog, some spaniel, mostly mutt.

"She ate something bad. I think an old muskrat down by the creek. She'll be okay."

"She didn't seem that glad to see me."

"She's been scared of all the soldiers. A lot come around the house. She hides under the porch."

"Well, that just shows she's smarter than some people I know. Wisht I'd hidden under the porch."

"Johnnie, you're not a coward. Are you?"

"No, I'm not. I'm just tired."

Andrew stood up, brushed the dirt off his pants legs. "Let's go home."

"Yep." John stood too, swatted Andrew on the butt, and they walked up the sloping river bank.

The little girl, her cat cradled now in one arm, waved.

North of Harrisonburg, June 4, 1862—Confederate Army

"Well it's just natural for us to think of them as fools, because so often they are."

Sutton laughed out loud, surprising himself, and Sparrow laughed too, although it looked like he was trying not to. Givens Woods, the skinny, sarcastic soldier Sutton had met at Charlestown, was arguing with Sparrow about officers.

Sutton had walked down to the edge of the little creek to relieve himself and had heard their voices, been drawn by them.

It was a strange argument, because both Sparrow and Woods seemed to believe about the same thing. But they were having a grand time tugging at the edges where they didn't.

"You just can't always know what all goes into their decisions, that's what I'm saying. We can't see it all, down here on the ground," Sparrow said, pacing at the edge of the water, splashing a little with his feet.

"And they can't see much from their exalted heights because they're blinded by the shine off their own damn brass," Woods said, spitting an accurate shot at a sapling.

"Well, they do think they've got a pretty straight line to the truth, most of them. But the good ones listen," Sparrow said.

"How many good ones are there, sergeant? Most listen only to the tones of their own voice because they love it so." Woods pulled up a sapling and slashed with it, as with a sword, slicing leaves off the limbs of trees that nodded down toward the water. "A lot of them are officers because they were big bugs at something else before that has nothing to do with fighting. They got used to people telling them how smart they are, people who want a good deal from their bank or to marry their daughter or just a word in public from the big man so they can look to others like they're close to him. And maybe they got to be big just because their father owned the store before them, and they're dumb as a post but can't ruin the business if they try because the town is growing so fast. You think that's going to make them smart about how to keep us from getting killed? Smart about how to get at the Yankees where they're softest, where their belly's showing? No, it just makes them loud and sure of themselves even when they don't know shit. They just think their commission as a colonel or a general makes them right. Now that's a fool, to my way of thinking."

Sparrow looked at Sutton, winked. "This boy's wound up, Will. You think he's right?"

Sutton leaned his head to the side, raised his eyebrows, not wanting to be part of the argument but willing to throw one log on the fire. "Plenty of Jackson's men have thought he was a fool on this tour through the Valley," he said. "Taylor's men were ready to tar and feather him last month."

On the way to Front Royal and Winchester in May, Richard Taylor's Louisiana troops had been force-marched from the Luray Valley on the east side of the Massanutten up around the south end of the mountain, then north to New Market and over the pass back into the Luray Valley, about three times the distance as they'd have had to cover if they'd just gone straight north up the Luray side. They'd fumed at Jackson and called him all kinds of crazy as they'd trudged up over the mountain, realizing where they were going.

"But there, that's it," Sparrow said, pacing again like a lawyer making a case. "They thought Old Jack was an idjit, same as people thought when he marched us east up the Blue Ridge and then turned us around to go blast Milroy over at McDowell. He starts one way and then turns tail and the boys think he doesn't know what he's doing. But he's throwing the Yankees off our trail, making them think he's going one way and then he slams into them from a direction they're not watching. If you don't know what's in Jackson's head of course you think he's a fool, marching you for no reason. But it works. We do the hiking and he does the thinking and the Yankees do the running when we hit them."

Sutton looked over at Woods, who was looking through the trees, not at Sparrow. "What do you say, Givey?"

"Yeah, he looks smart when it works, I'll give you that."

"Oh, come on, he *makes* it work, it's not an accident, for God's sake," Sparrow almost hollered, waving both hands up and down as he walked. "He had Taylor's boys marching in all their colorful get-ups and making all their rowdy noise so all the world could see them heading for the Valley Pike. Word would get up to Banks that Taylor's lead unit of Ewell's men was heading down the Pike for Strasburg where Banks had his main force, so he left Front Royal on the other side of the mountain uncovered, only those thousand poor Yankees there for show. So Old Jack cuts back into the Luray valley, hot foots it to Front Royal, rolls over that little force and cuts in behind Banks toward Winchester. It was beautiful, Woods. Banks didn't know where his ass was to hold on and cover it." Sparrow stared at Woods, trying to drill the point in with his eyes.

Woods turned his head slowly toward Sparrow, smiled and nodded and said, "There, sergeant, you made my point for me. It only worked because Banks is a fool. He's only a general because he was a big politician in Massachusetts, and Lincoln had to throw a bone to the crazy abolitionists up there. Banks doesn't know a thing about war, only knows how to gas in the Congress. Thinks because he had power there making deals that he knows something about leading troops. He couldn't recognize strategy unless someone held money out for him to show which way to go. And who pays the price for him being too stupid to know how much he doesn't know? Those dead Yankees we shot up there, the ones who push plows and bend rims around wheels and are just the little people who do actual work back home and don't swell up too big for their hats. They're following too many fools, and so are we. They'll get us all killed before this is over, and they won't know why we're lying there on the ground." Woods' voice had calmed and carried a sad weight that gave it authority. Sparrow held his tongue for a minute, just shaking his head.

"All I'm saying, Givens, is that we can't judge what our officers are doing because we don't know what they're aiming for and how they're planning to get there." Sparrow's voice was quieter now, too. "We think they're cockeyed because we see only the pieces we're walking over. They see the whole picture."

"Why don't they tell us what they're doing? We'd go more willingly and we'd fight smarter. Who made them the holy men who get to keep the enlightenment for themselves?" More heat again now in Woods' voice. Neither man would let this be.

"Sure, they tell us and we'd be so full up with pride at knowing what was planned that we'd just have to tell everyone we met and some civilian would pass it on to a spy, not meaning too but also excited by the whole sweep of it, and the Yankees would hear and be sitting there waiting for us. Then we'd be on the ground instead of the Yankees."

"Plenty of us are getting shot this way, sergeant. Haven't you noticed?" Woods' voice had quickly turned acid, the verbal shot wicked. The argument had suddenly gone hot.

"Holy Christ, it's war, Woods, whadya think is going to happen? Men are going to get killed." Sparrow was leaning toward Woods now, barking back, his big feet planted by the creek bed, his arms stretched at his sides.

"More than need be. But the officers don't care—the more dead the more glory."

"You're wrong, nobody wants the killing."

"Then why are we doing so much, and why are you just going along?"

The words slapped. Woods and Sparrow stared hard.

"You carry their orders," Woods yelled.

"And you better goddam obey them," Sparrow yelled back.

"Not when they're wrong. I'm sick of it."

What had started as a favorite pastime—complaining about officers—had taken on a cutting edge. Sutton saw the rifles, leaning against trees, one near Sparrow, one near Woods. He shivered. The marches had been too long and everybody was weary of it all. Overwhelmed. Facing death, and the need to deliver death while worn out as a horse ridden too far too fast. It tore at everybody. The anger here was useless, but an understandable result of a large body of men moving too much with too little food and rest.

"All right, my friends, that's enough. Don't get so riled," Sutton said, walking toward them both. "Your point is that a lot of our officers don't know exactly what they're doing. Who does know? We've never been here before. They're pulled out of their towns and their farms just like we are, thrown into this mess where nobody knows what to do. How can anybody be ready for this? Men from another state, men pretty much like us, coming down here by the thousands loaded up with guns and cannon balls and nobody knows quite why. It's all gotten beyond us."

The three men stood, looking at each other. Sparrow dug in his ear with a finger, Woods bent his legs and scratched at his crotch, looking up into the leaves. Sutton rubbed his hand across his face. "Let it go," he said.

"Shit," Woods said, turning away after a last glance at Sparrow.

Sutton let out a breath, his chest sinking.

"You think Jackson knows what he's doing?" Sparrow asked, his hands hanging at his sides now, shoulders down.

Sutton felt less sure than he wanted to sound. There was a falling feeling inside his gut as he realized how dependent they all were on the real answer, not just his.

"It seems so," he said.

He looked at Woods, who had his hand now on a thin tree trunk, leaning into it as he bowed his head. Woods said, "I think Will's right, nobody much knows. And that's pretty goddam frightening."

Yes it is, Sutton thought. Yes it is. The whole business is frightening as hell. This many men, with guns, moving up and down the countryside, hunting another huge bunch with guns. Not really sure what they were doing, but angry enough to argue with friends on their own side. Short of food, short of shoes, short of sleep. The movement itself grinding away, at the men, at the towns and farms, like a rising muddy river caving in its banks as it churns its way to the sea.

We can never go back from this—not as the same men, Sutton thought. We're all being worn away. It's too much, for too long. It's not what we were meant to do, with our strength, with our hearts, with our lives.

South of Luray, June 4, 1862

Bettie Verner thought the war was awful, even though she knew you weren't supposed to think that. She had just turned 20, and the world in which she'd thought she'd take her place was falling apart.

She and her mother were running the farm. Her brother, and most of the young men in the neighborhood, were off with General Jackson. Several had been killed; one came back with no feet. Her brother, as of the last letter a month ago, was still alive, but suffering from camp sickness that was making him lose weight he couldn't afford. So many men had died in camp away from the bullets. She prayed he wouldn't join them.

She knew she shouldn't dwell on her own concerns when her country was fighting for its independence. She followed politics, and agreed with secession. New England shouldn't be able to dictate how Virginians should live. Shouldn't be able to set tariffs that kept the South subservient to Northern money changers. Shouldn't be able to interfere with the South's economic system of slavery. And surely shouldn't be marching armies south to destroy homes and barns and fields. And men.

Her family had lived in the hills above Luray for three generations. Their farm was lush with wheat and corn, their cattle were healthy and fat. She loved watching them graze on a rounded swell of pasture, all faced in one direction, spaced like a wallpaper pattern, with the misty ranks of wooded mountains rising behind. Walking by the creek and seeing mountains in all directions, she felt an abiding sense of peace and belonging. She loved her life, and she was ready for more.

The family home was brick, two stories, with a broad gallery in front and a long addition behind forming the stem of a T. It was cupped in a soft hollow of the rolling land, surrounded by oak trees and about half a mile off the main road from Front Royal to Conrad's Store and Port Republic. From her bedroom she could see the mighty ridge of Massanutten Mountain and the trees at its base where the South Fork of the Shenandoah river flowed. Her best friend lived right by the river, in a stagecoach house next to a ferry. Bettie visited often, loving to hear from the people passing through stories of the rest of Virginia. They were not far from Washington, and the family had gone there twice a year to shop, see a play, learn the new fashions and talk about the affairs of government.

The Verners were well off. While life wasn't easy, it had a grace and a sureness. Her father was a lawyer and served in the Virginia Assembly. He was often in Richmond, and her mother had always run the household and farm accounts, reporting to him when he was home. The work of the field and the house was shared by six field slaves, a cook and a maid. But Bettie and her mother were always working themselves, sewing and cooking and canning, helping with the livestock. Her brother worked hard in the fields, fixing machinery, repairing the outbuildings, planting and harvesting. There was little leisure, but much satisfaction. They ate well, had the clothes they needed, kept a good store of wine and some of the finest horses in the Valley.

She was fully into womanhood and eager to make a family and a home of her own. She was proud of her body. It moved beneath her clothes with a force of its own, alive and ready. Trim at the waist, rounded above and below, arms and legs strong and taut. Her hair was the rippling colors of wheat in the sun, her eyes dark blue, her skin smooth and clear. She was said, she knew, to be lovely.

Virginia was the most beautiful place in the world, and the Shendandoah Valley the most beautiful place in Virginia. It had seemed life would go on here as it always had. A life of books and learning, bright conversation, laughing dinner parties, rides along the river, clever friends, sleep in deep quilts soothing tired bodies, and the church on the hill for thanking God for His gifts and for what was still to come.

Bur what would come now?

Everyone talked of Jackson. And of Ashby. These men were heroes, fighting to preserve Virginia. But to her they were agents of destruction. She didn't want the Yankees to win, of course, although she was afraid they would. But she hated the glorification of war and death. How many men could be sent home missing eyes and hands and legs? From the pulpit and the capital, Virginia women were exhorted to honor these badges of courage with their love and devotion. But who could look every day at a face shattered by searing metal? How many supporting limbs could be shorn away before the whole structure of life collapsed?

She was ready to live, but now she could look forward only to surviving.

Yankee troops had passed by their house several times already. General Richard Ewell's Confederate army had marched by at the end of May on their way to the fights at Front Royal and Winchester, and the Verners had given the men meat and milk and bread. The Federal army was now moving south down the Luray Valley, chasing Jackson and Ewell, who were now said to be on the other side of the Massanutten Range. The Shenandoah was the granary of the Confederacy, as every newspaper said, and the Yankees wouldn't leave it alone.

Many servants had already run away from farms in the neighborhood, and more would go. The Verners treated their people well, so no one had left yet, but somebody would. Maybe all of them. And the blackguard Lincoln aimed to free them all anyway. The slaves would never make it in the North, and the South would never make it without the slaves. She had read the abolitionist agitators' stories of terrible treatment of slaves, and she supposed it happened some. But slavery was sanctioned in the Bible, and as long as people followed God's commandments and treated them well, slavery was right. It was even helpful to some of the Negroes, for so many couldn't live on their own. And the North didn't want the black people to live among them. Some of the rabble-rousers in the North said the slaves should be freed and then sent back to Africa. Even Lincoln. How noble. Return them to savagery and Godlessness.

Theories. Punctured now by the reality of bayonets and cannon shells. People could argue all they wanted about the way things were meant to be, but she could see how things would be.

Her family was surrounded by a cocoon of wealth. That cocoon had been spun by decades of hard work and careful living, and the family deserved what they had. She was, however, fully aware that she was better off than most. But that was ending.

Not just men were being destroyed. But wealth. Around Winchester, down the Valley, many farms had been burned, their animals driven off, eaten or pressed into Yankee service. So many women and children there were homeless. What they'd once had would never come back, especially those whose husbands and sons had been lost in battle. And there were too many of those. There was so much debt in Virginia, she knew, that just one or two crops lost to war would put many families under forever.

How could any country survive with its cities and farms destroyed? Virginia's banks were sinking, money was scarce and worth less every day.

The life of Virginia was at a breaking point. If the war went on much longer, it would all be lost, no matter who declared victory on the field. It may already have slipped so far that it would fall even if the war were stopped today, she feared.

And how would it be rebuilt if the wealth that supported it was wrecked?

If slavery were abolished, how would they work their fields, tend their animals and put up their food? Would she work from dawn to dark, clothes tattered, fingernails ripped, hands hard and torn? Scratching for a poor living day to day? Hopeless.

And life without men was flat and dull. Fathers, brothers, lovers gone. Despite what those radical matrons of Boston and New York said about women getting the vote and having lives of their own, life here in Virginia for women was defined by marriage and children, by building a home and a future. And that was a full life. Being part of the church that took care of the poor, being partners in running the home economy, teaching the young people the values of fair and just human interaction.

She talked with men about more than household things. Some raised their eyebrows at her outspokenness. But she was hardly going to give up her intellect. She'd read widely, and debated well. She could cast as well-informed votes as any man, but why would she need to? She was part of forming the thoughts of her father and brother and neighbors, by how she talked, how she challenged, how she made them think. She believed in the roles of husband and wife, and she wanted to step onto that stage with a strong and thoughtful partner.

Who would that be? Did he already lie with the dead on the sad dreadful day after one of Jackson's battles?

How could people revere this man who destroyed? It was not by his choosing, she knew, but he was wrapped in the arms of the devil, and in their struggle, she thought, we all would fall.

"There they are," her mother said, stepping onto the shady porch. She pointed toward the river. Another column of blue troops was coming over a rise in the main road.

Her mother, Amelia, tall, her weathered face firm but tired, held a pistol flat with both hands against her belly between her hips. Bettie felt first fear, then pride when she saw her mother with the gun.

"Wouldn't you love to shoot one?" Bettie asked.

"Bettie, don't think such a thing."

"Do you believe it wouldn't be Christian?"

"Of course it wouldn't."

"Is what they're doing Christian?"

"No. But I won't be part of it."

"You may have to be, mother, and in a very few minutes."

"Then I'll do what I must."

"And ask for forgiveness?"

"Yes."

"Good for you." She loved this sudden flash of spirit. Her mother's brother Mark had already been killed in the war. Her mother cried for days, then stopped. She went on now with a flatness, a grimness that was too seldom relieved. She laughed on occasion when the women of the neighborhood came together to wrap bandages or sew clothes for the troops, but the laughter rose and wobbled like a wounded bird, then sank.

The work was endless in the house and on the farm, without the men. A cousin and two children were staying with them now, chased from Charlestown by the war. The cousin, Elizabeth Howe, was a sad and cheerless woman, and was so before her husband was killed and her oldest son captured by Federal horsemen. She added her gloom to the household, her dull presence sucking out light from the rooms.

"What's Elizabeth doing?" Bettie asked.

"Staring. At the wall."

"My God, that woman needs to wake up," Bettie said.

"Hush, she'll hear."

"At least she's not talking to that stupid dog of hers, like she always does."

"Dear, that dog is her last link to her life before..."

"Then why doesn't she play with it, or do something with a little life, get up, walk, get her skirt wet in the creek?"

"Hush, Bettie. She's had trials."

"Yes, and who hasn't?" Bettie was impatient with these people in her house. More than impatient. She just didn't like them. The children were bratty and loud. They came into Bettie's room without knocking, touching things, letting the dog on her bed. Bettie knew she should be charitable and kind to them. But she didn't want to.

"What if those Yankees come up here?"

"We'll give them water, like before," her mother said. She reached up to pick dead blooms from the basket of flowers suspended from the ceiling of the porch. The soft slipping sound of wind in the trees by the house was broken by the clatter and creaks of horses and wagons on the road down the hill in front of them. Just another little invasion wearing away at the life they had had.

"Will you show them the pistol?"

"Only if I need to."

Two women on the porch and one Colt revolver. Such frail defense. Although the women, old and young, were determined, could they stand for an instant if the troops rolled up to the house like a thunderstorm?

Bettie watched her mother's long fingers close around a rotted blossom of the fuchsia plant and pull it off the thin green strand it hung from. Then the fingers touched a pale white blossom that had just opened and was ripe inside with translucent pink and slick firm petals. The fingers dallied, petted, withdrew.

A cry came from a teamster down on the road. "Hyeee-yaw now, git, dammit."

For a moment Bettie pictured a ragged wave of men coming through the front yard, overlapping the front of the house, peering in the windows, circling to the back door, sweeping past the outbuildings, grabbing what they wanted from what the Verners had worked so hard to keep.

She was startled, and angry. Angry at these men she'd never seen, from places she had read about and once wanted to go. Would there ever be travel again? Would their father ever come back from Richmond, would they ever take the train again to Washington? Would they go to New York as they'd planned before this all started? If she could, would she want to? Had the war closed off the world? Had the war closed off her future?

How could these men take so much from them? How could they dare? How could it be allowed?

Maybe Jackson and his ferocity were the only way. But the Lexington professor and his troops were away beyond the mountain, no good to them right here, right now.

She looked at the gun barrel in the folds of her mother's pale blue dress. It was black and sleek, hard beyond stone. She wondered if she herself could hold it, push it toward a man. She wanted to be able to.

How did those soldiers do it? Perhaps they never thought.

A rider broke away from the column of men, turned up their road. They saw him rise and drop as the horse cantered straight toward the porch. His legs bowed in a grip around the horse's chest. Clumsy, Bettie thought.

He slowed the horse to a walk, rolled his shoulders in fatigue. Ten feet from the porch he stopped. He was thin, dusty. Brown hair stuck with sweat to his temples; he rubbed the moustache under his nose with the back of his hand.

"H'lo," he said.

The women said nothing.

"Ma'am, we want some food. Do you have bread, or meat?"

"You've left us nothing, sir," Amelia said.

The man tilted his head back, then shook it, smiling thinly. "You don't look too thin to me, either of you. All respect, you know."

The women said nothing.

"C'mon, give me something. I gotta go back with something, ma'am."

"You may have water for yourself and your horse. Your horse needs it."

Amelia gestured toward a pump to the side of the house, the movement of her left hand uncovering the pistol in her right.

"Not such a good idea," the horseman said, jutting his chin toward the gun.

"Nor yours," Amelia Verner said, scorn ripping through the simple words.

They stared.

The wind stirred the air, lifting the fronds of the fuchsia by Amelia's head. She raised her chin, her mouth shut tight, her eyes holding those of the man, a bank clerk from Brooklyn whose butt and inner thighs were rubbed raw from an ill-formed saddle.

He was hungry, but he was more tired. And he was purely sick of hostility.

"Kur-ryste," he said, and slapped his horse. It jumped, and so did Bettie, jolted from the trance of tension. The man pushed his horse to the side of the house without looking back at them.

In a moment he came walking back around the corner, leading his horse. He paused, looked up at the bedroom windows and around at the fields. He looked as if he'd just been dropped in a place he didn't recognize. He was about to speak again when the front door slapped open and Elizabeth's little dog tore out, yapping and racing toward the man and the horse.

The horse reared, and in one harsh rush of motions the bank clerk jerked one arm to check the horse and pulled his pistol in a snap and shot the dog, catching it in the neck, nearly tearing its head off.

All sound stopped, the clap of the shot erased as quickly as it came.

Four hearts thumped in shock—once, twice, thrice.

Then a child screamed from above, a torn lost howl.

The man looked at the bleeding, still animal. "Shit fire," he said, almost growled. "The hell with you all." He turned, stuck his left boot in the stirrup, grabbed the pommel with the right hand that still held the smoking pistol, and slung himself up on the horse.

"The hell with you," he said, looking down. He sniffed snot back up his nose, swiped at his moustache with his gun hand, tugged the horse around and rode away toward the column of dusty blue.

Crying burst from inside the house. Hopeless, bereft and ragged like a wound.

Bettie let her breath out in a rush and looked over at her mother. Only Amelia's shoulders had sagged; the rest of her hadn't moved, including her eyes, which stared at the empty sky where the rider's head had been.

Bettie didn't want to move, had no interest in this moment or the next.

"This is life?" she thought, standing small and empty on the porch, flies descending on the dog.

The blue troops moved slowly south. No one else disturbed the house.

New Market, June 4, 1862—Confederate Army

They'd fought a little rear-guard action at a creek south of New Market. Nothing big, just enough to get the blood pounding. Turner Ashby, Jackson's cavalry commander, had been his usual self, riding headlong at the Federals to stampede them when they came too close.

Maybe a dozen Union soldiers had fallen, some of them killed, some wriggling on the ground in pain, pushing with whatever limbs still worked to get behind a tree or an outcrop of rock to find shelter from the bullets and the horses.

Two of Ashby's men had been killed. Patterson Neff didn't know one, but the other, Thorne Moffet, he'd grown up with.

Some of the Federals had fought very bravely, and Neff told Ashby he admired their skill and the calmness with which they stood in their places and faced Ashby's troopers. Ashby told him someone once said to Jackson that he admired the brave ones on the enemy's side and felt sadness to have to shoot them. Jackson had said emphatically that that feeling was wrong. He wanted the brave ones killed. "Kill them all," Jackson had said. "Shoot the brave officers and the cowards will run away and take the men with them."

But killing the brave meant the best were being lost, forever. On both sides. The ones who'd survive would be the skulkers, the cowards, the ones who thought first of themselves and not of the cause. Who would be left after the war to put things together, to guide the government, to teach the families? Men like Thorne Moffet, a thoughtful, smart, funny school teacher who had tended his aged parents and served on the town council at Strasburg wouldn't be able to lead Virginia to recovery after the war was won. The noisy bullies who were tough on the peacetime streets but hid when the bullets flew would be the ones still standing at the end of the war.

And the northerners who would run the country the Confederacy would have to be neighbors with would be the ones who talked big but didn't step forward to fight. It didn't seem right. It didn't look like a good future.

Neff sat now on a fallen tree beside the creek, swollen after several days of rain. It looked like a good place to fish, small and fast like Tumbling Run in his neighborhood, in the lower Valley by Fisher's Hill. Home. This Valley. This Virginia.

Neff's pistol lay in his lap. He picked it up, felt reassured by its weight. The barrel was six inches long, black steel, nicked in a few places. From beneath the barrel he unclipped and pulled down the lever that prized the cartridges out of the cylinder. The mechanism was simple and clean. He pulled back the hammer, the slick double click of the action sounding solid and certain. It got your attention, this noise. Said something decisive was about to happen. Said, don't tread on me.

He held the pistol out at arm's length with his right hand, sighted on a bluejay drinking in the creek. The bird dipped its head in the flow and sluiced water back over its flapping wings, bobbing up and down. Neff tripped the trigger with his forefinger and lowered the hammer softly with his thumb.

He'd shot men with this gun. Held it inches from a man's face just moments ago and pulled the trigger hard.

Patterson Neff had ridden next to Ashby in the fight, caught up in his energy, his zeal. They'd ridden right through the creek a few hundred yards from here, splashing water on the men they were assaulting, knocking them down with the thick breasts of their mounts while the men were trying to reload. They'd shot the Federals with their pistols as they rose in the water from their fall. Blood had spurted from the forehead of the man Neff had shot. He'd seen the man's eyes, angry, then wide, then under the water.

Neff slipped the pistol into the holster on his left hip. It slid into its leather socket with a 'shuk' sound that he liked. It came out with a 'swoosh' sound that gave him confidence. He pulled it in and out a few times, then stopped.

He lifted his sword and put it across his thighs. The sword was lashed to his saddle most of the time. When he wore it slung from his belt, it clunked into his pistol too much. Still, he liked the sound of it clanking as he walked. The blade rattled in the dented metal scabbard and the sound made him feel gallant, dangerous. It wasn't a sound you heard when you went out in the woods grouse hunting, he thought. This was a sound that said you were hunting for men. If they needed to be hunted. If they were invading your home.

He slipped his hand inside the curved metal of the fist guard. The leather grip was coming loose again. He'd tightened it many times, taking the leather in his teeth to pull it taut. He now had twine wrapped about the base to keep the leather from unraveling. He pulled the sword out four or five inches, looked at the silver blade, pushed at the hilt and watched the blade slide back in. Then he pulled it all the way out, fast, and the blade rang as it swept out of the scabbard. He held it up in the sun, light running up and down its curved length. It looked medieval.

He was ready to defend honor with this sword. No, not honor. That's what you felt when you wore the sword to a dance full of officers in uniform and ladies in wide bell skirts. With this sword, in its creased and tarnished scabbard, he was defending something much less theoretical. Himself.

He slapped the sword on his thigh, lightly, then harder. You hit people with the flat of it sometimes to knock them aside. You could smack them unconscious if you hit hard enough, slam them off their horses.

Or you could chop with the blade. He had done that in this fight. As he held the reins in his left hand he'd slashed at a Union rider with his sword in his right. The northern trooper had fired at Neff with his pistol as they closed on each other, sending a bullet into the leather of his saddle, then two more horse strides and Neff had swung up over his own head and down past the Federal's. The sword had knocked off the trooper's hat and then sunk in his left shoulder. It had stuck there, four inches down, buried in bone. Neff pushed back and forth, and the man jerked to Neff's motion, the sword stuck in him as if in wood. Neff stood in his stirrups, leaned forward and shoved the man from his saddle. He fell, and Neff's sword was tugged out of his hand. Neff pulled his pistol and shot him.

He came back later for his sword. The Federal was still alive, a bullet in his belly and Neff"s sword sticking up above his head. Neff couldn't say anything. The man looked at him, his face sweaty, his mouth tight. The man blinked as Neff stood over him. Both were breathing hard. Neff felt tears start. The excitement and hatred that shot up his spine and filled his lungs in battle were gone. Now there was a terribly hurt human being lying at his feet in the drizzle. Looking at him. Like a deer you had shot but hadn't killed. It was still wild, it tried to get up but couldn't, it looked at you with cold incomprehension at your transgression.

"I didn't come to your home, sir, why did you come to mine?" Neff said, his voice choking. The man just stared at him. The gaze had neither hate nor forgiveness, just a cold resolve. To live, Neff supposed. To keep breathing and get home. Neff didn't think he would make it. But he heard a quick prayer in his head, asking that the man would.

"We'll go," Neff said. "A surgeon will come. Your men will take care of you."

Neff knelt, put his left hand on the man's left breast and levered the sword quickly up and out of the man's flesh with his right. It came loose without a sound, but the man gasped, once, twice, three times, four times, then quieted. His tongue came out, his eyelids fluttered. Neff took his canteen from his saddle, tilted water into the man's mouth. He drank. Neff took his handkerchief from his pocket, folded it over the sword wound, lifted the man's right hand and put it on the handkerchief to hold it in place.

"Hold this on 'til they come. God keep you." Neff stood, found the man's hat and laid it next to him. Neff was crying. The man still looked at him, level and ice cold. His breath came in small chuffs. Neff wanted to stay with him until help came, realized that was madness, stepped into one stirrup, swung into the saddle and rode.

He'd cleaned his sword in the creek with sand and leaves. He stared now at its edge. He lifted it above his head and very slowly replayed the downward slash. At his own shoulder's height he stopped the sword, gritted his teeth, shuddered.

The feel of his weapons gave him strength. But, right now, no peace.

He placed the sword flat on his thighs again. Bent at the waist, with one hand on the pommel, one hand near the tip. He rocked over the sword, bending its metal from the ends he held.

He said out loud, but just barely, "We have to get through this." The words came slowly, each one pulled through his tight chest. "We have to pass through this valley. God grant that our souls, not just our bodies, make it through."

South of Luray, June 4, 1862

They were so close. Was that freedom? Was freedom so close?

The blue-clad troops marched down the road, toward Conrad's Store, thousands of them. Well, it was a stretch to call them blue. Most of their uniforms were worn, muddy-looking now where the rain had soaked into the dust. They looked tired.

Was this the host of the Lord? Were these rough men the liberators of his race? That's what Henry Aaron Verner had heard from his brother Samuel in Lexington, who had the northern papers read to him by a black preacher, and who had told Henry. He had heard the stirring words of *The Liberator* and *The North Star* read to him, the calls for the black people of the South to welcome the Northern troops as they slew the infidel slave owners and freed the people.

Henry stood in a small patch of woods at the edge of the Verner farm, where he lived. He was 30 or so, several inches below six feet tall, strong in the upper body, with a large head and close-cut black hair, a small chin beard drawing some of the roundness out of his dark face. A hundred yards away was the road, and the blue troops.

Should he run to them? Should he race out on the road and throw himself at the feet of a blue captain and say, "I'm here, take me?" He'd heard of slaves who had done that, and they weren't always welcomed. He knew of several others who had simply run north when the blue troops came. Little word had come back. One or two made it to Baltimore, he'd heard, but he had no idea what their lives were like now.

These men looked too serious to bother with him. They were going to battle. Jackson was rumored to be south of the farm, by Port Republic. There had been fights up north by Front Royal and Winchester and Strasburg, he knew, and then Jackson's troops had gone up the far side of the Valley, on the other side of the Massanutten, with Federals chasing them. What would happen? Would these blue troops beat Jackson? Would they kill him? Would this part of the Valley then become part of the United States again? Would he be free? He hadn't been free in the old United States, so could he expect anything different no matter who won this war?

Henry trembled. It was a risk just standing here. He'd slipped out of the barn and run down the far side of the pasture, below a low hill that he hoped had sheltered him from the view of anyone watching from the house. For an instant as he ran he'd seen Miss Bettie standing on the front porch, watching the troops. He'd been terrified she would see him, and assume he was running away. Would she shoot him? He'd seen her practice firing a rifle in the hills above the house. The kick of the gun nearly knocked her over, but she'd kept at it until she was good enough that Henry didn't want to find out how close she could come. But he wasn't running. He just wanted to see. To stand close. To taste the idea.

Horses were going past now, pulling wagons. The canvas of the wagon tops was wet, the brim of the hat of the man driving the horses drooped over his face, soaked. Then came two cannon, huge fierce-looking things, aimed backwards now as they rolled, their black snouts dipping toward the muddy road. How many men could one of those kill? What must it sound like? Judgment Day, most likely.

So many men, so much might. They must win. How could anyone stand before them? Especially the ragged Confederates. He'd seen them come up this road a few times, too, and he'd been in Luray with Missus Verner when Jackson's big army came down from the Massanutten and joined the army of the bald-headed general. Those men looked more lively than these blue ones, but they were in such bad shape. Their clothes were old and patched, a lot of them didn't have shoes or soon wouldn't after a few more miles of marching. Those men had now marched all the way down the Valley and back up again, and now they had to go up against this huge column of grim men from the North.

Surely they'd kill this Jackson.

He'd heard of Jackson too from his brother Samuel. Jackson had started a Sunday school for blacks in Lexington. That had surprised Henry, but Samuel said it was just the way Jackson was. It wasn't that he particularly liked black people, Samuel said. He just thought they should have the Word of God. Jackson owned slaves himself and was hardly an abolitionist. Samuel didn't think Jackson wanted to improve the lot of slaves. He just wanted them to hear the Bible. Samuel had laughed and told Henry, "Yeah, there's plenty of slavery in the Bible, so it's safe for us to hear it."

But the black people loved the Sunday school, Samuel said. They loved hearing the stories, and they liked Jackson well enough. They didn't talk much in the classes, mostly they listened. They saved their discussions and arguments for home, in their small bedrooms, on the back porches or around the kitchen fire. That's when they'd talk about injustice, and whether it was God's will that the whites could be masters of the black people, and whether maybe the Bible lessons were being taught them to keep them content with slavery. They wouldn't show any of this to Jackson. They knew he wouldn't listen. But it was precious to be able to learn, Samuel said, to hear inspiring words from a man whose faith in God was so deep, and to have ideas stirred in them that they could bring back to their tiring days of work and their inquiring nights of talk. For allowing them this opportunity, Jackson was regarded as an unusual man in Lexington—in Virginia, for that matter. Even during the war now, Henry had heard, Jackson asked others to continue the school for blacks, wrote letters asking how things were going, sent money, pushed to keep his black children hearing the Word of God.

What would he think if he knew that these same groups of blacks also gathered around to hear the northern freedom papers read? Getting ahold of one was a rare occurrence, Samuel said, but when one was smuggled in, the people came eagerly, in twos and threes, to hear the other words. Were they from God? Or from madmen in the North? Would anything change? Would the slaveholding system that had brought Henry's ancestors from Africa to Santo Domingo to Virginia fall? Henry had never allowed himself to believe any such thing. He felt angry at the rabble rousers who talked about abolition, he felt a distant pity for the black people who sang about Jubilee. And he felt nothing but fear from the few whispered sentences he'd heard from bitter young black men talking about slave revolts, about weapons hidden away, pruning hooks, scythes, butcher knives. Whatever they did would fail, and then would come retribution on them all. Like with Nat Turner.

Henry kept a tight rein on his hopes, and felt that was best. Life at the Verners wasn't too bad, compared to some. It was wrong, he knew that, dead wrong for one man to own another. In heaven's eye, despite what the Bible said, it was evil. In time, maybe generations, it would stop. He hadn't expected it in his lifetime. But now? The Bible said that, after the flood, it would be the fire next time if man didn't repent and change his ways. And now, Henry thought, looking at the crowded road, in those cannon, in the cartridge cases of those thousands of men in blue, was this the fire?

Would it purify, or would it only destroy?

All that he knew about this war so far is that it had taken away the men and made everybody poorer. It hadn't made things better for anybody. The Verner women were doing things they hadn't done in years—like carding wool and trying to spin it, and not very well. The farm was short of everything, from food to hands. If the war kept going, no matter who won, it might just be that all that would come of it was more poverty, more hopelessness. The South might become a land and people too exhausted and played out to ever amount to anything again, no matter who ruled it. And when the black people were always on the bottom, if everything got worse for everybody, he knew who'd get the worst of it. The war might just change one master for another, leaving life for the blacks the same as it ever was.

This was a white man's war that hurt everybody, Henry had thought. But that Mr. Garrison, and Frederick Douglass, said something else. Douglass said that, although the war was being fought by the whites to preserve the Union, it should be turned into a holy campaign to free the slaves. Douglass wasn't hopeful yet, but he kept thundering, Henry knew. "Not a slave should be left a slave in the returning footprints of the America army gone to put down this slaveholding rebellion," Douglass had said, and Samuel had repeated the words to Henry, who remembered them.

And although his condition in life and his common sense made him suspicious of optimism, still he did allow himself, for one moment, as he watched the soldiers, to wonder—maybe this was the dark time before the storm. Maybe everything wouldn't be left in ruin. Maybe some light could break through.

The strength of this army walking in front of him gave him the courage to look at a glimmer of possibility: had the time finally come?

Henry muttered to himself, watching, "Lord, some say you haven't done such a good job looking out for us black folks, and I don't know much about that. But if you got anything to make up to us, and if you got any idea of redeeming that promise about the last being first and the first being last, this might sure be a good time to start. We black folks are as hungry as the whites here now, and working even more extra now that so many white men are gone to the war. Yes, Lord, if you think this is the time to turn things around, you go right ahead. We think it's mighty high time, begging your pardon, Lord."

Henry smiled at his prayer, at his brashness. He wasn't convinced praying did any good, but he was sure it didn't hurt anything.

Focusing again on the world in front of him, on what was instead of what might be, he moved south, a hundred yards through the trees, following the soldiers but still screened from their view. It gave him a little jolt to move farther from the house, a thrill of fear and possibility, and he started to run to keep up with the march. Moisture from the wet earth seeped into his shoes where the sole was tearing away. Branches slapped his face as he ran, the new pale leaves confusing his sight. He wanted only to keep up, to not lose the soldiers from his sight while he teased himself, testing the length and strength of his tether. He ran.

And he ran right into a man he never saw squatting beside a tree, hit him on the shoulder with his knee, and they both slammed on the ground and skidded. Henry had hit the ground flush on his chest, and as he struggled to gulp air back into his lungs, leaves caught in his windpipe and he coughed in sharp hacks. When he rolled over, he saw a rifle muzzle pointed straight at him, and behind it a man in a dirty shirt, kneeling as if in prayer, his pants still around his knees, his white gut hanging a little over scraggly dark pubic hair and a shriveled pale penis and thighs thin and white as bones. The man looked fierce and completely foolish at the same time, but the look in his eyes made Henry feel anything but humor.

"Christ if I'da known you's a nigger I'da shot you right off. But now that I look at you I don't think I wanna waste the bullet and make the noise. What the fuck are you doing here, boy?"

Henry froze, then barely moved his right hand, palm out, up in front of his face. "Don't, sir," was all he said.

"Where'd you come from?" the man said, keeping the rifle aimed at Henry with one hand while he pulled at his pants with the other. "Are you running? Do you think we'll take you in? We ain't got room for no niggers, boy." The man reached behind for some leaves, wiped at his ass, then stood, fumbling with his belt. "My guts are on fire and I can't even shit in this god-forsaken country without getting run over by a runaway. My God what I'd give to be back in Indiana."

Henry hadn't moved. He stared at the man, the muscles and skin around his eyes drawn tight as he watched for any movement of the rifle or the man's finger in the trigger guard. He flicked his gaze to the man's eyes, trying to read what he'd do. Henry wasn't afraid of being shot, although he thought in the jump of a heartbeat that it was a real possibility. He was afraid of the man thinking he was a runaway, of being taken back to the farm, of being hauled back to the Verners as a captured runaway slave. For years Northerners, for all their talk of abolition, had returned runaway slaves, making money at it, not knowing or caring about the hellish punishment that awaited the returned slaves. And it wasn't the punishment he feared either, it was the misunderstanding. He hadn't decided to run, he didn't think he was going to, and he didn't want the Verners to think that he had. It was a matter of dignity, he realized in a flash of emotion. If he was going to go, he wanted to do it standing up, as a man. He didn't want this foul-mouthed, dirty man from wherever Indiana was dragging him up to the porch of the house like a hound found running wild in the woods.

"I wasn't running. Sir." Henry spoke softly, eyes back on the rifle. He lowered his hand, but was still down on one knee.

"Yeah, sure, just like I warn't thinking about staying in these damned woods until my guts quieted and the fighting got over. We're both just too damned brave to stay out in the open, is that it?" The man spat and clipped his words in a harsh accent. He lowered the rifle now, looking around to see if any other soldiers had heard the commotion. No one was near. The marching went on beyond the trees, the sounds of hooves, creaking wood and shuffling feet a murmur through the protecting foliage.

"If you warn't running, where the hell was you going so fast?" the man asked.

"Just trying to keep up so I could see the soldiers, sir," Henry said. He gestured to his body and then the air above him with his hand, asking permission to stand. The man nodded and waved with his rifle, lifting its barrel from its aim at the ground to somewhere around Henry's stomach to show that Henry could stand but was still in this man's power.

"Why you so interested in the soldiers, boy?" the man asked. His face was darkened by the sun and by several days' growth of bristly beard.

"Just different. Just wanted to see," Henry said. He was hardly going to tell the man what he'd been thinking, the questions he'd been asking himself about what this army could do and whether it would mean anything. Henry was skilled at hiding his real life from the whites he worked and lived with every day. It was nothing to hide from a stranger. He didn't agree with the foolish way some blacks played the sweet-tempered jovial act around whites, although he knew that was just protective coloration too, like what the animals wore to not be seen. His own face to the white world was politeness without fawning and seriousness without being sullen.

"And what did you see, nigger, your saviors? That ain't why we're here, I'll tell you that." The man spat on the ground, wiped his palm on the side of his pants. "We've had niggers yelling 'Jubilee' all the way down here, and I'm sick of that there horse manure, I'll tell you. They just get in the way and eat up our food. We don't want you here, and we sure as hell don't want you back home." The man opened his canteen and took a drink. It no more occurred to him to offer Henry a drink that to offer one to the tree by his side. "Where do you live?"

Henry pointed back through the trees—"The brick house yonder."

"In the house?"

"No, sir, we have a cabin behind."

"Any men there? White men?"

Henry wasn't sure what he should say. He didn't like the idea of this man going to the house, with or without him now. The man didn't seem to be in any hurry to get back to the mass of troops on the road, and Henry assumed he was a straggler, if not a deserter. Men alone, or in pairs or small groups, were always wandering the neighborhood when the armies passed, stealing things and poking where they shouldn't be. The women of the neighborhood were terrified, including the black women. Nothing had happened yet, but Henry didn't like this man. But he held the gun. And all the power.

"No."

"So do you sneak in at night, boy, and grab yourself a little white bee-hind?" The man laughed, leaning toward Henry, apparently expecting an answer, if not a description. Henry only dropped his head and shook it a few inches.

"Ah, shit," the man laughed again, pulled a rag from his pocket and wiped his face. "What kind of women you got up at the house?"

Henry said nothing. The man lifted the gun. "Two. Missus and her daughter. And some relation woman staying, too." He didn't mention the two black women, the cook and the maid.

"How old's the daughter?"

"Don't know."

"Marrying age? Married already?"

"No, but could be."

The man looked up toward where the house could barely be seen through the trees, peaceful on its rise at the base of the foothills. "They got much food?"

"Not much, sir. Nobody does."

"Might be fun to be sociable. Might pay them a social call."

"The daughter, sir, she shoots. Rifle. Pretty good, from what I see."

"I be damned, the rebel bitch. Might enter into my planning, yes indeed." They both were still standing, two yards apart. Henry had no idea what was going to happen, or how this would end. He only wanted to get away, get back to the barn before anyone knew he was gone. It might already be too late for that. And with a Union army marching by, it wouldn't take long for the Verners to make an assumption about where Henry was. The soldier didn't seem much interested in Henry any more, hadn't said anything about taking him back to the house, but still he kept the gun pointed at Henry.

"Well, nigger, you go on now." Henry tensed, eager but waiting for something bad to come. "You get back where you came from, and if you see me by that farm of your white folks, you bring me something good to eat and damn quick. Hear? And I might want something else besides, we'll see." He looked toward the troops on the road. "I'm a scout, so I'm not going right back, but don't you think you can go to the army, boy. We don't want you. We don't give a damn about what happens to you as long as you stay out of our way." The man made a pushing gesture with his gun held horizontally between his fists, as if he were herding a crowd along. "Go dammit, and don't tell anyone you saw a Federal colonel."

Henry moved around the man, keeping his face to him, then backed through the woods, watching as he went. The man stooped down, picked up a rock and started to throw it at Henry, and then Henry ran, straight back through the woods toward the barn. All the big ideas he'd been playing with were gone from his head. All he wanted was the security of the barn or his tiny room in the cabin, the known feeling and smell of the wood around him, the few things he owned, the animals he tended. All he wanted was what had been. The soldiers, what they came for, what they might find, what they meant, could all wait. For now, he just wanted what he had.

The Northerner, a private not a colonel, but he liked promoting himself, watched the black man go. "Trouble with this war is chiggers and lice and niggers," he said out loud. "And not enough pussy, not by a damned sight." He laughed, out loud again. He looked at the runny mess he'd made on the ground, pulled his belt tighter, and thought about going up to the house. He turned, leaned down to look through the trees, and saw the column of his comrades still moving. Plenty of time to get me some grub, he thought. And maybe a treat, reach under somebody's worn-out calico dress and feel for paradise. It had been so long. Some men made do with other men at night, but that wasn't to his taste. He sat down for a minute, thinking of the feel of loose tits under thin warm cloth, and smiled to himself.

Henry stopped at the edge of the woods, where the corn started growing. He looked back to the road and saw the wagons at the end of the Federal column just passing by the turnoff where the road came up to the Verners' house. His chance had passed. He hadn't been sure he would take it, but now it was gone anyway. He was tired, tired in his soul. Tired of thinking of freedom, tired of thinking of slavery. Tired of keeping that insistent voice unheard, the one that cried, "I am a human person." Miss Bettie and Missus Amelia were all right to him, but mostly they didn't treat him like anything at all. Like a mule or a wheelbarrow, seemed to him. Part of the landscape, part of the tools that ran the place.

He liked the Southern soldiers who came by the house. They joked with him a little, some of them. Some looked at him strange. He'd been surprised when a couple of them said they sure wished they could afford a slave. He thought everybody had slaves, but the men told him that wasn't so. One even told him he wasn't fighting "to keep you in chains," but to chase the Federals out of Virginia so he could go home and just get his own work done on his own damned farm. "My mule is the onliest slave I got," the soldier, a small red-haired man with bad teeth, had said. Then he'd spit on the ground.

That Federal colonel sure didn't seem to want him, Henry thought. Wanted him as much as he wanted the shits, that was clear. Nobody wanted slaves, only the things the slaves could do for them, get for them. Nobody wants us as people, Henry thought. We're just part of what they keep in the barn to get things done. Hell of a thing. If this was God's plan, then God was a strange one. Why did he make us? Why did he make us black? Why did he mark us and chain us? Why did he make white people so sure we're the animals?

Why don't I just go up to the house and get supper? That's a question that makes more sense, Henry thought. Nothing much is going to change soon around here, it seems. The armies will fight, men will die, and we'll still be unwelcome, 'cept for our work.

Jackson. If he runs Bible classes, then he's probably got the Lord on his side. So he'll probably push those blue troops out of the Valley. Will the black folks who ran away have to come back then? Running is not worth a whipping, or being sold to Alabama. Henry would stay. His brother Samuel could keep talking about the big change that's coming, talk all he wants. He could keep reading the freedom papers, and Henry would listen. But he'd keep a hold on his soul, guard it from agitation, cup his hands to keep the winds from the flame of himself. Because that was all he had, that flame, flickering and flaring as the war blew by.

His skin and muscles jerked as a shot whanged from up at the house. Henry crouched. He heard a horse galloping down the road, from the house to the river. He saw the skinny Indiana man run out of the woods, pull on the arm of a soldier sitting in the weeds by the road, drag him to his feet and pull him south with the rest of the blue army. Indiana man won't bother us tonight, Henry thought. Hope no one does. He hoped he'd never see another soldier, blue or grey, again.

He heard wailing from the house, and turned to find out what new travail had been visited on this corner of the world that was his home, his prison.

Port Republic, June 6, 1862—Confederate Army

Patterson Neff sat slumped on the porch of the Kemper house in Port Republic.

Stonewall Jackson was inside. With Turner Ashby's body.

What a pretty little town, Neff thought. Rivers and hills, like his home down the Valley near Strasburg. You couldn't find an ugly place in the Valley if you tried, Neff thought, but this one was particularly handsome. Two rivers—the South River and the North River—came together at a point just a few hundred feet north of the Kemper house to form the South Fork of the Shenandoah. The Blue Ridge Mountains rolled like waves just east of town. Northwest of the house, across the North River, was a high rolling plain lush with grain. That was where Ashby had been killed.

The house was sturdy, two stories, high shoulders, a typical rich man's house. Beautiful pine floors inside, he'd noticed, although now they were getting scarred by spurs as so many cavalrymen went in and out, first carrying Ashby, then paying their respects. Neff wanted to look in the window here by the door to see Jackson, but he didn't think that was right. Give the man some privacy. Give them both.

The South River gushed over rocks between wooded banks just on the other side of the house across the street. High trees shaded the little cluster of homes held in the crook of so much water. I bet there's good fishing from that point where the rivers join, Neff thought. Although I guess we won't be having time to fish. Those pastimes would have to wait until the Yankees were cleared out of this Valley. When would that be? We are so far up the Valley, Neff thought, and two Yankee armies are chasing us. Seems we're going backwards.

Fremont had followed them up the west side of the Shenandoah Valley. It wasn't a pell-mell retreat, Neff had realized, as the Confederate troops under Jackson seemed to take their time. He and the other riders had enjoyed the trip, seeing towns he'd never been to before the war. New Market, Harrisonburg. They'd poked around in a cave above Harrisonburg, gotten some ham and fried chicken from a fat woman at a farm where the yard was full of clacking chickens and snuffling pigs. She'd even had red-eye gravy.

People had come out on their porches as the troopers passed. The whole Valley was porches, Neff had decided, as if people couldn't stand to give up on the beauty of the vistas and go inside. People had yelled to them, asking where they were going, why they were riding south. Asked where the Yankees were. They looked stricken when told that Fremont was coming behind. The troopers had yelled that they were drawing the Yankees deeper into the Valley to stretch their lines of communications and crush them with one blow. The women on the porches looked like they weren't so sure, and neither had Neff been.

But they'd reassured the homefolk. "General Jackson won't let you down, he'll take care of Fremont, don't you worry. He's coming down a path he won't find his way out of, that's the truth," they called, mocking the nickname Fremont had earned out in the Rockies and California—the Pathfinder.

They'd fought several rear-guard actions, mostly firing cannon at the Yankees and taking some shots in return. Occasionally there'd been a rifle fight when the Federals had gotten too close, but mostly it was a lark. Riding and shooting and yelling. A lot of Ashby's troopers were gone, taking home horses they'd liberated from Banks up at Winchester. Ashby didn't hold too tight onto anyone, let them do what they wanted, most times. That's why the men loved him.

But Ashby could fight, and the men would fight hard for him when they had a mind to. They'd put a lot of Yankees on the ground.

Ashby had been made a general during all the fighting in the Valley, even though some said he didn't deserve it. Camp talk said Jackson had been angry that Ashby's troopers weren't at Winchester where they could have scooped up thousands of the retreating Federals. Ashby had been off to the east, fighting Union cavalry. And a lot of his men were off on their own, gathering up the spoils of war. Undisciplined, some would say. But they were horsemen. Cavaliers. They rode hard, but went their own way. Ashby didn't lead them so much as ride before them, showing by example what a horse soldier could do. Neff had been with Ashby at Winchester, and heard Ashby say he was pleased with his men's performance. They'd ridden for most of two days without stopping, and Ashby was in his glory.

Then, two days ago, up at the other end of the Valley now, they'd turned on Fremont near Cross Keys, southeast of Harrisonburg. Ashby had seen a good chance, found ground he liked, and asked for infantry. They came up, and together the foot and horse soldiers had battered Fremont. Ashby had had a horse shot out from under him, then a little while later another. This time, when he stood and called out to rally his troops, he took a bullet full in the breast. Dead in an instant.

Fremont had been stopped, but not broken.

A shock had settled on the Confederates. Many men had been killed since this moving carnival of marching and shooting had started at Kernstown two months before. But Ashby was the best-known cavalry commander in the war, and the first famous general to fall, and his loss would sadden all of Virginia. He had seemed so cavalier about the dangers always right next to him that his men had never thought he could be killed. He'd had such joy and spirit in the daily defense of the cause he believed in, he made everyone around him believe that they would prevail, no matter how tough or long the fight. A few of the riders around him thought Ashby would prefer the fighting never end, as he'd found his place in it, found the place in himself that came most deeply alive. He'd fought partly to avenge his brother, killed early in the war, and he fought hard and earnest.

But now the fighting had ended, for Ashby.

The shock was still there. And the southern troops were withdrawing again, into the fields around Port Republic. The war was gathering close here, as armies flowed together like the rivers. Jackson seemed to be preparing to fight Fremont on the west side of Port Republic and then Shields on the east side, attacking the two armies in sequence.

Neff heard nothing from inside the house. He thought back to just a few minutes earlier with some amazement.

In the gathering darkness, Neff had been listening to the low voices of women inside when he'd heard the clatter and creak of horses. He'd heard the tinkle of tin cups tied to the backs of saddles, he recalled, a sound that always pleased him. Suddenly, turning off the main road into the little lane just feet from the porch, there was General Jackson and two others. Neff had been so surprised he'd forgotten for a moment to stand. The general had paused in his saddle, looked up at the second floor of the house, over to the South River nearby, then back up the main road to the covered bridge crossing the North River. It was as if, even now, he had to know exactly where everything was.

General Jackson had taken his cap off as he stepped up onto the porch, his boots clumping on the wood. Neff treasured the moment, sad as it was. He'd never been this close to Jackson. Neff had seen Jackson's high forehead, his brown hair pressed down on his head, sweaty. His head was down and his beard pressed into his collar. He'd looked—hurt.

Neff had said something about the tragedy, the loss.

"God's will," was all Jackson had said, in a low voice edged with pain, and stepped inside.

Neff stood now, wondering in the quiet. Was he praying?

Jackson's faith was deep, everyone said. He was a deacon of his church. He wished never to march or fight on the Sabbath, although often he had to. He had religious services held regularly in the army.

Neff was certain Jackson was sorry to lose Ashby. It appeared Jackson had truly liked Ashby, although Jackson never seemed really close to anyone. They had had their differences, over discipline, and early on over whether Ashby would have an independent command or serve under Jackson. But Jackson couldn't help but admire the dashing rider who helped bring victory.

Was Jackson, in that shrouded little room, seeing something that frightened him? A fallen general laid out in a coffin.

Several aides had been shot next to Jackson in battle. The general exposed himself regularly to enemy fire while reconnoitering the ground he would cover to get at the Yankees.

So much iron and lead had been in the air these months.

Did he look at Ashby's still body and wonder when he would be there?

And if so, did that frighten him? Or did he have such faith in God that he could see death as only a transformation? Could any man truly look at the face of death and not tremble, at least for what he'd leave behind, if not for the unknown future?

Jackson loved his wife, Neff was sure. He'd seen her come into camp when the army was in Winchester. And Jackson surely must love this Valley, he fought so hard for it. Would he be afraid of going?

Neff would.

Later that day they were going to carry General Ashby's body over Brown's Gap in the Blue Ridge and take it to Charlottesville. Too many Yankees in the neighborhood to try to bury him at home.

What would Jackson feel as Ashby's corpse went over the gap in the mountains? Neff knew that, for himself, something light and joyful, that could illuminate the dark days of the long struggle, had passed.

Neff walked a few steps away from the porch. Tried to listen to the water tumbling over stone in the river he couldn't quite see. Tried not to think what was next.

Earlier, when he got word of Ashby's death, Jackson had been writing a dispatch to John Imboden, another cavalry commander. At the bottom of the message Jackson had written, unsteadily, "Poor Ashby is dead. He fell gloriously—one of the noblest men and soldiers in the Confederate army."

Imboden would carry that slip of paper with him for years, until it tore to tatters.

One of Fremont's officers would later write that Ashby "was a man worth to them regiments, a blast upon whose horn was worth a thousand men. When we found the brave Ashby was slain, there was no rejoicing in our camps."

It was a strange war. Men killing men they respected.

Night, and sadness, lay on the mountains.

Inside the Kemper house, Jackson stood in the parlor doorway. Ashby's body lay just beyond. Behind Jackson was the room that was the office for the Kemper family business, the transporting of produce and goods by boats down the Shenandoah River that made Port Republic, so far up the Valley, truly a port.

In the parlor, the family furniture had been moved and Ashby's body placed in a simple pine coffin by the window in the far corner. Beyond that window was the road that ran from the bridge that crossed the North River past the Kemper house and, a lifetime beyond, ran south to Lexington. Where Jackson had lived, once, a life that seemed so out of reach now.

During the day people had come, as people do in small communities where neither tragedy nor joy is private, and looked through the window to see the fallen Ashby. Their hero. He'd been placed there so they could see. It had been both reassuring and frightening for people to see him, so small in his coffin. The war had come to the neighborhood, fighting had happened just a few miles northwest; the Yankees were so close, almost here.

They had heard so much about this dashing man, who had chased the Yankees all over the Valley, that now they had to see him. Even just this small quiet remnant of him. It helped them to see it was a real man who had done so much to frustrate the enemy. Just a man like them. Maybe that meant other men could do it. Yet it was also frightening, that this man, who had danced so close to death so many times and sprung away, had now been killed. Brought down. To this small box. In this still house. How many others would die?

A woman looked up at Jackson, started when she saw his face, nodded at him, then gestured with her head toward the door. Jackson nodded his head in turn, then folded his hands in front of him. The woman gathered the knitting she'd been working on into a bag, said in a whisper, "Bless him, and bless you, sir," and then slipped past the general and through the door into the office, leaving two candles burning in the room. Jackson shut the door behind him.

After a few moments, he leaned one knee forward—to take the weight off the leg, to start walking toward Ashby, to start to collapse, he wasn't sure. But the movement made the leather of his boot creak, and the sound stopped him cold.

It was so still in the house.

He held his breath. Then leaned a little more weight on the leg he'd put forward, and the floor beneath him creaked. And he stopped again.

It was so still in the house.

Where Ashby was had never been still before. The man was movement, impetuosity. Daring and endurance. Jackson shook his head at the memory. Ashby knew intuitively where the enemy would appear, where they would go, what they would try. And he went just there, and harried them, stopped them, drove them. Who could replace him?

Jackson looked around the room. Shadows flickered on the wall. A few framed pictures, a desk, a hutch, a low table, a rocking chair. He looked through a doorway on the far wall, into what appeared to be a dining room. Deep shadow. Here, in this parlor, on the mantel a candle, and on a small end table, a lantern. Next to the coffin.

The coffin. His eyes flicked past it. Then returned. He didn't want to look at it. But the light pulled him. What was there pulled him. The center of the stillness. The source.

Night air slipped through the window, brushed past the skin of his hands. He felt its softness. Outside, a frog peeping a small noise; beside his ear for an instant the chirring of insect wings. But these tiny sounds didn't dent the stillness.

He took a step, the swish of his pants was a windstorm, the exhaling of his breath a cry. He stopped again to stop the noise.

He could see now, a step closer, the dark black hair and beard in the coffin. He took another step, the creaking of his boots and the floor and the leather of his belt and the jangle of his sword a storm of sound, and he stopped again.

The stillness seeped back in. Jackson sank to the floor, there, several feet from the coffin, his right hand catching his weight as his knees buckled, his sword scabbard banging on the cut lumber of the floor. His ankles hurt as they bent, tired from riding and walking, his knees felt like sharp bone cutting the planks of the floor. His head drooped. Boot toes, knees, his right hand on the floor.

He couldn't move farther. Could barely force his left hand up to pull off his cap. Couldn't reach to set it anywhere, so it stayed in his hand until the hand dropped to his thigh and the cap rolled away on the floor. Jackson sank forward, doubled up now on the floor.

Stillness.

His breathing. Barely audible. He opened his mouth for air, it was dry and his lips and tongue made clicking sounds as his mouth came open. His back, bent low above his hips, burned with strain.

His forehead touched the floor. It was gritty, cold.

So bent, he had to pull each breath, as from a well.

Into his ear slipped the "click, clock, click, clock" of the timepiece on the mantel. He heard it for a few seconds, sound from a world where the living measured time, and then it slipped away again. He tried to hold onto it, but then it was too hard, and he let it go, and the silence flooded back.

He could feel the weight of the body in the coffin. Feel it as Ashby's horse had felt it. But then it had been quick; now it was dead weight. He could feel the back of the skull, the shoulder blades, the spine, the hip points, the heels. The weight of the body pressing down on the wood of the bottom of the coffin. He could feel it.

He rested there, his mind slack, his chest to his knees, his body and Ashby's body a mingled weight. A burden. Ashby's laid down. Jackson's still to carry.

I have caused so much death.

Silence.

Why? My God. Why?

Silence.

Is that my role?

Silence.

I have caused so much death.

Silence.

I would rather be planting lettuce. Fingers in the deep black earth behind my house. Lettuce in rows, straight, small, the plants so frail.

Rows of soldiers. So frail.

I have caused so much death.

Silence.

He opened his eyes. Right before him, the crack between boards in the floor, barely visible in the dark.

I am a man of God. I am a religious man. I have sat in church hour after week after year. I have sung, I have prayed, I have studied the Bible.

Why must I cause so much death?

Silence.

These Federals. The soldiers, the generals. I served with them, before. I know them. Must I kill them? Must we kill each other?

Silence.

I would rather be dancing with mi esposa.

He shook his head, the skin of his forehead now just above the dirt of the floor.

I am not questioning, Lord. I am just saying, this is hard.

Silence.

And you would say, that it is hard does not matter. If it is right, it is to be done.

A hard breath now, taken in through shudders.

And that is the question I cannot ask. Is it right?

Silence. The stillness of the room was thick, heavy, the air was no longer flowing through the windows. All sounds had stopped. All air.

Is it?

Now there wasn't even silence. There wasn't even breath.

His mind had stopped. The whirring, the pulsing, the searching. Stopped. Nothing.

Nothing.

He felt his heart beat. Deep. Hard. Strong. It kept going, as if it knew where. As if it knew why.

This is a trial, Lord.

A gasping breath. A shudder.

This is a trial.

His eyes were pressed so tightly shut all the little muscles hurt around them. Shut it all out. Shut it all away.

Stop thinking. Stop asking. That way lies despair.

Empty yourself. And then faith will fill the void.

His right hand, now a fist, pressing against the floor.

It must be.

I must.

His body shook, for just an instant.

He was alone.

So much killing.

He raised his chest, his shoulders, his head. There were bits of grit on his lips, in his beard.

It is what I've been given to do.

His knees pressed into the wood planks.

He looked at the coffin.

He closed his eyes.

I know my men say they can tell when a battle is coming, because I am in my tent all night, on my knees. Praying. They can see my silhouette.

I am trying to put it into your hands, Lord.

And trying to understand those hands.

I am trying to put it out of mine.

Yet that is a shirking.

Is this what I am to do?

It is for my hands to do.

He spoke aloud. From the Forty-fourth Psalm. Reaching for the words. For the comfort. For the fire.

> "Thou art my King and my God,
> Who ordainest victories for Jacob.
> Through thee we push down our foes;
> Through thy name we tread down our assailants.
> For not in my bow do I trust,
> Nor can my sword save me."

He thought, pulling deep in his memory for the words. Haunting words.

> "Nay, for thy sake we are slain all the day long,
> and accounted as sheep for the slaughter."

He drew in a ragged breath, his jacket tight over his chest.

> "Rouse thyself! Why sleepest thou, O Lord?
> Awake! Do not cast us off for ever.
> Why dost thou hide thy face?
> Why dost thou forget our affliction and oppression?
> For our soul is bowed down to the dust;
> Our body cleaves to the ground.
> Rise up, come to our help!"

Jackson pressed his forehead once more to the dusty floor. Stayed bent over for a long minute. "Bowed down to the dust," he said again. "Slain all the day long." His voice was low in the quiet room.

This man, whom others saw so often standing so firm, was now lain low. No stone wall now, but loose earth. Scattering in the wind.

Where do I go now? How?

Captain of a ship in the dark. Where is my commander, where is my crew? I see only the deck, heaving and rolling, and just beyond the rail the deep and the dark. The wind from every quarter, tearing my garments, lashing my face. No compass, no glass.

Here is a man who had no parents. His father died when Thomas was two, leaving the family so poor his mother sent him off to live with an uncle. Then she, ever so warm, ever so distant, died when Tom was seven—when a boy is most in need of warmth.

In the spare rocky hills of northwest Virginia, he pulled his own life together. Grew up with uncle Cummins, with hard work at a mill, long nights of study. He reached for the order, gathered the boundaries, the organizing principles, the firmness of religion. Then of the army. Because the world itself was so chaotic. So far beyond his understanding. The tangles of fate, the harshness of chance.

So he held in, to hold on. Tightened. Gripped.

Beyond this center that he reached for and held, was there no gravitational pull, no centrifugal force, nothing that binds? Out there, would all fly apart, out into endless space? And emptiness?

Not if he held. The manual of arms. The code of honor. The virtue of discipline. The scriptures of the Lord. The guidance of the anointed.

These things, these certainties, would stand up to the gale. With these, he could stand firm. He needed them to hold to. To hold on.

From this solid footing, from this high ground, he could see to make his way. See just enough for each step. And one step opened the next. In an ordered world, in a disciplined march. In the rigor of effort.

He stood so straight because if he once started to bend he would fall with the burden. He understood that he could not hold himself up. Not himself. Not alone. So he held tight to the word and the way and the will of his God. And, too, to the order, the clarity, of the firmness of the military.

And with these certainties he created a frame that held up a structure strong enough to stand. And so he went forward. To steep challenges at West Point. To frontier forts barely hacked from the tangled scrubland of Florida. To hot dry dusty landscapes and barking cannon in Mexico. To lockstep lessons in airless rooms at the Virginia Military Institute. To drillgrounds in Richmond and bloodstreaked hills in Virginia. To ranks of church pews, to midnight prayers in tents. To leading men where no man would readily choose to go. And the certainty he had found, the structure he had built, had held him up as he held to it.

He had to hold.

Given form and strength by the discipline he had chosen, he could then, sometimes, let it ease. To open to the movement of the music in Mexico after the war. To dancing with his Anna in their comforting Lexington parlor. To the sweeping rise of the mountains beyond their farm outside the town. To the beauty's of the morning. The grace of growing plants.

To admire the wild abandon, the daring, the speed, the single-mindedness of this young man, Turner Ashby.

Jackson had deep passions, although so few saw this. And he was careful, careful to never go too far, give way too much to the passion. That was self-indulgence, he thought. He would dance with his wife, romp on the floor with children, feel the glory of the sun on the mountains. But not too much. Take the gifts, and turn the joy back toward God. The joy itself could be a trap. He could like something too much. And then it would be centered on him, not on the gift, or the giver.

He would not let himself go. Hold in, hold on, hold tight.

But now, alone in this small quiet room with death, he was unraveling.

This man, Ashby, had so much promise, so much energy. Since his brother had been killed he had become so unfettered, so unleashed.

So committed—to cause? To revenge?

So passionate. And Jackson had found Ashby so alluring, so engaging. Jackson had let his appreciation of Ashby flow into that place inside him where life burned so bright. Even in the terrible darkness of this war, here was a light.

And now he was dead.

And now here Jackson was, at the end of the march, at least for this day. Prostrate on the floor.

And sinking.

No.

Not now. Not after all this.

He pulled deep for the boundaries. For the edge that would hold him. He would not go over.

He couldn't quite find it. Just beyond his reach. More effort, and he groaned.

He must not let himself fall. Into himself. Into his sadness. Into his fear.

He felt, from the inside, the bones of his thighs, of his back, of his chest. He felt for the discipline, reached, summoned, the outward shape of the vessel. Could he find it? Could he touch it? Could he hold it, so it could lift him?

His hand opened slowly.

Moments passed. Pictures flashed—dappled sunlight tumbling through deep woods as dark horses wove among the trees; an arm, Ashby's arm, flashing up to flick his riders away from Federal cannon unlimbering; firelight, tired men talking, then looking up at him as he passed, trust on their faces; the opening in the trees of a wooded mountain pass, his way to the enemy's rear and another chase; enemy columns melting away like sugar cubes in water. His wife's white face in the hallway, expectant and happy with the day and their presence together in it.

And then, there it was.

The southeast corner of his house, as he stood on Washington Street. The stone of the foundation, rugged blocks, pulled from the spine of the earth. The brick of the walls, the trim square windows, the chimney tall and solid. His home.

The structure. Of his life.

He could hold on to this.

And he grasped.

And the sun sailed from behind a church steeple, and light touched him.

He stood, slowly, stiffly, the legs pushing up, the boots scraping on the floor, the sword jangling. He could smell the sweat, of his horse on his legs, of himself in his uniform. He could feel the weariness in his muscles, in his bones. He lifted his face to the ceiling. Saw shadows dancing. A fly, jumping from one beam to another. His eyebrows were pressed together, the skin on his broad, high forehead wrinkling into a taut knot of pain. His grey-blue eyes closed to slits, his beard moved on his collar as he worked his mouth, slowly.

Sorrow flickered across his face. He would not allow himself to doubt, but he felt so deeply the anguish of endless killing. Not just his anguish, the pain inside him. But in so many others, in so many homes. On so many hillsides.

"I don't surely know," he said aloud, softly. "I don't know, but...." For a flicker of a second he had a glimpse of himself playing on the floor with the children of friends, laughing, tumbling with them. A smile started to stretch the corner of his lips, then died. "These children must have their freedom, and the Federals cannot burn their homes, cannot send them off as refugees. Cannot kill their fathers. Cannot be allowed."

Feeling form and strength return, he squared his shoulders as if back at West Point. Brushed the grit from his beard. "They must be stopped. You are using me to stop them. I would wish it otherwise. But these children must have their lives. Their future."

Resolve.

He felt now both solid and open. He had found the timbers again, the frame that held him up. But he also felt as if his skin were gone, the surface of his body open, the wind flowing through.

He looked again at the coffin. Rough wood. The room's clutter pushed aside. Little grace. Ashby shot in the chest, a fresh jacket pulled over the wound, a red rose laid above it.

I am called a champion of war. But I am nothing, Lord. I am yours. You are all.

So much killing. Do they think I like it? I call for it easily enough, and often enough, true. But it is because you call for it. And therefore it must be.

As little as I understand, I believe you are guiding me. To do this killing that I would wish not to do. But we do not choose.

I am almost certain…

He put his hands to his thin lips.

"I must," he said, again aloud.

"They could stop it. Any day. Any hour. Leave us alone. Leave us in peace.

"Until then, we must fight. And I will not shrink from it."

His eyes less clouded now, the beginning of light behind the grey, Jackson finally stepped to the coffin.

And here lies a young man dead. Such a young man. Dead.

He looked at Ashby's face, sunken beneath his thick black beard. Pale, when once it had been so deeply tanned. Just a day before, so deeply tanned.

Heavy eyebrows. A broad face. Thick brush of black hair. Eyes closed. Forever. No expression will ever play over that face again. No elation. No anger. No fear. No surprise.

This face. It could be mine.

His beard is thicker. His eyebrows much more full. His nose flatter. His hair more lush—my forehead creeps up higher each day. His face was much more a playground for expression than mine. But not now. Now, the face of death.

I've seen so many dead.

But he is so…here.

Jackson's eyes locked on Ashby's white eyelids. Jackson stared, moment after long moment, and then sight faded. Ashby's face faded. Time passed, and the very quietness of the room disappeared. To nothing. No sound. No stillness. Just nothing.

And Jackson felt, from in the open cavern of his chest, a long, wide, flat plane. Slowly spreading. Then flaring faster out, all directions, flat, wide, broad, colorless, only speed and distance. Nothing to see, only that broad flat plane pulling, so huge it made him unsteady, tipping forward, leaning into and over the plane. He was spreading, thinning, flying out, everywhere. Gone. To vapor, to wind, to sailing. To empty.

He was lost, for minutes, hours. Flying, the spare, endless plane. The white of mist. Hearing gone, breath gone. Him gone.

Flat space. Far, and far. Forever.

All gone, into infinite white geometry.

And then, beyond distance, a hint. Of shape. Here, barely, then gone, in the mist.
Coming closer. Sailing in, so slow.
The shapes, a fluttering.
Trees, leaves dancing? In a wind he could not feel. Because there was no feeling.
Only these shapes, ethereal. In mist, beyond nothing.
Trees, surely. The shapes of trees, fleeting in and out of vision.
Their limbs bent gently. A sparkle below. A flow. Water? Movement. Eternal and
only now, slipping by. Light flickering on a ripple.
A river. And beyond it trees. Surely, but hard to grasp.
Time. More clear now. Closer. Sure. And he stopped. And all stopped. Here.
A river. And over the river, trees. Shade. Shelter. Welcome.
And peace.
Here.
It is.
And he understood. And he would go. Not now. But soon.
Over the river. And into the shade of the trees.

South of Conrad's Store, June 7, 1862—Union Army

Emerson Grady came full awake. It was dwindling night, barely light.

He instantly came into the realization of the absence of John Nichols. His friend. Shot. Disfigured. Shattered. Killed. At Kernstown. Ten weeks ago.

It wasn't an awakening with some indistinct haunting feeling that something wasn't right. It wasn't an awakening where he automatically turned his head on the ground to look for the tumbled lump wrapped in a blanket that was the friend he'd marched south with. It wasn't that his muzzy nighttime mind reached out for the thought of Nichols and it slowly dawned that he was gone.

He woke right up into loss.

They would march south in an hour or so, and Nichols would not be next to him. Again.

Grady stared into the branches and leaves above, just coming clear against the thin morning sky.

Just gone, he thought. Just plain gone.

Like smoke. Dissolved in air. Nowhere.

He was surrounded by men. Sleeping, snuffling, stirring. But he felt completely, achingly alone.

He heard a skittering to his right. Rolled his head. Saw a squirrel on the road. Walking across. Like an old man. One skinny leg, then another, halting, slow. Was it lame? Had a stray bullet caught it? No, not possible. But it moved so slow, deliberate, jerky. Maybe a wagon wheel had rolled over it yesterday. Grady felt a wave of sadness surge through him. Poor little thing.

Then, with a spindly paw touching the beaten grass at the side of the road, the squirrel arched its body up and did a little leap into the next patch of grass. It continued in fluid pouring hops, up and down, over the grass and into it, over the grass and into it, like a tiny porpoise, passing beside Grady and hopping lightly toward the trees that covered the swell of a foothill.

Grady grunted. Didn't smile, but his mind had liked seeing the squirrel move like any old squirrel on any common day.

He sat up. In an hour or so they'd move. Toward Jackson. Surrounded by men, he'd march alone. Toward Jackson and God knew what.

Port Republic, June 8, 1862, morning

It almost all came apart. The bravery and initiative of gunners from Ohio and riders from Unionist West Virginia had almost snatched the battle from Jackson's hold—in fact had almost snatched Jackson.

Suddenly there were Yankees in the streets of Port Republic. While Ewell was holding off Fremont north of town, Jackson was going to send his troops across the South River to go after Shields. But Shields didn't wait, and Jackson was caught napping. Everyone in the Valley army was exhausted, and Jackson failed to post enough men to guard the crossings of the South River. The advance Federal cavalry and artillery unit came across the river and scattered the few Confederate pickets. Shouts and hoofbeats rang through the town. Jackson, alerted on the veranda of Madison Hall south of town, raced for the bridge across the North River, coming under fire from the Yankees. He barely made it through. Two members of his staff were captured. A small Confederate force of riflemen and three cannon kept the Federals from the rich wagon trains parked south of the town. At the other end of Main Street, the Yankees rolled a cannon to the south side of the North River, aiming straight down the covered bridge. If they could hold the town and hold that bridge, Jackson would be caught between the Federal pincers, Ewell's men isolated to be hit by Fremont, and a small force and all the wagon train stuck defenseless south of the river.

But Jackson had responded instantly. He had ordered a cannon from the Rockbridge Artillery on the north side of the covered bridge to fire on the Yankees—"Let 'em have it," was his short fierce order to Captain William Poague—and then grabbed the nearest Virginia company and sent them down to charge the Yankee-held bridge. They ducked under one blast of the Federal cannon and raced across. More Southerners came up from the town and the Federals were chased back across the South River, sped along by cannon balls, galloping away to join Shields' later infantry advance.

It had been a near thing. Daring on both sides had run headlong into a tough little fight. After 50 miles of marching, shooting and parrying, the momentum of the forces gathering on the two sides of the two rivers had teetered, and the fragile balance had almost tipped. Jackson had to keep from fighting the two Union armies at the same time, had to deal with them one before the other, or he'd be overwhelmed. The balance would hang and waver again many times in the hours to come.

Jackson's men, and Ewell's men, and Fremont's men, and Shields' men, were gathering now in the fields and hills beside the rivers—the North River and the South River, which joined at Port Republic to form the South Fork of the Shenandoah. The water flowed, and men flowed, like tributaries racing toward a rocky tumbling falls.

Port Republic, June 8, 1862, night—Confederate Army

The ground was hard, the gnats were hungry, the noises that Sutton was usually too tired to hear now echoed and bounced around in his head. The night was slow and empty, and Sutton, though exhausted, could get no rest. He heard, as if each noise were amplified and carried over as a gift just for him, men coughing, slapping at bugs, cursing at the next man over who inadvertently kicked his neighbor in his sleep. Guards switching their rifles from one hand to the next, with the metal of the ramrod rattling against the metal of the barrel and the wood of the stock. Two men toward the edge of camp, telling a story and laughing, one with high-pitched giggle that twanged at Sutton's tired nerves. Closer, an officer answering the questions of a sergeant, mostly saying, "I don't know, Roy, we probably won't know where we're going until we get where we're at." Then the snare-drum clatter of a horse riding in fast, braking, then the stretching scritch of heavy leather as the rider lowered himself from the saddle.

Give up, Sutton told himself. Sleep won't come.

He sat up. His hips hurt, and a spot between them just above his tailbone. Sometimes it felt, as he turned over while sleeping on the ground, that the muscle and ligament that held the bottom of his spine to his hips was tearing. He was afraid at times like this that he would break there, about the midpoint of his body, and never be able to use his legs again as the bottom half of him fell off. It scared him, his body coming apart this way, but it was also kind of a funny thought—a guy who stopped at his belt.

Usually, after walking around a little, the strength returned to his lower back and he felt all right. He wondered when the problem started. He remembered having to stop his plowing several times this past year because of the fiery pain. Now it followed him into the march and the campground.

He had a right to be tired. Jackson had marched his army from Kernstown at the north end of the Massanutten to McDowell way to the southwest, back down past Winchester and almost all the way to the Potomac, and then back up the Valley past the south end of the Massanutten to Harrisonburg and now the little town of Port Republic. Up and down the Shenandoah Valley, twice. With plenty of time for shooting at Federals and being shot at by them.

And yesterday. The fight against Fremont near Cross Keys. The memory of it had kept Sutton awake. Echoes of screams, explosions, the rushing wind of cannon balls, the thud of bullets, the torn ground spilling into the air. His ground. The fight had happened on his farm.

His mind, spinning, shut off thoughts of yesterday. Just closed.

Sutton flipped his blanket off of his aching legs, reached with trembling muscle-strained arms for his shoes and pulled them on. Every time he tied the laces he feared feeling and hearing the snap of the string he used for laces. Or the rip, like that he felt in his back muscles, of the leather itself giving up its fragile hold.

He stood and stretched. A man next to him let rip an enormous explosion of gas. Another man nearby threw a canteen at him. "Keep that to your own self, I'm downwind, brother." Other men laughed. Sutton could hear a banjo being plucked near a fire beyond. Nobody was sleeping much, it seemed.

Sutton walked up to a man, at least 10 years younger than he, who seemed to be trying to hide his boyish face behind a beard the size and color of a haystack. "Any more excitement tonight, lieutenant?" Sutton asked.

He looked into the eyes of the lieutenant, Peyton Morse, seeing uncertainty, a bit of fear. Was this boy in farther than he could handle, like a dog stuck in a badger hole, unable to go forward or back? Were we all? Sutton wondered.

"No, thank God," Morse said. "How you doing?"

"Can't sleep, think I'll walk a little. It's all right, I won't go far."

"I'm sorry, Sutton, that the Yankees have your farm now behind their lines," the lieutenant said.

"They can have it," Sutton said, and walked slowly out to the road. He'd walked or ridden to Port Republic probably 200 times, every couple of weeks for the eight years he'd farmed just west of the town. He'd walk around its few streets and see people. Ask how things were going. Talk a little.

The work was hard in this neighborhood, but it was rewarding. There were a few big landholders, but mostly lots of smaller farms. People generally worked the land themselves; a few owned a slave or two, a few more rented a slave now and then. But slaves were expensive, and little farmers like Sutton couldn't afford them. So they did all their own work by their own hand, generating their own sweat, taking their own satisfaction, wearing down their own bodies.

Sutton had no objection to slavery, just like he had no objection to the stately big houses the richer families had. Both were simply beyond his reach. Because he couldn't afford a big brick house with wings and outbuildings didn't mean someone else shouldn't have one. Sutton felt he had no right to tell someone else how to live or how to work his land. He might be envious, if he told himself the truth, but that didn't mean he was against building fine houses, or owning slaves.

He came into Port Republic regularly to buy supplies, sell a few things. People from the countryside brought their produce to the Port to have it shipped by barge up to Harper's Ferry. It was a busy little town, and he liked it. It felt centered. Held in the arms of two rivers, bordered by gradual hills.

Standing, scratching at his hair, his thoughts jumped for a second to yesterday's push back and forth across the fields he had plowed. The line of soldiers in blue pushing with stabs of flame at the line of soldiers in grey and brown. The cries of anger, the cries of pain. But then his mind veered away from it. It wanted to go somewhere else. It was searching for something else. It led him, pulled him, dragged him.

It was the why of it.

Not why was it all happening. But why was he in it. Why he kept at it through all the death, all the dirt, all the miles and nights of hard ground.

"Ever fish in these rivers, Sutton?" the boy lieutenant asked, and the question took a moment to get through.

"Uh, yeah. Sometimes. Pretty good trout. Some bottom fish."

"It's a pretty place. I'd like to come back here when there aren't Yankees."

"Me too," Sutton said.

"You thinking of staying here?" the lieutenant asked. Meaning now, not after.

"You mean when the army leaves? No, sir, I'm in for the war. I'm not sure why, sometimes, but I guess I am."

"We're just doing it because we have to, I guess. Doing it because places like this are so pretty, maybe."

"Must be. There must be some reason, eh?"

"Hard to find on a night like this."

"Yep, true enough."

Sutton looked at the boy again. The fear seemed to be eased, maybe just by talking.

This was a strange night. Couriers and generals kept riding across the bridge and down Main Street, to the big house at the south edge of town, Madison Hall, where Jackson had made his headquarters. Everybody was exhausted from so many days of marching and fighting. Hundreds of men had disappeared, broken down by the marches, unable to go on. Those who were here, sprawled on the ground in and around the Port, were edgy even in their weariness. They'd heard rumors that Shields and his Federal army were just across the South River. They knew, because of two days of cannon thunder and flying bullets, that Fremont was just to the west. Both Yankee armies had been chasing them for days. Nobody knew what Jackson planned. They'd handled Fremont roughly yesterday, but he hadn't gone away. Now there were Federal armies on both sides of the Valley army. Looked at one way, Sutton thought, Jackson was trapped.

"You think General Jackson knows what he's doing, lieutenant?"

"I wouldn't ask that so loud, Sutton. His staff boys are all around."

"Well, they wonder sometimes too, from what I hear," Sutton said. "But what do you think?"

"He fights like hell, Sutton. And he says he marches us so hard and so fast to gain the best advantage against the Yankees so we spend the fewest lives, and I guess I believe him. He's marched us up here for a reason, must be. This is good ground for a fight."

Wind whispered in the leaves above them, and in the wet bottoms by the rivers frogs were singing in choruses. Sutton shuffled his feet, reached in his pocket for his battered pipe, just to hold something in his hands. "Why? Why is this good ground?" he asked.

The lieutenant turned and looked below them as horses pounded over the covered bridge across the North River. He saw lights on in several of the houses of the town. Many of the townsfolk had left, but quite a few were still here, the lights showed. Although armies had passed through this neighborhood before, this was the first time the fighting had come here. People weren't sure what to do. When the Federal cavalry hit the town this morning, civilians ran for the woods. It was a jarring, sad sight for the Confederate soldiers, seeing so close the cost of war in their homeland.

"Well, if you're going to fight two Federal armies, the rivers here will keep them separate so you can fight one at a time, if you do it right. This bridge right here is the key to the whole thing," Morse said. "It's the only one still standing in the upper Valley here. We've burned all the others to keep the Federals from concentrating. So we can move over that bridge to bring our troops together to fight first Fremont, like we did, then Shields. We've got the interior lines here, and that's always an advantage."

Sutton was surprised by Morse's knowledge. He was so young—but then there were colonels and generals in their twenties in this war, he knew. Men rose fast if they were good fighters and leaders, and if enough of their superiors got shot. Then Sutton recalled that Morse had told him one other night when they talked that he had grown up in Harrisonburg and gone to the VMI for a year before dropping out. Never got to Jackson's classes, but he'd studied a fair amount of military science.

"But there's no bridge across the South River there, just the ford. And we're always slow as molasses going across fords," Sutton said.

"That's why they're stringing those wagons across the river." At the east edge of the town, they could just barely hear men driving horses and wagons to the river. A group of black pioneers was fixing wagons together and putting planks across them to make a rickety temporary bridge. Port Republic, at the junction of the two rivers, had crossings to the north and the east. For Jackson's army to fight Shields, it would have to cross both rivers. And it looked like that's what was going to happen tomorrow.

"We've hurt Fremont, and he's moving slow," Morse said. "From what I see— and I'm only guessing, but it makes sense—it looks like Old Blue Light is going to leave a few of Ewell's boys north of the North River to keep Fremont occupied again tomorrow and bring the rest of the troops across both rivers to attack Shields to the east. Shields and his Federals are coming down from Conrad's Store, it was his boys that raised hell in town today. Made Jackson skedaddle."

Sutton laughed, a relief to think of Jackson high-tailing it through the town, racing for the bridge. "Did you hear, lieutenant, that he had time while racing out of town to scold Dr. McGuire for his language?"

"I heard something like that, what did you hear?"

"McGuire was loading wounded into a wagon from the church on Main Street, and swearing at his drivers. Jackson yelled, 'Doctor, don't you think you can manage these men without swearing,' and then he tore off." Sutton laughed again.

"Always the upright instructor, even when he's leaning across the neck of his horse to keep from getting shot," Morse said, smiling with Sutton.

"That bridge may have saved Old Jack," Morse said. "It's all about bridges here. See those boys putting kindling and powder kegs on the covered bridge? We can burn it down, drop it in the river, anytime we need to isolate Fremont. And that wagon bridge across the South River, we can cross it and pull it up after us to keep Fremont from following us, or keep it up and cross back over if the fight against Shields goes against us, pull it up then to keep him from following. Flexibility. Gives us room to maneuver."

"Seems like we need it," Sutton said. "I'm not real easy about having Yankee armies on two sides of us."

"Me neither. But I think Old Jack loves it. He's keeping these armies occupied so they can't leave the Valley and go against Richmond, and he's got them right at his fingertips where he can have a battle whenever he wants one. He likes that. He's a fighter."

The two men stood together, looking down on the bridge and the town, hearing men and horses moving in the night.

"Do you like the fighting, lieutenant?" Sutton asked quietly.

Morse looked over at him. He knew Sutton had been in a lot of battles and firefights in the last three months. And he knew it must have been shocking to fight in his own neighborhood yesterday. "I heard Jackson say once at the VMI, at a general convocation, that nobody really likes fighting battles. But he must like it, he's so good at it. They say his eyes light up—Old Blue Light."

"I never know how eyes can light up," Sutton interrupted, "but I guess they do. Mine squint."

"Mine close, at some of what's in front of them. Yesterday, I saw a man with just white neckbone sticking up from his shoulders. Head torn off by a shot from Fremont's cannon." Morse was quiet for a moment, then said, "I'm scared before a fight, but then once I'm in it, I like it. God forgive me, but I like it."

Sutton nodded, wanting to hear more. "What do you like?"

An owl's eerie hoot came through the night. They both stopped to listen. A single rider walked his horse across the bridge, the clop-clop of its hooves echoing off the roof. A man behind them woke up shouting on the ground, "What, what, where are they coming from?" The man beside him hushed him, said, "It's night, Billy, it's all right, it's all right."

Morse looked down at his hands, touched the butt of his pistol in its holster. "I feel alive, I guess. I know what I have to do, it's right there in front of me, and I do it." He paused, then added, still looking down, "It's defending Virginia, and it's keeping them from killing me and the boys around me. But that's just part of it. There's a thrill that runs through my body that has nothing to do with right or wrong. It's just, I don't know, accomplishing something. It's clear what needs to be done. I like seeing where there's an opening and sending men into it, getting them to see what I see. I like moving them."

He looked up at Sutton. "And I like killing the Yankees. I like seeing them fall. Getting the men to hold their fire until the bastards are close and then yelling 'fire' and the guns rip all along the line and the smoke blows out and the Yankees fall like wheat before the scythe. It's massing power and taking them down.

"I don't know, Sutton, it makes my guts tight, but it also makes me feel light and fast. It's, well, Lord, it's like being with a woman, holding that power and then releasing it all at once." He stopped, no more words coming, embarrassed by what he'd let out. "I like it, though maybe I shouldn't," he finished.

Morse straightened up, swung his arms to wake himself from the reverie of talking. "Sutton, you should get some sleep. Drag your blanket over by these trees, away from those clods who're making so much noise."

"I suppose we'll be at it early."

"Always are," the lieutenant said, swiping at gnats in front of his face. "Old Jack always starts at early dawn, except when he starts the night before."

"That's it, that's the case in fact," Sutton said, and they both laughed a little.

Sutton turned, looking east into the darkness of the plain beside the Shenandoah. Listening to Morse talk about fighting, Sutton had understood what he said, but realized he didn't have the same feelings. Not the same thrill. That wasn't why he was in this army, the night before another battle. What was it?

He had no answer. He kept looking into the night.

"This high ground we're on, lieutenant, it looks over those fields across the river. That's where we'd fight Shields, if he's down this far, isn't it?"

"Probably right."

"If Fremont got this ground, he could put his cannon up here and sweep us off that field even if he can't cross the river," Sutton said.

"Ewell will have to hold him."

"It's all a pretty delicate dance, it seems. Everything has to go right."

"It's a chancy thing," Morse agreed. "But it always is. Jackson's got to make it work."

"So do we."

"And you'll need some sleep to do it."

"Yes." And Sutton walked away to try to find some rest. Before it all started again.

North of Port Republic, June 8, 1862, night—Union Army

The water rippled silver as it flowed around the gravelly downstream point of the island.

Jones' Island, an officer had said the name was as he put Emerson Grady and a few other Federal soldiers out here on picket. The land on both sides of the South Fork of the Shenandoah River tumbled down to the grassy flats, wet and soggy now with high water. The island was long and thin, Grady had seen in the fading daylight, curving around a bend toward Port Republic. The kind of place where Grady would have liked to sit on the bank, watch the cottonwood leaves shiver in the wind, find a deep spot to drop a line. In other times than these.

Shenandoah. Meant daughter of the stars, some college boy said. A few stars shimmered in the water by the island, a dancing trail of reflected flecks of light. Come all this way. To see this. I've seen it. It's pretty enough. Now let's go home.

They'd come farther down the road today. Another short march closer to—what? To Jackson? To a fight? To a bullet? A small troop had made it into the town today. Almost bagged Jackson. Made him scurry like a rabbit. He slipped through. They couldn't hold the town. Rebel cannon blew a few of Shields' men off the bridge. A little taste. A turn or two around the dance floor before the ball opened for real.

"Grady." A hissed whisper from his left. Parker. "You awake?"

"Better be," Grady answered in a low, breathy grumble.

"You think they'll come tonight?"

Grady tried to see ahead, over the small heads of wheat that bobbed in the occasional breeze. "Don't know. Don't know how bad Fremont beat them up."

"Maybe they've had enough."

"Maybe. We thought that before, Parker. And Jackson turned on us. I don't know what he's doing."

"I wish he wouldn't do it to us," Parker said. He shouldn't be so close, should move farther left to watch nearer the road. But Grady supposed that, like him, Parker felt alone, scared, about to fall off the far edge of the earth in the dark foreign night.

Quiet for a few moments. Frogs. Crickets. The buzz of mosquitoes around Grady's ears. Mosquitoes went for the ears, gnats for the temples. Coordinated attack. More than Shields and Fremont had been able to do. Fremont fought Jackson alone, when the two armies should have hit him together, from the two sides. Shields hadn't made it in time. Bridges were down behind them, so the two armies couldn't connect, couldn't even talk. That Massanutten Mountain in between them like a sentinel. A barrier. A column in Jackson's army. Now, at the south end of the mountain, where the two armies should have been able to tie in together, Jackson was aiming his cannon at them.

Maybe I should just wade or swim out to that island, sit in the brush, back against a tree, and wait this one out. Let it happen around me.

I suppose I won't. I'll stand here while they try to roll over us. Or I'll rush them with the others, trying to break them before they get in a line of battle. I'll stay for it. Not much else I could choose.

The water's not all that deep, it doesn't look like. We could wade across and hook up with Fremont. But it would take so long. When a river's at a man's chest in a ford it sweeps him off his feet. The equipment sogs and pulls him under. Even at shallower crossings, we move slow as a turtle at the water's edge. We'd bunch up, be perfect targets for those Rockbridge boys and their artillery.

The night goes so slow on picket. Drags, sags, fades, pulls you down to dull and thick. Then your breath and heart jump to full run with any noise. Could be the feet carrying the body that's raising the musket that's aimed at your head. God, what I wouldn't give for a dull summer night in Pennsylvania, Grady thought.

Parker hissed again, "I don't think they're coming."

"Might still. Keep looking for them. They're tricky bastards." Grady walked a little, toward the river, back. To keep his blood flowing. Wake up his head.

A shriek, high and thin and shocked, as an owl hit a rabbit or something, out on the island. Grady shivered, shook his shoulders to roll it off him, the noise of the pain and the desperation.

Then just quiet, frilled with rustling leaves and tripping water. Alone out here. Very   damned   alone.

Port Republic, June 8, 1862, night—Confederate Army

The woods were thick and tangled here where the South River flowed into the North River to form the South Fork of the Shenandoah, on the eastern edge of the half-abandoned town of Port Republic.

James Sparrow, exhausted, could not push his eyes closed. He buzzed with random energy.

I'm coming apart. Can't. Gotta hold together on guard duty. But, this pressure inside, feels like it's flinging pieces of me out in all directions. I'm spinning, whirling out like drops from a flung wet towel.

Dead bodies in Port Republic. Just a few. Scattered. Where the Federals hit us. Surprised us.

Dead torn bodies. Lots of them. Back on Sutton's farm. Would the Federals push through from there, come screaming now at my back? More of them out ahead in the dark where they'd raced in from Shields' front yesterday. Ready to come at me from those dark fields and trees in front. Christ, they're everywhere.

Jeez, they got Ashby. How many can we lose?

My thigh muscles. Feel ripped, squeezed through a mangle. We gonna march back all the way to Tennessee?

Sounds to the right, at the river. Wagons being pulled into the stream. Black men shoving horses. Entreaties, curses. Horseshoes clashing on wet rocks. Making a bridge over there. So we can cross and have another fight. Stand in front of each other's bullets again, cur-riste.

This musket weighs like stone. But soon's I lay it down they'll come through that dark, those little evil flashes of light from their barrels. Coming at me. Again. Jesus won't it stop?

I've been eager for them other times. Bring 'em on, mow 'em down like wheat. Lay them in shattered pieces on the ground. Rake them limp and broken into trenches. Cover them up, move on to find more ground that will hold them. Bury them all. It's hopped me up, lifted me, the thrill, move where you've got cover and catch them where they don't. Pick a man's chest and squeeze, the kick of the gun butt solid and satisfying on your shoulder front. *Did* something. Bam. Do it again. Push 'em back. When you all hold and then fire at once, the crashing flight of sound down the line on both sides of you at once like a rattling flight of geese all lifting off a lake, you feel extended along the right and left, all the line as one, the power of men's will together.

Now. Just scared. Used up.

My shoulders. Feel heavy as pumpkins. Can't straighten up. Stooped like an old old man.

So tired I could drop. But my head would still be pulsing, glowing coals. Fermenting stuff in a jar, bulging at the lid. My eyes.

Everywhere at once a clear spattering sound rushed him, shocked him, front and sides and back and above. Noise dropped and wrapped him and every muscle clenched and his mind exploded as he jumped.

Fat fast raindrops. The sky, the leaves, the air full. Half a minute and it stopped. Pieces of him pulled back together. Breathing kicked back in, his skin held him again. He was wracked, could hardly stand. His head swung forward, eyes reaching. Toward…?

Just dark. Some swaying tree branches. No northern lines, no silent men drifting at him like taut sailing ghosts.

He heaved a huge breath. Shook his arms and his chest and his belly. Aw, God, I used to have fun, make fun. At the beginning of all this I was lively as a goat in springtime. I'd make men laugh, pour japes out on the marching column to make it move the smoother. Enliven the men and they'd enliven me. Make us all roust about, slap some butts, dance along the line and holler at them to step lively 'cuz we was going to a ball dance, step along now ladies raise them dance pumps and kick in line. Have to have some *fun* out of this boys, 'cuz we're out here on a lark, camping where we want, pissin' in the grass, no wives to tell us what to do and what to fix and where to spit our chaw. We're having some fun now, boys, don't you know how to *prance* and make this line move with some *spirit now,* by damn! Oh, I could get them all rolling along, dancing in a line like a quivering snake, raising their muskets in a rippling row, shaking their fannies as they pranced along, laughing like kids out of school on the first fine day of spring. I could *lift* their spirits, make them *fly* for just a few minutes, forget about the guns and wounds and friends not here, and that would lift me just as sure. The men liked to be in my march, we'd have some fun of it. Might as well skylark, boys, we could be dead by morning, laid out on the cold cold ground and then you'll wish you could *move* them legs and *wiggle* them hips like the girls you can't get near now 'cuz you smell so rank and you are so damn far away from that sweet little honey pot, yessir. *Move it* while you've got it to move, move it while it can, learn yourselves to dance away from those flying Minie balls, just dip and flourish your long ugly arm and let that bullet pass on by boys. Let's let those Yankee sops know we've got some *juice* in us now, pick it up. Oh, yes, I could get them moving like a pack of blacks in the nighttime quarters, jigging and skipping 'cuz they're ain't nothin' else to do. Had me a tambourine I'd slap against my leg and make everybody jiggle as we walked. I'd flip a cap off with my fingers, pinch a cheek and slip my arm inside some scared boy's wing and we would strut ourselves along with a slide left and a sliiiiide right and the other boys would whistle and hoot and soon that scared little mother's son wouldn't know where he was but he was smiling big as an idjit at a bonfire, having him some fun. And we all would laugh and clap in time and the officers would wonder where we got the whiskey but I'd call out we're just drinkin' in the sunlight sir and marchin' off the miles. I poured it on and spread it around and wrapped the joy and laughter I teased out of them around my shoulders like a mantle of riches. I could make a whole afternoon of sore feet and worrisome miles just slip on by. And it made me feel just bully. And that's why I done it so much, to keep me flying, because otherwise I'd just crash on the ground and dig my face into the earth and cry a flow up to the Potomac, I would. I would. So I laughed at the fear and I danced with the devil and I kicked up dirt all along these Valley miles because it made me feel good to make those boys feel alive. While they could. Dance in the face of the beast, what else can you do? Turn your ass and slap it to say the hell with you, you ain't got me today, I'm mine and I'm still here and you can't have me if I laugh at you. So we laughed, and we pranced, and we kept ourselves from falling apart, and I poured my soul out in the air like a little boy jumping off a haystack and I got us all to jump. I was a contagion, I spread my grin through the stumbling ranks. I was a conflagration, I spread my fire all up and down the line and they reflected the heat and warmth right back on me and we kept ourselves going 'cuz we didn't have no choice in the matter, we was there to jump in front of guns and hurl our metal at the Yankees' soft fat bodies and chase them back above that Mason Dixon line if we could live that long and push that hard and run that fast. It was a joy to light up those faces, lift up those chins, goose those spirits up so's they could stand and look it in the face. And spit and wink and draw a bead on another man they'd never known.

Sparrow breathed heavily, staring in the dark. The dance in his head slowed, sputtered, stopped. It was my way. But I don't have much of it left anymore.

A scuttling in the brush and electricity ripped up Sparrow's spine and flashed white in his brain and jerked his arms up with the musket. Small and low, waddling through the leaves. A porcupine or hog. Nothing come to kill him.

But maybe the very next noise would be it.

By God I got more life to live. More sunrises to see rosy violet in the morning clouds. More curving hips to touch, more soft arms to dance entwined with. Don't let me go down here, don't let me go down here.

I would so miss the taste of water just from the well, so cold it clenches as it soothes. I would so miss the snap of an apple on my teeth. The rush of a quail's wings. The smell of hay just cut flowing like a mist up from the glistening green. I would so miss the quick smile that falls like the beat of an angel's wing across the face of a pretty woman when you showed you were interested and she was too. That promise of something, that promise of a soft warm ride to heaven. God those bright white petticoats, those legs flashing pale glory, I ain't seen near enough of those.

Not enough yet. There's more I want.

It's hard to keep alive. Not just whole, no metal through your body, no sickness in your guts, but just hard to keep *alive. Lively.* Jangling around and bouncing. I got me more livin' to do. And here I am with a gun in my hand and half of Pennsylvania out there aiming at me. So I'll damn sure shoot first and I'll damned sure shoot clear and I'll get me out of this. Whole.

I will.

He reached his hands up, gun held in both like a bridge above his head, and felt the wind through his arms. Flowing. Alive.

I will.

He shivered.

God I hope so.

Port Republic, June 8, 1862, night—Confederate Army

Thomas Jackson stood on the bank of the North River, looking into the darkness of the covered bridge. The bank by his feet tumbled down through brush about a dozen feet to the river—the water skittered between rocks, the light from burning campfires sparking on the running waves. The rushing sound of water was comforting, although among the thousands of men lying on the ground, and in the apprehension of what was to come again in the morning, there was little comfort.

In the ripples above a riverbed rock, Jackson saw sign of both eternity and the ever-shifting present. Small flashes and endless flows of time.

Tomorrow. We'll fight again. Hold Fremont. Take Shields.

Then, perhaps, over the mountains to join Lee at Richmond. Turn back McClellan.

Jackson let his shoulders sag for a brief moment. He hung his head, shook it slowly, raised it again. Looked across the river. Straightened his back, blew breath out his nose, nodded to the dark.

How much longer?

He stood now facing north, at the head of the Shenandoah Valley. Behind him, a long march, was his home, that he hadn't seen since the war began. His parlor, where he practiced his lessons. His garden. The walk down the hill and then up another to the VMI. Nearby, his church. Lexington. Graceful houses, quiet days. In front of him, the long Valley, where he'd marched his men so fast so far. My foot cavalry, they call themselves now. He smiled, his beard spreading. These men, they do wonders.

I have hidden them in the mountain gaps, marched them up one side of the Valley and down the other. I have dropped them on the Federals like a hawk from nowhere. Surprise, audacity, speed. They outnumber us. These armies in the Valley, they add up to twice my numbers, more. So I take them in pieces, throw everything I have where they are weak, where they don't look for me. McClellan with his hundred thousand men waits for everything to be ready, for each horse to be shoed, for each haversack to be filled. We, we have so much less, so we don't wait. I don't wait. Nothing is ever ready. We are never fully ready for this bloody work. Can never be. So let's get on with it. Hit with what we have. Hit hard. Hit ruthlessly.

It has worked, this month. With God's grace, we have scattered the Federal armies in the Valley. If He wills it, we will beat this last army of Shields' tomorrow, roll them back up and out of this Valley where they don't belong.

Will that end it? Will it ever end? How long can we make less do more? These men, I would not lose another one, we've lost so many. I've sent so many to their death. But if we hit those people hard, hit them fast, this will be over sooner.

He blinked. Lowered his eyebrows over his weary face, his thin lips opening for air. Is that true? Or does the North have so many men that this will never end? Can we not make them weary of war, weary of death, weary of losing battles? Can we stop this? My Lord I pray this will be over soon.

General Thomas Jonathan "Stonewall" Jackson slapped his gloves against his thigh, stretched his jaw. He pulled air deep into his chest, straightened, kicked his boot in the gravel of the road.

Tomorrow we'll try once more. We must beat them. Destroy them. They cannot have Virginia. I must press them, and press them again.

And for an instant, there was an electric charge flashing around his heart, sparks dancing along his nerves. His eyes surged wide, his teeth clamped. He could see, in the dark, faceless Federals blown backwards as if by a hurricane wind. He lifted, riding it. The rush of it thrilled through his soul. He swallowed, as if taking in drink. He could love this, he could.

He shivered, his muscles loosened, all along his body. A bitterness came in his mouth. He chased away, banished, any thought but duty. This was his to do, just his duty. Clear before him. To be done. Because it must be done, that's all. No more. God save me.

The night was once more still, and so was Jackson.

He gazed again across the river, then closed his eyes. Bowed his head, in supplication and in weariness. And prayed again. One arm raised in the dark.

Port Republic, June 9, 1862—Confederate Army

Bullets pinged off stones in the field by the river. Men yelled. The battle was on. Orders were to move ahead, press the Federals, fold them back off this field. But they weren't giving much ground. All around where Givens Woods stood, men were falling to their knees, turning their backs to reload as if that would protect them, leaning forward with their heads down, hands holding hats on, as if in a high wind. Men were flung down by the impact of the Minie balls, tossed up in pieces by the cannon shots.

Woods tried to keep his head down. He was a good soldier. Nothing too brave, certainly no hero. Heroes didn't live too long, he'd seen.

He'd also observed that, although there were a few hotspurs who tried to make a show of their actions leading up to a fight, once it started, people mostly just did their jobs without much flair. They just got down to it, taking chances only when they had to, to put more pressure on the Yankees or to save a friend who'd been shot, maybe. Many, like Woods, were grim about it. They'd walk into hellish fire, but they wouldn't cheer over it. Oh, he'd heard yelling and rah-rahing on the battlefield, but most men didn't do that.

Woods was pretty realistic about war, he thought. It was a nearly sure way to get yourself killed, if you stayed in it long enough. The best way to not get killed was to just do what you were supposed to do and not get out of line. No volunteering for special details, no running out in front of the boys, no grabbing for the fallen colors, no standing when there was something solid to crouch behind.

He would fight for Virginia, like his friends from Rockbridge County, but he wouldn't go out of the way to win the war all by himself, whether with a rifle or with passionate talk around the campfires. And he'd try to give the Yankees hell, but he'd rather chase them back North than kill them. He didn't hate them. He just wanted them gone. So he could go home. He'd shoot at them, and he'd aim true. But he wouldn't take much delight in hitting someone. That person, though a soldier in blue, was a man just like him. Talked funny, but the uniforms of the ones he'd seen looked almost as raggedy as his, the faces looked almost as desperate once the shooting started. A lot of them were scared, when you could see them close enough. Some were just resigned, like he was. Most, he figured, wanted what he wanted—to go home.

Today, Givens Woods didn't think he'd make it home. Ever. He'd had that fearful premonition—knowledge, almost—that this was it.

His friend Colton Ramsey had been killed at Cross Keys. Woods hadn't seen him fall, but he saw him dead. Albert Paxton, his other messmate, was sick, had been left behind at Harrisonburg. Woods went on now with men he didn't know as well. He hadn't seen Sutton, the quiet, curious man he'd met at Charlestown, since the fighting at Cross Keys yesterday. Or was it the day before? The fighting happened on Sutton's land, some of it. Strange. Maddening, no doubt, for Sutton. What a monster this war was, trampling fields and lives. And homes.

Home. "I'll never make it," he said. He ripped a cartridge with his teeth, poured powder down his barrel. He looked around, above him at the blue punctuated with floating white clouds, sun pouring down on the wheat fields by the Shenandoah's south fork. Take it in, boy, he thought. It will soon enough disappear, for you.

Dirty grey smoke drifted over. The fighting roared around him.

Before the battle opened, he had handed the man he'd marched with a letter he'd quickly scrawled that morning. To his mother. "Make sure she gets this, will you? You know?"

"Sure. Yeah. Don't worry. It's fine. I mean, you're fine, you'll be fine."

But the man had flinched.

Woods knew. He just knew. He had no idea how. He'd heard of this, many times. He'd believed it. But now, it was different. It was him. It reached into his guts. It squeezed his lungs. It was a thrill beyond fear and terror. It was the edge of a tremendous fall, and he couldn't pull his breath in as he teetered.

This could be the fight. This would be the day. This might be the moment.

Right very now.

He'd known it. But he'd walked into this field, he'd stayed in line. He'd fought. He'd moved on orders. He kept at it, kept at what he'd done for months because that's what he did. Not because he thought, not because he believed, but because that's what he did.

He shot some more. He tore cartridges. He loaded. He shot again. He wouldn't stop, until he was stopped. Bullets whipped past him, splashed into ground and thunked into men. He didn't flinch, but he was in thick slow breath-sucking wonder. Was he wrong? Would it not happen?

Then.

Now.

Here.

He saw something coming fast at him, almost tied to his eyes by a pulley and line that was being whisked so quick by unseen hands. Right at him, direct line, but tumbling a bit, it was slow at first, barely seen, picked up by his fast-turning eye that scanned the field for danger, then suddenly a rushing tiny black shape that was done hovering and dancing while it decided and now it was shooting from the background of green leaves and pale wheat sheaves, growing in mass and speed as it flew at him like a tiny homing bird unleashed and slung across the world. At him.

It grew leaping in his field of vision and then—*for a rushing timeless moment it all suspended and he was in another summer day as a little boy by a stream watching fish flash over rocks. His knees were dirty, ripped a little with a fresh tear leaking clear fluid into grains of gravel stuck in the skin. Bugs, mosquitoes and gnats, were squished in a black smear on the white skin of his right thigh, a wing and a couple of bent legs sticking up. He was kneeling at the edge of a fast but small sparkling stream behind the cabin where he grew up in a foothill swell of the Blue Ridge mountains. Summer, summer, summer, summer. So much time. The world just peeling back, opening its secrets to a boy who would poke under bushes and pull up deadfall from the tumbled mast in the woods to see what lay and worked and writhed beneath. To a boy who would stare for what seemed hours at the silvery unseeable surface of water and the long-leg bugs that strode across the trembling fluid and at the quicksilver flash of minnows tipping sideways as they sluiced over what proved to be a perfect skipping stone. Wind stirred the sumac and it shusshled above his head, draping the sound of long warm summer around his shoulders like a worn piece of well-known flannel. A bird trilled as it dipped in air above the stream, he looked up, and then*—the hard black shape rushed up and he was ripped away as the bullet just smack hit him and...

And then there was nothing.

Port Republic, June 9, 1862—Union Army

It was a ripple, this little hill, in front of the main wave of the Blue Ridge. A smaller rise piled up at the foot of the mountain.

Trees had been stripped from part of the hill to feed a charcoal furnace. The little flat open place was called the coaling.

Federal cannon had been dragged up there, to fire down on the Confederates in the field below the hill, where they'd bunched up as they came out of Port Republic to attack Shields' men. The effects had been brutal.

Rebel troops had attacked the battery twice to stop the slaughter, taking the ground, then losing it again. Emerson Grady's Ohio regiment was now being sent up the hill to beat back what would surely be another Rebel attempt to take the guns. The coaling on its modest rise of high ground was the key to the battle.

Grady was exhausted, and didn't see how he was going to get up the hill, much less fight when he got there. It had been a hard fight so far, and a long march before.

They'd walked with Shields up the east side of the Shenandoah Valley, this part called the Luray Valley for the little town at the base of the only pass through the Massanutten Mountain that split the Valley in two. On the other side of Massanutten, Fremont's army was marching, also toward Jackson. The aim was for the two armies to join and destroy the Rebels.

But Confederates had burned the White House bridge across the South Fork of the Shenandoah at the base of the Luray-New Market pass. They'd burned bridges farther up the river too, toward Port Republic. The spring and early summer had been wet, and the river was full and high. Shields and Fremont couldn't reach each other. Unless they could join at the southern end of Massanutten, they'd fight separately.

That made Grady and the troops nervous. As had the continuing march up the Valley. Each step took them farther from Washington, farther from Federal territory. Fighting at the downstream end of the Valley, around Winchester, had meant they could always fall back across the Potomac or east across the Blue Ridge to the trains at Manassas. They could always get away from Jackson.

But now Jackson had lured them 50 miles up the Valley. Were they chasing Jackson any more, or was he pulling them into a trap?

In peacetime, the trip would have been lovely. This part of the Valley was narrower than the western side, and stunningly beautiful. The Blue Ridge and the Massanutten rose majestically on either side, heavy with trees and misty blue-green. The mountains were restful to look at, soft rounded variations on a continuing theme. The ground between the mountains swelled up and down like a rolling sea, crested with woods, dotted with two-story farm houses floating in rich grain. The South Fork of the Shenandoah curved back and forth against the base of the Massanutten, and creeks curled down the hillsides to the river.

But on this march the countryside seemed ominous to Grady. The mountains pressed in. Room to maneuver narrowed. As they neared Port Republic, the little hill on the east, the left as they marched, jammed them close to the river. Except for the clearing of the coaling, the hill was thick with dark woods. It seemed a tight spot.

And then the Confederates came marching to meet them. Not very many at first, but more were coming up from the town. The Union men looked west, to see if Fremont would come to the heights across the river, at least place artillery there to help them fight back the Rebels. But nothing appeared. They were on their own. Two armies chasing Jackson deep into his own country, they should have been able to overwhelm him and put an end to this upstart's deadly annoyance so the blue troops could concentrate on Richmond and end the war. Should have.

Smoke puffs bloomed above the wheat to the south. The frightening rip of rifle fire, first in bursts, then in sheets, chilled Grady's spine. Minie balls flicked through the leaves, and it was all happening again.

Grady's Ohio unit had gone in with an Indiana regiment on their right and a Union Virginia regiment on their left. Grady had heard that every Confederate state except South Carolina had sent men to fight with the Union. He thought this extremely strange, and wondered what these Virginians must be feeling as they started firing on their countrymen. Then he realized they were all countrymen on that field. Or had been. He looked to his left, and saw the Western Virginians were pouring it on.

Grady walked close to the Rebel line, knelt and fired. With the heightened senses of battle, he was almost sure he could see his bullet pass between two men and then past three more men behind, yielding nothing.

His next shot, he was sure, found the chest of a tall Rebel and dropped him into the wheat. The wheat shafts themselves were being cut by the Union bullets as if by a scythe.

The jumbled swirl of time in battle came upon Grady again. A few minutes would stick slow in front of him for what seemed an hour, and then a dozen minutes would blow by in a blink. In a break in time, he could see in microscopic clarity the white bone broken like thin slats of wood and sticking through the skin all around the hole where a bullet had smashed through the forehead of a man next to him, the hole broken through right at the border of the white skin that was always under a hat and the tanned skin that the sun had darkened. Grady looked at this ruin for a long time, it seemed, while men moved and fell and shot around him.

Then an hour's worth of time raced by in a flash in the wheat. His barrel heated, his stomach muscles cramped to a wall of pain. Then, slow again, Grady step by step walked forward, the river on his right, stopping every two or three steps to load and fire. For a time he and the men around him, who pushed messages and meaning back and forth to each other with their hands and jutted rifles because the shooting ate up any voice, had to stop and then slip sideways left toward the road to get a better angle on the Rebels and to take what help they could from the cannon in the coaling. But this still didn't stop the men in front of them from shooting and shooting and shooting. As Grady watched some fall, more came up through the wheat behind, as if extras racing to the stagefront in a play. Why would they come up here just to get shot, he thought to himself in a lull in his mind when he forgot to keep loading his gun, the paper cartridge with ball and powder inside held at chest level by his hand for several minutes, it must have been.

Time dropped suddenly into another track and raced around him, and the din of screams and yells and rippling cracks of gunshots dropped on him like a cloud-burst and he was pushed back by the force of bodies and billows of smoke and air made hot and hard by the flying bits of lead.

It went on and on now, fast and slow together, and he'd never done anything but hold a searing rifle barrel in his callused hands in a bulletswarm chaos of bending breaking bodies.

At the north end of the Massanutten mountain, two and a half months ago, Grady's Ohio regiment and Sutton's Virginia outfit had shot at each other amid the stone fences and woods of Kernstown. Grady's friend Nichols had been killed, his head and guts splattered on the bloody ground. Who knows what barrel the bullets came from? It didn't matter. It was just a mess of killing and maiming, men looking into each other's angry frightened faces and shooting right into them. No aim but to survive.

Now, many long marches later, more dust and gunpowder soaked into their roughened skin, these two units were shooting face to face again, pushing each other back and forth with lead and flame across a ruined field by a lovely river. The curved rampart of the south end of the majestic Massanutten presided over the horrible scene, as had the similar heights of the north end of the mountain in March. If seen from the mountain, the matter below would have looked small, a nettlesome brash disturbance tucked in a corner of a sweeping prospect of mountains and forests and hawks sailing the summer air. Seen from over the steel sight of a rifle barrel, it was a hellish maelstrom of smoke and sweat and stink and cries and parts of bodies being ripped from the normal web of muscle twitch and blood flow and nerve signal that added up to life—a hand tilting a glass to a mouth, say—before the war.

This time, as Grady's unit saw by hand signals the order to climb to the coaling on their left above the field, Grady swung his rifle up once more and let go the charge he'd rammed down the barrel a minute ago. He had aimed only in a general way at a clump of men in front of him, across a little wagon-wheel indentation in the ground. He saw as he turned away one man spin around as if tripped in a game of tag, and fall.

And this time it was muscle and blood vein of William Sutton's leg that was shredded and torn by the screaming cone of lead. Who knows what barrel this bullet came from? It didn't matter. There were guns aplenty, aimed north and south, doing their dirty business with random horror.

Grady climbed the hillside up to the coaling where the cannon smoked and bucked. There were bodies dropped in piles around, horses and men. He stepped over them, sat down, his lungs whuffing like a steam engine on a grade, and loaded his rifle just in time to hear an ungodly warbling howl break through the trees to the south in front of him.

This would never end. This would never ever end. He raised his rifle as a new burst of the ancient hideous storm broke over him.

Port Republic, June 9, 1862—Confederate Army

"General Jackson sent us to take this battery, and that's what we're going to do, lads. Close up here, and let's be ready to move." The Confederate captain was calling in a hoarse whisper to the men crouched around him. The Federal cannon in the coaling on the hillside were ripping Jackson's troops in the field below.

The Confederates had come out of Port Republic, trying to cross the South River on wagon beds laid end to end in the stream. Men had backed up at the makeshift bridge and the troops had slowed to a crawl. Some of General Richard Taylor's Louisiana troops had waded across, used to living around—and in—water. Then a fast march east with the rippling gunfire off to their left. They saw men walking back from the battle, drifting singly or in pairs, their heads down, their rifles, if they had them, drooping from their hands or upside down on their shoulders.

"I don't see no blood on those shirts, boys, best turn around and join us, get back in it," a man near Alain Guidry yelled at the soldiers. It was always like this at the back end of a battle, shocked and wounded men wandering away from the storm of sound and metal. The battered men paid the fresh troops no heed.

Taylor's Louisianans turned northeast and trotted into the woods, pushed on their way by James Sparrow, sent back from the fighting in the wheatfield to guide the fresh troops. Sparrow slapped his hands together and shouted at Guidry and the short line of marchers, "Go to it, boys, there's plenty for all, get in those trees and jam those cannons up their asses, will you now? Yes, my boys, go to it!"

On the hillside now they could see through the trees ragged lines of Confederate troops giving ground slowly down in the flat fields by the river. More troops were coming out from Port Republic, and the fighting wavered back and forth on the plain.

Taylor's men moved as fast through the thick brush and trees as they could, aiming at the Union battery in the coaling. The Union gunners couldn't see the

Louisianans in the trees, but they sent shells crashing into the woods where they thought the Rebels must be.

"Those bombs scare hell out of me," said Tommy Bresnehan as he ducked next to Guidry, his friend from a small settlement just upriver from New Orleans. Guidry was a farmer, Bresnehan a ditch digger. They were a long way from home. Ducking at the shells made no sense, Bresnehan supposed, but it made him feel better.

A howling swish flew above them, then an explosion and a deafening crack splattered the air, and a tall tree, 80 feet high maybe, splintered in the middle and disintegrated in flame and smoke and the top dropped vertically like a spear, slamming to the ground, collapsing on itself into sharp hot white fragments.

"Holy Jeeesus," Guidry whispered to himself, stunned and frozen in the brush.

Bresnehan shook shards of wood out of his long scraggly hair. "Gotta duck the trees, too, I guess. Even old Jack ducked when he came under cannon fire up by the Potomac last winter," Bresnehan said as they started walking again. "They were breaking up the locks in the B&O canal and the Yankees were shelling them all the while. Old Jack was standing in the trees on the Virginia side and they dropped a couple shells right near him, and he ducked, boy. Shows he's got some sense, and I'm following his lead."

"Once, they say. He ducked once, then got over it," Guidry told him. "Never ducked again." He smiled nervously, then patted Bresnehan on the shoulder, jerked his head forward. They grinned at each other and moved on.

Branches slapped their faces and tore their sleeves and pants. They had to push their rifles straight out in front of them to get through the brush. They had to step high over the deadfall—not easy when you're nearly running.

They were close now. Some of the cannon in the coaling were firing down into the fields, plowing great holes in the Confederate lines. They could feel in their muscles the slam of the cannon as the pressure waves crushed the air against them. For a fragment of a second they could hear the shells whistling out over the wheat field, then another "FWHUMP" of air and noise as the shell burst on the ground amid the southern troops.

The higher pitched, sharper sounds of muskets told them Union infantry was guarding the cannon they were after. It was going to be purely awful.

They stopped, looking through the trees ahead. As he knelt, waiting for the order to charge, Guidry looked at a clump of brush and twigs a few feet in front of him. It had eyes. Guidry jerked as he realized he was looking at a man, crushed to the forest floor. The man's butternut pants and dirty beige blouse blended with the fallen twigs and bark on the forest floor. The man was partly covered with dirt, shattered wood, leaves. Guidry couldn't see all of the man—wasn't sure all of the man was there. Guidry realized the man was a Confederate who'd been hit, apparently by cannon fire, in an earlier assault on the battery. The man was facing Guidry, away from the battery. His shoulders were embedded in the forest debris, his head pushed up at a painful angle. Guidry could make out a belt, a thigh, one shoe, not much more. A cold silver glint of light was reflected in the man's eyes. He blinked two or three times, nodded his head a fraction of an inch at Guidry. Didn't say anything, at least nothing that could be heard above the explosions.

Guidry shivered. I'll have to make sure not to step on him when we move.

"All right boys, Old Jack says we must take these cannon. Fix your bayonets, save your fire 'til you can see something to shoot at. Let's move in smart and let's have those guns," the captain called, louder this time to reach the 30 or so men in the woods.

Just because Jackson says we must doesn't mean we can, Guidry thought.

"Stay close to me, Alain, I'll keep them off you," Bresnehan leaned his head over next to Guidry. "Hey, remember," and he opened his jacket and showed Guidry the letter in an inside pocket. A letter to Bresnehan's parents, in case he was killed.

"I remember, Tommy. But you'll give it to them yourself at the end of this war. Now let's hunt us a couple Yankees." Guidry quickly looked to the left and right to see where the others were, then watched the captain. Guidry's dark hair, sharp face, stubble of beard made him look dashing and dangerous, but he felt only tightness. Eagerness to get it over with, to pass through the shooting to something safer on the other side. To something quiet.

Bresnehan wore a straw hat crushed shapeless around his head. His hair beneath the hat was reddish blond, his ears were large, his white face was dirty. His eyebrows were way up on his forehead. He half sat on the ground, his shoulder turned against the pressure from the Union battery. He looked forward, over his shoulder, then grinned back at Guidry.

"Good luck, boyo," he mouthed.

"God bless us both, Tommy," Guidry said back. He quickly crossed himself, then the captain yelled and shoved his raised arm forward, and Guidry and Bresnehan pushed off the ground and leaped forward.

The quavering banshee rebel yell warbled in front of them as they ran, then a blast of air knocked Guidry sideways. The six-inch tree next to him shattered and tipped, felled by one ax blow of a federal cannon shell. He tripped, over the wounded man he'd forgotten was in front of him, and he hit the ground hard as another shell ripped the air above his head. He saw an arm pinwheel in the air to his right, attached to no body.

He sprang to his knees, then his feet, grabbed his musket from the fallen leaves and sticks, flicked sweat out of his eyes, looked forward and saw flashes of light quickly smothered in smoke at chest level in front of him. Rifle fire, he thought, and twigs and leaves snicked off the branches around him. The sound of quick pops rippled in front, then firing came from his right back at the Federals. He ran, slammed into a tree, shook himself, took two more steps and saw a man in blue with a filthy face aim a pistol at him. Guidry dropped and fired and the man fell away, clubbed by a musket butt swung from his left. Guidry started to reload, dropped the cartridge, then ran on with his bayonet pushed out in front of him. A shot hit a tree by his head and splintered wood into his face, knocking his head sideways and he fell again.

Up once more, bleeding and running, he broke into the clearing. A cannon two feet to his left roared and jumped and he was knocked to the ground again, deafened and stunned. He heard nothing for a few seconds, then sound slammed over him like a wave. Men yelling, rifle bullets hitting cannon barrels, gunstocks hitting skulls, horses rearing and screaming, shots, grunts, bodies hitting the ground, bones snapping.

Just ahead of him he saw Bresnehan sawing at the neck of a horse with a stout knife, his other hand locked in the horse's mane, the horse's head jerking back and pulling Tommy off his feet. "Kill the horses," Bresnehan yelled over his shoulder, looking wildly for his comrades. Just as blood poured from the horse a Federal soldier smashed Tommy's neck with the butt of his rifle, tossing Tommy sideways into the wheel of a cannon. Guidry stabbed at the soldier with his bayonet but missed, dropping his rifle, then grabbed a stone the size of a breadloaf and flung it at the man. It bounced off the man's shoulder and he spun away, knocked over by another rushing Confederate soldier whose head then snapped back as he was hit by a shot from the edge of the clearing where a knot of men in blue were standing and firing. They melted away as more Louisiana soldiers broke from the woods and leveled their guns, flame spouting from the muzzles.

Guidry found a musket at his feet, kneeled, ripped a cartridge, loaded, leveled and fired at the bluecoats backing away in the trees.

The Federals were giving way, and too many horses had been wounded or killed for them to bring the guns off with them.

But they hadn't gone far. From the left, down the hill, a line of Federals lay flat on the ground, shooting, rolling sideways to reload, and shooting again. In the trees in front of the Louisianans, more smoke and more shots.

"Turn it, turn the gun," the captain yelled, his left arm hanging shattered, his pistol in his right hand jabbing the air. "Come on boys, turn this gun and give it to them." The captain leaned into the cannon's left wheel as two soldiers grabbed the right wheel and another the cannon's trail. They swung the big gun around, shoving against the rocky, uneven ground. The captain pushed aside a tall man from the cannon's butt end, sighted, then stepped aside and the tall man with glee jerked the lanyard and metal and flame slashed out from the muzzle and cut down men and trees at the far edge of the clearing. A moan came back through the trees, and fewer rifle shots now.

Then the Federals on the hillside rose and charged, a dozen or so brave and frenzied men. For a second Guidry could see the trim white house on the river flats behind them and the fringe of trees that marked the Shenandoah making a bend, then blue-white smoke erupted from the thin Federal line and bullets were whining off the metal of the cannon, chipping wood off the spokes, thunking into men on his left. Another cannon had been turned, and Guidry saw two Confederates duck as the cannon erupted. Caps and bodies and rifles flew backward down the slope as the shot took the Federals, then smoke billowed over Guidry and he heard a wail and a lone voice holler, "Let's git."

The hillside emerged from the smoke and a handful of Federals were running. Rifles around Guidry cracked and two of the men fell skidding on their faces. Some of the Louisiana boys ran, jumping and stumbling, down the hill in pursuit. A fat Union officer stood steady and yelled "Damn you die" as he brought up his pistol and dropped two of the soldiers. His pistol clicked empty and he lowered it, waiting with clenched teeth and searing eyes until a bullet through his face ended his stand.

Below, the Federal troops were now running back from the tattered golden fields of hay and clumping up in the narrow opening of the woods where the road ran north toward Conrad's Store. Blind flights of steel balls from canister shells jerked a dozen at a time to the ground. Some stumbled brokenly to their feet, some lay still on the roadside. From his left, on the river flats, Guidry could see solders from Virginia sweeping down on the chaotic retreat of the Federals. Then he sunk to the ground, done.

When Tommy Bresnehan awoke, the scene was still. His eyes saw rocks, a shattered rifle butt, broken spokes from a cannon wheel, chewed ground, a ragged shoe sole close to his face with a leg stretched beyond, bent at the knee, connecting to a body twisted on the ground, an arm trailing back at a broken angle, a head with tousled hair turned to the dirt. He moved his head with pain and saw next to him a rumpled jacket on a man cradling a musket. He raised his eyes and saw a sharp, lined face with dark eyes, blood and sweat trailing through black grime on the cheeks. Guidry. The face moved, something close to a smile, dragged down as it rose by exhaustion.

"I thought we'd lost you, Tommy," Guidry said. "Don't move yet."

An arm of the jacket moved and Bresnehan felt a hand light on his face, then his neck.

"How you feel?"

"Busted up," Bresnehan said, his voice a low grumble. "How do I look?"

"Busted up."

"I think a cannon ball hit me."

"Yankee rifle butt. Right here." The fingers pushed tenderly into Bresnehan's neck. He felt a stab of bright pain through the broad ache, sucked in a breath.

"Broken?"

"Not if you can move your head." The fingers moved, pushed some more, more sharp stabs. "I think you'll live."

"Many killed?"

"Lots." Guidry jerked his head toward the slope below them. "They're taking them off." Bresnehan's eyes followed Guidry's motion, and he saw a long row of crumpled men lying in the dirt, feet together, arms folded over their jackets and shirts. One's shoulder was torn open, a mass of red. One had only shoulders, half a neck, a skin flap and an ear.

"God," Bresnehan breathed. "The Yankees?"

"Running. Those that can."

"The guns. They're ours?"

"Ours now."

Guidry leaned down to help Bresnehan up to sit, turned him to lean against the wheel of a caisson. Bresnehan moved slowly, jerkily, winced, grunted, settled. "We turned them, the guns?"

"We killed them with them. Gave them their own iron."

"We didn't want it."

"No, we didn't. They needed it more than we did, that's what we decided."

"And we gave it to them. The bastards."

"No, Tommy. They fought like hell. They were brave, or they were crazy. They were just like we are."

"But they were trying to kill us. Here in our own home."

"It's not our home, Tommy. We're states away."

"It's our country."

"*Is* it now?"

They looked at each other, limp and weary.

"It's our country, Alain. It's ours."

"Will it be?"

"We'll make it, make it ours. Ain't that why we're here?"

"Who knows."

"They're gone."

"For a time."

They looked at men carrying bodies down the hillside to the flat ground by the road. Other men there were digging trenches. They heard men softly talking to the wounded above them on the hill, heard one man crying "Oh, oh, oh, oh, ohhhh."

"Lie still, Zack, please lie still. We'll stop this. HEY, over here, man come and stop this bleeeeeding, can't you stop it? Zack, Zack, please lie still."

"Oh, oh, oh, oh, oh."

Weeping.

Bresnehan saw a tall, aristocratic-looking man in a general's uniform standing with a group of men, pointing toward the north. "Is that Taylor?"

"Yep. He came when we'd finished. Said we'd done fine. Ewell was here too. And Jackson."

"Jackson?"

"He came here. To congratulate us. What was left."

"What was he like?"

"Lit up. And sad, somehow, at the same time. Looked down the hill and said 'Press them, press them.' Said we'd been the key to the battle, that we'd won it. He thanked us. It was pretty good to hear."

"I wish I'd seen him."

"That old boy there, the big one with the red beard? He was straddling a cannon when Jackson rode up. He whooped at Old Jack, hollered, 'We told you we'd take these guns, general, we told you.' Hollered like a madman. He's a wild one from that bunch that works the docks in New Orleans. Learned how to fight in the Quarter, just took it up here to Virginia. Didn't need a drink to be drunk today. Drunk with whatever glory there is in this. He just kept whooping at Jackson. You'd have liked it, Tommy, you like to holler."

"What did Old Jack say?"

"'God gave us this victory,' is what he said. God's got strange hobbies, you ask me."

Bresnehan smiled, for the first time since the morning.

Port Republic, June 9, 1862—Confederate Army

William Sutton could hear the tickle and trill of the South Fork of the Shenandoah off to his left. In front of him, sheaves of wheat, a soft honey color glowing in the afternoon light. Particles of dust, tiny chips of wheatshaft floated in the air, caught for a moment in the sun. That horizontal sunlight. It always made things look so full, rich, rounded.

Back home, just a few miles and a world away, sometimes the afternoon light had stopped him in his tracks. Behind the mule, pushing the plow through the thick dirt of the Valley, he'd stop as the last afternoon sunlight streamed over the

Appalachian ridge, the western border of the Valley. It filled the bowl of the Valley with gold—the wheat dipping in the breeze, the furze of corn silk lit with fire. As the land rose up the side of Massanutten, its trees took in the sunlight and bulged forth from the mountain, each leaf illuminated, painted by hand, the depth of the trees brought forward by the light. Like when he ran his fingers through the deep auburn of his wife's hair, and it took a little while to fall back into place, lights flashing inside, a flow of color, each strand bright. Deep. Full. The whole world alive.

Sutton tried to keep thinking about Martha. As he looked at the wheat sheaves ahead. He'd ridden the road to his right many times. Up the Luray Valley to Conrad's store. To get supplies for them. The beauty of the Luray Valley always charmed him. But he liked his home place better, at the foot of the Massanutten, just behind him where the two valleys joined. There were rivers all around. The South River, the North River, and the peaceful place where they came together at Port Republic to form the South Fork of the Shenandoah. To the north of his place, his and Martha's, the North Fork of the Shenandoah.

He could feel the power of all that moving water, gathering. Pulling itself in from the hills, from the rises, from the richest country on earth. Rolling down the Valley, caressing both sides of the Massanutten, tumbling together at Front Royal and making its run to Harper's Ferry and the Potomac. The water. Gathering. It was one of the only things, that and Martha, that made him understand what God must be like. If there was a God. He used to think so.

In some of the few moments of ease he'd given himself as a farmer, he'd sat on a rock in the Potomac, just below Harper's Ferry when he'd been there to visit friends, looking upstream at the B&O bridge that shot across the river and into the mountain tunnel on the Maryland side. A couple of hours before sunset. Just sitting, staring at the confluence of water and light. Listening to the hushed liquid rush of the river—lulling, hypnotic essence of peace. The falling sun arced into his eyes from above the Ferry, that sweet little Virginia town sloping down to the rivers joining. The big river was slow among all those rocks. Moving, always moving, smoothing the stones. Straining toward the sea, but not too hard. Nothing seemed hard as he'd sat on that quartz boulder, the sun's flecks glittering on the water and sparking the stone. This was his Valley, his home. It didn't belong to him; he belonged to it.

Back at the head of the waters, Martha had died in '61. They never knew what took her, but it took her fast. There was that. It shook him, sure enough. But that wasn't what scared God away. From him. Or him from God.

It was the blood on his own fields.

He didn't know why it had come. But the war came. They had crossed the Potomac, the Northerners. And it was started. He hadn't made it to Manassas in time for the fight, but he had gotten there for the blood. All over Henry Hill, slick in the trampled grass and weeds. Drifting down Bull Run. To the sea. Not too hard. Just seeping along.

The Northerners went away after. Skedaddled, the Virginia boys loved to say. That was it, wasn't it? They'd stay on their side. In their country. This country was ours, just leave us the hell alone.

He never understood why they came again.

They'd been licked, fair and square. They'd bled on ground that wasn't theirs. They had no right to draw blood there. Or to leave theirs there, soaking the soil. But they came back. Strong. Fierce.

Why couldn't they leave us be?

Tariffs. Nullification. States' rights. Slaves. The territories. Popular sovereignty. Black Republicans. Secession. The Confederate States of America. What the hell did it mean? What the hell did it matter?

Just don't come here, this is ours.

He'd joined boys just as angry, just as strong, just as fierce. To defend the Valley. That's all he knew. The Valley. It was his. He belonged to it.

They shouldn't be here. It wasn't theirs.

Now, after this fight, while he lies in this once-sweet field, they're running again, the Yankees. But not him. His leg. Torn there behind him. A weight, a pressure, a throb that won't let him go.

Up ahead, in the rich light among the sheaves. A hand. Not a whole hand. The little finger was gone. The palm half blown away, red and white shreds fraying out. Flies on it. Busy. No arm nearby that he could see. No man.

That hand had once held the handles of a plow, he'd bet. Or maybe trimmed a hoof and hammered shoe nails. Maybe once lifted a woman's hair. Felt the swell, the firmness and the giving all at once, of a woman's breast. Left hand, it looked like. Right breast, then, unless from behind. Then left. A glory either way.

Martha gone, but he could feel her presence as the little army stumbled across his fields yesterday.

His fields. They'd fought on his fields.

Shoes tattered, some feet bare. The fight at Cross Keys. He'd marched with Ewell's boys across the ruts his own wagon made, the furrows his mule Minnie had turned. The little rise Martha walked across to bring him water. And her smile, a little word. That made the work, the sweat, worthwhile. That's what shoved God away. Not the cannon blasts, although those scared the holy Jesus out of him. Hellish loud. Not on this place. Not where he'd stopped to look at wildflowers in the afternoon light, glowing stronger just before its fade, and heard the buzz of grasshoppers below. The rip of metal tearing the corn, spanging on the rocks his plow had raised, splattering through men he'd known since kids.

It was the blood.

Running into the dirt. Pooling dark by the roots of the corn his hand had put in the ground. His determination had raised from the dirt. Now it was fouled. Like the barrel of his gun, gummy with scorched black powder. Nothing could come out. The earth was fouled, tarry with black blood. The life that for years pushed up through that soil couldn't pass now.

Sutton hadn't felt the howling emptiness of terror when the cannon barked and shattered. He hadn't felt gravity slip away when the muskets—so many—spattered their sound and lead across the fields. Sure, he was scared. But he held on.

It was the blood.

On his ground. Something was so wrong. So out of place. He'd worked that ground, nurtured it and it had nurtured him. Now dark blood, violet where the light hit, glistening like oil. Flowing down his rows. This just couldn't be. This just wasn't right. Not this place. Not here.

Now Martha was gone. She'd flowed away, her last essence, pushed by the runnels of blood.

The Yankees stopped. He and the boys had bought a few miles, with blood. Such a price. For ground that was already his, wasn't it?

Behind them while they fought in his fields, Jackson, Old Square Box, holed up in Port Republic where the rivers joined. Yankees on the other side too, across the South River, Shields' army. There were so many Yankees. They seemed everywhere.

So we hit them on that side too. That's all Jackson knew, his messmates said. Find the Yankees and hit them. No great strategy, no smart plans. Just find the Yankees and hit them. If not, they'd be all over you. You'd go down. There were so many.

So across the South River and into the wheat field by the South Fork of the Shenandoah Jackson sent them at dawn. Unit by unit. Throwing a cupful of water on the fire at a time, hoping it wouldn't get too big before you could reach another cupful. That's how Jackson threw them in. Pell mell. Whatever he could grab. He didn't care who got killed, just throw them at the Yankees.

And they got slaughtered. Here beside the lovely river. Jackson threw us in next. We did better, but a lot of us went down too. Hard.

That man, wherever he was now, without his hand. So many lost so much. Lost it in this field.

And now it was quiet. Nothing much moved but the flies. That hand sure as daylight couldn't move. Any more. Could it still feel the broken wheat shafts it lay on? Was there touch? Could it remember the breast, the hair, the weathered splintery handle of the plow? Gone.

So much gone. God was gone, banished by the devil's work in Sutton's own dirt at Cross Keys.

Even Fremont's cannon on the rise across the river were silent now. Arriving finally at the end of the battle, they'd blown holes in the men coming to help the wounded. Bastard. Some of the Virginians were going out to help the Yankees who'd been shot, but they got out of there fast. "You can have 'em, blow 'em back to hell, General, and fall in after 'em," he'd heard one man yell, the last voice he'd heard close to him. That was an hour ago, maybe. Maybe more. He was losing track of the day. All he could tell was the light, that was fat awhile ago, was thinning now. And so was he. He was leaving himself, it seemed. Part was looking out the eyes to see that hand in the wheat. Part was drifting away. Trailing into the air like smoke after a fire. Rising into a world where God was gone.

Port Republic, June 9, 1862—Union Army

Shields had failed. Instead of trapping Jackson between his troops and Fremont's, Shields was now in retreat. And not a particularly orderly retreat.

Emerson Grady no longer cared about the outcome of the battle. He was alive, and that was the most important fact. He had an ugly trench dug in his left forearm by a Minie ball that all but missed him, and that had stopped bleeding now and only stung. He was dirty, and could taste dirt still. A shell had exploded right in front of him in the wheat field. The metal fragments had missed him, but he'd been slammed onto his back while dirt rained down on him. It was in his hair, down his shirt, down his pants, up his pants legs.

His shirt was soaked in blood, from a horse whose neck had been slashed next to Grady up in the coaling. It was starting to dry and stiffen. The blood reeked.

Every muscle he had was sore. His back ached, he could hardly move his shoulder where a rock had hit him, and the fronts of his thighs felt like they were on fire. But he kept walking. Fast. Because there were still cannon booming behind him.

"I think it's only horse artillery following us," a slouching man next to him said. "I don't think there's any regular troops still coming."

"Oh, that's a mighty relief, friend," the man in front of Grady shot back. "I'm damn glad I'll only be killed by horse artillery."

Some laughter rippled down the broken ranks, but it was tired. Everybody was tired.

They'd marched hard down the Luray Valley, past the serrated end of Massanutten Mountain, all the way to Port Republic. Then they'd fought tired, and got no help from Fremont across the river.

They'd been beaten, and now they were running from the Rebels. A depressing and useless few days. Enough, Grady thought. This must be enough.

As he walked, hardly able to hold his heavy rifle, Grady thought about his 13-year-old son. Robby had been so intrigued by the rifle. Robby and Carlyn had seen Grady's unit off at Cincinnati, and Robby couldn't keep his eyes off his father's rifle. He didn't seem to worry much that his father might be shot, he was just awestruck by the gun.

"Are you going to carry this all the way to Richmond, father?" he'd asked, hefting the rifle as his father handed it to him.

"That's what they tell us, son."

"Are you going to shoot people with it?"

"If I have to. I don't think the Rebs will let us just walk into Richmond, boy. We'll have to fight them for it."

"Father, have you, I mean, have you killed anyone before?"

"No, Robby, thank God I haven't."

"What will it be like, shooting a man? I shot a deer, remember? I didn't like it much. What will it be like?"

"I don't know. I don't look forward to it. Maybe I won't have to find out."

He missed his son. Robby was so full of curiosity, gobbling life up. Starting to talk to girls more. Learning fast in school, asking his father questions about subjects Grady knew nothing about. He wanted to be with his boy, helping him discover the world.

Instead he was running down this road. He wanted to be in his own rocking chair, smoking his pipe. He'd rather be in his hot mechanic's shed, sweating and swearing while he beat on some irksome piece of metal. He could picture the beaten-down mud around his shed where grass would never grow. Could see the rabbits eating the beans in his garden. Could see the tar patch on his roof where he'd fixed a hole that still leaked in a heavy rain. Give him any tedious task at home now and he'd think he was in heaven.

He knew this battle wasn't big enough to end the war. The Valley was just a sideshow, and nothing here would stop the war. Even a defeat would be palatable if it brought an end to the fighting. He believed in the Union and all, and he didn't want the Rebels to win. But it wasn't a matter of beliefs, or even of pride, any more. It's just that there was too much killing and he wished it would stop. But he was afraid it never would. And he was afraid he wouldn't be able to stand that thought much longer.

He wouldn't run away. That wasn't in him. He'd made a commitment and he'd stick. Besides, a lot of deserters got caught. And what would he tell Robby? Carlyn would understand. She'd welcome him back no matter what. She just wanted him whole.

If they could decide it all in one big battle, and let the winner have his way, that would be fine with Grady. Roll the dice, take your shots, and let's decide. Fair enough. Go your way if you win, Southerners, or come back and be quiet if you lose. Let's get it over.

But these battles just bled you and slammed you to the ground and wasted you. Then you had to get up and do it again, those of you who were still alive, still could walk. It just kept on, deciding nothing. Just killing.

Much more of this, there'd be nothing left of the South and nobody left in the North. Is that where this was going?

"What happened, Captain?" the man next to Grady called to an officer riding down the line against the direction of the retreat.

"We got whipped," the rider said.

"I can tell that, sir. How'd that sonofabitch Stonewall do it?" the man asked. "And where was that useless Fremont?"

"Keep a civil mouth, soldier. Jackson pinned Fremont down across that far river with Ewell's troops, then came at us with his own," the officer said, turning his horse to walk with them a few paces. "Then he must have snuck Ewell back across both rivers and hit us with the whole force, there were so many of them. That's what knocked us out of our artillery position, seems to me, and after that the game was up."

The rider reined his rearing horse, told the men to stay in line and keep stepping smartly.

"We're doing that all right. Can I borrow your horse, sir?" the man said, to laughter. "Can't Fremont come up behind those Rebels? These boys here would turn around and fight them again if we could squeeze those bastards between us and Fremont, wouldn't you boys?"

"You go," Grady said, as they all kept walking north.

"I think Jackson burned the bridge," the officer told them. "There's smoke back there. But it looks like Fremont's got some cannon up on the bluffs above the river now."

"Lot of good that does us," the footsoldier said, slinging his rifle upside down from one shoulder to the other. "That old boy's got the pluck of a snail."

"Keep in line there, men, less mouth and more foot. Keep it going," the officer said, and his horse's hindquarters flexed and pushed as the rider spurred south to keep the column moving.

Jackson played us, Grady thought. Lured us up this valley to nowhere, then played us like a bullfighter parrying two bulls. Waving his cape at one, swirling on the other, confusing both, making himself a blur then slipping the sword in when neither knew what was coming.

Grady pushed his cramping legs a little harder. He didn't want to see this bull-fighter prance any more.

Port Republic, June 9, 1862—Confederate Army

It was raining, but Sutton woke because he hurt. His consciousness slammed back into his burning body, dropping in like a stone. The muscles of his thigh were ripping, over and over. They'd clenched around the tear, the shredding the Minie made when it looped through his flesh like a shooting star. The Yankee who fired probably never looked, never aimed. They were running beside the Shenandoah, the Federals, probably wondering what the hell they were doing in Virginia, and the Yankee probably just swung his musket around and pointed at where he'd been, squeezing off a shot and praying for the damnable war to end, before he did.

Now Sutton's leg was coming apart in the dark. The grass smelled sweet, lush, over by the river. The wheat stalks were sharp where they pushed against the flannel of his shirt. He smelled his own sweat, maybe some piss, who knows what happened when he got hit.

The pain was like the worst burning flux when your bowels tear open, hot, from bad food. This was happening in his leg, the big thigh muscle, like his guts had been rerouted and the muscle couldn't hold.

The dirt beneath his face was getting wet with the night moisture. He could smell its richness. This was where he'd lived. Was it where he'd die, pressing against this dirt as he'd pushed at it for a living all these years? It would fit, he thought.

Awake, wet, pinned to the ground and to consciousness by the gash ripped in his leg by a man he'd never seen, he tried to calm himself by thinking. By looking back. There may not be a forward. He breathed deeply to steady his body. The wooziness from the pain ebbed a bit.

I'm lying, busted, the fluids of my life draining into the ground a few miles from my own farm. Maybe someone will come and take me from this field, patch me up. Maybe I'll just die here. But I can do nothing now myself. But think. Keep my head going, if nothing else.

How did I come here?

Yes, it was the Yankees. Yes, I was mad, biled, at them coming where they had no right. Yes, it was my little farm they couldn't have. And some it was Virginia. Virginia for the rich men is an abstraction, a way of living to be loyal to, a place where breeding over generations has made men proud. But to me it is the place I find so lovely, the place where peace and grace sweep down the valley and wrap you around with beauty. Like I never thought I'd have.

The Valley, the Yankees. But something moved me to take action. And to keep going.

A goad, a spur. A light.

It was Jackson.

That strange man.

Why follow him?

It certainly wasn't his warmth, for he has none. Some officers, even generals, walked along with their men sometimes, sat with them, talked with them. He'd only heard of one time Jackson had joined the men around a campfire. That was after Kernstown, when a man called out to the general to join him and his mess-mates for a bit of stew from the pot. To the man's surprise, Jackson had come over and sat down. He'd said little. The man, brash, said to Jackson they'd surely been whipped that day. "General, it looks like you cut off more tobacco today than you could chew," the man said. The others around the fire were shocked at the mountain man's audacity, but Jackson only said, "Oh, I think we did very well." And that was that. He soaked up a little more heat from the rail fire, then got up and left.

And it wasn't just that Jackson was successful. Yes, men liked generals who gave them victories, but they liked just as well generals who hardly fought. Look at those Union boys falling all over McClellan. He hadn't done anything yet but drill the men and preen like a rooster.

Jackson did give them victories, even when it seemed they weren't in any way possible. He seemed to know where the enemy's armies were, where they were going and where they were the weakest. He seemed to be able to see through the mountains. And he seemed to be able to see into the hearts of the Union generals and see them quaking. When they hesitated, he'd be on them. He knew just where they quivered with uncertainty, and he hit them just there. He'd beaten everyone he could find these last three months in the Valley. That made men believe.

But Jackson's victories had come at a high cost—for the men who fought on the line. Again, McClellan. Partly his men loved him because he was so careful of them. Wouldn't fight until everything was just so, and until he knew the odds were good. But Jackson went at it whether or not the men were rested or the odds were anywhere close to favorable. And once in, he expected you to fight to the last. He'd court-martialed Dick Garnett for withdrawing his men from Kernstown. Didn't care that they had no bullets left. Stay and give them the bayonet, stay and die. That's your duty.

Why didn't men run from that kind of stubbornness? But they didn't. They followed Jackson. Did almost anything he asked, or at least tried. March 25 miles again today, after the same march yesterday and a few hours on the wet ground in between? Yes, sir, here we go. Sutton had done it too. Marched right along. Knowing Jackson would throw them at the Federals, exhausted at the end of the march, even against four-to-one odds.

Did Jackson care about the lives of his men? In an odd way, Sutton thought, he did. He'd throw men into the maw of cannon, knowing they'd be blown apart. He'd march right up to a bigger Union army and kick them in the face. But Jackson did it, Sutton thought, because he believed the best way to put out the fire is to blast straight into it. Don't scrimp on lives now, so that we don't keep whittling away lives month after month, year after year.

Day to day you might be shocked by that, abhore that, if you're the soldier in front of the cannon. But in the long run it seemed right even to Sutton, lying here. This wasn't a dance or a debate. This was war. And a lot of the men, including Sutton, felt 'let's get to it. Knock the bastards down and let's get home.'

Sutton's whole body was cramping now. He wanted to turn over on his back, but when he tried he couldn't get his hips to turn. He wanted to look at the sky. Maybe in a little while.

The main thing about Jackson, Sutton finally realized, was that he was so sure. So very, very sure.

Sure that the South was right. Sure that the North was wrong. Sure that the invaders had to be turned back, and sure that they could be.

Sure that the cause was righteous.

This war was more than confusing. It was chaos. All the killing. All the blood. All the severed arms and legs and feet and hands piled up outside the hospital tents. All the young lives ruined. Sutton no longer knew what was right. And Sutton no longer thought God was in this war.

But Jackson seemed never to waver.

You needed someone who knew, because *you* couldn't know any more.

How could God be on either army's side when they both did so much killing? Wouldn't God damn them all for the destruction they were causing? For the mindless slaughter, for the rows of men left dead in the fields?

Jackson didn't seem to wonder. He seemed to know. He rode that little sorrel horse along like a farmer going to town, just another day of life. The man was quiet as he rode right up to the beast of war, as if he had the strength of God's blessing wrapped around him like an old wool shawl. Not a flicker of doubt or fear. He was sure.

It was in his eyes. Calm, steady. If God meant them to win, they'd win. If God meant them to die, they'd die. That faith seemed to give Jackson a peace amid this storm.

Sutton didn't have that faith. So he followed Jackson because he did have it.

And following, he'd gotten his leg blown open. Did that make him a fool? He'd hated it all, including Jackson, two days ago in the fight over his own fields. And now? Staying with Jackson had earned him this place in the dirt.

He wondered. If he could ever walk again, if he could ever stand, would he follow Jackson again? He wanted it all to be over. Wished it had never started.

But Jackson. Solid. Certain. Refused to be anything but successful. Knew he carried the sword of the Lord. Knew, so no one else had to. Sutton breathed deeply, slowly closed his eyes, and let it all go. If the war went on, and if he went on, he knew right now lying in this field that if he followed anyone it would be this strange, quiet terror who'd just worked such hideous magic all up and down the Valley of Virginia. Yes. He would follow. This man. If he could. If he lived.

"Any Virginia boys out here?" a voice called in the dark. Sutton heard boots swishing through what was left of the wet wheat, saw a lantern. Someone was coming to help him.

The battles were over in the Valley, for a time.

Shields and Fremont drifted north, in tatters. They'd boasted that they'd bag Jackson. But, deep in his own country, the VMI professor had turned and beaten them. Brilliantly, savagely, thoroughly.

The Valley Campaign would stand as one of the bloody landmarks of military strategy, not just in this four-year fratricidal tragedy, but in all the sad, stirring story of war.

Jackson had marched his men 400 miles in 32 days, fighting almost daily, wearing out men and horses and shoe leather and four Union generals and their armies. Those armies counted twice as many men as Jackson's, but Jackson had spread them out across the Valley with his feinting and marching and slashing and swept them away one by one in five major battles. He'd captured 4,000 prisoners, 26 guns, and enough U.S. supplies to deeply embarrass Nathaniel Banks and the North. The campaign had kept thousands of troops away from McClellan's glacial push toward Richmond, and given Lincoln in vulnerable Washington a stiff case of the fantods.

It had all cost Jackson 1,000 casualties. A low cost for the advantage gained— unless you asked the men shot to pieces by Federal lead or broken down by the marching.

But the men had always pressed on, most of them. They'd followed Old Jack, been driven by his stern demanding conviction that war was won by finding the enemy's weakness and hitting him, over and over until he yielded. They'd trudged, and loaded, and fired, been shocked off their bare feet by the searing concussion of exploding shells that heaved the earth from beneath them, gotten up and trudged some more after their general, mad as some thought him. Several times during May and June weary southern soldiers had written home that they'd heard waves of cheering rolling from the back of the ragged marching line toward the front, as Jackson came galloping along on his little sorrel horse, his cap raised to recognize his men. His foot cavalry. His band that followed him they never knew where, but into what they always knew would be tough brutal fighting that might send the northern host home.

There was glory, and bodies, enough for any zealot, for any patriot, for any storyteller.

For Jackson, ever faithful to his Old Testament certitude, there was a message in the smoke and blood. Ewell would always remember his commander turning to him as Shields retreated and saying, "General, he who does not see the hand of God in this is blind, sir, blind."

Whether it was God, or good generalship and good aim, Robert E. Lee was grateful. Outside of Richmond, with 100,000 Yankees coming at him—fewer than would have been had Jackson's victories not held so many in the Valley and around Washington—Lee sat down to write to Jackson.

"June 11, 1862. Your recent successes have been the cause of the liveliest joy in this army as well as in the country. The admiration excited by your skill and boldness has been constantly mingled with solicitude for your situation."

Lee hadn't known what to expect from Jackson. He feared it could all go up in smoke at any time. The professor had performed well at Manassas, not so well in the mountains around Romney, nor at Kernstown. But in the past several weeks Jackson had electrified the South, marching everywhere, risking everything, knocking out Federal army after Federal army.

Lee had taken a risk, giving Jackson his head. If Jackson was beaten, Shields and Banks could descend on Richmond from the west, while Lee and Johnston were shielding the city from McClellan to the east. "Solicitude" was a polite word for the concern Lee felt as he waited for news from the Valley. But Lee was a polite man, one who didn't get exercised. He could take a potentially fatal risk and never show it in his face, his breathing, his hands. So he left Jackson in the Valley, gave him Ewell, waited to see what trouble they could stir up for the Yankees. If they couldn't badger the Federals, "those people" as Lee always called them, then he'd bring Jackson to help fight McClellan. If only Jackson didn't get himself destroyed and lose the gamble for Lee on two fronts.

"Boldness." That was Lee. And he saw that in Jackson. Link Boldness to skill and judgment and they could win this war. Could beat the ponderous Federal army that hadn't yet found a commander who knew the word. "Boldness."

"Thank the Lord," Lee whispered to himself as he handed the note to an orderly to be telegraphed to Jackson.

Port Republic, June 18, 1862—Confederate Army

Two men sat near Sutton, leaning against the worn white wall of a small store where recovering wounded were gathered. One had a rag around his head. They had just come out to be in the sun. Sutton, lying under a tree, could hear them talking.

"The man's eyes. They're cold. They're icy cold."

"You seen 'em?"

"Yeah, he stabbed right through me with them.

"At first it was like he didn't see me. He was looking at something beyond me and it was like I wasn't there. I was with a passel of boys from my company when Jackson and some other officers came by. We stood where we were. The Yankees were around, so nobody cheered Old Jack. Not even to get his goat."

"Get his goat? Whadya mean? Why would you cheer to do that?"

"He doesn't like it. He gets red in the face and flustered to beat all when you cheer." The man laughed, his mouth showing in his ragged red beard, happy to tell this one. "So of course we do it every time we can."

The smaller man, with the bandaged head, asked, very curious, "What's he do? Lord, I'd think he'd shoot you if he doesn't like it. I'd never do nothing to cross that one, I swear."

"Shoot us? For cheering? Nah. It just makes him ride faster on that funny little horse of his. To get away from it. Lord, the boys do love to see him go."

"So you're not cheering 'cuz you like him?"

"Oh, some like him, all right. Well, I don't know as it's liking. It's trusting, maybe."

"Trusting? Christ, he gets most of his men kilt. Got me hacked all to hell. Look at you, without your arm. We gonna trust this man?"

The bearded man looked at his left arm, which stopped where it should have bent with an elbow. "He didn't do this, some damned Yankee did. But maybe you're right, maybe it's not trust." He looked away from his stub, out beyond where Sutton lay on his side. The man was quiet for a time, then said, "It's respect, but in a funny way. The man's just damned good at what he does. He gets it done, and doesn't care about the cost. Because the cost of not getting it done—

you know, a march or a flank attack—is much damned higher. On us, in the end."

"Yeah, well, that's where we always take it. In the end, no matter what. But you cheerin' him to make him run, that's not respect to me. You're makin' fun of him."

"No, no. No, we're not. But we're *having* fun. Damn well better, my friend. What's more fun than jabbing the one above you? Maybe we do it because we respect him, but I think really we do it because it keeps us from thinking about the awful parts of all this. Or maybe it just breaks down the boredom. That's the worst." The bearded man stopped, pulled a weed, stripped the soft green part of its stalk through his front teeth with the one hand left him. All around the store were wounded men. Some sat, saying nothing. Some talked in pairs. A few walked, one trying to get used to a crutch because a shot leg could no longer hold him.

"But you were saying you seen him. Those eyes."

"Grey. They looked like ice to me. Some people say he can be kind. Merry even. But all I saw was cold." The man paused, letting the scene form again in his mind. "It was out of Harrisonburg, and we were marching toward Cross Keys, Fremont on our tail. We were taking that break once an hour that he allows us sometimes so we can march all day."

"God he likes to make us march," the shorter man said. "He's a maniac for it, like for lemons."

"Oh, come on, you pulled in by that lemon story?"

"Whadya mean?"

"He doesn't like lemons any better than anyone else. It's just he became a hero after Manassas, so every little thing about him gets exaggerated. Everybody likes fresh fruit, any kind they can get their hands on when all we've got to eat is raw corn and old meat. So Old Jack eats a lemon, somebody writes something about it in the paper and pretty soon everybody in the Confederacy is sending him lemons. It's part of how a legend gets all crosswise."

"All right, so no lemons. But he does like to march us, you can't deny that."

"No, I surely can't."

The short man pushed himself up by his hands to get his rear off the ground and scoot it up closer to the wall of the store so he could sit up straighter. As he moved, he yelped.

"You all right?" the bearded man asked.

"By Jesus that hurts."

"I thought it was your head that hurt, not the other end."

"It is. It's where that damned New Yorker or Ohio bastard or whoever it was sliced me with his sword."

"Your head hurts when you move your butt?"

"My head hurts when I move anything, partner. It's all connected. You'd be amazed what you use them muscles on your head for. Your scalp, I guess. I never knew I had muscles up there, and now it's like they're tearing all the time."

The bearded man wiggled his ears, raised his eyebrows, scrunched up his cheeks and eyes, and could feel the muscles tightening and moving under his hair. He nodded a little, having learned something.

"You were in the fight for the coaling, weren't you?" he asked.

"Yes, brother, and I'm barely here. A lot died."

"Somebody with a sword cut you?"

"Damned officer. Tried to cut my head off. I threw up my rifle and it blocked him. I think somebody shot him right then too. I saw red in the air. Though that could have been from me. Then I don't remember nothin'."

"That was a hard fight. All over. From the town to the river to the coaling."

"You got yours by the river."

"Yep. Pretty place to get shot."

They'd talked before about when and where and how they'd been wounded. They would talk about it again. It was foremost in their lives—lives that seemed more vivid to them now because they'd been so close to death.

"Well, like I said," the bearded man resumed, "Old Jack just looks right through you with those eyes. But then for a second it was like he saw us, me and the men I was with. We were leaning against a fence, some sitting on the ground. He'd been looking at space, I think he was remembering the ground we were marching toward, the rivers and hills. He was seeing what would happen. Then his eyes changed and he saw us."

"The ones it was gonna happen *to*," the short man said, and laughed a little harshly.

"It was like he built a tunnel with those eyes, carved everything else away and just shot a shaft of bright focused air between him and me, and then him and the man next to me. He just bored in."

"Did he smile, say anything, nod?"

"Nothing. But you felt—seen. There was some kind of connection. I felt pulled. His face didn't change, as I recall, but it was like he recognized me, and the others, and just with his eyes he pulled us in."

"That's crazy, ain't it? Pulled by a madman."

"Not a madman. But he looked driven, driven toward those rivers, where they came together at Port Republic. And once he looked at us, we just looked like part of the journey to him. So we were. And we went."

"And we got shot. Or you did. I got sliced like a melon."

"Yes, we did. And now we're here. And we'll go with him again when we get healed, if we can."

"You might, brother, not me. One get-together with a big ugly sword swung by a ugly ol' Yankee is plenty enough for me. I'm stayin' wounded."

"Up to you. I reckon I'll go back at it, long as there are Yankees in Virginia."

"Yeah, and as long as Jackson keeps you hypnotized with them eyes. Me, that feller's sword broke the spell."

The two men settled against the wall, the taller one reaching with his one arm to tilt his hat forward. They were ready now for a nap, in the sun, their wounds having earned them the rarest thing in the army—repose and peace at the same time.

Sutton was four days out from his time on the operating table—a door laid across a table. The doctor had thought first to amputate, then dug for the bullet, bandaged the leg and let Sutton go, mostly whole. The doctor was keeping him close to the store that had served as his surgery and now was a place for men to heal, or die.

He'd been carried off the field in a donkey cart and taken to the store south of Port Republic with dozens of others. Jackson's army had spent a few days around Weyer's Cave a little farther south of the Port, then gone over the mountains, no one knew where. The Yankees had backed off after the battle.

What had been a tempestuous whirl of marching and fighting had now subsided into the quiet of a country road and woods and settlement. Women cooked food, stirred laundry pots, stood with baskets against their hips talking while wiping sweat from their temples with the back of their wrists. Kids ran down the dusty road chasing summer. Dogs barked beneath trees. Old men sat in porch chairs and talked, slowly, with the space of years between their words.

The war had moved on, leaving Sutton behind in the wreckage.

He didn't mind it today. This was a pretty place. Across the road, birds danced in the branches. In a clearing, a woman in a long pink dress was sharpening knives on her little back porch. Most of the wounded men around the store were dozing or talking quietly. One man, in a blue jacket, was writing another letter. Every time Sutton saw him he was writing. Sutton didn't know if the man was a Yankee prisoner or a Confederate soldier wearing a Yankee coat. If he was a prisoner, he was treated well, just like the other wounded.

Sutton had passed out when the doctor worked on his leg. When he woke up, he felt every muscle in his body had been pulled and wrung like a rag. He could barely breathe or move.

Then, on the second day, pain came rushing into his leg like scalding water and had lapped there like waves against rock ever since. But he loved the pain, because he still had a leg to hurt. So many limbs had piled up outside the window of the store it was like something out of stories about hell. Sutton took the pain, with gratitude.

He couldn't walk yet, but soon, he told himself. For now he stumbled, leaning on a crutch, letting go like a fallen tree when he had laid himself down clumsily in the grass outside the store.

He loved the grass, he loved the store, he loved the minutes of the day. Because he was alive.

And he was still curious to hear the talk of others, about Jackson. Even though he should have had his fill by now of the man and his marches and his murderous battles. Along with his wonder at being alive, he felt a heaviness, a weight of experience he didn't want.

The wind lifted his sandy hair. The tickling at the roots as the hairs moved made him think of the scalp wound the man nearby had suffered. Sutton rubbed his palm on his head, feeling what was below. The muscles that you never thought of. The bone plates of the skull that protected your brain. Except against the darting metal that he'd seen break enough head bones. At least I still have my eyes, Sutton thought. Didn't get shot there, like some. All my fingers are here, my leg stayed on, I didn't get shot between my legs where some poor fellows had. Good God, he thought, what would you do about that? He squeezed his thighs together almost without thinking.

The men were still talking about Jackson. He heard the word "crazy" and then they laughed. "Crazy like a hunting dog, crazed for game," the one with the beard said. "Knows exactly where to find it, I swear Old Jack can smell those Yankees."

Sutton laid back. The sun fell warm on his shirtfront.

And he slept.

Fredericks Hall, June 23, 1862—Confederate Army

"I'm sorry I didn't recognize him, sir. My God, I can't believe it. What a fool I was. Was that really General Jackson?"

Captain Draper laughed again. It had been a delightful, if slightly terrifying moment. As captain of the guard, he'd been called from his tent in the middle of the night by someone saying a Confederate officer wanted to see him on the road.

He'd been sleeping in his uniform, so he'd scratched his hair into some semblance of order, brushed his coat quickly and slipped it on. He'd grabbed his hat and walked toward the checkpoint. Confederate troops from Richmond had been moving toward the Valley the last couple of days, so they'd had a lot of people passing back and forth. Then came the order that no one was to pass back toward Richmond. Draper hadn't known what it meant, but orders were orders and they'd kept a close watch here east of the Shenandoah Valley on the road that paralleled the Virginia Central railroad from Gordonsville toward Richmond.

He didn't know what this commotion could be, but he wished he'd been left sleeping. With Jackson fighting up and down the Valley, Union troops moving north of the Rappahannock and McClellan creeping up on Richmond, everybody was nervous and there was precious little sleep.

As he'd approached the clearing by the road, he'd seen Private Weiss standing by two mounted men. In the dark he hadn't seen who they were until he got right up to them. One he hadn't recognized, but the other he had with a quick trip of his heart. There, wrapped in a rumpled coat with his cap pulled low over his eyes, was General Jackson.

Jackson, with evident enjoyment, told him the story. The two riders had approached Weiss at the checkpoint. Weiss had challenged them, and the second rider had said they were Confederate officers on army business. Weiss wouldn't let them pass. Then the rider had said they had urgent messages for General Lee in Richmond and must get through. Weiss had said his orders, straight from Old Jack, had been to let nobody through. He was sorry, but he couldn't let them pass.

Then the rider with the long beard had leaned out of his saddle, commended Weiss for adhering to his orders, and asked that the commanding officer of the guard be called. Weiss had been reluctant to have Draper awakened, but he'd called for another soldier to go for the captain. Weiss wouldn't abandon his post himself.

Draper had come and told Weiss who the bearded man was, wished Jackson good luck, and let the riders pass. Departing, Jackson told the private and the captain that if all Confederate soldiers would obey their orders as well as Weiss had, the country's independence was ensured. Then he'd touched Little Sorrel on the flank and cantered off down the shadowy road.

Weiss had been too shocked to even salute. He was still befuddled and embarrassed.

"Why didn't he tell me who he was, Captain? Then I wouldn't have made such a fool of myself."

"Would you have believed him? Would you have let him through?"

"Well, yes, he's General Jackson."

"Then you're lucky he didn't tell you, private. If you'd let him pass, he'd probably have arrested you. He's a devil for arresting people who don't follow orders. He arrested one of his own cavalry lieutenants as a spy in May for asking too many questions about where the army was going. A day later he arrested an officer for abandoning Front Royal to a larger Federal force without a fight. Col. Zephanier Connor of the 12th Georgia." Draper looked seriously at Weiss. "'How many men were killed,' Jackson asked Connor when the colonel reported he'd lost Front Royal to Shields. Connor told him 'none.' 'And how many were wounded,' Old Jack asked. When Connor said 'none,' Jackson said he hadn't put up much of a fight and arrested him."

"That's frightening."

"That's Jackson."

"Oh, lord, I said my orders were from Old Jack. I called him Old Jack to his face."

"He's heard worse. At least you didn't call him Tom Fool like some of his own soldiers do."

"Oh, lord, captain." Weiss said, his shoulders sinking. He shifted his rifle to his other hand and looked down the dark road where Jackson had ridden away. He shuffled his feet; he couldn't stand still. "What do you think he's doing?"

"Going to talk with Bobby Lee, plan some more trouble for the Yankees. But nobody will know what he's planning until the second it happens. That man tells nothing to nobody. I hear he told General Imboden 'always mystify, mislead and surprise the enemy.' And he does that, better than anybody in either army."

"So that's why we're sealing off this road?" Weiss asked, drawing his jacket tight against the night chill.

"I reckon." Draper took off his hat, swept back his hair, tugged at his trousers where they'd snagged on his boot when he'd pulled it on so quickly. He swept his gaze around the woods. "There are plenty of spies around, Pinkerton's men are always out trying to find what we're up to. But you don't need spies to find an army. Civilians always tell where we're moving. They tell the Yankees to scare them, get them to leave. But now nobody's moving. We're stopping them, like you did Jackson," Draper said, laughing again. "We've shut this countryside down. And you stopped General Jackson. Boy, you'll have something to tell your grandchildren, won't you?"

"Captain, don't tell the other men what happened, will you? They'll think I'm an idiot, they'll ride me forever."

"I can't tell them, Weiss, the general would jail both of us if we told anyone he was here. But I wish I could. It's a lesson, and Jackson made the point. Stick to your orders. He commended you, private, you should be proud."

"Oh, brother, proud as a mouse hiding in leaves, Captain."

"Good night, private. I believe I'll go back to sleep, if I can. Stand your post." He turned, then looked back. "Oh, and if General Lee wanders by, you'll know him by his white beard. And the halo." Draper walked off, and after a few steps tossed his head back and laughed again.

You never knew what would happen, he thought as he went back to his tent.

Jackson's secrecy kept the Federal commanders from knowing what was happening. Jackson rode 50 miles that day to see Lee, and 50 miles back that night. He moved his troops by train and hard marches from the Shenandoah Valley to the north side of Richmond and joined Lee in the Seven Days battles that shoved McClellan back from the Confederate capital. By moving troops in view of captured Union officers who were then paroled, by planting misinformation with residents of the Valley, by sealing off roads and by pushing little screening forces against Fremont and Shields after Port Republic, he pushed the Union forces back down the Valley toward the Potomac and kept Lincoln's men from knowing where he was until he appeared on the Chickahominy to attack McClellan's right wing at Richmond.

Jackson moved his troops unusually slowly in the fighting around Richmond, wearied by a strange inertia that some attributed to exhaustion after the Valley Campaign. He estimated that he could get his troops to Richmond faster than in fact he did, so he wasn't in position when the fighting started. He stopped his troops short of battles already under way, and he marched, with poor guides, along wrong roads. People would argue for decades about Jackson's performance, whether he was dulled by lack of sleep or whether Lee's battle plan was too complex to work. Although the Seven Days battles saved Richmond and pushed McClellan's huge army against the James River where he could shelter under his heavy gunboats, they cost thousands of lives and Lee was unable to hit McClellan with the killing blow that would stop, or at least stalemate, the war.

But without the maneuvers and pluck of Jackson's foot cavalry earlier in the Valley, without the courage and daring Jackson showed in pitching into several Union armies in succession, more Union troops would have been freed from northern and western Virginia to join McClellan, and Richmond may well have fallen.

Jackson's tactics in the Valley showed what he could do at his best, and were a preview of bloody victories to come. Cavalry commander John Imboden remembered Jackson saying, "always mystify, mislead and surprise the enemy if possible, and when you strike and overcome him, never let up in your pursuit so long as your men have strength to follow....The other rule is never fight against heavy odds, if by any possible maneuvering you can hurl your own force on only a part, and the weakest part, of your enemy and crush it. Such tactics will win every time, and a small army may thus destroy a large one in detail, and repeated victory will make it invincible."

Jackson's troops in the coming year—through Cedar Mountain and the stunning flank march at Second Manassas, through the blood at Antietam and Fredericksburg—seemed invincible. And so did Jackson.

Until Chancellorsville.

South of Port Republic, June 26, 1862—Confederate Army

Sutton stretched out his leg, as far as it would go. It was stiff, and wouldn't extend fully, but the pain was lessening. He could stretch it a little farther today before the pain hit than he could a few days ago. Soon, he thought, he could walk almost normally. Could trade his crutch for a cane.

He thought of a man in his company who, before the fight at Kernstown, shot himself in the foot as darkness fell over the little valley of Cedar Creek. The man had not wanted to fight, but couldn't find it in himself to just walk away. He'd aimed his musket at his toes, but shot too high and blew off half his foot. The rest had to be amputated, and the man went home a cripple for life. Crippled in his spirit, too.

Sutton had seen many men in the Stonewall Brigade simply walk away. Called it French Furlough. They'd go for awhile, go home to see family if their home wasn't behind Federal lines, go to see friends if it was. Most would come back. They'd get extra duty for punishment, maybe be sent to the pioneer corps to cut trees or dig latrines. Sometimes they'd be put in the guard house for a week or two, and on rare occasions they'd be bucked and gagged in front of the regiment. But it was very common to straggle, fall off the march for a day or two, and it was fairly common to just disappear for a week or more at a time.

War was hard. The marching was hard, the absence from family, from the normal things of life, like pumping water or shooting birds, was wearying to the spirit. Seeing friends and acquaintances dead on the ground, bent over silent rifles or toppled cannon, was killing to the soul.

Sutton had had enough. He'd marched all up and down the Valley. He'd been in more fights than he could count. He'd seen his regiment cut in half, with sickness and tearing wounds and desertions and death. He'd seen rifle shots tear the wood of his own house, seen cannon balls plow the ground of his own fields, ripping the roots of his crops. He'd seen too much blood, some of it his.

He'd killed men, he was pretty sure. He'd pumped enough lead into the Virginia air to take down a company of Yankees.

While they'd beaten the Federal armies, they hadn't destroyed them. Hadn't stopped them. They were still in Virginia, still in the Valley. Apparently Shields and Fremont had both gone north down the Valley, but no one was sure how far. Jackson had taken his troops out of the Valley, most likely to Richmond to help out Bobby Lee, so there wasn't likely to be more fighting in the Valley for at least a few weeks. But it would all come back. The same ground would be fought over again, the same clashing views of how life should be lived and governments should behave would be tested again with fire and terror.

And what would it do?

Everyone had thought one battle and it would be over. It had been a year now. The North wasn't going to let us go, Sutton thought. It had sent hundreds of thousands of men into the South to force us into staying in a government we no longer wanted. Did that make any sense? And the South was spending its blood and its treasure at a profligate rate to stand on its own principles, to run its affairs without interference from the bankers and politicians of the North. How long could this go on? How long can we bleed?

In the past few days he'd been happy to just be alive, and to have his leg, hurt as it was. But what had happened in the past few months kept sinking into him, deeper and deeper, like a chill to the bone that the Valley sunlight couldn't reach.

I've had enough, he thought. I'm done. At least for awhile. I need to be sent off to refit. To graze in a pasture and fatten up and let my wounds heal and nerves knit back together.

I need to not be shot at.

I need not to see a man one day and then never see him again.

I need to be away from dying.

Men were leaving the little settlement by the river. Some were going home for more recuperation, if they could get to their homes. Some were going right back to the war, to their regiments. Some were going back who shouldn't, who weren't completely healed, but they felt they had to go. Be with their boys.

It was time.

The weather had cleared and it was lovely in the Valley.

Sutton limped down to the South River. Slipped down the bank, stood on a rock at the water's edge. He looked down at the dead leaves pressed into the mud, the broken sticks tumbled against stones by the current. He let the sound of moving water flow through him. Sun fell in spots and patches through the shivering leaves, on the water, on the birds darting through, on Sutton.

I'll go to my brother's, he thought. His brother Ab had moved to a little town near Raleigh years before the war. He was lame in his right leg from being kicked by a mule and hadn't had to serve in the war. But his son was a drummer boy in a Carolina company. Ab could use the help at his place.

I'll go. Far away. I'm done with this Valley.

From behind Sutton came noise of stones slipping and twigs snapping. He looked around and saw a big man coming toward him, walking carefully sideways down the bank to be sure of his footing.

James Sparrow. He stood above Sutton, nodded, and sat down on a flat rock beside him. He looked at Sutton, then down, pulled his pipe from a pocket and began to fill it.

"How you doin', boy?"

"Hah, glad to be drawing breath. You?" Each man was happy—mightily relieved, in truth—to see the other, but they didn't make a fuss over it. Sutton's eyes brightened with surprise and pleasure when he saw who it was, and Sparrow's face and little nod showed satisfaction at finding his friend.

"Tired as a horse pulling fat women to church. Dead through to the bone," Sparrow said. "That's God's own truth."

They both smiled, and Sparrow offered Sutton his tobacco pouch, which looked like a dirty rag with a collection of dead mice in it.

"Lost my pipe."

Sparrow heaved over on one ham, reached in another pocket. "I got another, this old cob, if you'll use it." He handed it over, a battered corn cob with a stub of twig sticking out of it.

"Looks good to me," Sutton said, and he filled the pipe and the little clearing by the river drifted with smoke.

"You look like you're doing better," Sparrow said.

"Mm," Sutton said. "I'll walk again."

Sparrow looked hard at Sutton, puffed, nodded. "You also look like your spirit is low, brother," he said.

"I'd say."

"I heard you got hit," Sparrow said, leaning his head back to jet a stream of smoke into the air. The breeze from above the bank rolled the smoke in a flattening cloud back over Sparrow's black hair and beard. "Hell of a fight."

"More than I was ready for."

"Coming at us from both sides like that. Seems like if they'd have attacked in concert, they'd have had us."

"They came at us plenty hard, from where I was," Sutton said with a small shake of his head. "Why didn't it work?"

"Old Jack kept them apart. And their fear of him slowed them down. I'm thinking his reputation is his real long arm now, not his artillery. It softens them up, makes them queasy in their bellies. Makes our close work more effective once we get to them," Sparrow answered.

"Plenty close, and barely effective enough, I'd say."

They paused, each involuntarily replaying scenes from the battles just past. The screams and explosions and confusion seemed a world away from this flowing river capped with green leaves and bird song, but they'd seeped into the two men so deeply that their minds and senses were infused with the crashing bloody chaos of war. It would take months, years, of peace to make it all fade away.

"How'd you find me, Sparrow?"

"Been asking. I figured trying to find you would give me time to rest. Wanted to see how you're doing, if you needed anything."

"I need for this war to be over, can you fix that up?"

Sparrow laughed, shaking his barrel chest, his chin riding the swells of his thick neck. "Wish I could, my friend. Don't we all? But leave it to Jackson and he just might do it."

"If he leaves any of us standing," Sutton said quietly.

"How bad's your leg?"

"Ball just scraped the bone, the surgeon said. Another eyelash and I'd have lost it. Ripped up the muscles pretty good," he said, kneading the flesh above his knee. "Thing's stiff as a pump handle."

Sparrow tossed a stick in the river, watched the ripples. "You goin' back to the regiment?"

"Nooo," Sutton said, long and slow. "No, I've had it, least for awhile."

They smoked, Sparrow scratched at his beard, Sutton leaned back into the ground and roots and stones. The sound of the swishing water mixed with the shushing leaves, and they just listened for awhile.

"You gonna stay here?" Sparrow asked while looking over the water.

"No, there's not much here left. I'm going to Carolina, to my brother Ab's. Knit, heal. See if I can see my way to come back. Or maybe I'll just sit there."

"Wouldn't be so dumb, that sittin'."

"What are you going to do?"

Sparrow spit between his teeth into the water, a quick hissing "tsssvit" that streamed a translucent line into the sunlight. "I had me a couple days rest, now I'm going to catch up with the boys. They wouldn't know which way to walk or when to squat and shit without me yelling at them."

Sutton looked over at Sparrow to see if he was smiling. He wasn't. "Why are you going back into it? Why, really?" Sutton asked.

Sparrow cleared his throat, looked at his pipe, then at Sutton. "Everybody makes a choice. Choose what you gotta do. I'm going to see this thing through. Whichever way it goes, I'm going to be part of it. It's all there is right now." He breathed deeply. "It's so big, it pushes everything else out, for me. It's all I can see. Like a cyclone pulling up your neighbor's barn, you just have to turn toward it, can't look away."

Sutton nodded. Sparrow shrugged his shoulders. "That's it, for me. But I ain't been shot. You, my friend, you need some rest. Back away for awhile, it's a good idea."

"Good or not, I've got nothing left for this right now. I don't think I could lift a musket if a Yankee had a bead square on me," Sutton said.

"Yeah," Sparrow said. "I know. I mean, I haven't been through what you have, but I feel for you."

"Funny, Jim, I've known a lot of men in all this marching and fighting, and gotten close to some of them." He looked at the twig he'd been twirling in his hands, bent it, snapped it and jumped a little when it broke. "A lot of them are gone, like Woods killed just now in the fight by the Port. But you...you stay around. And I thank you. I'm glad you came to find me." He looked briefly in Sparrow's eyes and nodded his thanks again.

"You be careful," he told the bigger man. "I don't have any more friends to lose."

Sparrow dipped his head. Saying he'd be careful seemed ludicrous in this war where missiles flew from a mile away to tear up whole chunks of forest, where bullets from a hundred guns at once whipped all around you. So he didn't say anything, just tipped his head and pursed his lips.

They talked by the river for another half an hour, of Harper's Ferry where Sparrow had run a store, of the advantages and beauties of the various parts of the Valley, of how much of a crop might get in with the men gone from the Valley. After awhile they came back to talking of where Jackson might have gone.

"Old Blue Light's lookin' to find some more Yankees to tear up, probably around Richmond, and I want to be there for it. Got to go, Will."

Sparrow looked over the river for another minute, pulling in the sight, the sound, the peace. Then he slapped Sutton on his good thigh, rose slowly like a geologic force, arched his shoulders back over his elbows, groaning with the stretch. Sounded like a bear.

"I'll see you again. This war's gonna stay for awhile."

He looked down, reached out his big right hand, blackened with dirt and powder stain. Sutton reached up and took the hand in his slighter one. They grasped for a moment, then Sparrow pushed his right leg into the embankment and started climbing.

"You take care now."

"You too, Sparrow. Stay low."

Sparrow's laugh was deep and rumbling. "That ain't so easy for me, but I'll damn sure try."

And he walked over the top of the river bank. Sutton sat, alone, feeling an emptiness fill in behind Sparrow like a weather front dropping dirty grey clouds.

Two days later, with a medical pass that should convince any provost guards who stopped him that he was permanently disabled, although he knew himself that he was recovering, Sutton started out of the Shenandoah by Brown's Gap. He hitched a ride with a passing farmer, and as the horses struggled up the Blue Ridge hillside, Sutton could see a glimpse of the golden, beaten wheatfield by the river where they'd fought. He turned forward in the wagon, shutting out the sight.

PART THREE

THE WILDERNESS

"The people who survived the sword found
grace in the wilderness."

—Jeremiah 31.2

Gordonsville, August 18, 1862—Confederate Army

"You have to do it."

"Why?"

"It's orders," James Sparrow said.

"Oh, that's good. We're gonna win the war with orders to kill our own people." The man turned his bearded face and spat on the ground, a speck of white saliva catching on a tiny curl of hair below his lip. His sunbrowned face was bunched up and his mouth turned down in a frown of pain and disgust.

Sparrow hated this. In all the terrible bloody march of two years of war he'd never had to do this.

Flat dark clouds were sliding across the sky from the west, erasing the clear shining blue above Sparrow and the men. Around them, the forested swells of middle Virginia rolled up to this clearing where ranks of soldiers stood in a hollow square. To Sparrow's left, a long line of men, watching, quiet, sullen, looking down at their hands, at the dirt they were fighting for, at the men across from them on Sparrow's right who were drawn up in another line. And behind, the third line of the square, more men, their faces blank, looking up, looking to the side, looking anywhere but at the four men alone in the open end of the square. These four—one round and short, one lean and bent, one tall and proud, one hunched over his clasping hands trying not to weep—sat on wooden coffins. Behind each coffin a trench dug in the ground. A gust of wind lifted the long brown hair of the proud one as he stared at Sparrow. The man's eyes were fixed, his expression firm and neutral, holding with his eyes the last shard of dignity he would ever have.

Behind Sparrow were twelve soldiers of the Stonewall Brigade. Chosen by lot, they were the firing squad. Their rifles had been loaded by others. Eight had full charges in them, four had only powder and no ball. They wouldn't know who fired the shots that killed the deserters.

"You're going to tell me this is going to stop it?" the bearded man turned back to ask Sparrow.

"No."

"There'll be no more desertions if we just kill these four?"

"I don't know," Sparrow said, trying to fight off his own confusion, his own building nausea.

The wind glided between the men and fluttered the kerchief around Sparrow's neck. There was coughing, a low grumble as men behind Sparrow leaned toward each other.

"I just know we can't have desertions, we've got to have everybody in the ranks if we're going to beat the Federals. They've got so many men, we can't have ours going home," Sparrow said, his head down as he talked to the bearded man.

"Shhhhit," the man spit out the word. "Men are gonna go if they have to. We don't want runners anyway."

"It's orders," Sparrow said. "From Old Jack." And if you don't follow the order, Sparrow thought but didn't say, you'll be in front of that rifle damn quick, not behind it.

They did need every man, Sparrow knew. Jackson had just beaten Pope at Cedar Mountain, and now they were after the retreating Federals. But McClellan's army was still down by Richmond, and there were hundreds of thousands more bluecoats all over the boundaries of the Confederacy, pushing in. They had so many men. It would take a miracle to beat them. And will. And discipline. Jackson knew that. War wasn't a choice, once it was started.

But these four men. Probably scared, sick. Maybe a sick wife at home, or a dying father. Or they just made the very damned reasonable choice not to be in front of scraps of hot flying metal anymore.

But Jackson said stay and fight. The more who stayed, the more would go home at the end. And there would be a home to go to.

A magpie cried out. A lieutenant walked up to Sparrow. "Are your men ready?" the lieutenant asked.

Sparrow hesitated. It was starting and it wouldn't stop. Couldn't. "Sure," he said. "Soldiers, raise your rifles." He couldn't tell if he'd said it out loud.

The twelve riflemen looked at Sparrow, at each other, then slowly raised their rifles. Twenty paces away, the four men's eyes went wide, then closed. Except for the proud one. He stared still. His chin forward, his lips a thin line, his thoughts unreadable. Perhaps at home.

The lieutenant stepped up. A tenseness pulled the lines of watching soldiers taut. Fear leaked into the square, touching a chill to the four and all the others. Nobody moved.

The lieutenant gave the order, quickly rifles cracked, the dusty blouses of the four men jumped in red gouts, their bodies were flung backward and they were dead.

The echo of the shots came back from the trees and the low hills. Grunts and "hooh" and "uhh" from the men still standing. Birds on the wing, startled loud by the sharp reports on this quiet afternoon. "Shoulda shot Jackson," a voice said, low.

"Form up!" Sparrow shouted. "Left march!" and the line to Sparrow's left turned and marched past the bodies. All the men in turn were marched past the bodies. To see. To take the lesson. To try to understand what was beyond their experience, beyond their ability to take in. They marched, looked, not a word, and the wind blew through the disintegrating square of men, formerly farmers and cobblers and coopers, now just tired men shuffling in line, their spirits fallen out of their chests.

Sparrow stood. His stomach was trembling, his fingers shaking. Christ on high, I hope Jackson knows his way through this, he thought.

The four men lay in the dirt, their eyes closed to the clouding sky above.

Near Raleigh, North Carolina, Sept. 1, 1862

Abner Sutton's left hand was bleeding. He'd cut it with a tobacco knife, deep in the web between his thumb and forefinger. The harvest was just beginning, and Ab had let loose a rich string of curses when a fast stroke had cut more of him than the plant he was holding.

His wife Rosalyn had wrapped the hand in a dish towel after cleaning the wound, and had told Abner that he ought to have the doctor stitch it up. Ab cursed again and said he didn't have time.

"You should listen to her, Ab," William Sutton, his younger brother, said. They were sitting on the porch of Ab and Rosalyn's house, a few miles west of Raleigh. "I saw a lot of men patched up in Virginia, and the surgeons have gotten pretty good at putting them back together. Had a lot of practice." Will snapped off a bite of apple and gestured at his brother with the remainder.

"Aw, the good doctors have gone north with the armies," his brother said in an angry growl. "We just got quacks left around here. Wouldn't let them touch me if I was cut in half with a scythe."

It was late afternoon, and the men could smell the aroma of a savory stew that Rosalyn had cooking inside. Ab pulled the cork on a jug of whiskey, poured a little on the crook of his thumb through the towel, winced, and took a swig of the liquor to help with the pain. "You want some?" he asked Will.

"Yeah, don't mind it," Will said, slinging the dregs of cold coffee—or what passed for coffee in the Confederacy—over the rail and holding out his cup.

"Well, it feels good to sit. Guess I can use an evening on the porch, holding down these rocking chairs," Ab said, looking around at the fields of corn and tobacco that stretched from the front of his house down to the dirt road and the stream beyond. "I could get good at sitting, but it don't get you anywhere," he said, setting down the jug and lighting a thick cigar, clumsily because of his bad hand.

"You watch out, Ab, you might get a taste for the easy life. Might become a gentleman and just sit here telling people what to do." Will raised his eyebrows and rocked back in his chair.

"About as much chance of me becoming a gentleman as you becoming a general, Willie," Ab said, blowing smoke across the porch.

"Yeah, that's about fair," Will said, and they both kept rocking.

Abner Sutton was six years older than Will, shorter and thicker, his fair hair thinning. He was a pleasant man, generally, but the strain of working a farm with very little help had tarnished some of his brightness and brought frustration and anger closer to the surface more often than before the war. His face, always youthful, had darkened some and today wore the stubble of several days without a razor. There was grey now dotted in among the black whiskers. He breathed heavily, like a man who never quite catches up on his rest.

He'd been glad to see his brother coming up the road two months ago, but shocked at the shape he was in. Thin, wasted, pale, limping on his left leg. It was Ab's right leg that had been shattered by a mule years ago, and he knew how hard a limp made the everyday motions and tasks of life. He'd tried to keep his brother in the bed in the corner of the little parlor or in the rocking chairs on the porch, but after a week or so Will had started moving around the farm, helping with repairs and feeding the hogs and chickens. Ab had welcomed the work, but tried to get his brother to take it slow. Rosalyn baked and cooked as much food as they could put their hands on, trying to restore Will's color and spirit. It had been working, little by little.

Will had found the routine of the little farm calming, the satisfaction of the work restorative. His leg was better, less stiff with the regular exercise of chores and walks, able to bear more weight every day. He still used a cane on walks, but went without it while bending in the chicken coop and working in the garden. He put a little weight on in his chest and belly, and the exhaustion had started to seep out of his muscles and bones.

But his head still rang with the phantom sounds of gunfire when he lay down some nights, and inside he still felt tattered, like a battle flag shot and ripped by the wind. But less so every day.

The two men had not been together for a dozen years. In the past two months they'd found again how easy it was to be around each other. They'd laughed over times on their father's farm near Harrisonburg, remembered sparking some of the girls, compared their merits, talked about how age and childbearing had sat with them. Ab caught up from Will on what had happened to the boys they used to lark with—some of them dead now, most in the army. One of their best friends had moved to western Virginia where Union sentiment was strong, and neither of the brothers could find fault with that. Men did what they had to as one country tore away from the other.

Ab took another pull from the jug, poured another for Will.

"Bobby Jansen down the road told me there was another big fight up in Virginia. Stonewall jumped the Yankees, snuck behind them again. Those sorry Northern generals just don't know what to do with that Stonewall of yours, do they?" Ab said.

Will reached down to the newspaper he'd laid beneath the rocker, flipped it open on his lap. "I picked up a paper in Raleigh today, and it's quite a story all right," Will said. "Fought again at Manassas, and the Yankees are barreling back to Washington. John Pope, the conceited bastard, got his own army shoved up his backside with a hot ramrod. Deserved it, from what you read."

"That Pope's a braggart, damn sure served him right. 'The Rebels have never seen the backs of my western troops,' he said when he took over after McClellan played out. Well, Willie, those friends of yours up in the army have seen the backs of Pope's boys now, runnin', and with a stripe down their pants too." Ab laughed, and so did Will.

"He's nothing like General Jackson, that's certain," Will said. "Jackson doesn't say much, just gets things done. Pope, he says too much, and has things done *to* him. General Jackson must have particularly liked this one; I bet he hates a bragger."

"Do you wish you were with them, Will? Something like this, does it make you want to be with them again?" Abner asked the question in a low voice, his words coming slowly. It was clear he'd been thinking about it.

Will looked down at his hands, rubbed his finger under his nose, leaned forward so his elbows rested on his thighs, his hands clasped in front of him. He didn't answer for almost a minute. When he looked up at his brother, Sutton's mouth was drawn thin, the muscles around his eyes were tight, and a distant but simmering pain showed on his face.

"I know what you mean, Abner," Sutton said. "A victory like this, it sounds grand in the newspapers. I don't mean any disrespect, but it's different when you're reading about it at home. It sounds like all lark and glory. It says here in the newspaper that Jackson's men were eating tinned lobster and carrying off hams when they hit Pope's supply line at the railroad at Manassas Junction. Absolutely got behind him, cut the railroad and burned up what they couldn't eat or drink or carry off. It sounds glorious, and I'll bet the boys had themselves a time."

Sutton rubbed at his mouth with his right fist, brushing his lips with his knuckles. "But what you don't read about, Ab, is how many boys broke down on the road as Old Jack pushed them to get in Pope's rear. You don't read about the ones who wore out and died on that fast march. The ones who despaired because they just couldn't move their legs any more." He paused, looked at his brother, who was looking at him. Abner's face was still, he was listening. Sutton thought his brother must be wondering what he'd missed, must be thinking, all at the same time, that he'd missed what was the biggest damn thing that had happened in anybody's life in the South and that he was glad he'd missed it. Sutton felt a little sheepish at pushing the horrible parts of war at his brother.

"A lot of men's lives are breaking apart up there," Sutton said, more quietly now. "You should be glad you're not in it, Ab. Somebody's got to keep things going, keep raising food and families. Keep living."

"Do you miss it?" Abner asked.

The question took Sutton unprepared, although it shouldn't have. It hit him in a place where he was queasy. Something had been restless inside him, now that he could walk pretty well. He liked being on the little farm well enough, loved seeing trees that he knew didn't hide people moving for an angle to shoot from. Sleeping in a bed again was lovely. Waking to the sound of birds, not guns, was giving him a calm he'd thought would never return to his bones, his muscle, his mind. Eating hot, soft food was a pure delight. Seeing a woman move was...perfect.

Getting away from the Valley filled with war had been a salvation. He'd felt his mind, and his soul, were ripping. So many men, everywhere, sweating and stinking. No place for just yourself. Movement, all the time. Never a rest for days on end. Men bent over next to him with churning guts, pain that sliced like a bayonet through their middle. Men dead on the ground, of pneumonia, scurvy, scarlet fever, smallpox. Wounded men staring haunted through pain into fear of a future they couldn't imagine.

But as the days in North Carolina piled up like fat white clouds, as no bugles called him to put his tender life in front of hot rough cannon, he'd felt the peace that was seeping into him twist and stir under a cold wind.

There was a pull.

He'd found it surprising. He hadn't been sure he was going to go back to this war. But he'd been feeling, wondering, almost yearning.

What was Sparrow doing? Was he still alive? All those other boys he'd marched with, how were they? Would they build shelters tight enough to keep out the winter snow in the months ahead, digging into the earth, piling up brush and cutting logs for walls, stringing tent halves for a roof, forming a rude chimney with wattle and sticks? What would those nights be like in winter camp? What would they all be talking about? Would anyone have a complete pack of playing cards, or would they have to alter their games again to fit the amputated decks?

What would they eat? Would they keep having victories before the winter came? How many would be left behind, dead in the trampled fields?

He hadn't paid much attention to the battles around Richmond after he'd left the Valley. He was too weary, deadened at the core. But when the battle of Cedar Mountain came in early August, when Jackson and his men, Sutton's companions on all those hard marches, swept Pope from the fields cradled by the mountainside, Sutton had felt a rush of pride that he hadn't known would come. They were beating the Yankees. His friends. His brigade. His army. McClellan was cowering under his gunboats' protection on the banks of the James River, and Pope was being chased north at gunpoint, his bluster blown back at him in cannon smoke.

And now this second fight on the plains of Manassas. Jackson had done it again. Disappeared, turned away from where Pope was looking for battle, and marched like hell until he dropped down in the Federals' rear and crouched like a lion waiting to rip up the first soft thing that came by. And rip Jackson did. Almost destroyed Pope, even when he got help from some of McClellan's brigades pulled up quick from the peninsula below Richmond to join the fight. Jackson, and Longstreet too once he'd come up with Lee and the rest of the army, had torn the bluecoats to pieces.

And Sutton, prodded by his brother, had to look at how he felt about it. And he felt part of him was up there. On the rocky rise by a railroad cut where he just knew many of the men he'd walked and talked with earlier in the summer now lay dead, blood stiff on their worn-out clothes. And on the dusty roads north, marching fast and exultant with his comrades who'd made it through the fight and were now pushing the Yankees back toward the Potomac. He felt he was with them, because he knew what they felt like, how much their feet hurt, especially the ones with no shoes, how excited and giddy they were to still be alive, to not have been taken under by the random bullets that sought any flesh to root in, how hungry they were but they didn't care right now because they were chasing the game, how angry and thrilled they were at once to actually have the chance now to get those goddam Northerners out of Virginia for good. How amazed they were at what Jackson had gotten them to do.

How proud they were of themselves, and of their general.

How alive.

Sutton stood. He fidgeted. Shook his good leg to stretch it, kept bouncing it just a little at the knee. He looked at Abner's jug, shook his head just a tic. Let out a long breath.

"I don't miss it. It's a hard thing to miss. Like a disease. But you have it so long, maybe you get used to it." He looked down from the spot under the corner of the porch roof he'd been aiming his eyes but not his attention at, focused on his brother's tanned face.

"The Yanks, they have this expression. 'A big thing.' They call something major 'a big thing.' Like when a commanding general is changed, when McClellan took over from McDowell, that's a big thing. Some soldier goes into the hospital feeling poorly and gives birth to a baby, because it turns out it's been a woman disguised as a man to fight next to her husband, that's a big thing."

"That's happened?" Abner asked, amazed.

"Yep. Couple of times I've heard of. There's some women want to fight, want to be with their man. Stay disguised and nobody knows."

"Can't the men tell?" Abner asked. "I mean, when the boys stand up by a tree and piss, what does this woman do?"

William laughed and shook his head, and Abner chuckled too. "It's a strange war, a weird situation that draws somebody like that," Abner said.

"That's it, though, Ab. It draws you. It does draw you. It's the biggest thing. I don't know if it's good or bad, it's just big. The biggest thing. So big it takes almost everything out of your control. It puts you right up against the most awful things you've ever seen, smashes your nose right into it."

Sutton put his hands flat together, as if in prayer, and pressed the edges against his mouth. He breathed through his steepled fingers, once, twice.

"You see it. You turn away." He pulled in a few more breaths. Turned away from Abner, looking into the trees beyond the porch. "But then you turn back to look again." He was almost ashamed to say it, but it had the unmistakable feel of truth as he thought it, and even more as he said it. And he felt like saying truth to his brother. Wanted to feel close to Abner, because he was starting to feel loose, untethered.

Still looking at the trees, he said, "I thought my soul blinked out when Martha died, blinked to black like an ember just then done burning. Then that battle on my farm…" and he blew out of his pursed lips, a sound like blowing out a candle flame, "that blew the ember clean away. I thought." He shook his head, once left, once right, slowly.

"Everything was wrong. I didn't give a damn about the cause. And it wasn't that I was afraid I might die, because after a couple fights you realize, really know deep down, that you could be gone in the time it takes some store clerk from Cleveland to flick a trigger, gone and never coming back. No, it was that there was so much…" he lifted his shoulders, opened his hands to frame his face, "…death. Smashed men. Sick and dead. Shot and dead. Fell and dead. Just dead. All over. Everywhere."

He chewed on the inside of his mouth, squinching his face over to the left, unconsciously biting at his own flesh.

"Life's red blood gushing out of them, worse than cutting a pig's neck, I'll tell you. You feel like you'd been knocked into another world where nothing you used to know applies. You just keep moving through it, somehow."

Abner nodded his head, listening, taking it in, glad that his brother was talking.

"And when you move through it, when you're able to keep moving, there's a lift to it. Like you've escaped hanging. You're sent back to your prison cell and, and you're so darned happy to see the other men in the cells around you that you think it's the best place in the world. Because you're still alive." Will's voice was soft now, as he got to the center of it.

"You almost weren't, and others aren't, but you are. And, God save me, it's a thrill."

Abner tipped his head a little, thinking. He wasn't sure what to say, if he should say anything. He wasn't sure he understood. Wasn't sure he could. "But you're out of that prison now," he said. "Why do you want to go back?"

William grunted, the muscles on the left side of his face lifting his mouth and bunching the skin around his eyes in half a smile. He looked over his shoulder at Abner. Said, "I don't want to go back, Ab. But I think I am going to." He shrugged his shoulders, realizing he'd just named a decision he'd been thinking about in the woods and the fields and the night for a week. "It's the draw. It's the Big Thing."

"Duty?" Abner asked.

William shook his head, narrowing his eyes. "No," he said, surprised at how clear he was. "No, at least that's not the main reason. Might be better, more noble if it were. But no. It's something about me." He soughed breath through his nose, rubbed his fingertips into his right cheek bone. Dropped his hand. "Maybe finishing it. Maybe just being there. While it's going on, I need to be part of it.

"I am part of it." His voice was firm, sure.

"I don't think I really want to be, but it's pulled me in. I think, some way, part of my soul is back up there. It's started to grow back, to heal, here with you and Rosalyn. May never be—full, again. But it feels like part of me is still up there, in Virginia. Somewhere around where Jackson is. Somewhere close to the fight."

He looked at Ab, to see if what he was saying was connecting with his brother's understanding of the world. To see if it could. "I think I need to go back and hook into that part of me again. I've been broken, it feels like, and the fire up there, well, it might just weld me back together." He nodded. "Finish the war, and get myself whole again, if that's possible."

He raised his eyebrows a little, flicked his hands open like he was holding something, and said, "When I can walk a little better, Abner, I'll have to go back."

"You don't have to, Will. Plenty around here who aren't. Men hurt much less bad than you. They're sitting it out."

"May work for them, Ab," Sutton said. And didn't say any more.

Abner looked at his brother, leaned forward, and with both resignation and approval in his voice said, "Well, it seems to me it's like a great big tiger just walked into your front yard, and it's just standing there looking at you, twitching its tail. And you feel like you've got to go out there and touch it, because you've never seen anything like it before. Don't even think that it's likely to bite off your hand, or worse. You just got to touch it." Abner raised his eyebrows, looking to see Will's reaction. "Maybe it's that you got close to it before, but this time—you've got to touch it, grab hold of it."

William Sutton's smile was sad and appreciative. His brother had it. He'd listened. He'd understood.

Sutton would go back for the tiger.

Camp Baylor near Bunker Hill, Oct. 12, 1862—Confederate Army

The bayonet was stuck in the ground that was the floor of the tent. Into the ring that fixed the bayonet to a gun barrel, a candle stub was stuck. The flame gave off a fair amount of heat on this cold afternoon, but more importantly, it illuminated the faces of the cards the men were holding. After the devastation the Stonewall Brigade had met in the West Wood at Sharpsburg, the rest here in the lower Shenandoah Valley was well earned.

One man with a large belly that was surprising to see, given the short rations the men had been on during the Maryland campaign and how little food was still being produced in the Valley, laid down a hand of cards and proudly said, "Euchre, what do you think of that, about time."

Groans came from the others, and then a pair of tattered boots slid to a stop outside the tent and a bearded face dropped into view in the opening, almost upside down, and the man outside said, "He's coming."

"Who?" the man with the winning hand said, and the other said, "Old Jack."

The man with the ample belly leaned over and looked outside the tent for the messenger, but the bearded man was already several tents down the line, spreading the word. The man with the belly saw men coming out of tents, pulling on coats and throwing things back into the tents as they turned to walk down the beaten ground of the camp toward a gathering about a hundred yards away.

"Better hide those cards away, J.J. It's prayin' time."

The big man, kneeling, tipped his head back, looking at the canvas roof of the little tent and said, "Holy Jesus, and just when the luck is starting to come to me."

"You're lucky to still be drawin' breath after all the metal those bluecoats threw at us up by Antietam Creek, J.J., what more luck do you want?"

"Just another sweet hand, that's all I'm asking," the man said, looking at the cards on the ground as another pair of worn, chapped hands swept them into a deck and tucked them under a flap of a knapsack.

"Hell, I don't wanna go to a prayer meetin'," J.J., the big man, said.

"Then don't go, nobody's taking roll," a small man called Boyd said. "But don't you think you need it?"

"Need what?" J.J. asked. He was on his knees still, his thick hands on the dirty thighs of his trousers, looking up at Boyd.

"Some salvation, some praying to try to get closer to it."

"I been close enough to eternity just marching with Fool Tom Jackson all over creation. Don't think I need to be told I'm in danger of hell by some chaplain that never saw the flash off a musket barrel." He looked at the men leaving the tent, shook his head, knowing he was beaten. By a general who loved to pray.

And Jackson did love to pray. And to see his men praying. There'd been an awful lot of praying in the camps since Sharpsburg—revival meetings, chaplains everywhere, men on their knees all over.

Behind J.J., a man who'd been sleeping sat up and scratched at his hair. "Ol' Marse Robert says that gambling you and the boys do is the worst thing there is, J.J.," the man said. "Says while we're struggling for our sacred rights as a nation we gotta keep ourselves pure in our ways. Seems to me you could use a little church time to see the error of your behavior."

J.J. snorted. "Well General Robert E. Lee can kiss my ass if he thinks I'm not going to do a little card-playing and dice-throwing out here. This is the most god-damned boring life there is, when we're not getting shot at—what's he think we're supposed to do out here, Sparks, darn socks sittin' in a circle?"

The man called Sparks—his name was Sam Peyton but he'd been called Sparks since setting his pants on fire by sitting too close to a sparking campfire after the battle of Winchester—pulled on his socks and laughed. "I'd like to see you say that to General Lee, I surely would." Sparks didn't have shoes any more, but he thought putting on a pair of tattered socks dressed him up a little for a prayer meeting.

"I probably wouldn't say it just like that to the general, I give you that," J.J. said. He looked over at Sparks. "You going?"

"Yep."

"Why? You're no church deacon."

"I'm going 'cuz the general's going." Sparks stood and bent over, leaning a hand on J.J.'s shoulder as he eased around him in the small tent. "Boyd, I'll walk with you," he said to the third man who was still standing outside the tent.

"Wait, now, Sparks," J.J. crawled out of the tent and grabbed Sparks' sleeve. "You don't even believe in God, you told me that."

Sparks, his head tilted and a little half-smile on his face, looked at J.J., who stood almost a head taller than Sparks now that he was upright. "I don't, most times." He nodded, said, "I sure wish I did believe when the fighting starts. These prayer meetings don't hurt, and maybe some of the God talk will stick to me. I could use the protection if it does." He smiled. "Besides, I like the singing."

Boyd, a believer, looked at Sparks and shook his head. "You can surely come along, Sparks, but you're not much more ready to receive our Lord's grace than he is," jutting his chin toward J.J.

"Think I'm a hypocrite?" Sparks asked Boyd.

"No, I don't, I'm not judging you, but I'm not sure your mind or your heart's very open."

Sparks put his long arm around Boyd's shoulder and leaned ahead, starting them walking toward the chapel in a beaten-down field shaded by a few trees turned color with autumn. "Well, now, Boyd, it makes the general feel good to see us at the prayer meetings, he likes to think he's leading us to the Lord. So I'm doing this for Old Jack even if I don't get much out of it myself."

"I don't believe General Jackson likes a man who's not straight about what he is," Boyd said, shrugging off Sparks' arm. "There's no man more honest about things than Old Jack."

"No, that's true, he's brutal honest. I've heard he's even been critical of Robert E. Lee, says he doesn't hate the Yankees enough. That's an open heart for you." He looked at Boyd, who just looked ahead while he walked. "But we can't have Old Jack thinking he's leading a pack of heathens out here in the wilderness, now can we? So I'll march along to the prayer meeting to make him feel better about all this." Sparks waved his hand to take in the camp around them, the stacked rifles, a wounded man sitting bent over his bandaged arm, the hills, the war. He grinned and hollered over his shoulder, "Come on, J.J., get a little religion with us, you got no game now anyway."

J.J. shook his shoulders, brushed off the front of his shirt and started after them. A few steps along he stopped, turned back to the tent, dug in his pocket and threw a pair of dice through the flap, then ran after Boyd and Sparks. A big sergeant walking down the line of tents, man named Sparrow, saw J.J.'s motion and grinned at him. All around them, men were walking toward the open-air chapel to be part of Stonewall Jackson's Christian army.

That evening, Jackson wrote to his wife about the minister's sermon—"It's a glorious thing to be a minister of the Gospel of the Prince of Peace. There is no equal position in the world."

Winchester, Nov. 21, 1862

"You made him a lunch?"

"Well, yes, of course I did. I'm not going to have the man go halfway across Virginia with no food, Reverend."

The Rev. James Graham laughed at his wife, Fanny. Ever the mother, taking care of whoever came to hand. In this case, she had packed a small sack with bread, cheese, apples and some pie for General Thomas Jackson, who had spent most of the day with the Grahams in the Presbyterian Manse in Winchester.

"And how do you know he's going halfway across Virginia?" the reverend asked, smiling.

"Well surely not from General Jackson, you know very well. But everyone says he'll be going to join Lee at Fredericksburg, and, well, I just wanted him to remember us as he rides."

She looked down at her hands, picking at her apron. "I hope the Lord protects that man," she said.

"I pray that He does too, and He will, if that's His plan," the reverend said. "He's done a pretty good job so far."

His wife looked up at him. "There's been a lot that needed protecting and haven't gotten it."

The minister nodded, a shadow of pain slipping across his face. "I know, Mother. It's hard to understand." He rubbed at his balding head, then nodded slowly. "There are a lot of questions, but I don't think we're supposed to know the answers. We are just required to have faith that it all works to the good."

Fanny Graham shook her head, turning half away. She was so tired of the war.

"It is hard, Reverend. I'll try to borrow your faith, you seem to have enough, always." She tried to be cheerful, but it hurt her to see Jackson leaving, again.

The first time had been just before the battle at Kernstown, just a short way south of Winchester, on March 11 of this year. It seemed so long ago—so much had happened, so many marches, so many battles, so many deaths. So many times Winchester itself had been taken by the enemy and then liberated again by Valley troops. Back in March, Jackson had come to the Manse and told the Grahams he was taking the army away, leaving the town open to Federal invasion. He had wanted to fight Banks rather than give up the town where he had spent the winter, but his commanders had advised against it, and he had decided it would be too dangerous to fight when so outnumbered. He had stood in their parlor, his eyes shining, frustration and dejection showing in his face, apologizing to the Grahams but saying it would all work out for the good. At least, that's what he'd prayed for, with Fanny and James Graham there in their home.

And the Yankees had come to Winchester, several times. They broke into homes, some of them, searching for food or silver or worse. They closed down businesses and required people to have permits to move beyond the town, they threatened arrest to any seccessionist who wouldn't sign an oath of allegiance to the Union. Food became scarce, as fields went unplanted because no young men could stay in the area. Battles were fought north and south of the small town, and wounded, bleeding men flooded Winchester's homes and churches. Antagonism was so high in the occupied town that, once as the Federal troops left with Jackson's army on their tail, women of the town had shot at the blue soldiers. Fanny's mother, she wrote in a letter to General Jackson's wife, killed two blue-coats herself. The last time the Federal troops had left, they'd burned down the depot and several warehouses, including a powder magazine that had shattered windows all over town when it exploded. The on-again, off-again occupation of Winchester had been wearing, depressing, maddening.

And so many Winchester boys had died—on fields just outside of town, bleeding on sofas in the homes of friends, crumpled on hard ground many days' march from home.

Since that first time, when Jackson had said he had to take the troops away, his Stonewall Brigade had fought all up and down the Valley, then around Richmond, then shattered the miscreant Pope at Cedar Mountain and slammed him in the rear and flank at Second Manassas. Then the Virginians had marched into Maryland, liberating Winchester and Harper's Ferry on the way, and run into McClellan's hosts at Antietam. The troops said Jackson had sat his horse in the middle of the Potomac ford after that grizzly battle until every one of his boys had crossed back into Virginia.

Then a respite. Jackson had his troops back in the Valley, resting and refitting—which meant he was trying to get some shoes and blankets out of Richmond. The Grahams had hoped to see him, sent word for him to stop by and visit. But the troops had started moving, once again marching in worn ranks out of Winchester, and the minister and his wife feared they wouldn't get a visit. But then he came to tea.

The Grahams' house was a home to Jackson. He and his wife, Anna, had stayed there for almost two months the previous winter, after Jackson had taken over the Valley command. They ate together, the four adults, and played with the Grahams' four children. The general and the minister talked long into the night about spiritual matters. When a messenger came with a question of war, Jackson would always walk down the street to another house that served as his army headquarters, keeping the Manse free from military meetings. Fanny recalled now the most touching and in some ways incongruous aspect of the general's long residence with the family—how he would romp and play with the children, bringing young Alfred into dinner by crawling along on hands and knees with the child riding on his back, Jackson bucking him like a horse and jostling out squeals of laughter from the little boy.

Now the children had asked to stay up and see the general, their big, bearded, laughing friend. Fanny had agreed. The family had had a lovely evening with Jackson, whom Fanny called "our general." Jackson told them about the presents he regularly received now, because of his fame, some from as far away as England. Gloves, boots, saddles, bridles, and more stockings than he could ever wear out. "Our ever-kind Heavenly Father gives me friends among strangers," he'd told them, smiling with surprise. They'd talked of Anna, and how much they all missed her at the table that evening. Jackson's wife was pregnant, and he showed great eagerness for the child to be born, while wondering aloud when he would be able to see it. It was clear to the Grahams that Jackson wanted peace to come so he could go home. It was just as clear that he would never leave the front while the war was on. Officers had to set an example and not leave the army for personal matters. If everyone *in* the army was actually *with* the army, Jackson said, the war could be shortened and independence won.

The Grahams marveled at how Jackson seemed able to put the war aside and enjoy a domestic evening with friends. There was no gloom about the general, despite the horrors he'd been so immersed in—the bloodiest day in American history just two months ago at Antietam, a cornfield reaped by bullets and soaked in gore. He delighted in the children, avidly discussed God's will and how to discern it with the minister and his wife, enjoyed the good food and seemed absolutely at home in the Manse. It could have been an evening five years earlier, with no war swirling outside, only the company of dear companions of the heart and soul.

And then he had gone.

Out into the night, and off to join his marching troops. Heading for winter quarters east of the mountains, or perhaps looking for another battle.

The world knew Stonewall Jackson as a commander who brought iron and fire on the enemy with a sorcerer's magic and a merciless speed. The reverend and his wife knew Thomas Jackson as a thoughtful, gracious, committed Christian who could never stop smiling around children and who would deflect any praise toward God and his troops.

"I think he'll be all right, Mother," Reverend Graham said, placing his hands on his wife's round shoulders. "He is a man of God, and it seems that, I don't know, some sort of light travels with him."

"I hope so, Reverend. I wish he hadn't had to go so soon."

"Oh, you know, he's stopped here several times during the war, and he'll be back. I pray he will."

She nodded, then looked at him. "How can a man like that be so humble, Reverend? Did you hear him say again the credit for his victories belongs to God? He's a lesson, a model of a Christian man. His modesty would seem affected in others, wouldn't it? But he is just so real, so…soft, almost," she said.

"Except to the Federals. He's steel and slash with them," the minister said, sitting down in a wingback chair by the fire. "Last winter, several times, he'd talk with me about the war. Never at dinner, you noticed. Never with the family. But in our evening talks he'd lay out his philosophy of war for me, because I asked. He sounded very hard. But for a purpose, almost a Christian, humanitarian purpose, I finally realized. He said the business of a soldier is just to fight. Not to march or dig breastworks or stay in camp, but to strike the enemy, invade his country and do him as much damage as possible in the shortest possible time."

"That sounds so destructive," Fanny said. "Not like the man who kisses and tickles our children."

"Just what I said to him—so destructive. And he said it was precisely the opposite. By prosecuting the war with vigor and speed it would be brought to a quicker end, and lives saved overall. He was so sure of it. Sure that was the right way. And you've seen how he's moved so quickly since last winter, surprising the Federals with such impetuous blows. He told me Napoleon never waited for everything to be ready—he acted, he marched, he struck like lighting."

Both the Grahams sat looking into the fire.

"He can be like these flames, I'd say. Burning, or comforting," Fanny said. "Coming from the same source, doing two very different things."

The reverend nodded, and grunted his agreement.

"It *was* good to see him, wasn't it?" he said.

"Oh, yes, James. He's so—consoling. We've been through so much—although I know many others have truly suffered, and we have not. But, it's been so miserable, being in enemy territory, not being able to do the little things we normally do—going where we choose, meeting whomever we like. Having a town with stores and people walking about. But somehow it seems better when he's here. I think about the deprivations less, the fear."

"And when he's here, he's got that army. Those Stonewall boys. That helps calm some fears, all right," the minister said through a smile.

"Yes, old Banks or that damned Pope—excuse me, dear, but he is awful—won't come around when the Valley army is here, and that's a relief. But there's something about the man, just himself, just the general, that makes me feel better, more at peace. He looked so healthy today, and he laughed so much with the children, you could just see the joy on his face. And seeing that gives you a happy feeling, a feeling that the world is a comfortable place, a fine place. I wonder if he knows, knows that his joy is so contagious?"

"I don't think he's that conscious of himself, at least that way. He thinks of life as a gift, and would be surprised at people who don't take joy in it, and thank God for it." The minister thought for a moment, wondering if he really understood Jackson. He thought he'd come close, after many long talks, minister and student both eager to understand the depths of life and faith. "Strange how a man of war, one who's so masterful at it, can make us feel peace. But he does. Just another contradiction. There are so many, my dear."

"Yes, so many. And another one is how tired I feel from feeling so good. I'm going to bed, Reverend. And with the general gone, you have nobody to talk to, so come along too."

"I will, in a moment. I'll just say a prayer here, by the fire, for the general."

"Our general. And pray that he likes my lunch, too, and then come up," she said, kissing the top of his head.

James Graham laughed at his wife, and thanked God for a spouse, and children, and a friend like Thomas Jackson, who could give him the gift of mirth. So precious in these dark days.

Moss Neck, below Fredericksburg, Feb. 23, 1863— Confederate Army

Mountains and rivers. Jedediah Hotchkiss dreamed of them. Curving lines, winding lines. Randomness that coalesced into patterns that showed you the way to winning a battle, or a war. Hotchkiss spent endless hours capturing mountains and rivers, fields and forests on paper. Thin tracing paper, mounted on heavy paperboard. Squares to get the scale right. Pencil, India ink and watercolor to make the maps tell their stories.

The mountains and rivers were part of Jackson's arsenal, part of his strategy, part of his army. Alive. By moving his men across them, in and out of them, he almost made the geographic features shift on the earth to fit his design, to shield his army from the enemy, to hide and mystify. Jackson brought the mountains and rivers alive. And Hotchkiss, Jackson's topographical engineer, was the dissecting scientist who opened up the mysteries of the land and trapped them on paper. The chemist who reduced the terrain to its basic elements so Jackson could choose just the right place, just the right angle, to move or feint or hide or jump.

Hotchkiss loved the ground, and what it could do for you. And so did Jackson. As Hotchkiss sharpened a colored pencil with his knife, he wondered if Jackson could still appreciate the beauty of a hillside or river's curve, or if all he saw were angles of attack and cover from artillery fire. Hotchkiss had heard that steamboat captains said the magic and beauty went out of the river when you had to look at each leaning tree or ripple of water as something that could, this trip or next, rip the bottom out of your boat. Hotchkiss had to admit he could seldom just look at the wind blowing leaves on a hillside—he was automatically measuring elevations, thinking of contour lines, reducing the natural world to something manageable in front of him. He suspected Jackson, however, could detach from the practical and just take in a graceful rise of mountain. Jackson so loved Virginia that the land must still have a soul to him. That's why he fought so hard for it, Hotchkiss decided.

Jackson knew most of the ground in the Shenandoah Valley and had an instinctive feel for elevations that would screen his movements from the enemy, shortcuts that would speed his marches, river crossings that would let him slip away. But still he'd had Hotchkiss draw maps of everything, so Jackson could see far beyond what was immediately before his eyes.

In this war, you could only see as far as a treetop or a hilltop or, for the Federals, a tethered observation balloon would let you. So the man who knew the land beyond his eyes' reach had the advantage.

Around Richmond, Jackson hadn't known the land as well, and his performance in those battles was plodding. Here, in central Virginia, around Fredericksburg, Jackson had been studying the land all winter. His feel for it was strong now, rooted. And as usual, he was looking well beyond the ground on which his troops—and the Yankees—were camped now.

Hotchkiss was working on two maps this evening. One showed the battle fought last year at Cedar Mountain. The map was for the official record, but also for Jackson's memory bank. The battles at Manassas showed that ground once fought over in this much-trampled country between Richmond and Washington could any day become a battleground again.

The other map was in front of him now, as he looked up from the wavering light on the table to see a figure in the entrance to his tent.

"Boswell, come in, how are you?" Hotchkiss said, pleasure evident in his high voice as James Keith Boswell, an engineer on Jackson's staff, stepped in.

"I'm cold, my friend, and still sick. It looks like Christmas out there, and it feels like we're in the North." The snow that had fallen yesterday was still over a foot deep. Boswell's boots were wet from the walk, and he worried about the men in their huts. Low, dark, smoky places the men built dug into the ground with ill-fitting logs for walls and canvas roofs. Not much more than badger holes, and the winter so severe for Virginia.

Hotchkiss found his friend's observation uncannily apt. We may in fact be in the North before much longer, Hotchkiss thought to himself. The day before, General Jackson had given him secret orders to prepare a new map of the Shenandoah Valley and the country to the north, extending through Maryland

and into Pennsylvania. All the way to Harrisburg, the capital, and Philadelphia. Far beyond the current theater of war. The audacity of it had shaken Hotchkiss for a moment, but he knew Jackson's hope that a thrust into the belly of the North and destruction of coal mines in Pennsylvania could shorten the war and help bring independence for the South. He realized he should be surprised by nothing the general thought about. Audacity was a fitting description of Jackson. And he was always thinking aggressively, always many moves ahead.

Boswell flopped in a camp chair, pulled off his gloves, and asked what Hotchkiss was working on.

"Maps," Hotchkiss said, uncomfortable at not feeling free to tell Boswell what the map covered. But the general had a padlock mania for secrecy, and Hotchkiss had to honor that. He pulled a broad sheet of paper over the map of Cumberland County, Pennsylvania that he was reducing to fit his overall map of Jackson's projected campaign.

"That's a surprise," Boswell said, smiling. "I thought you might secretly be writing a romance of the dashing General Jackson and his crusade."

"Dashing is not a word I've heard used about the general. Fits Jeb Stuart better, don't you think?"

"Mmm," Boswell agreed. "I guess I haven't heard that word either. I've heard a great many other words applied to our general in the year I've served his pleasure and his displeasure."

"Haven't we all. If he was everything we hear him described as, he'd be a saint and a foaming madman all at once," Hotchkiss said, leaning back in his chair and turning down the lamp on the desk.

"Pretty good description, Jed. There's romance in you indeed; better catch it on paper and make yourself famous with Old Jack."

"I'll leave that to Cooke, he's the writer," Hotchkiss said, referring to John Esten Cooke, a novelist serving as an aide on Jeb Stuart's staff.

Then Hotchkiss caught Boswell's reference to a year on Jackson's staff. "It has been a year now, hasn't it?"

Boswell nodded, and his voice came out serious. "Day after tomorrow. One year to the day. It seems much more like 10. One year for each battle I've seen."

"It has been hard, hasn't it?" Hotchkiss said.

Boswell nodded, and looked ruefully at his friend. His face, though youthful, showed around the eyes what he'd been through in the year, what he'd seen in the battles. "By now we all know how foolish our ideas of glorious war were. At least I know I was a fool," he said. "I've seen too many corpses now, too many houses with only a chimney sticking out of rubble, too many women and children turned homeless, to be able to think it's anything but just awful. Virginia— Virginia is ravaged."

"Why do you stay?"

"There's nowhere to run."

Simple fact. No flourishes of patriotism or romance. No Walter Scott. This man has been around Thomas Jackson, Hotchkiss thought. He just says what he means. That was one of the reasons Hotchkiss had come to like Boswell so much. One of many. Boswell, at 24 young like most on Jackson's staff, was an engineer who'd done railroad work before the war. He had a sweetheart behind enemy lines in Fauquier County, and he worried about her, worried that the state, and life, would never be whole again. Boswell had joined Jackson's staff at the beginning of the Valley Campaign last year, and friendship had grown and deepened quickly between him and Hotchkiss. The intensity of war made weeks and months seem like years, so Hotchkiss felt he'd known Boswell for a very long time. Acquaintance grew into camaraderie, which grew into a deep-flowing connection of shared joy and fear as the two faced together the manic emotional ups and downs, soarings and crashings, of Jackson's campaigns. And they shared an affection for the general, a man who was known mostly for sternness and distance. But they could feel his concern for them and for the rest of the staff. Although in battle Jackson would without hesitation send them into the hottest fire to deliver messages or steer troop movements, in camp he was a part of their lives, sharing meals and talks, laughing with them as they joked and jibed to let off the pressures of this unnatural life. He asked often after their health, always shared any food that was sent him by local families, and encouraged them to pray and take part in religious services so their spirits wouldn't wither in the soul-wasting moral chaos of civil war. He even let them slip off to see their families when the army came near their homes, something he seldom let other men do and never did himself. He cared for them, although he couldn't take care of them. Nobody could truly take care amid the random instant deaths and maimings and diseases that seemed to live in the very air and could fall on anyone at any time.

This winter at Moss Neck had been a time for finding some unaccustomed pleasure and peace, for deepening friendships, for taking stock two years into the war, for looking for meaning or a way to survive without it.

Moss Neck was yet another of the lovely places Virginia held out to ease the worn soul. Looking for winter quarters in mid-December after the ghastly battle of Fredericksburg, Jackson had come to Moss Neck several miles southeast of that town. At first he had insisted on camping in the woods and not taking the offered hospitality of the Corbin family who owned a mansion nearby. Sitting cold around a wintry fire, with his wagons still miles away at Guinea Station, Jackson disappointed his young staff by insisting that he and they share the hardships of the troops. The lack of food didn't deter him, but when a dead tree fell smashing into the campfire and when he couldn't sleep on the cold ground, he relented and made for the mansion, for one night's rest by a fireplace and decent food. For two weeks or so after that Jackson stayed in a tent on the grounds, still saying no to a room in the house. Then an earache and Dr. Hunter McGuire's orders convinced him to take up residence in a small office building on the grounds, and that became Jackson's home for three months.

Here, near the winding Rappahannock River, Virginia is more subtle than in the Shenandoah Valley. The earth rolls, thick woods open onto lush farm fields, creeks and streams create graceful curved cuts in the low hills. The river itself, broad and slow, loops past high bluffs, creating thickly wooded points or "necks".

The Corbins had built Moss Neck about a mile from a bend in the river, on a gradual hill deep with oak woods that overlooked fields and pastures, the River Road to Fredericksburg and the Rappahannock gorge.

Designed like an English country residence, Moss Neck had a two-story central building with a broad porch and white columns across the front of both levels, a cupola on top and spacious one-story wings thrown wide to both sides. It was breathtaking, startling in its graciousness and size in the midst of this forested countryside.

In the yard was a three-room office, where the Corbins kept the farm's records and ran the business. One room was a library, and here, amid fishing tackle, ladies magazines, agricultural books, deer antlers, framed pictures of race horses and hunting dogs, Jackson spent the winter. Jeb Stuart, a frequent visitor, was fond of poking at Jackson about his sumptuous surroundings. In his saber, spurs and black-plumed hat, Stuart strode around the room, looking over the paintings of horses, prize bulls and a fierce rat terrier, and chastised Jackson for his low taste in art. One of Stuart's favorite memories, which he cherished for the short time left him, was of Jackson blushing and smiling and going along with Stuart's pretense that the pictures had been chosen by Jackson himself. When Stuart goaded Jackson about the racehorse paintings, saying the old women of Virginia would be gravely disappointed at this show of moral degeneracy, Jackson had smiled and told his friend that perhaps he had had more to do with racehorses than Stuart suspected. As a child he'd raced horses for his uncle Cummins at Jackson's Mill in northwest Virginia, leaning far forward on the horses as they pounded around the four-mile track. Stuart, the one man who could always make Jackson beam with pleasure, was surprised and pleased to have Jackson join in the banter. Even Robert E. Lee helped in rallying Jackson, during a Moss Neck Christmas dinner of turkey and oysters when Jackson's servant Jim wore a white apron to wait on the table. You're only playing at soldiering with all this fanciness, Lee taunted Jackson—you'd better come to my headquarters to see how a real soldier ought to live.

Good food, smart company, laughter in a fine house—it was the closest Jackson had come to the kind of life he was fighting to protect since staying with the Grahams in Winchester the winter before.

But the pastoral setting of Moss Neck lost much of its former peace and solitude as it was transformed into an army camp. Trees by the thousands were chopped down for fuel and shelter, the clearings rang with the tramp of drill and parade, the Stonewall Brigade Band played right in front of the house, sometimes lilting tunes, sometimes dirges for soldiers dead of disease.

The beaten ground became muddy, some men slept in "gopher holes" dug in the snow or the earth, soldiers complained bitterly of men who weren't sharing their hardships in the army, and deserters were flogged. Three deserters were sentenced to be shot, and the Stonewall Brigade's general Frank Paxton proposed to Jackson that the three draw lots and only one be executed. Jackson refused, insisting on discipline and expressing disappointment in Paxton, but President Jefferson Davis commuted the sentences.

But there were daily visitations of joy for Jackson. Janie Corbin, five years old, would run out to see the general every day in his office, in the midst of his reports and meetings with officers and congressmen. She would play on the floor, cutting out paper dolls, taking his gifts of an apple or a piece of cake he had saved for her. People in the yard could hear Jackson talking and laughing with Janie as she played. It was a blissful distraction for a man who had yet to see his own baby daughter Julia, born since he left for the army.

Jackson's greatest concern this winter was the spiritual state of his troops, his greatest desire to lead a converted army. A religious fervor had swept the army in the past two years, and the Stonewall Brigade had, at the beginning of February, built a log church in the woods at Moss Neck. Some said the men gathered there more for physical warmth than spiritual sustenance, but the general was glad to see them congregate and helped lead them in prayers.

He felt earnest prayer by faithful people would more likely bring peace to his torn country than all the armies Jefferson Davis could put in the field. "If we were only the obedient people that we should be, I would, with increased confidence, look for a speedy termination of hostilities," he wrote his wife that January.

Moss Neck was an interlude of calm, of life, that felt a world away from the war. For Jackson and all his staff.

In Hotchkiss' log-sided tent, the fire burning in a crude hearth, the mapmaker looked closely at his friend Boswell.

"You're tired," Hotchkiss said.

"To the bone. To what's left of my soul. This pretty place here, we're only hiding. The war is out there. The Federals are across the river, and they'll come over again, as soon as Spring breaks. Then it will all start once more. They're having snowball fights out there now, the men, regiment against regiment. Before too long they'll be back to muskets and lead. I don't need to see any more, Jed. No more widows, no more dead, no more glory."

"'War is the greatest of evils.' That's what General Jackson said to me just before Christmas, one night when we had a long talk. He must be tired of it all too, don't you think?"

"I don't know," Boswell said. "I don't see him getting tired of anything. He never seems to rest. He's always doing something, even here. Getting reports on provisions, ammunition, deserters, courts martial, the man never stops." Boswell opened his overcoat, the warmth of the fire starting to reach him. "But he said war is evil, eh?"

"Yes. What do you think?"

"Some of the men would say he likes it. Likes it too much. To be attracted to something evil, now that's temptation."

"Well, maybe everyone's wrestling with that demon," Hotchkiss said. "Perhaps that's what explains all the praying out there."

The two men fell quiet. Hotchkiss fiddled with his maps and pencils, Boswell stepped over to the fire and tossed another chunk of wood in. The wind blew, flapping the canvas roof of the shelter. Smoke drifted between Hotchkiss and Boswell.

"The war's brought some good, Keith. Your friendship, for one thing."

Boswell turned, an impish expression suddenly replacing the dark look on his face. "Oh, that's sweet of you, Jed, and I feel the same. But I'd rather we'd met at a dance, don't you know?" He smiled. "And don't go all girlish on me now, there's plenty doing that out there in the camp." The unexpected remark, and the return of some welcome liveliness to Boswell's face and voice, surprised Hotchkiss and made him look up from his table.

"You don't say, now?"

"It's a long winter, a long war."

"Not that long," Hotchkiss said, laughing.

The tent flap opened, cold wind blew in, and James Power Smith, another of Jackson's young staff members, ducked into the hut.

"Oh, a Presbyterian congregation, here we go," Hotchkiss said. Smith, like Jackson and Boswell, was also Presbyterian and had been a divinity student before the war.

"Prayer meeting?" Smith asked, looking around the smoky little space. Hotchkiss laughed.

"No, we're grousing," Boswell said. "And we're liking it, so don't try to cheer us up, old man."

"Got any coffee?" Smith said, pulling up a cut stump for a chair.

"Oh, yes, my lord, we have coffee, and cakes and pies aplenty, whatever you'd like for a sumptuous repast," Boswell replied, pulling a linty, half-chewed biscuit from his pocket.

"Well, I got half a ham from the ladies of the Corbin castle, and if you're especially kind to me I might share it," Smith said.

"You, my very dearest friend, are a prince, I've always said so. Hand it over," Boswell replied, holding both hands out and bowing his head.

The three passed around the cold ham, talking of how the soldiers were doing, how everyone was getting ornery and tense from the cold and the mud and the endless drilling. Hotchkiss thought to himself that fighting, strangely, always seemed to revive the men, and that soon this waiting would be over. And if Jackson carried through his idea of going north, crossing into Pennsylvania, some of the men would be thrilled to bring the war to the homeland of the invaders, while others, who signed on only to defend their own homes, would sheer off and take French furlough. Whatever happened when the travails of active campaigning resumed, some men who were now complaining loudest would look back on the months at Moss Neck as a stopover in paradise.

"Armies aren't meant to sit in camp," Boswell said. "They rot from the bottom, like a pumpkin on the ground."

"Oh, it's only we officers who are accomplished at sitting about?" Hotchkiss asked.

"Indolence is an art, and if you work hard at it you can master it, that's what I've found," Boswell said, a smile now back comfortably on his face as he found his natural gregarious rhythms returning. The gloom of war could not be a constant companion to this irrepressible young man. "Eating, conversing, inhabiting parlors, keeping shirts white, this is hard work, and only some of us have the talent for it."

Smith laughed and said, "You can't touch Crutchfield for laziness, Keith. That man finds war a serious affront to his sleeping schedule." Stapleton Crutchfield commanded Jackson's artillery, and was, like Boswell, a garrulous and lively member of the staff family. "And nobody can talk as much as Reverend Lacy, at least according to Dr. McGuire's rather constant complaint." Lacy, a minister from Fredericksburg—Presbyterian, of course—had been called to camp by Jackson to organize and augment the army's chaplain corps.

"Lacy does seldom seem to inhale, although he aims to inspire, I'm sure," Boswell said.

"But he's doing a lot of good," Smith said. "He's tireless. Meeting with the troops, meeting with the other chaplains to encourage their work, trying to bring more ministers to the army. So many of the men are joining the church, and nothing pleases General Jackson more."

"Seeing death so close does bring men to the pew, that's sure," Boswell said. "And, seriously, I'm glad too that it's happening. If nothing else, it keeps them all occupied with something other than the fistfights that have become a regular sport out there. And it gives them some other songs to sing besides that 'Lorena' and 'Home Sweet Home.' I've heard those enough for this lifetime."

"Oh, camp life is hard on your artistic sensibilities, my poor man," Hotchkiss said. "We'll try to issue some new song sheets to the boys. But I find I like how the men sing. It's a comfort, and the only sound in this war I'll care to remember." Hotchkiss rubbed his hands together, said it was hard to hold his pencils in this cold. "Did you hear the story that the general was walking through camp, looking at the men huddled by the fires chafing their hands, and an officer with him said the cold was so hard on the poor devils. And Old Jack leaned over and corrected him, saying, 'Call them suffering angels.'"

Boswell shook his head, Smith laughed. "He's always watching other people's language," Smith said.

"Oh," Boswell said, rounding his voice to the tones of a preacher, "I think it's a lovely parable that shows the mighty Stonewall's great and saintly compassion for his men." He tipped back in his chair. "At least that's how the ladies of the South who are warming up a new spot in the Trinity for General Jackson will interpret that little story as it passes into legend. If indeed such an exchange ever happened at all."

"Half of what's said about the general is fantasy," Smith agreed. "A man who's so quiet about himself leaves plenty of room for others to talk about him. And talk they do. Other than food, and home, and maybe lice, there's nothing they talk about more."

Boswell, although he edged his talk with sarcasm, was as impressed as his friends by the general's hold on his men. The soldiers would complain about Jackson loudly to each other, about his working them so hard, and they'd complain right to him when they got near enough, about bad food and late pay, but they talked obsessively about him and most were truly proud to be in his command. And so was Boswell.

"Talking about talking, go back to Lacy," Hotchkiss said. "Is he making progress with the chaplain corps?"

"Some," Smith said. "He's having them preach in their own brigades and then switch with another and preach in that brigade. So each unit will hear from two ministers, and that's to the good."

"Especially if their own's a dull preacher, begging your pardon, reverend, something you would never be," Boswell said, nodding to Smith.

"Oh, variety is beneficial, I know that. There are many rooms in the mansion," Smith said.

"Some better furnished than others," Boswell couldn't resist adding, and the others laughed with him.

"Are more coming in, preachers, I mean, to be chaplains?" Hotchkiss asked.

"Some," Smith said again. "Many seem to think they can serve Lord and cause better farther away from the guns, it seems." Boswell, across the little room, snickered. "But General Jackson has made it clear," Smith continued, "that he welcomes all men from all faiths. Don't ask what denomination they are, he's said, just ask if they preach the Gospel, and bring them in. He's very open-minded about this. We have Roman Catholic priests now as chaplains, you know. There's so much work to be done."

"Jackson's spending as much energy and attention on this as he is on drilling and reorganizing the army," Hotchkiss said. "Has Lacy reporting to him right along with the quartermaster and division commanders. And Jackson's holding the chaplains to their duty, telling them they can't go home because the soldiers can't either, that it would set an example that secular concerns are more important than the business of redemption." Hotchkiss laughed, thinking what the chaplains must feel like being drafted into Jackson's Christian army.

"He says organizing the chaplain corps is the most important work in the army," Smith said, nodding his head as if hearing Jackson say it, and approving.

"Does he really think that? I mean, why? I know he's religious, and so am I. But this is war, not a tent revival," Boswell said.

Hotchkiss leaned forward, looking at Boswell. "You have to remember, this is a man who would love to be a minister. 'I cannot think of anything more glorious than being a preacher,' he's said. And I think he means it. He loves talking religion. He'll do it endlessly with Lacy, with Dabney when he was here, with you, Smith, it seems like."

There was a rap on the tent frame, and a face ruddy from the cold, with a hawk's nose above a chestnut beard, pressed into the opening between the flaps.

Hotchkiss, facing the tent door, smiled with pleasure when he saw who it was, then he stood. "General, how are you? We were just talking about you."

Jackson leaned in, swatted at the snow on his boots and pants with his cap, then straightened to his height of just over six feet. "I would say you need more to occupy your minds, then. Perhaps I need to assign you more tasks, all of you?" His voice was warm, the edges of his mouth showed the hint of a jest; he liked these young men.

"Actually, sir, we were talking about faith," Smith said, "but you came here looking for something?"

Jackson nodded, his left hand rising to finger his beard, looked at them each in turn, then said, "I was looking for Major Pendleton, but I would be happy to join your conversation for a moment, if I may, as you are treating a topic more worthy than that you first mentioned."

The young men, of course, said they'd be pleased if he would join them, and Jackson leaned one thigh against Hotchkiss's table, idly slapping his gloves on the tabletop, near Hotchkiss's covered map of Pennsylvania. "What were you saying about faith, then?" His eyes were intense, even though his posture and the setting were relaxed. The men felt for a moment as if they were in a school room. Then Smith said, "We were talking about your chaplain corps, and the importance of faith in the camp."

"And do you think it is important, is needed work?" the general asked.

"Yes, sir, it gives men comfort," Smith said.

Jackson nodded, didn't speak for a moment, waiting to see if anyone would say more, then added, "Oh, it provides much more than comfort."

They all looked at him, and Smith raised his hands, inviting elucidation. "The Gospel, a bright faith, gives the men guidance in this most trying time, in these cold camps so far away from their families," Jackson said. "But it is also guidance for life beyond the war. If we can bring men to faith here, that faith will serve them for the rest of their lives." He paused, and the little gathering of men nodded. He stroked the fingers of a glove, his thumb coming back to a frayed place on the index finger where the reins had worn the leather. "Faith improves everything we do, I believe." He looked up, pushed dark hair behind his ear. "Faith makes a shoemaker better at his work, following the Gospel makes a tailor more punctual, more careful, more faithful to his promises. It's laid out there for all of us, in the Gospel, and if we can put God's charge into practice in all our endeavors, we will be better for it and our work and its results will be better. For all time."

Jackson fiddled with the gloves while his eyes strayed to the small fire. "Fidelity to duty is honoring God," he said quietly. "An unshaken faith is what we owe God, and in return we will have peace of mind, peace in the soul." He nodded slightly, and was still.

Boswell shifted his feet and looked up at the tall thin man before him. "Doesn't this war, General Jackson, shake your faith?"

Jackson nodded, taking the question in. Boswell didn't know if the nod meant, yes, the general's faith was shaken. As Jackson stayed quiet Boswell felt that the nod simply meant a larger yes, a yes to a faith that answered all questions. He felt as if he'd asked a question in logical language and had gotten an answer in a few bars of music.

"All things work together for good to them that love God," Jackson said, his voice taking on a richness as he warmed to his subject. That was his answer to almost any question, Smith knew. It didn't seem a full answer, in terms of the questions asked, but it did seem full to Jackson, as if the answer meant far more than the question.

Taking up Boswell's inquiry, because it troubled him as well, Smith asked, "But how can the inhumanity of war, the cruelty we see every day, the disease and death and maiming, not shake one's faith in God?"

"Is your faith shaken, James?" Jackson asked.

The others felt a tightening in the room, as the abstract question was made so personal, so present, so quickly.

Smith lifted his face, his features open with thought, and said, "Yes, it is shaken, often, and yet I still believe. And," he went on, haltingly, "I'm not sure, not sure how those two things go together."

Jackson nodded again, as if hearing a confession and not judging the one confessing, his faith neutral. He responded with a calm, level voice, "We do our duty and leave the consequences to God. That is how we show our faith, live in our faith." He looked at Smith, leaned ahead, reaching one hand a few inches forward. "I think that is the only way. We can raise the questions, although they are painful. It is natural to question. But we cannot question the answer." He leaned back again. "And the answer is faith."

This was logically unsatisfying, Boswell thought as he watched Smith nod, even circular, but its simplicity had an emotional appeal. It was unreasonable, literally beyond reason. But it said the answer was faith; Jackson clearly said the answer was faith. Not *in* faith, but it *was* faith. The answer.

"Do you fear for your own life, General?" This was Smith again, asking a question few men on a battlefield openly asked one another, although it was on almost everyone's mind.

There was a moment of quiet, and muffled voices from outside could be heard, along with the wind rippling the canvas.

"We must cheerfully accept God's will—whatever it may be, including death or wounding," Jackson said. "That is our duty, and in fact our privilege. If we conform to His will we won't agonize over why something has happened. It is God's will, and we can't know His purpose. But all things work for the good for those who believe, so if we just acquiesce, accept, all will be well."

Smith knew Jackson believed this, knew these words came from deep inside his faith. The calm tone of his voice—not arguing, not trying to convince anyone, just telling—made the words solid and common as the ground.

"But, do you fear?" he asked again, surprised at his own temerity, but feeling that Jackson's very quietness invited the exploration.

Jackson looked back at Smith, cocked his head a little to the side, and smiled. A small smile, but it reached his eyes, and there was a little "hmph" in his throat, almost a chuckle. He looked as if this time he'd heard the very specific question and was truly examining it, examining his own feelings. And he said, "No," as if surprised. Surely he'd had to have thought of it before, Smith thought, and then realized with a fresh astonishment—he was often astonished by Jackson—that perhaps the general never really had thought so clearly about whether he was afraid. Perhaps he just did his duty and lived in his faith so easily, in his faith that whatever was would work for the good, that he had never looked at the result that faith brought him—lack of fear. And when he looked, and found there was no fear, he was pleased.

That, Smith thought, was a truly amazing faith.

Looking at Jackson, who leaned there with a little smile on his weathered face, Smith saw the calm that his faith gave him. A simple calm. Here was a man who had studied war at West Point, been under killing fire in Mexico, and had led troops all over Virginia for two agonizing years. The government—two governments—had had enough faith in him to put the fate of men and perhaps nations in his hands, and the men themselves had the faith in him to follow through sickness and death and disappointment. Jackson was a rather tall man, but only of average build, nothing huge or unusually strong about him. He was not loud, in the camps or on the fields of war. Yet he gave off an intensity, as of a steel spring bent and ready, on the battlefield, and it poured out of his sparking blue eyes and his alert raptor's face and his quick slashing hand gestures. In camp and on the march, he was less tightly wound, but never fully relaxed. He seemed ready, all the time, for whatever would come next. Smith knew some called Jackson stiff, and that was his reputation as a teacher at the VMI, but to Smith it wasn't stiffness. It was that Jackson never slouched, never gave in to gravity, never gave up the posture of a man thanking God for the blessing of being alive, never wanted God to think this man was wasting God's gifts through inattention or lack of caring. Jackson seemed up and alive, taking the world in, watching what was coming, always thinking about what was next. And yet with all this activity seemingly going on in his mind and his soul, which Smith thought he could see in the intensity of Jackson's eyes, there was also this sense of calm that the man gave off. It was incongruous, calm from a man of such action and intensity, in the midst of an endless war. But it was there. Right now it was there. Calm from lack of fear, calm from abundance of faith. As much as his relentless conviction in battle, this spiritual calm was what gave Jackson his power, the power that drew men to him, made them give up their fate into his hands.

Hotchkiss, still thinking about the issue of fear, leaned forward over his table and said, "Look at Jeb Stuart, who seems to revel in the danger of a fight. Men call that courage. I wonder if Stuart is more reckless than courageous." He twined a pencil through his fingers. "But perhaps true courage is being able to accept that God has us in His hands. Not to protect us, but so that whatever happens, even if we're shot and killed, it will be all right. One is personal, Stuart's, and the other is beyond one's person, it's not about yourself. It's about God. Does that sound right?"

Jackson nodded, crossed one big boot over the other, didn't like the posture, stood straight again. "I don't think it's a matter of courage," he said, "and I don't think it's a matter of fear. It's about faith."

"We can't know what's going to happen, so we must let go and trust in God," Boswell put in.

Jackson pursed his thin lips, then opened them and said, "We must let go."

It sounded like a mystery to Boswell, a conundrum, almost a Buddhist puzzle. By letting go, we receive. Grace. Peace. Freedom from fear.

"So," Smith said, "it's that acceptance of God's will that shows true faith, and true faith ensures you will be saved. Not saved in this battle, but saved for eternity. You must accept whatever happens—not just death, but defeat, which for some is worse—or you will not be saved." The men—Smith, Boswell, Hotchkiss, Jackson—were still, listening to the fire crackling, and to their thoughts. "It's hard," Smith said, and Jackson said softly, "Oh yes." Hard, Smith thought to himself, to hold on to what is least tangible at the time when the physical world around you is most terrifying. Hold on to this precious fragile thing in the wind of the most devastating storm. Hard to do, while so easy to say. And that's what Jackson did. And that, Smith realized, was a very large part of why the man was so magnetic. It was his faithful ability to hold on in the storm, to cup his most treasured possession while his very flesh could be torn from him by a shell. And not care. As long as he held it. His faith. His obedience.

He could do what it was hardest to do, in the hardest place to do it, the middle of a raging battlefield. And the men could feel it. And they followed him. Because he had it. Because they wanted to have it too. The faith. The conviction. Add to that his strategic genius, his single-minded drive, and you had an invincible force. That invincibility was what men wanted in war.

And it came from letting go.

Smith looked at Hotchkiss, whose brow was knitted, and at Boswell, who was looking away as if through the tent canvas, and at Jackson, whose features were composed and calm and who was looking at him.

Boswell interrupted Smith's thoughts. "Isn't there also a practical side to this chaplain corps, General?" he asked. "I've heard you say that a converted army, warriors for Christ, will enjoy the spiritual favor of God. So if we pray, and if we believe, and if we model ourselves on the Gospel, and if our cause is just, we will prevail. Yes? So, in a sense, isn't the chaplain corps, the spreading of faith, being done to make the men better soldiers, to get us victories, to win our independence?"

Boswell held up a finger and added, "And if that's the reason, isn't that a worldly one, not a selfless Christian one, and doesn't that mean we're not simply being obedient to God? Aren't we trying to lead God, not follow?"

Jackson raised his eyebrows and looked again at Smith. Smith felt the general wanted him to answer, again as if in a classroom.

"But Keith," Smith said, "General Jackson sees beyond this war. What you say is right, he, you" and he looked back at Jackson, "think a converted army will be more successful, but that's not why you have faith or want the soldiers to." He felt a bit timid, trying to speak for Jackson, but Jackson was nodding. "This war is temporary, faith and life are eternal. Faith can help win this war, General Jackson believes, although I have to say I'm not so sure, but it's not *for* this war. It's for the men and their souls. Forever."

Jackson stood straighter, then leaned and spread his long fingers on Hotchkiss's map table. "I do believe that if we can marshal the men's faith, we can win this war, if that is God's will," he said. "But James is right, it is not for this war alone that I hope the men find faith, and that I believe we must do everything we can to help them come to faith. Obedience to God gives you many temporal benefits. It makes you calmer, takes away your anxieties from trying to understand the workings of this world. It harmonizes your mind and heart. Here and now it gives you peace. But the ultimate reward is salvation. That's what faith provides. Even if this army is defeated. Even if we're killed. If we have faith and do our duty, we will be saved. For eternity. That's what I want for the men," he said, then added, "and for you."

He lowered his gaze and said softly, "And for myself. I must admit I don't always feel that faith as firmly as I should. That is my trial." The others could barely hear his voice now. "This war is a test, and I don't always meet it. But we must all try."

The staff men were silent. Hearing Jackson confess to any faltering of faith was more startling than seeing him make a mistake on the battlefield.

Jackson pulled on his gloves, swept his hands down the front of his uniform coat, and said, "Thank you for including me, and I will pray that you hold on to your faith. That we all do. These are trying times." He nodded to each of the men, and salutes followed him as he turned to the tent door. "And now I will see how we're doing at providing food for the men—our suffering angels." A final affirmative nod of his head, the hint of a grin, and he was gone.

In the flickering light Smith looked at Boswell. Hotchkiss looked at Smith. It was quiet in the timbered tent. Hotchkiss set his pencil down.

"So we have to let go," Hotchkiss said softly. "Release ourselves into our faith?"

"Yes," Smith said.

"That's hard," Hotchkiss said.

"Don't I know?" Smith replied. "I'm aiming to be a minister and I can't do it, not like Jackson."

"Well, it's hard to release in this damned war," Boswell said, thinking of the year just passed. The scenes of devastation. The mangled men. "I can't get it out of my mind, and I fear for the shape my soul is in." His head was bowed, and Smith clapped him on the shoulder.

"It's reassuring to know General Jackson sometimes struggles too, with faith," Smith said. "Makes me feel better. Because clearly his questions are answered by that very faith itself. Perhaps the asking makes the answer stronger."

Hotchkiss stood. He looked down at his maps, at the lines that showed the ways to get at the Federals. At the breaks in the mountains, at the crossings of the rivers, over which war would pour. He put his finger on the Potomac, the last river over which Jackson wanted to send the Federal armies, back to their own country. It was a long way from this peaceful place near the Rappahannock. Many rivers to cross.

"That must be why we all stay so close to Jackson," Hotchkiss said. "His soul is lit like a watchfire by his faith, and we see it in the darkness, and we feel its warmth."

Boswell smiled, his face showing he was not fully convinced, couldn't yet unquestioningly embrace—maybe even understand—what Jackson had said. But he felt a part of this little group of men trying to make sense of it, felt a comradeship that eased him. He'd keep going with them, and keep searching with them when they had a little time to think and talk about it all. This night had been both unsettling and encouraging. He'd keep at it. And he'd keep going with Jackson, in the light of the man's faith. "Staying close to Jackson in the dark," he said, pulling his coat around him. "That's going to be my watchword. That's what I will do."

And he would.

And it would kill him.

And after that, the mystery.

Below Fredericksburg, April 21, 1863—Confederate Army

The riverbank made James Sparrow think of William Sutton. He'd last seen Sutton on the bank of the South River in the Shenandoah Valley, after the battle at Port Republic last summer. Sutton, because of his leg wound, could hardly walk yet when Sparrow found him. The Rappahannock here, falling from the east slopes of the Blue Ridge Mountains and running to Chesapeake Bay, reminded

Sparrow of that river and that meeting. He missed Sutton. Plenty of men around him now, of course, and lots that he liked, because he was a gregarious man. But Sutton had been quiet, serious most of the time, a good thinker and a man who would listen to Sparrow. And when Sutton talked, it was usually about things that Sparrow himself had been thinking about but not saying to anyone—the harder parts of being at war, why they were there in the first place, the fear of it, the closeness to death.

Sutton had been somber when Sparrow had seen him last. He'd almost gone up the spout, and that will cause a man to settle in on himself, Sparrow knew. Sutton had gone to North Carolina, to his brother's farm, and Sparrow wondered if he'd ever see him again.

Sparrow had walked almost to Hamilton's Crossing, far upstream from the Stonewall Brigade's camp south of Fredericksburg on the Rappahannock. Having broken up his winter camp at Moss Neck to be closer to Fredericksburg and the Federal army, General Jackson had been staying at William Yerby's home, and now his wife Anna was with him, and their little daughter Julia. The men were spread out on the higher ground overlooking the river, with pickets down by the shore. Even though there were plenty of Yankees across the river, often in plain sight, it had been a calm time. As Sparrow walked, he saw a crowd of men in a flat field by the river playing baseball, running in the field like boys, shirt tails flying, everybody hollering and laughing. He'd passed another group on their knees praying with a chaplain, a common sight this winter in the camps.

The new Federal commander, General Joseph Hooker, was getting his army in shape but wasn't doing anything much with it yet that involved the Confederates. Word was that Hooker would have to wait until May or even June to move, because so many of his men's enlistments were up that he'd have to wait until the two-year men left and were replaced by fresh recruits. But they'd been drilling over there, and the Federals that Sparrow talked to across the river seemed proud and full of piss and vinegar again.

Down by the water, a group of men crouched at the river's edge, working on something. Sparrow walked down the bank, digging his boots in. The men looked up at the noise.

"Evenin', sergeant," one said. "Got any tobacco you want to contribute for tradin'?"

Sparrow saw the board the men were floating in the shallow water. It had little sacks on it, and a folded, worn newspaper. One man was pushing a couple of newspaper pages onto a stick, making a sail that would fit into a hole they'd whittled in the board.

"Nope, but looks like you got plenty there. What are you after, coffee?" Sparrow said, squatting on his haunches, the stones of the river's edge squeaking under his boots.

"Anythin' we can get. Coffee, maybe, sugar if they got it."

"Hey, Billy, can you float a cow over here?" a small man near Sparrow who was arranging the cargo on the board yelled across the river, and the other men laughed. *"We been eatin' roots and weeds here and we're famished. You got plenty, send it on over now."* The men laughed again, wryly, because the jibe was sadly close to the truth. The Confederate soldiers were on short rations because the single railroad line up from Richmond could only run two trains a day with barely enough provisions to keep the men alive. It seemed infernally crazy; Virginia was such a lush land for farming, but the rickety Southern railroads couldn't carry enough supplies to its main army. Lee was said to be worried that his men wouldn't be strong enough to fight once the Yankees finally moved, and he was harrying Richmond about it every day, the men said.

"We send a cow over we're coming over with it, Johnny!" a loud voice called back from the opposite bank. *"And we're coming soon enough, you won't have to worry about rations cuz we feed our prisoners good."*

"Heyaah, my ass," the small man said in almost a growl to himself as he fixed the stick-sail onto the board. *"You come, we'll do you like we done Burnside,"* he yelled again. *"C'mon an' try us, we ready for you'uns."*

The man, with a battered hat and dirty blue jacket taken, no doubt, from a dead Federal after the battle at Fredericksburg, stood up and swept his arms back over his head to crack his back. "Someday that damned Lincoln's gonna find hisself a general that can fight and get those boys to do what they got in 'em, and then we'll be in trouble. Cuz there's a mess more of them than there are of us."

A boy so young Sparrow hoped he was a drummer leaned over and pushed the little plank boat out into the river, the light wind caught the newsprint sail, and it headed across.

In December General Ambrose Burnside had crossed his huge Federal army over this lazy river on pontoons, swept into Fredericksburg and headed for the heights behind the town. There Lee had his men entrenched, and the Confederates, outnumbered two to one, had mowed down the Union soldiers mercilessly, endlessly. A head-on assault against an entrenched army on higher ground. Suicide, but Burnside had kept pounding his troops against that Confederate stone wall. Men fell and died in neat, ordered rows.

"It's good that war is so terrible," Lee had said as he watched the battle, "or we should grow too fond of it."

Jackson's troops, with Sparrow in the middle of it, had fought off Federals who'd crossed the Rappahannock below Fredericksburg. Jackson had been everywhere on horseback, astonishing his men with his natty appearance as he'd replaced his normal worn-out uniform with a bright new one given him by his friend Jeb Stuart. He exposed himself to hot fire, including ranks of Federal cannon booming away from the heights across the river, but he hadn't been touched. When he'd beaten Burnside's men back onto the river flats, Jackson of course had wanted to charge and end it, but Lee said no because of the massed cannon across the river. Piling up dead men in bloody blue uniforms by staying on the defense here suited Lee. Burnside's army limped back across the Rappahannock, and that was it for one day.

Since then the Federal troops hadn't done much. Tried to march upstream a month later for another crossing, but it rained so much Burnside's wagons and cannons and men bogged down in mud so deep mules disappeared in it. After that, Burnside was cashiered and "Fighting Joe" Hooker took over the biggest army on the planet. Lee wasn't too scared, the men said, because he called the new Federal general "Mr. F.J. Hooker."

The sun had fallen behind Sparrow and the little group of men at the riverside, and in the growing darkness it was now hard to see the farther shore. Sparrow could just make out about half a dozen men across the way, sitting on stumps and fallen trees, holding fishing poles out into the current. On his side of the river, a little ways upstream, he could see two more Confederates standing under a long curving limb of a willow tree, their long poles dipping toward the ripples of the moving Rappahannock.

"I hope Jed and Cyrus catch them some fish, it's the only fresh food we get," said a lean man with two fingers missing from the right hand he was scratching his dirty hair with. "Sergeant, you got a line on any food? We gonna get some decent rations before we have to fight these fat boys across the river?"

"All we get is a quarter pound of bacon, day after day, and that ain't enough to even make us sick of the monotony of it," another man said. "Damn."

"Aw, we don't want you to get soft by eating too much," Sparrow told them. "There's plenty of food, we just want you to be ornery enough to give those old boys hell when they come at us."

"Where's the food?" the drummer boy said, standing up fast and looking behind Sparrow, as if to find a wagonload of hams.

"'Cross the way, boy," Sparrow said, jerking his head to point with his chin across the river. "That's where Old Jack always gets his food, from the Federal commissary."

"Well, they ain't giving us none today," a tall man said, spitting into the river. "Gonna be fish again, if we're lucky. Cyrus," he yelled to the men by the willow, "you getting' anything?"

"Just getting tired of waiting," a voice came back to them.

From over the river, a silvery noise floated across the water, lilting and soft. A band had started playing in the Federal camp. It was hard to tell the tune at first, but then the horn sounds wove together with a drifting sureness and the men could hear it was "Home Sweet Home." One by one, the Confederates sat on flat stones at the river's edge and fell silent, listening to the music. They looked down at the water, tossed a pebble or two in, one swished a fallen cottonwood branch over the dancing surface of the river gone lavender with the reflected color of sunset.

The music stopped, and the evening sounds of frogs and crickets filled in, then the jumpy notes of "Yankee Doodle" darted across. The men listened, bobbing their heads, and then the drummer boy said, "There it is!" and took off running downstream where the men could just barely see their little boat's sail standing out against the dark water as it came back from the Federal shore. A few minutes later the boy returned with a sack of coffee and another of tea, and a note that he said he couldn't read. He stuck out his hand in front of Sparrow's face, and Sparrow reached up and took the note, the torn page of a book a little wet along one edge.

"We bin toled to stop tradng with you. Giving away secretes. No more news paper. This is the last." Sparrow handed it back to the boy when he'd read it. "I guess Hooker's mad about us knowing what he's doing from reading the northern newspapers. Thinks he's going to stop his boys from communicating big military secrets."

"The hell else we gonna do?" the tall man said. "Those boys over there are about as bored as we are. We'll keep doin' our tradin', just won't let the officers see." He bit into another hunk of tobacco, his lined face showing disgust at what a man with brass on his jacket thought he could make ordinary men do.

The band had stopped again, and the tall man yelled across—"*Hey, Yank, play something for us now. It's our turn.*"

"*Hire your own band, Reb,*" one Federal shouted back. But before a reply could come from the south side of the river, the Northern musicians hidden behind the riverside fringe of trees started the first notes of a soft-flowing tune. Sparrow cocked his head, trying to place the song. A small man with a moustache that fell down both sides of his chin smiled and said quietly, "*Maryland, My Maryland.*"

Again the little cluster of men went quiet, a few leaning back on their elbows to look for the first faint stars in the darkening sky beyond the budding branches above their heads. Sparrow liked the music, but he also felt funny, dislocated, listening to the band. This could be any spring night in any town square, he thought. Hard to imagine what the two groups of men on the opposite shores would be doing to each other in a few days or weeks. Unsettled, he stood, said good night to the men he'd been sitting with, and walked back up the river bank.

Coming out of the trees, he looked up at the shallow hill rising beyond the riverside fields, and saw the flickering yellow lights of campfires decorating the night. He heard deep voices singing, shook his head and kept walking.

He knew he couldn't walk as far as Fredericksburg, and didn't want to. He still had visions in his mind of the broken city. The Federal bombardment that had preceded Burnside's crossing in December had shattered the lovely old town. Fredericksburg had been founded in the 17th Century at the head of navigation on the Rappahannock. George Washington's mother and John Paul Jones had lived there. Sparrow had an aunt who lived there now, in a small brick house that had taken several cannon shots from the Federals. He'd visited her when she'd returned to the city after the battle, and they'd both cried in the small parlor where a cannon ball had smashed a ragged hole through the outer wall and the oak flooring. The roof was torn, the front door was gone, and the cellar was a mess from the cannon ball that broke through the floor. Most of the jars of food his Aunt Elizabeth had put up were turned into shards. Her bedding was gone, mirrors broken, her pictures slashed and the few books she'd owned thrown out into the muddy street and stomped to a pulp. The Federals had ransacked the town, doing more consistent destruction to civilian property than they'd done anywhere else in the war, so far. No one was quite sure why this had happened, but it made the thought of the town bitter to Sparrow.

Still, his aunt wouldn't leave. Like many of the 5,000 or so residents of Fredericksburg, she had returned and tried to put her life back together. Even now, with Hooker's huge Federal army wrapped along the north side of the Rappahannock like a threatening snake, she was adamant about staying. Sparrow had gotten Elizabeth to promise to leave when the Federals started to move again, but he wasn't sure she would.

This night was confounding. Lullingly beautiful. The materiel of war was piled behind him. Cannon balls in pyramids next to huge tubes of iron and brass ready to launch it against dentists and teachers and farriers and farmers marching across lush cropland. Fifty thousand rifles were on his side of the river, maybe 90,000 on the other side, cold metal and wood now but, when touched off, hot launchers of death and scythes that sliced off arms and feet. Men now playing cards or writing letters to their mothers by a stub of candle would turn to killing at the click of a clock hand. Thirty times more people were in the hills and road-sides around Fredericksburg than had ever been there before the war, and they'd come not for a great tent revival but for an organized ritual of killing. Yet tonight was as lovely and poignant a night as he'd ever spent. Men fishing, joking, singing. He'd even heard of Yankees who'd swum the river in recent days to talk with the Southerners on the other side, and Southerners who'd done the same to the north side. Getting to know each other. Killing time together.

How perfectly strange.

He tried to put it all away from his mind. If Sutton were here, he'd probably talk about it all with him. But Sparrow was alone, and he tried to think just about the rhythm of his walking feet.

He turned back downriver after a time, walking back toward the Stonewall Brigade's camp. Things were quieting down, the big army camp settling like an enormous livestock farm, the sounds of coughing and rustling and calling out to one another gradually fading.

When Sparrow came by the place where he'd seen the men pushing their trading boat over toward the Yankees and had heard the army band playing, he paused. The Confederates were gone from the riverside now, and he presumed the Yankees across the river had also returned to their camps. He looked at the water sliding by a few feet below him, the muted reflections of a few small camp-fires riding atop the ruffling waves. Then a bugle sounded in the Yankee camps, its tone softened by the distance. Muted, plaintive, laden with emotion, it slowly tolled out single notes. "Duh duh Dah. Duh dah Daah. Duhdahdah, duhdahdah, duhdahdaah. Dah dah Daaah, daah dah duh. Duh duh Daaaaaaah." The last note thinned, receded, and drifted away into the night.

Taps.

Newly adopted as the evening benediction by the Yankee chief of staff, General Daniel Butterfield. A gift now to the thousand lonely men bedding down on both sides of the river within the reach of its grace.

Haunting, and beautiful. Like this night.

Near Raleigh, North Carolina, April 25, 1863

William Sutton was sure he had lost his damned mind.

Tomorrow he would leave for Virginia. To return to the war.

And here was Eugenia Carpenter, young and, from what he could see and imagine, soft. And here. Now.

Sutton was helping a neighbor of his brother Abner's move furniture. A relative had died, and Sutton and the neighbor had brought chairs and chests and a bed and other pieces by wagon down a winding mountain track to this house a few miles from Abner and Rosalyn's place. It hadn't been hard work. Eugenia had helped them here at the house, taking the lighter objects, bringing them water.

The neighbor had been wounded a year ago and lost the use of one arm, but was still strong, although Sutton could see the imbalance of the man's muscled chest and biceps beneath his sweaty undershirt—rounded and firm on the right side, withered on the left. Forever.

Eugenia was the man's niece, fled from Winchester. She was almost 30, she had said, plain, her face round, her smile rather crooked, a small tooth distractingly missing near the front. But she had the figure of an angel beneath the loose muslin dress she wore. Sutton felt a tug every time she moved, swaying like a warm moist summer breeze that slowed you down and made you feel every inch of your skin. When the sun had been just right this afternoon, behind her, he could see the hazy silhouette of her long, firm legs beneath the long skirt. It had made the work go too fast. He didn't want his eyes to be gone from this sight. He didn't want the day to end.

Just now she was bending over one end of an old settee that she and Sutton were moving to a spot on the front porch from which the family could watch the road come up the curving valley of a little creek. Her end of the settee had slipped from her hands, and she was bending down to grab for a better hold. And Sutton could see, had to see, couldn't turn away from, the front of her dress fall open, just enough. Through the tangle of loose laces at the top, Sutton's eyes roamed over the curving tops of her breasts, in shadows but lighted just enough by the late day's sun, hanging down with a delightful heft of gravity, but pushed up by the dress and the strain of her bending to bulge at the top where the fullness of the breasts stopped in the tightness of the skin below her collarbones. When she shifted to her left, her foot scooting on the porch floorboards, both breasts swayed sideways, a tandem motion that moved your soul. He could see the cleft between, dark and lush defining the light softness on either side. His eyes were drawn. He hardly felt the wood in his hands, the floor under his feet. She shifted one more step, and her breasts swayed again, touching against one another's roundness, caressed by the soft fabric of the dress that held her like two hands from behind. Sutton's breath caught, he could barely be heard as he said, "One more step should do it," wanting really to crabwalk that settee all across Carolina. At this last step her dress opened more to the side and Sutton felt like he was falling as the full fine shape of her left breast became visible. Glory.

"I think that's far enough," Sutton said weakly, blinking and putting down the piece and forcing himself to stand and look out over the porch rail and not at Eugenia any more.

"Yes," she said, and straightened up and looked at him and he looked quickly at her and tried not to look at the shape of her pushing out of the muslin or the small bumps in the middle of the swells and maybe she was lonely—there were so few men—but he wasn't going to stay and he absolutely knew that when he was lying in a tent back in Virginia with gunfire in his brain he would have proved that he was crazy. Not staying here with this woman or some other to see what might happen in a real life. But could there be real life any more? He had no idea.

He huffed out his breath as if he'd worked hard at moving the furniture, slapped his hands up and down past each other. She smiled, pushed back her hair over her ear with her thin pale hand, said thank you and drifted off the porch through the door into the house.

He felt dizzy for an instant, from standing, from something. Her shape, her skin, in his mind he suddenly found he couldn't separate them from torn shapes and torn skin. He closed his eyes. At Kernstown, Winchester, Cross Keys, Port Republic, what you saw in the fighting and after was so awful that you had to shut down some of the part of you that feels. He had done that. Most men had, he thought. A veteran told him to, and it had taken time, and he'd had to hold tight to himself to make it work. Now, he had to keep it shut down, or he might lose hold of everything.

Nostalgia. What you once had and might not get back to. Or never had but wished for so much it seemed you did. He missed his wife and he missed the feel and smell of a woman and he missed just lying down with someone. But what it seemed he missed more was the war. Or else he wouldn't be going back, would he?

Sutton looked at the door where she'd gone in. He stayed on the porch until the neighbor came out, the job now done. The two men talked a little, the neighbor wished Sutton well, said maybe Sutton would see Eugenia again sometime in the Valley when all this was over. They shook hands, and Sutton walked down the steps and down the road toward Abner's. A hundred yards away he looked over his shoulder at the little house and there was no one on the porch and he turned and kept on walking.

The next morning at earliest dawn he and Abner drove the wagon into Raleigh and Sutton got on the train. The car slowly rocking under him, he tried not to think of what he was leaving or what he was going toward. He was just going. He had signed up with a North Carolina recruiter and would join a Carolina regiment, not his old Virginia group. That way he'd have a new start, he hoped, while still returning to the Stonewall Brigade. Something familiar, something new; a balance that might work.

He didn't want it to, but as he looked out the window the vision of that woman's breasts came back, although not so clear now. As the train swayed north, he was almost glad the vision was fading, although he knew he'd want to call it back sometime soon and it wouldn't be there. He'd be alone with the war.

Guiney's Station, April 29, 1863—Confederate Army

The Rev. Beverly Tucker Lacy had taken Anna Jackson to the railroad station in an ambulance. Her husband couldn't accompany her, as he had ridden to the shattering sound of cannon fire after Jubal Early had sent word that the Federals were stirring from their winter camps across the Rappahannock from Fredericksburg.

Mrs. Jackson had stayed with the general for the past nine days, at the gracious home of William Yerby south of Fredericksburg, bringing their daughter Julia for her husband to see for the first time since she'd been born. It had been Anna's first visit since the time they'd spent together at the Grahams' in Winchester more than a year ago.

Now the war was returning, and Anna Jackson and her daughter were going back to her family's place, Cottage Home, in North Carolina.

The little train station south of Fredericksburg was a carnival of moving men, boxes, handcarts, horses, recruits with rifles held high on their shoulders, civilians lugging trunks and valises, porters and slaves trailing their employers and masters through the crowds. A few wounded men were already being brought to the station from the first skirmishing by the river, their groans lost in the noise of yelling, of screeching wheels, of boots on brick pavement, of clopping hooves and shuffling feet.

A train pulled in, chuffing steam, and among the troops and newspapermen stepping down on the platform, William Sutton jostled away from the cars. He'd been three days traveling on the rickety Confederate rail system from North Carolina.

"You're just in time, Will, the ball's about to open," a strong voice called from among the crowding people. Sutton looked toward the voice, and saw James Sparrow.

"Couldn't stay away?" Sparrow said, stepping between the moving men. "Welcome back to the killing floor."

"Well, Sergeant Sparrow, it's a surprise to see you. And I'd say staying away was pretty good," Sutton said. "But I was afraid you wouldn't have much of a chance this spring without me. Duty calls, even through the woods of Carolina. How are you, Jimmy?" Seeing the big man smiling through his tangled beard was a welcome pleasure. Sutton hadn't expected to see anyone he knew until he got closer to the army. And then he'd mostly see strangers, because he had come this time to join Carolina troops from near his brother Ab's farm. He wanted to come back to the war, because it wasn't going away, and because he wanted to feel it again, but he wanted some distance from what had happened in the Shenandoah Valley with the Virginia troops. But seeing Sparrow made him feel like he'd arrived somewhere he was supposed to be, and made the second-guessing he'd been doing on the train—about coming back—slip away.

"I'm tolerable, and you look pretty fair for a casualty." Sparrow grabbed Sutton by the shoulders, and Sutton put his hands up on the larger man's thick biceps. They nodded at each other, grinning, with no more words for a few moments. Sparrow pulled Sutton over to a bench, Sutton put his gear on the ground and wiped his face with his sleeve.

"What are you doing here, Jimmy? Just come to make sure I didn't get back on the train?"

"Sure, looking for deserters. Naw, I just helped bring Old Jack's wife to the station, she's going back to where you came from. We're getting ready for a fight, and the general's sending her home. She was here with their baby, and Old Jack got to see the little one for the first time. Beats looking at us, I'm damn sure of that."

"You've come up in the world, squiring Mrs. Jackson."

"Oh, I just happened to be there when Reverend Lacy was getting the ambulance hitched, asked if I could help. Glad I did, too, she's a fine lady. You could meet her."

Sutton looked down at his clothes, worn to begin with and now rank like his body from days of travel. He held his arms out from his sides, showing the condition he was in.

"Hell, she won't care, she's been in camp with Old Jack several times, she knows what soldiers are like. Come on. She's got time before her train. Could be hours, the way things go. Or don't go."

Sutton's curiosity overcame his reticence, and he followed Sparrow through the milling crowd to a small porch area beside the station where a small woman with dark eyes and dark hair sat with a sleeping baby and a slave, Hetty.

Seeing them, Sutton hung back. He was tired from the long rail trip, and he knew he smelled bad. But it was more than that. He had thought of General Jackson as a mystery, a man half legend already and half riddle. He had heard so many contradictory things about the general, listened to every story he could, pored over any newspaper accounts he found, made a study of this strange man. The troops held him in awe while they treated him almost like a talisman that would, while putting them in gravest danger, somehow assure their safety. And now here was his wife, the person who knew him best. It was like he was coming up to the window of a house at night, eager to look in, but hardly daring lest he see too much. Still, he truly wanted to look. He blinked, shook his head, and stepped forward after Sparrow.

"Ma'am, Mrs. Jackson? I'm sorry I went off for a minute, but I found a friend who was wounded with your husband's army in the Valley," Sparrow said, reining in his normally boisterous voice to try to seem more gentlemanly.

Mrs. Jackson looked up, smiled and nodded to Sutton as Sparrow introduced him. "I would shake your hand, Mr. Sutton, but I'm afraid Julia has me occupied."

"Very pleased to meet you, Ma'am," Sutton said, looking into the eyes that looked intently back at him. "I've just come from your home state."

"Oh, where?"

"Near Raleigh, my brother's place, where I've been recuperating."

"I hope you're well," she said, her voice quiet yet strong above the hubbub. Sutton nodded. "Carolina is such a pretty place, don't you think?" she said.

"Yes, ma'am, the hills remind me of the Shenandoah, some ways."

"Can we get you anything?" Sparrow asked.

"No sir, just sit with me, if you don't mind. I feel a trifle lonesome, even in this crowd." She adjusted the blanket as the baby stirred, hitched her higher on her shoulder. The two men took chairs the station agent brought them, along with a pitcher of water and a glass for Mrs. Jackson.

They talked of Carolina, a little stiff at first, as neither of the two soldiers quite knew what to do in the presence of General Jackson's wife. But she put them at ease, a well-bred but not stuffy woman who seemed strangely comfortable, although visually quite out of place, at this station teeming with the comings and goings of a great army.

Sparrow asked her if she was uneasy about the coming battle. "Oh, some, of course. But General Jackson has such faith in Providence and says all things work to the good, and I must put my faith there too, and I do so. Still I can't help but worry, just the same. He takes such chances."

"That's what beats those people across the river," Sparrow said, and she nodded in silence.

After a little idle conversation, Sutton gathered his courage and asked her about her husband. He'd never have a chance like this again, to get a feel for Jackson. "If I might ask, Mrs. Jackson, what is the general like, back home, in Lexington?" He surprised himself with the question, and Sparrow looked at him with his eyebrows up and a trace of a grin.

She looked at Sutton for a long moment, wondering perhaps if the man were impertinent or just showing with his curiosity how much he and the men felt connected to her husband. "He's private," she said, and Sutton lowered his head, looking at the ground. Anna let the pause hang, then smiled and said, "He's gentle. Surprising, isn't it? No one who has seen him only here, among these rough ways of war, would guess what his domestic side is like."

"Tell us," Sparrow said, wading in now that Sutton had started and Anna had given them a little glimpse. "You know we respect and admire the man, and would follow him into hell, begging your pardon. And have, many times," Sparrow said, laughing at his own words. "But I can't say we know him. Maybe the men on his staff do, or the big generals like Early or Ewell, but we don't, really."

She was quiet for a moment, most likely wondering if her husband would want her to respond. But being with him in such joy as he saw and played with his daughter, and then having to leave so quickly, had left her with emotions roiled and close to the surface, and she felt talking about her husband would ease her. And she knew there was a bond, a connection forged in fire that the soldiers felt with her husband, and she thought that must be helpful in fighting the war, in getting the men to do what her husband—and the South—needed. And she thought, although she knew it probably wasn't logical, that their affection for the general might help them protect him in battle.

"You may not credit this," She said with a playful look. "My husband gave up dancing when he joined the church, although he used to love it in Mexico after the war, he says. But still, some evenings, in our own home, he will dance with me, gentlemen, when the spirit moves him. Of course, he closes the shades," she said, smiling and looking down.

"What dance?" Sparrow asked.

She looked up sheepishly. "The polka." Her mischievous smile quickly followed their delighted ones, and they each chuckled over their private pictures of the unlikely scene of the general prancing about his house with the curtains drawn.

"So he can let himself go, and have a lark?" Sparrow asked.

"Oh, yes, with abandon."

Not a word, Sutton thought, that would ever come to mind had he not heard it from her.

"He often hides behind doors in our little house, and leaps out at me to surprise me as I come past," she said, tossing her head. "He is a playful man." Sutton and Sparrow nodded at her, taking this in without a word.

"He laughs, just like a little boy, and his face fairly beams, especially around children."

She saw skepticism in their expressions. "You haven't seen this?"

"No, ma'am," Sutton said, "but we don't see him much, at least I haven't."

"And there aren't many children handy," Sparrow said.

"It's a pity, you should see him when he's laughing. But I suppose there isn't much that prompts you to laugh here." She was quiet a moment, looking over the men moving handcarts of supplies and carrying stretchers bearing men taken by sickness.

"Oh, we often have to laugh, ma'am," Sparrow said. "If we didn't, we'd have to wonder why all this was happening, and I don't think we'd find an answer without driving ourselves crazy."

"Yes, laughter helps, I suppose, like faith," she said. She sat without saying anything, and they sat respectfully quiet as well. The baby still slept, and Mrs. Jackson passed her to Hetty to hold. "The general was so pleased to see our Julia. Carried her around, held her up, called her a precious angel." She laughed to herself, and when the men looked at her questioningly, she said, "He was often told this week that Julia resembled him. And he said, every time, 'Oh, no, she is too pretty to look like me.' Often he would kneel over her cradle, and just gaze at her for the longest time." She shook her head, sorry that the general's enjoyment of their daughter had been cut short.

"My husband enjoys laughter and children for the same reason, I believe, that he takes such strength and satisfaction from his faith. He has had much sadness in his life, and he has needed some way to balance that. His father died when he was a little boy, and he was taken in by relatives when he was six because his mother couldn't support him. Then a year later his mother died. Our daughter is named for her; he felt his mother's loss very deeply. He feels," she said, looking at them closely, "everything very deeply." She held her hands in her lap, one on top of the other, palms up. She ran the knuckles of her right hand across the thumb of her left absently as she thought. She looked off to her right, toward the distance, over the heads of the people at the station.

"His wife, his first wife, Ellie Junkin, died in childbirth just more than a year after they were married, and the child died too. And we lost one baby, before Julia," she said very softly. "He was shocked at the deaths, I would say. They hurt him deeply. But he didn't wallow in his feelings. He doesn't. He took a lesson from Ellie's death, he told me. To eradicate ambition and resentment, and to learn humility." She nodded slowly. "It's a strong man who can do that."

Sutton wasn't sure how humility fit with a man who was so certain of his judgments and his cause, but he thought he shouldn't air his questions, even though he sensed Mrs. Jackson would enjoy engaging in such a discussion. He also wondered if perhaps Jackson hadn't allowed himself to really take in his wife's death, had maybe too quickly turned it into some kind of tempering for himself. Sutton had felt his own deep grief at his wife's death, though, and knew how debilitating it could be, knew you had to pass through it. Martha's death, and the ferocious battle on his own farmland, had made him break loose from his idea of God. He wondered if anything like that ever eroded Jackson's convictions, or if the man were shockproof. There was no way to phrase his questions that wouldn't seem like criticism of her husband, even though that wasn't what he would have meant. So he asked something safer.

"What does the general do, when he's home, with his time?"

Anna laughed. "Oh, he's very industrious. He sees laziness, indolence, as a high sin. He rises at six, walks, studies his lessons. You know he was teaching before the war." The men nodded. "After classes, he studies and reads again for an hour or two, then has dinner with me. The afternoon he might go to our little farm outside of town to see to things. He loves to garden. He would write me letters when I was home in North Carolina, telling me how my flowers were doing, about a new kind of lettuce he'd planted, about hoeing turnips and hilling celery. He even put up tomatoes when I was gone—that surprised even me." She smiled at the men, who seemed by their faces to have a difficult time picturing Jackson with jars and boiling water. "He is very taken by the natural world. He will come home from his morning walk and tell me about the birds he's heard singing, how lovely they are. The world sees him as a soldier now, but I know he'd rather be in our little back yard, tending to his plants."

"I hope he can be doing that again right soon, ma'am," Sparrow said. She tilted her head, looking at Sparrow, a fleeting yearning in her eyes showing how she wished this too.

"He keeps his mind always active, exercising it the way he does his legs by walking. He won't read in the evenings, by artificial light, because of his weak eyes, but I read to him sometimes. And he'll sit at night, absolutely still for an hour or more, facing the wall to keep out distractions, going over the next day's class lessons in his mind."

"What would you read to him, ma'am?" Sutton asked.

"History, poems. We read much of Shakespeare a few summers ago, and the general—no, he was a major then—would have me mark in the book passages he particularly liked. He loves a beautiful turn of phrase."

She looked at the baby in Hetty's arms. "He hasn't been home since the baby came, and of course that would break up his routine. We'll see how his life changes when he returns after this..." and she waved her hand at the activity around them.

"People say he didn't want the war to come," Sparrow said. "Is that true? Was he against secession?"

She looked down at her hands. Then, looking up at them, she said, "He hoped for the Union to be preserved, voted for Union candidates in the last election. He wrote to his nephew before Virginia seceded, saying, 'I am in favor of making a thorough trial for peace, and if we fail in this, and the state is invaded, to defend it with a terrible resistance.' I remember his words very clearly; he read them to me. 'A terrible resistance.' But he didn't take this lightly. He said many of the people who were advocating war had no idea of its horrors. He had seen it, and he didn't want any more of it. He said he looked on war as the sum of all evils." She paused, and Sutton thought how strange this was, that the man who brought such precise hell down on the enemy, and was so religious, could call war evil and still practice it so thoroughly well.

"It may well seem odd to you, but I have never heard any man express such utter abhorrence of war," she said firmly.

"Then why does he fight, Mrs. Jackson?" Sutton asked.

Her face showed a fleeting grimace of pain, then she composed her round features into a sternness that echoed the general's. "He sees it as his duty before God to stop these invaders. But he never wanted it to come." She looked up at the blue sky, a fleet of white clouds sailing. "He prayed regularly, with our minister, that the war could be averted. When Governor Letcher called on him to bring the more advanced cadets from the Institute to Richmond to help drill the new troops, he obeyed on the instant. But when he had them all assembled on the parade ground at the VMI, he still prayed with Dr. White that, if it was consistent with His will, God would still avert the threatening danger and bring us peace."

The two soldiers, the small woman, the slave and the child sat in silence as before them the train was loaded with passengers and freight. Anna Jackson reached again for Julia, then said to the men, "But God saw fit to let the war come, and there must be a reason for it. My husband believes God has ordained this war, perhaps for purposes we cannot know. He believes the North must now be punished. But I do fear it, gentlemen. It has already exacted such a cost. So many of the young men we know from Lexington have already been killed or maimed. So many families there have known such grief."

She stood, and the two soldiers shot up a moment behind her. "Do you think this battle will be bad, gentlemen? What do you know of General Hooker on the Federal side? They say he is a fighter."

"He's a blowhard, ma'am," Sparrow said. "But he does have one hell of a big army over there." Sparrow wiped his nose on his jacket sleeve. "But your husband and Bobby Lee will chase him. If he comes across the river, ma'am, we won't let him back over."

"Are you on the general's staff, Mr. Sparrow?" she asked. Sparrow laughed, saying, "No, I'm just a soldier. I just came along with Reverend Lacy to make sure you were all right, and to get out of camp for a while. And I'm glad I did, Mrs. Jackson. It's been a pleasure."

"Will you be near the general, when…when this begins?"

"We are in his corps, ma'am, so we'll be where it's hottest," Sparrow said, thinking too late what picture this might draw for the general's wife. But she did not seem nervous, and Sparrow decided not to try to give her any false reassurance. She knew her husband, and knew what risks he would take in a battle.

"Fight well, if it comes to that," Anna Jackson said to the two men. "Take care. Mr. Sutton, you have already taken a wound for the Confederacy, surely that must be enough. Stay out of harm's way, if you can."

Sutton nodded, and thanked her for her kindness. "But I'm afraid we're all in harm's way, aren't we, until we send this Yankee army back out of Virginia," she said.

They walked with her to the train, helping with her baggage. As she stepped up onto the car, Sutton said, "Travel safely. You're surely going back to a pretty country, Mrs. Jackson."

"It is pretty, Mr. Sutton, but it is not my home, not since I left it to be married. I miss the Valley, Mr. Sutton. Don't you?"

Sutton felt his throat catch and his chest constrict. He'd tried not to think much of his home since leaving the Valley after the fight at Port Republic. He could only nod to her, and whisper a blessing for her to himself. She looked at him intently, with her head tilted, thinking things she couldn't say to a stray soldier she'd just met and would never see again, then tipped her hat and turned into the car.

Sutton felt a twinge of loss as her skirt swept from his sight. He felt so weary, and nothing had really started yet.

As Anna Jackson's train pulled out of the station, thousands of men in blue started wading south across the fords of the Rapidan and Rappahannock rivers. Pouches full of powder and lead bounced on ranks of marching thighs.

Yet another round of horror coiled in the darkening woods.

The Wilderness, May 1, 1863—Confederate Army

Jeb Stuart was like a cat that ran because it just had to, skittering rugs across the wood floor as it turned, digging its claws, jumping quick to a chair or table and off again. Jeb Stuart rode. He exulted to see the mud kicked up by horses' hooves as his troops leaned into a turn, galloping. He was alive on a horse, and he had to run. He felt the jolting speed from his stirruped arches to his jaws as the horse beneath him, part of him, stretched and pumped and flew.

His breath was always shallow in battle. The excitement of a boy when things were just too good, mixed with the thrilling fear of punishment for things done wrong. Stuart wasn't fearless. Nor particularly afraid. When on a patrol, or a dash for his own lines, or hollering orders for cannon to unlimber, he was taut, strung like a bow. His breath couldn't reach the bottom of his chest, stayed just under his collarbones, trapped and stinging. He was nerved. He was tight as a drumskin. The only thing that eased him was speed, reckless headlong speed.

He loved to run. He had to run.

If not, it all might catch up with him. The terror. The splendor. The risk of all. The lilt. The lifting flood of emotion when he saw the enemy break and run. Made the enemy break and run. Back where they came from. Where they should never have left. But thank God they did. Or he wouldn't have this rushing, this riding of a tidal wave, this breaking crest that would fly him to perdition or to paradise. He didn't much care which, it seemed to him. It was the ride that mattered.

Stuart understood what Lee said, "It is well that war is so terrible; we should grow too fond of it." It was an addiction, heartier than opium. It took Stuart. So he rode to stay ahead of it. Just ahead.

This day, in the thick woods called The Wilderness west of Fredericksburg and south of the Rappahannock and Rapidan rivers, the armies of the United States of America and the Confederate States of America were moving into place around a crossroads at Chancellorsville. Stuart, long-haired, dashing, egotistical and brave, had ridden far to the west, where the Union line would end. The day had been lovely, the spring green riotous, the breezes from his run bracing and cool. The air was full of the electrical tension of gathering armies, and Stuart had transformed that building energy into speed through his legs and his horse's.

While running, he had found something so extraordinary that he had to bring it back and lay it before Lee. He knew what would happen. Lee would snatch it up like a hungry man grabs a piece of fresh bread. And he would hand it to Stuart's friend Jackson to wolf down.

And the Yankees would pay the bill.

Stuart had ridden in his favorite manner that day—wide-ranging, free of complex formations and plans, the cavalier loose on an adventure. Reconnaissance. Test and probe, peek and run. Dash and twirl and dash again. He had ridden around to the west of the huge Federal army that was spreading like a plague in the woods south of the Rappahannock River. Not around the whole army this time—he'd done that twice before, all the glorious way around, Yankees chasing him through occupied ground but unable to touch him as he flew with his men—but out beyond the lines, where the order and plan of the great strategists frayed away and unforeseen things always happened.

He had found opportunity—to grow more fond of war and at the same time end it. He had found an opening, a mistake, work undone, precautions not taken. He had found the right end of Hooker's lines left unprotected.

Armies when they chose ground and prepared for battle found some way to anchor the ends of their lines. Men in line facing forward could be defeated by shots from the side. Shifting 90 degrees under fire to confront and shoot at an enemy off to your side without shooting into the comrade in front of you was a difficult and time-consuming maneuver. So shots from the side—enfilade fire—could shatter an otherwise strong formation and send men running in terror. In the worst case, the line could be rolled up from the end, with fleeing men shattering nerves and formations down the line and making it all come apart.

To avoid this, the ends of lines were often anchored on natural obstacles, such as creeks or swamps or mountains. If these weren't available, the end of the line was at least curled back strongly so that some troops at the end faced 90 degrees to the side to guard against a flank attack.

But the Union troops of Oliver Otis Howard hadn't done this very well west of Chancellorsville. They'd made only a weak little curve at the end of the line, almost as an afterthought. But it wouldn't be enough. The rest of the line faced south, and nobody was paying much attention to what might come from the west. The Yankee army was so big, their lines were so long, Hooker's plan so strong, the Confederates could never match this menacing force.

Except here, where the line was weak, where the ponderous Yankee army was vulnerable as an animal's soft belly.

The sight made Stuart's heart rear and gallop.

Hooker's right was 'in the air.' A flank attack could roll right along the line, through the cook fires and soup kettles and stacked rifles and chatting soldiers and right up the ass of that blowhard Hooker. It would be wonderful. So delicious it would be sinful.

Stuart's grin split his thick red beard, he spurred his horse and the wind took the plume of his hat, and he flew. "Heeyah, let's go," he cried to his horse, and then he laughed into the wind.

Get some troops around this end. A lot of them. Fast marchers and hard hitters. That was Jackson.

His friend Jackson. They were a strange pair, people said. Stuart so flamboyant, Jackson so reserved. But, Stuart thought as he rode, he could always make Jackson laugh. He could break through. At Moss Neck, Jackson's winter quarters, Stuart had had such fun with Jackson, joking about his grand lodgings. A woman of the neighborhood had sent Jackson some butter for his table, and imprinted a game cock on the mound. Stuart had said, Look, General Jackson even adorns his butter with his family crest. Everyone had laughed, and Stuart had looked at Jackson, whose shoulders shook and face broadened and beamed with laughter. Laughter, like a child's. The man had playfulness inside him, and only Stuart, and children, and his wife Anna, could unlock it.

People didn't know what was inside that man, Stuart thought as he galloped back through the woods to find Robert E. Lee and change the course of the war.

Jackson's single-mindedness, his ferocity of purpose, was all locked on the Federal army. If they could bag them now, in these tangled woods, and trap them against the Rappahannock and press them to destruction, Jackson would put away war without a backward glance. Stuart, he knew himself, would miss it, would still want the aliveness that death so near sparked in him. But Jackson would let it go. And his gentleness would return as he went back, to his study, his work with the church, that Sunday school for blacks he ran, his wife and daughter. He would still be as wrapped up in God, but he would enjoy again the things of the world. The light on the mountains, the walks through Lexington, his garden, the yearning young men in his painful classes at VMI, a quiet meal at his own table.

It would almost be worth it, Stuart thought, to lose the glory war was to him so he could return this world to his friend Thomas Jackson. What a loss to the world of arms, to return Jackson to civilian life. The best soldier Stuart had ever known. But he would bring Lee and Jackson this gift of the Federal army weak and vulnerable. And he would see.

Stuart rode. He hummed to himself as the hooves below him pounded a clattering tattoo on the stony forest road. "Her bright smile haunts me still," he hummed. A lilting tune, a lifting ride.

Stuart rode, to bring the fearful force of war flashing out of this forest of second-growth trees so thick they could hide an army. So thick they could hide a victory. A victory that would end the war.

Stuart rode because he had to. To stay just ahead of it all, and to get fast to what came next.

He couldn't know, yet still somehow he knew, that in two years' time it would all catch up to him, at a little crossroads called Yellow Tavern a hard ride south of these woods tearing by.

It would catch up to so many in the years, and the days, ahead.

Chancellorsville, before dawn, May 2, 1863—Confederate Army

It was Jackson's supreme hour of greatness. It was breathtaking in its boldness. Many times he had marched around his enemies, suddenly appearing on their flank or their rear, casting them into confusion and fear.

This would be his finest, and his last, march.

Joseph Hooker's Union army curving from Fredericksburg up toward Chancellorsville was huge, 115,000 men to Lee's 60,000. Lee kept almost 12,000 of his men with Jubal Early guarding Fredricksburg, leaving his odds facing Hooker even longer.

Now, near the Chancellorsville crossroads west of Fredricksburg, the battle would come. Unlike Fredricksburg, with its stone wall and hill that had decimated the Union attack under Ambrose Burnside the winter before, this battle would be free form, amid hills and woods and clearings. In the beautiful Virginia countryside that had been wrapped in war for nearly two years. In the thick of the Wilderness.

Stuart, breathless, brought the word that Hooker's right was vulnerable. Jackson immediately proposed hitting it.

In the night, under a canopy of trees, sitting on a discarded Union cracker box by a little fire, Lee and Jackson conferred. The moment, though brief, became legend.

"How can we get at those people?" Lee, his voice low and rich and just short of eager, asked his most aggressive lieutenant. Jackson drew in the dirt in front of them with a stick, said he would swing far to the left on a flank march and come in behind the Union army. He had done it in the Valley, he had done it at Second Manassas. Lee knew he could do it here.

Quietly, calmly, Lee asked his most trusted lieutenant with what force he proposed making the march.

Jackson raised his head. "Why, with my whole corps," Jackson said. He looked in Lee's eyes. He saw there the briefest start, while his own eyes remained level and locked. Ever laconic, ever decisive. With those few words Jackson proposed taking two-thirds of Lee's forces at Chancellorsville away from the looming Federal army. Almost 33,000 men, leaving Lee only 15,000 to hold back the Federal host. A bare curtain against the impending storm.

Wood cracked in the fire and Lee's eyes caught the flame. Even Robert E. Lee, who risked so much so often with such calm, was stunned for a moment. With Early at Fredericksburg, he had already divided his army in the face of a superior enemy force. Now he would divide what remained, with 72,000 Federal soldiers right in front of him at Chancellorsville. It was unprecedented. Daring to the point of foolhardiness or genius.

Lee looked up from the fire at Jackson, read the resolve. Thought for only a brief moment, then gave a single nod. "Very well," he said, and it was unleashed.

A 12-mile march with an entire corps of men. The move that would shatter the Federals. And lose Lee his right arm.

Jackson stood. There was much to be done. Starting now. He stepped away, firmly. Then quickly stopped. He looked back at Lee, still sitting by the fire. The two men stared at each other. They both knew what they held in their hands—or almost held, if they could reach out and seize it. Jackson's lean features showed no movement. But his eyes were bright. Reluctant to part, yet with hearts racing at what might be, they held the moment and each other's gaze. Then Lee nodded again. Jackson pursed his lips together, slapped his gloves once on his thigh, turned and walked off.

He got from Jed Hotchkiss, his mapmaker, a view of the land. He got from Rev. Tucker Lacy, his chaplain who had preached in the area, information on the roads. Lacy found him a local guide. A few hours later, at his favorite hour, "earliest dawn," Jackson started his men.

On the march, Jackson's men came under cannon fire early on, and in one opening in the woods were attacked by Union General Dan Sickles' corps. But Lee's other troops, Stuart's cavalry, and the cover of trees protected them, and they shrugged off the challenge and kept walking. Jackson's foot cavalry from the Valley, striding at the Union army's weakest point. Again.

Seeing the troops in motion, General Joseph Hooker, the Union commander, convinced himself that the Confederates moving south and west were retreating. It's what he would have done against such odds. But he wasn't Lee. And he wasn't Jackson. Even if he could imagine such a risk, he'd never take it. Although pickets reported movement in the woods, Hooker couldn't understand what it meant. Although the war's own near history should have taught him the move, he didn't catch it.

And he paid. And his men paid. And the north came within a few musket shots of losing the war.

The woods west of Chancellorsville, May 2, 1863— Confederate Army

The march had been strangely peaceful. At the beginning, Sutton had just been tired, and that was true of most of the men around him in the Carolina regiment. They were quiet, moving because they were told, not knowing, as always with Jackson, where they were going.

They headed west toward a little settlement called Catharine Furnace, waded across a shallow creek called Lewis' Run, then dipped to their left, marching steadily southwest. Away from Hooker. They walked, most of them, with their heads down, like pack animals, just plodding to get to the end.

Where the road from Catharine Furnace intersected the Brock Road, they turned left, south, exactly away from the masses of Federal troops that had crossed the Rappahannock and the Rapidan to get at them. Some of the men were confounded. Were they retreating? What had happened to Jackson? A few said that when Jackson retreated there was always trouble in it for the Yankees, because he was just finding a good place to turn on his pursuers. Others said Jackson and Lee must be giving in to the superior numbers Hooker had crossed the rivers with, that Jackson was moving south to find a better day to fight. Quite a few didn't care a damn, just walked in a trance that two years of war had made familiar to them. The marching would never end, the shooting would never finish it, and all most wanted to do was stay alive and please God get some decent food.

Then, after a short time going south on the Brock Road, the column turned to the right, into a little trace that wound westward through the trees. Thin trees, many of them, second growth because so much wood had been cut for the furnace that made iron, but the place was thick with them. The flat ground between the trees was strewn with fallen branches, rotted leaves, thick under-brush going green with the lengthening spring. Small animals rustled away, snakes slid off the little road, birds lifted and fell in dipping flight.

And as the trace turned right to the northwest, and then to true north, heads lifted, faces looked inquiringly at one another, eyebrows raised in question, then thin smiles stretched across the lined skin of the men's countenances.

Heads nodded now. Steps quickened. Packs were shifted between shoulders squaring with awakening strength.

"Here we go."

"We're in for it now."

"More Hooker is."

Sutton felt himself straightening, standing taller as if after a nap when blood starts to flow to your limbs again like water gathering from rainfall and then running together to move, unstoppable.

A man next to him said through a stick he was chewing like a tobacco plug, "The Old Blue Light is lit, boys."

Soft laughter poked through the huffing breaths of faster walking.

"He's a sly one, Old Jack."

The rattle of canteens and bayonets and buckles grew, pants legs slished together, ragged boots kicked small stones clicking across the dirt.

These men, Jackson's foot cavalry, had been here before. Not in this particular overgrown woods, but on this edge of excitement. Racing past the flank of slow Northern boys held back by slower generals. Sliding through the hole left between Fremont and Shields in the lower Valley, across the rising ground and over the bridge at Port Republic, up the Rapidan and through Manassas Gap to perch like a spreading eagle on the bloody shoulders of the too-slow too-timid too-bewildered prey.

The men said there was a battle light in Jackson's eyes at times like these. It kindled their own.

"We're going around his right," a man said, a smile bunching around his eyes.

"Old Jack will march us almost to the Valley again, hell almost to the Ohio," another said, his tone between complaining and wonder.

"But we're getting around Hooker."

"You think so?"

"Sure as day, brother, we're outfoxing him."

"You don't think he knows we're out here?"

"Would have tried to hit us if he did, all spread out like we are."

"We're gonna get him?"

"We're going to bring him hell, friend. Drop it in his lap while he's sitting there counting his troops."

Union General Joseph Hooker had in fact accomplished one of the great marches of the war, pulling his huge army corps by corps away from Lee's front at Fredericksburg, crossing two rivers and dropping down on Lee's left flank and rear without Lee at first having an inkling of the danger. Hooker's men had been pouring south for two days before Lee caught wind of it. Destruction hovered behind Lee's left shoulder.

Then Hooker paused. He wanted Lee to attack him on ground of his choosing. But bad coordination, bad telegraphy, bad orders and bad ground kept him from pulling his forces together in the strongest combination and cost him the initiative. Lee started shifting around to face him, and Lee and Jackson conceived of this counter flanking move. It was like two fighters twirling around each other, one shifting behind the other's left, the other then dancing around behind the first one's right. The knives were out and flashing as they whirled. The first to strike behind the arm and up between the exposed ribs would have the day.

"You think he won't be ready?"

"He was out here two days before we knew it, now we're sliding in behind him before he knows. And we'll move, that's the difference between old Joe and Old Jack. Jack will hit him, and then the ball will open and we will lead him to the ground."

Sutton thought they were too sure. It might not happen like that at all. But as he marched he couldn't quell a hopeful feeling. Maybe this time they could do mortal damage.

The early morning had started cold, but now it was a lovely day. Recent rains had laid the dust on the roads, not enough to make them muddy but enough to keep the dust out of the soldier's lungs and to keep down the telltale sign of a marching column that might alert the Federals.

The men marched four abreast because the roads were so narrow. They walked hard for 25 minutes, covering a mile, then rested for 10 minutes. They stopped at midday for a skimpy meal—15 minutes. Jeb Stuart's cavalry covered the column's right flank, but no scouts rode ahead. Jackson would let nothing show Hooker what was coming.

Once, Sutton saw a commotion up ahead. Riders were coming back along the column. "It's Old Jack," a man said, and it was. Sutton could barely see him, could just make out the fresh new uniform, the tilted forage cap low over his brow. The men were not allowed to cheer, but Sutton saw, row by row rolling like a wave, battered hats and caps lifting off the marching soldiers' heads as they gave their tribute to their general. Jackson lifted his cap in return salute, turned and galloped toward the front on Little Sorrel.

The excitement passed, and the men settled into their pace. Sutton felt a pressure growing like heat inside his breast. Fear, anticipation, a sense of forces pulling him beyond his own control.

This part of Virginia wasn't like the Shenandoah Valley, Sutton's home. Or once his home. It was flat out here, lots of ground covered by forests. Little streams. Pretty enough, but in a funny way he felt closed in. The mountains of the Valley gave his eyes something to rest on, drew his vision up to the green crests. Here, everything was right in front of you. Trees right in your face, maybe a clearing and then more trees. He thought about the Valley as he walked. Missed it.

Pebbles had snuck into his left shoe. The men were striding so fast he didn't think he could take the time to get them out. Didn't want to fall behind. He kept walking, but the things were rubbing him raw.

"I've got to get stones out of my shoe," he told the man marching next to him. "I'll catch back up."

"Sure, suit yourself," the man said, and Sutton, slightly ashamed, was sure the man thought he was ducking out. Sutton skipped over to the right side of the narrow road, lowered his musket and sat down, reaching for the laces of his shoe.

Around him were stragglers. Men who had given out. Some would rest a bit, then get up and press on. Others were done, at least for the day. Some would never rejoin the army, Sutton knew. He'd heard about an underground railroad of Union sympathizers that helped Confederate soldiers get through the lines and to the North when they wanted to desert. He understood that in his bones and his feet, but not really in his soul. Fighting these people for so long, and then give up?

He tipped his worn brogan up and shook out the stones. His foot was red. Hurt. At least he had shoes, he thought. A lot didn't.

He tightened the laces, then felt suddenly very tired. He shouldn't have stopped; it was hard to get up now. He looked around, saw two men stretched on their bellies on the side of the road, asleep. Just beyond, a long, thin man lay curled up on his side, his arms around his knees, his face pressed into the dirt. Near him, another man—big—sat leaning against a tree, inert like a sack of flour. A short man with spectacles was trying to talk to him, but the sitting man was just staring, not reacting at all. The man's face drooped, his mouth hung open, his eyes didn't move, were vacant. The short man pulled at his sleeve, but couldn't stir the sitting man. The short man looked around at the marching column, fear and confusion in his face.

Sutton looked more closely, started, his chest jumping, his vision focusing on the sitting man's face. It was Sparrow. James Sparrow, his friend from the Valley, the man he'd talked to Jackson's wife with just a couple of days ago at the train station. What was wrong? Was he hurt?

He stepped quickly over to Sparrow, asked the short man what was happening.

"The sergeant, he's played out," the man said, agitated. "Just came over here and sat down, almost fell, didn't say anything. I can't get him to move."

"When?"

"About 15 minutes ago. We got to get going. Our regiment's way up there," he said, pointing forward.

"I know this man," Sutton said. "Jimmy, Jimmy, how are you, boy?" he said to Sparrow. Nothing registered on Sparrow's face.

"Can you get him going?" the man asked. Sutton knelt by Sparrow, touched him on the shoulder. Still nothing. "You go ahead," he said to the other man. "I'll stay here 'til he comes around."

"All right, mister, you gotta get him back to us. He's never done this before. We're going into a fight and we need him. Tell him." He looked at Sparrow, wiped at his forehead with his palm, then turned back to the marching men and trotted away.

Sutton sat down in front of Sparrow.

"Hey, old man," he said softly.

Sparrow blinked slowly. Swallowed. Said nothing. The blink made Sutton think at least Sparrow had heard him. Maybe knew it was him.

"It's me, Will. You rest."

Sparrow didn't move. But he sighed.

"Long way to walk, Jimmy. But it's a nice day for a stroll. Did you get tired of the scenery? Or the company?" Sutton ran his hand up and down Sparrow's left sleeve lightly as he talked.

"Too bad about that Federal army out there, it would be a much nicer neighborhood if they were back in Philadelphia or New York or wherever they were spawned." Sutton talked softly. "Say, you want some biscuits? Some boys in my mess had a contest to see who could make the best biscuits. I think some used dirt because we didn't have much flour, but some of them turned out all right." He dug in his haversack, pulled out a dull brown glob, held it up.

Sparrow moved his eyes, flat as the biscuit, then moved them away again. Moved his head about half an inch, left, then right, slow as if it were rock.

"I don't blame you. Maybe we'll get some better food up there, from the Yankee commissary. You're coming, aren't you?"

Sparrow tipped his head back farther against the tree, closed his eyes, breathed in slowly through his nose. Then a short shallow groan.

"Tired," he said, so low Sutton barely caught it.

Sutton looked at his friend's face, nodded. Sparrow was pale, his eyes sunken, the flesh of his face slack and soft like the faces of dead men Sutton had seen.

"That's right, you've earned tired," Sutton said. "Jimmy, everybody leans on you like you lean on that tree. It's your turn to be tired. It's all right, now, you rest a bit. Then we'll get going."

Sutton took out his canteen, tried to put it in Sparrow's hand. The fingers didn't move. Sutton left it there, resting on Sparrow's curved still hand. They sat quietly for several minutes, behind them the noise of the marching men a steady shuffle in their ears.

Sparrow turned his head a little, slowly, so he could look at Sutton. He stared for awhile, as if focusing slowly. His broad, normally open face looked strained. He said, with effort, "'S'worse. Scared."

Sutton looked back at him, understanding but not knowing what to say.

"Scared. Will. I'm…scared." Sparrow kept looking at Sutton, wanting him to hear.

Sutton thought. Some men would find it easy to say they were scared, all the hell they'd been through and all the hell the war still promised, including a fair ration of it waiting just up this pretty little road. But Sparrow had always been a big bluff jovial man, the kind who kept things light and seemed to spit in fate's eye.

So he knew he was hearing from deep within James Sparrow. The laughing defense was gone. Something had stripped away the barricade Sparrow had built around him. Maybe just all the marching had worn him down, or all the burying of men who died in camp of typhoid or dysentery. All the parts of men ripped off in bloody flensing rips. Maybe just all the days and nights of a war that would never end. Something had worn through to Sparrow's soul. And it was bleeding, here by another track for Stonewall's foot cavalry.

Sutton put his hand on Sparrow's knee. "Jimmy, what we're doing here, we'd all be fools not to be scared as hogs in fall." He stopped, wet his lips. "We're scared. That's what we live in. And it's tiring as hell. But we walk through it. Because there's nothing else to do. But maybe you can't do it this time."

Nodding, Sparrow grunted.

"Jimmy, you keep everybody else going all the time. You're cheerful, you make us laugh, you poke at us."

"Yeah," Sparrow said, his croaking voice surprising Sutton. And it took a toll, Sparrow thought, but he couldn't tell Sutton that.

"That's hard work, my friend," Sutton said, his thoughts going where Sparrow's were. "You keep the fear away from us by laughing, by making us think of other things. You do the work for us and maybe now you don't have enough left for yourself."

"I, Will, I got nothing." The voice ragged, worn through like threadbare cloth.

"Yes, I don't blame you," Sutton said, nodding.

Sparrow rolled his head so he could look straight at Sutton. Words came now, several in a row. "Back there, a shell burst near us as we walked. Nothing too bad. Happened a hundred times before. But this one. Wasn't even that close." He swallowed hard, Sutton lifted the canteen to his lips, Sparrow drank, Sutton poured some water in his cupped hand and rubbed it on Sparrow's forehead. "But it blew up and, and it broke me. It was like something started to leak out of me. Like those observation balloons across the river, like air going out of one of those."

Sutton nodded, raised the canteen to Sparrow's face again. He was glad Sparrow was talking, and wanted to keep him going, keep him engaged. This time Sparrow took the canteen in his own hand, drank, coughed, sat up straighter, shook his big frame and twisted his butt around on the ground for a more comfortable position.

"Aw, Will, I just, I just got so tired. More than tired. Sick of this all." His voice sagged. Sparrow looked beyond Sutton, saw the marching men as if for the first time, raised his eyebrows and shook his head.

Looking back at Sutton, he said, "And scared, Will." He said it low, his head down but his eyes looking up at Sutton. "Scared, so I can't move."

When Sutton didn't say anything, Sparrow went on. "This happened once before to me, Will," he said, sitting farther forward, pressing his hands into his back. "Before Port Republic, in the Valley. I never told anybody. Got scared the night before, but I talked myself out of it." He looked down. "I don't think I can this time."

"You scared to die?" Sutton asked.

"I don't know. I'm just scared of moving."

"That shell, it didn't hit you, back there when it exploded?"

"No," Sparrow said. "A piece bounced off me, still hot, and another fragment cut a man next to me. It didn't hurt me, but it...it knocked me, it sucked my courage out, I don't know, it scared hell out of me." He closed his eyes, rubbed absently at his foot, kept talking.

"I walked, I kept marching, but some of me was knocked back, to September, to Second Manassas, a fight so bad…you weren't there, you were in Carolina, recuperating, so you don't know what we went through." His eyes were still closed, but he had stopped all motion and he was back somewhere Sutton hadn't been. "I don't know why it reminded me of that battle, but it kicked me right back to the railroad cut where the firing was so hot. I couldn't shake it. Kept walking, like in a fog, and couldn't shake what I'd seen, back then." Sparrow was quiet for a moment, and they could hear the sounds of men on the road, occasionally stumbling and swearing, a few talking eagerly of what they would do when they got the drop on Hooker.

"We're stealing a march sure," a voice on the road said.

"Won't those Yanks be surprised?" another responded.

"If only they're not waiting for us," a third said.

"If they are I'm just tipping my hat and going home," someone else said, and there was laughter.

Sparrow's voice came back at Sutton's side. "We started that fight up on a ridge above Groveton. We came out and showed ourselves, just a little, like a tease, to the Yankees marching by on the Warrenton Pike below. Rufus King's men, New Yorkers, I think it was. We showed ourselves, like to tell them their time was up. Lobbed some shells at them. And then it started." Sparrow stopped, his head fallen down on his chest again.

"Tell me, Jimmy." Odd to be sitting here, another great march going on around them, armies moving for the kill, and we two just talking, Sutton thought. But that's what's needed now. I've got to let him go through it, or he'll never come out the other side. This man has pulled us along, I can pull him now. Or try to.

An officer yelled at them, "Come on, get back in line, no skulking." Sutton waved his hand away, nodded, signaled that they'd come. The officer walked over and kicked one of the sleeping men. "Move, you son of a bitch, get up and fight with the rest of us." The man didn't move, and the officer walked on.

"What happened, Jimmy?"

Sparrow looked up, his eyes clouded. He wasn't just remembering, he was seeing it again. Full color. "Well, they hit us back. It was hard, hours of fighting, and they shoved us back into the woods. We holed up there like badgers." He plucked at the canteen. "That ground up there, it's all broken up, trees everywhere, skinny, tall, the ground a mess. But we got back to a railroad cut, no tracks laid yet, they hadn't finished building it. Gave us cover. Some places just a trench, some places a mound, or a long ridge, where the rails would go eventually, maybe six, eight feet high in one place. We clung to it."

Sutton was kneeling in front of Sparrow, trying to block out the columns of men marching behind. He looked over his shoulder, saw men like a great snake moving, water beyond the road, a little flooded spot sparkling between the thin poles of the trees. He looked back at Sparrow, whose eyes were looking at the ground.

"The Yankees were coming through the trees, couldn't come in formation because of the trees and little runs of water. Moved like a mob, coming right at us. We said wait to fire until we could see their faces. And they came, and, Will, I could see their faces. Beards and lips and…fear. I looked into their eyes as they came up to our little high ground. And then we shot them down."

Nothing more came. Sutton said, "You've shot men before, Jimmy."

Sparrow gave a low "hmmm" of agreement. "But this was, so cold. It was like they were walking through the woods, looking for something. Like they were going to discover something, maybe just a good place to camp, some fresh water. We looked into their eyes and shot them down."

Sparrow laughed a little, a sound without humor. "It was all angles and lines. That's the picture I kept seeing just now as I walked. Like a geometry lesson. The long lines of the rifles as we swing them up, a whole long row of them in line, it seemed to go slowly, and then those long rifles went down at the barrel to lower so we could fire down at the Yankees. Then there'd be a jerk and shudder as the pieces were fired and another line would shoot out, from the muzzle. The fire spit out in a line, and you could almost see the line the bullet traveled. The Yankees were so close it was like the flight of the bullet wasn't much longer than the length of the gun, so there's another line as it shivvers into some poor man's breast and jerks him down, right on the same line, same angle, he falls at exactly the angle the gun was held. All lines." It was there, before Sparrow's eyes again.

"The line of the railroad cut, the line of the incline they tried to come up to get us, maybe just eight feet, but like a mountain when there's those lines, those guns, pointing right at them as they tried to climb. They'd slip on the fallen leaves, wet and moldy. You couldn't tell if they were falling because they'd slipped or because they'd been shot. But they went down, rolled, broke. I don't know why those lines stay with me.

"It went on for a long time. Men, our men, were falling all around too. We fought like animals backed up against their den." He stopped talking again. Then, "We ran out of ammunition. Grabbed more from the cartridge boxes of men who'd been shot. And then it was rocks." He laughed again, still mirthless. "Rocks. I saw Jackson at one point, standing behind us. 'Give them the bayonet,' he yelled. Will, I've never seen a Yankee stuck on a bayonet. But I saw some that day get their heads crushed with rocks."

He stared now at his open hands, his head moving side to side.

"I saw Jackson standing there, arms wrapped around, chin down, peering into the smoke like Old Scratch."

He looked up at Sutton. "That scared me worst of all. That man. Smoke all around, ripping sheets of it, drifting. And he's staring like he's trying to kindle a fire with his eyes.

"He's getting worse. Something. He's getting in deeper. Throwing bigger pieces at the Yankees. He was moving a big corps through those woods, squeezing them through like meat through a grinder. In the Valley the battles were never this big. Now he's going more full out, putting bigger pieces in the fire. Moving larger forces."

Sutton felt a flicker of dread.

"That's what scares me now, Will. Each time it's getting bigger. Something monstrous is going to happen. I feel it all moving now, it's like the ground is moving now. He's pushing more and more, like a beast that can never satisfy its hunger. What's going to happen this time? This one's big. We'll all be pulled in. To this pit. This pit of fire." The last words were soft, and that was it. Sparrow had said what was inside him, what was pushing up inside of him.

Sutton nibbled on the edge of the biscuit he still held. Spit out a piece of something, a twig. Sparrow's image of Jackson hung in his mind. Of bigger forces moving. And since Second Manassas there had been the horror by Antietam Creek, and the bodies piled up at Fredericksburg. Bigger all the time, more fuel piled on the fire. More forces pulling in to some dark center. They were moving just behind the two men, the long column on the road.

"It is getting bigger, Jimmy," he said, softly. "I think that's what it's going to take. The people who thought the war would be short were wrong. From the beginning. I think we all knew that. The Yankees' pride won't let them give in. It's going to take something—enormous."

And it was going to take Jackson. Pushing them all. Putting in everything he had. Everything they had.

Sutton was torn. He wanted to send his friend away, to someplace calm. To patch himself back together. To grow over the wounded places.

But there just wasn't time. Sparrow was right. Something big was coming together here.

"This will end, Jimmy, but not until we end it. They're not going to give up. We have to finish it," Sutton said.

He looked at his friend. Wished he was sitting on a porch somewhere. Wished they both were.

But this river was pulling, speeding up, running toward fast water at the rocks. It was going to take them all.

"Jackson's going to kill us all," Sparrow said, his voice low, sad, sure.

"No. He's going to kill a lot of Yankees. Enough to end it. Maybe today, Jimmy. You need to be there."

Was that true? Sparrow could just fade away into the woods. Many did. They stayed away from the battle, came back later with lies, some with shame, some without. Sparrow didn't need to be part of this one.

Was it that Sutton needed Sparrow to be in it?

Shouldn't he want his friend safe, away?

They weren't even in the same regiment anymore, wouldn't even fight together. But Sutton realized he wanted Sparrow to want to be there. Something was wrong if he didn't. Not just with him, but with the whole thing.

Something would be wrong inside Sutton.

And it was more than that. What if they fell short by just a little? One man, Sparrow, couldn't make any difference. But Sparrow led. Sparrow lifted. Sparrow helped men throw themselves into the fight. That could make a difference.

Sutton thought he'd try. Try to make Sparrow see what he saw. What Sutton had felt when he was back in North Carolina hearing about the fights Sparrow had been in. What made Sutton come back to the army.

He'd try, and then he'd let it go.

"Listen to me now Jimmy." Sutton sat back on his haunches, gathered himself. Started to say what was inside him.

"There's a man up there who needs you to get up and walk toward those Yankees. Now I don't know, exactly, why that should matter to us, what Old Jack wants. I laid there with my blood pouring into the Shenandoah soil and wondered that myself last year. I'm not certain I came up with the right answer. And I had to go away to let it all settle in my mind, because I was where you are now. It wasn't just that I was wounded. It's that something had gone out of me. But I kept thinking what it was that Jackson was doing. And it pulled me back.

"He wasn't putting his arm around our shoulders. He wasn't giving us glorious speeches about patriotism and right and might. He wasn't telling us that he was our friend and that he was looking out for us. He wasn't telling us that the other side was evil, that those men who fought for the North were bad men who needed killing. He wasn't telling us anything. He just looked at us with those cold steel eyes and pulled us to our feet with the magnetism of his own will. His own certainty. That this road was the road that Washington walked. And that if we were to have a free country and be free men we had to walk it too. And we had to walk it long and damned fast so we could hit them where they are most vulnerable, least ready, so that we could have an end to this.

"He walked us straight into the hottest fire so that we could quench it. He didn't flinch, he didn't equivocate, didn't tell us it would be all right, he just saw where he needed to go and he went. And he expected that others would see the same thing and do the same. Just go, along with him. As simple as that. Hard and fast and brutal. So that we could have done with this, and have our country. Not run by anyone else. Not occupied by anyone else. Not anyone else's but ours. And if we made mistakes in how we ran our country, why then they'd be our mistakes and we'd have to deal with them. By our own lights, with our own way of stumbling toward what's right. And he had such certainty, he *has* such certainty, that he would not allow you to drift outside of his magnetism. You could choose not to be there, you could choose not to be part of his orbit, and then he would leave you behind without a thought and go on with what he had. But if you were part of his, his solar system, then you would be pulled along by him and you could not stray any more than the earth can stray from the pull of the sun that holds it fixed on its course."

Sparrow was looking at him now.

"That man is a river, and once you lay down in those waters you are the river's and the river will pull you rushing to the sea," Sutton said. "That man is a force, that man is a law of natural science and you cannot escape his gravity.

"Because he will have this, Jimmy. This victory. He will have this moment of watching the Yankees running tattered and broken and bleeding across the last river of Virginia, and then he will lay down his sword and he will kneel in the soil of Virginia and he will weep with the wounded and the widowed and he will let you free. Only then, he will let you free."

Sutton stopped. He breathed fast, shallow breaths. Never in his life had he said so many words at once. Never in his life had he given a speech. And only two men heard this. James Sparrow, and William Sutton. And they both felt it hit deeply inside them. And they were both surprised by it. And they both knew it was true.

"Jimmy, you've got to stand up and walk toward those Yankees. And you've got to help the rest of us make that walk. You've got to help me, Jimmy." Sutton wasn't pleading, although he very deeply felt he needed Sparrow to come. He was just stating a fact, of the war, of comradeship, of what it was like being in Jackson's corps. "Jackson's pulling at you, with the strength of that vision of those people crossing the river. He's pulling at me, and we've got to go now. Now."

Sutton stood up. He had thought he would just let Sparrow go. But he couldn't. He had to do this. He held his hand down toward Sparrow. "Jimmy, I'm marching with you. We've got to go. Now. We'll do this together. We'll go. Both of us. I need you."

And Sparrow, looking up, with no words left, reached up to Sutton's hand, grunted as he lifted his bulk from the ground, wavered on his feet for a moment, reached down and slung the strap of his rifle over his shoulder and lifted his knapsack to his back and faced north. And took one step, and then another, next to Sutton, and then they went.

"He's going to kill us, Will," Sparrow said, but he walked. Sutton didn't say anything more. He knew there'd be killing enough. And whoever made it through might see a different world. For now, they just walked.

Hours later, as the sun lowered in the west and Sutton and Sparrow and thousands of others came to the end of their march and the beginning of their lightning strike, the German soldiers under Union General Oliver Howard would look up from their cards and their ease and their fresh beef cooking and see rabbits and deer racing out of the forest from the west. And behind them, where they couldn't be, Jackson's men.

Chancellorsville, May 2, 1863, 6 p.m.—Confederate Army

It was a rout. Exhilaration poured through Alston Powell, once a baker from Valdosta, now a rifleman in the Georgia brigade that led the assault on Howard's German troops who had thought the battle was miles away from them on this suddenly awful afternoon. Powell's chest was huge, his feet were flying over the ground, knees bent then straightening pumping like pistons branches slapping at his face his arms smoke wafting past him as if he ran through dirty clouds while a scream ripped from his throat no thought just go and go and go and push them into the river. He'd fired his musket a hundred yards back, not aiming just pushing it at the blue of the coats of the men running away from this explosive charge of Jackson's. He thought he should reload, he didn't have his bayonet on, but he just kept running, swept along by the massed rolling yells of the men all around him.

He ran, leaped a log, crashed into vines hanging from the branches, slashed with his gun, spun and tripped and fingers on the leafy earth ran ahead right out of the fall to keep up the chase. Keep them going, don't let the Yankees stop. It's ours now, we'll flush you from these woods and shoot you as you fly.

Ahead, men in blue hopped over fallen trees, darted through the thickets, only a few turned and fired, a puff of smoke and then they wheeled and ran on faster than they'd ever run before. He could hear no noise from those men, only the yelling from the others around him, the Yankees' run was grim while the

Southerners screamed their thrill at seeing the blue boys go. The frustration of having Yankees in Virginia for so long was streaming out of them now in screams and taunts and the high banshee hunting cry of the warbling Rebel yell.

"Come on Yank, I'm going to have them pants," one Southerner hollered, and others laughed as they ran. Dead Yankees meant new clothes for the ragged Southern soldiers.

"Run out of them boots, sojer, save me killin' you for 'em."

"You're ours now!"

"Go on, skedaddle home to hell," to more screeching laughter.

And they ran.

Powell's lungs felt like they were tearing from his breastbone and finally he stopped, stumbling to break his momentum, his thighs trembling and hot inside like brake pads scorched on an iron wheel. He fell to his knees and ripped open his cartridge box, bit into a paper tube, stuffed powder, ball and wadding down the barrel, pointed the gun forward and stood on shaking legs. To his right he saw men from his brigade running on a road, unimpeded by the thick woods of the Wilderness, and Powell crossed through the trees and reached the road. The afternoon sunlight was pouring low from behind him, making the leaves glow where he looked above. Smoke drifted ahead and men ran in front of him and Powell couldn't see very far down the road. But he knew the Yankees were there and that they hadn't turned to fight back hard yet and that if he just kept running maybe they never would.

Then he heard a lower pitch of yelling, the Confederates ahead hollering something surprised back behind them, and then men were pitching headfirst off the road to right and left as if the turnpike had risen in the middle and tossed them off like a bucking horse. Nothing registered in his head, he had no idea what was happening, not even when he saw ahead now in a clearing down the road a small gang of men in blue beside two cannon wheel to wheel in the middle of the turnpike. He couldn't put together what it meant not even when greyish smoke cascaded out of one barrel and men ahead of him were spun and slashed and flung backward and then the sound of something whipping past his ear and something slapping against leaves and smacking against trees and then Powell knew that the Yankees had fired a cannon straight down the road at the running Confederates and he froze and stopped and slammed down on his butt sitting in the middle of the road and watching the group of bluecoats doing something at the back of the second cannon. His hand was on his rifle which was standing straight up like a lance, his mouth was open and there was no noise coming out of it, only spittle flicking from his lips as his breath huffed in and out.

"Down!" someone yelled.

"Get the hell off the road!" Noises behind Powell, feet pounding, equipment rattling, men swearing.

"Yankee cannon dammit."

Smoke again, billowing thick from the second cannon, a flash of bright yellow in the midst and more metal flying.

"AAAAH-eeeee" a scream tearing through the woods. Men were running sideways now ahead of him, ducking low and diving into the woods. A man hunching off the road about 50 feet in front of Powell flung his left arm up in a splash of red and the arm and part of his face came off, pieces of him bright in midair in the horizontal sunlight. Powell ducked his head and pulled himself into a ball and started to roll as stones jumped sparking on the ground around him. The front corner of his coat was ripped backwards as a grapeshot ball tore through it and Powell kept rolling toward a thick tree at the side of the road. He heard again branches snapping and the thwack of metal hitting men and his ears were ringing from a roar he hadn't known he was hearing. He reached the tree and said "Thank you Jesus" and he closed his eyes and waited for the world to end.

One more cannon blast—enormous, crushing the air and stomping the ground—and Powell could feel the tree he lay curled behind quiver as metal thocked into it, he heard fast painful expulsions of breath behind him as men were hit, he held his head with both hands and pressed his face into the leafy moldy earth and a beetle crawled in his mouth and he spat that and dirt and twigs out and he pressed his forehead to his knees.

"Get goin', that'll lay those fuckers down for awhile, now roll that goddam gun," a harsh voice yelled from up the road, and rifle fire crackled from the Yankees as they shot to keep their pursuers from standing up again as the cannon rolled away.

"Let's go!" someone near Powell yelled. But no one moved.

Off to the right, a man was crying.

Ahead, a voice called out, "Jamie, I been hit, it's bad, God it's my guts and my chest, Jamie, Jesus, come on here."

There was firing off to both sides, and men yelling, but nothing here where the cannons had stopped the Southern charge cold.

Powell rolled over on his hands and knees, peered around the tree. Smoke, as if the forest were on fire. Drifting, it turned tree trunks to shadows then consumed them whole. A few men on their knees, some lying on the ground, a hand up or a leg bent. Some lying, flat, as if tossed away.

Powell noticed he was shaking. He didn't have his rifle—saw it now on the road. He started to go after it but found he couldn't leave the lee side of the tree. But he had to move. With his hands flat against the trunk, he sidestepped three, four times to get on the road side of the tree. His right hand slid over something rough, splinters jabbed his hand. He looked, and saw the bark of the tree had been shattered, as if chewed, by the grapeshot. Powell closed his eyes, pushed away from the tree, took a halting step, then another, then rushed into the road and knelt by his rifle, picked it up and loped back to his tree.

His breathing was shallow. He looked around. Men were looking at each other, as if waiting for a signal. Everybody was leaning, but nobody was moving.

Powell tried to think. To calm himself. He was more afraid here than he'd been in other battles, where the firing had gone on for what seemed like hours. Why? Why was this so bad? At Manassas, he'd known what was coming, that's what he figured. He was marching against troops he could see, could see they were shooting at him, and he expected they would be. It was frightening, but he just trudged ahead and shot back at them. He knew what was happening, had time to prepare himself, even just a moment, as he walked into the battle.

Here, he'd been running, elated, chasing men who were overwhelmed by the surprise of the flank attack, and no one expected them to turn around. Even though, if any of them had thought for a second they would have known that's what trained troops would do, that eventually they'd try to hold some ground. But no one thought, they just ran, pent-up anger and excitement and fear and relief flooding through them as they saw the Federals take off like frightened rabbits. And then, slam, it turned in less than a heartbeat and suddenly now they were the prey, in the sights of those huge brass guns. The soaring emotions slammed to the ground like a bird shot in midflight. Fear had smashed him like a bludgeon.

He looked around again. The others still watched, the road, their comrades. Powell no longer felt his heart would explode. He walked away from the tree.

"Let's be after them, then," said a short sergeant with a face half hidden by a red beard. Powell didn't recognize him; so many units were mixed together by the speed of the attack and the thickness of the woods. This time a few men started to walk back into the road.

"Not thataway," a man holding a red spot on his shirt sleeve said. "I'm staying off that derned road."

A small group came toward where Powell was standing and started moving forward, 20 yards off the road. "What about them that's hurt?" the man bleeding from the arm said, tucking his rifle beneath his good arm.

"Stretcher boys will come behind us," the sergeant said. "Let's go after those Hessian bastards. Come on."

A last look around by Powell and a few others, and the group began to move. Powell built up to a trot, wary now, no joy, no lift to him, just a run toward his duty and the hope that this might end it. To his right, across the road and through the woods, heavy firing. Ahead, nothing. But somewhere in the thickets up there those cannon were waiting again. Powell ran, making no noise this time except the sound of the breath whistling in and out of his mouth.

It was getting darker in the Wilderness, shadows touching and embracing into a thickening gloom.

Not far behind the Georgians, Captain Robert Wilbourn, Jackson's signalman, saw a strangely peaceful sight. He'd seen Jackson's eyes glow with increasing intensity as the attack rolled through the woods around the Orange Turnpike, seen Jackson lean from his saddle and shake the hand of a major who was firing canister shot up the road with his horse battery. Then, as the attack rolled on, and Wilbourn could hear cheering from the troops ahead, he looked over his shoulder and saw Jackson slowly raise his right hand in the air, stopping Little Sorrel for a moment as he gave thanks to the God whom the general was sure was guiding the victory.

Then, quickly, the peace was over, the hand came down, the general leaned forward and slashed his hand out over his horse's head as if trying to reach the retreating Federals and called out, "Press them, press on," and Wilbourn spurred his horse to keep up as they all surged forward.

South of Luray in the Valley, May 2, 1863, dusk

It had been a very pretty spring. The flanks of the Massanutten in front of the Verner home, and the Blue Ridge behind, were soft again with new green. Trees blossomed with flowers, dogwoods and redbuds randomly decorating the forests with vivid color. The azaleas in the front yard were heavy with white, like lush silk lace spun in stunning profusion on the drooping low branches.

The beauty was mocking. Bettie Verner stood on the front veranda, her spirit unlifted by the land's slow glide into summer.

Few soldiers had been in the Valley lately. But little of normal life had passed this winter.

There had been a few parties, but no one felt light enough for much celebration. Talk was low, smiles forced.

The nation was shrinking. New Orleans gone, much of Tennessee, most of the Atlantic coast.

Death had claimed so many more sons of the Luray Valley. The enormous fight at Fredericksburg, the insidious wasting of disease in the snowy camps. One house after another, already short of food and laughter and hope, donned black crepe and took in small clusters of murmuring friends come to share mourning.

Now, Bettie knew, the armies were moving again, up the Rappahannock away from Fredericksburg, to some bloody tryst in the wild woodlands near Chancellorsville.

They had hoped since First Manassas that one fight would end it, and then one more. But nothing ended it, and the newspapers filled day after day with the names of men gone, or maimed and wasted.

Her neighbors idolized Robert E. Lee, what he was able to do with such small armies and short supplies. His daring, his calm gentility, his quiet resolve. And Jackson, his stone-solid stands, his lightning marches and strikes, with every battle infused the weary people of the Valley and the South with swelling pride and vindication of the new nation's cause. The people cleaved to these generals for signs that the nation would be all right, that there would come the independence to go again and forever the way that the people had always gone. The victories lifted the people's hearts. They read the newspaper stories and gathered in every word of the fortitude and conviction their generals expressed, holding the hope to their breasts like a trembling small animal quick with the promise and lilt of life.

But there was that relentless man Lincoln, and so many hundreds of thousands of faceless stern men in blue flowing south, and no victory ever ended it.

Bettie Verner stood, the wind blowing her worn skirts around her legs so much thinner now from the lack of the plenty that once blessed this farm. She hugged herself, her hands reaching easily past her small breasts to her sides, fingers feeling the ridges of her ribs.

Her head was bowed. She didn't see the burgeoning swell of spring. She saw only armies marching, ragged and grim, toward more deaths and wounds. More was coming. That was all she could feel. The weight. The forlorn tightness in her chest. The cold around her heart.

Tears slipped past her eyelashes and ran, like blood from torn skin, down her cheeks. She rocked back and forth, her silent crying wetting the worn wood of the porch. She wept, alone, as the light thinned and faded.

Chancellorsville, May 2, 1863, dusk—Union Army

Night couldn't come quickly enough. Perhaps with the dark, the horror would stop.

"Where's Danny?"

"I don't know, back there in the woods."

"Did you see him get hit?"

"No, but I didn't see him running with us either, after we got past the cannon."

"Did you ask around?"

"Who's to ask? Schmidt's gone, so's Webster, and Heffernan. Haven't seen Wieskopf either, have you? Ohhhh, Jeesus." His breath was ripping through his lungs, his chest heaving.

"I don't know where anybody is. It's all mixed up. Stirred by the devil's bloody fork. Christ, where did those damned rebels come from?"

"Was it really Jackson?"

"Yes, Christ, they say he can just appear anywhere, like an evil shade."

"Lord high priest, don't say that."

The older man looked around, trying to see into the shadows. He wasn't superstitious, but this night he wasn't sure of anything. His whole command had been blown sideways through the thickets and trees by the explosion of rebels come howling out of the woods to the west. Half the men he'd been marching with for years had been trampled under the rush. He, Emil Dietrich, a corporal, had been unbuttoning his pants to relieve himself in the weeds when the attack broke over them. The younger man next to him, Karl Pierach, had been sprawled napping on the ground when Dietrich ran over him, stomping a boot into his belly and waking him to the chaos that fell like a meteor amid Howard's German corps. Dietrich had grabbed his rifle. Pierach hadn't, but picked up one of the hundreds strewn in the brush as the soldiers ran for their lives. They'd stopped now and then to shoot, gathered in little clusters of stubborn frightened men around a stand of trees or a low rise or a battery of cannon.

But nothing had stopped the rebels.

"Emil, did you see Pfeffer back there?"

Dietrich shuddered. He couldn't think of it.

"Did you see him? Jesus Holy Mother, did you see what happened? Emil, did you see?"

"Yah." He paused, and shuddered. "Did he ask you?"

"Oh, Christ, Emil, he pleaded. But I couldn't. Maybe somebody did, but we were all running. It came so fast." Pierach's voice stretched up, almost breaking. He was shaking his head, his eyes wild with the memory, searching the trees above them.

Dietrich couldn't stop the vision coming back. Pierach was crying now into his dirty hands. Firing still came from behind them, in ragged spatters and pops in the black woods.

Little Hans Pfeffer, his thick black moustache, his sharp little eyes behind round spectacles hooked into the mass of dark hair flowing over his ears. Sparkling and cheerful all the time. Laughing, laughing. Keeping everybody feeling good. But now. On the ground. Prisoner of gravity and pain. Pulling the wreck of his body with his hands gouging into the earth. From the small of his back down, a glistening mass of white and yellow and red and purple. Guts and meat and bone. Smashed flat by a cannon ball. A crushed man. Like a bug smeared on a floor. Dietrich shook his head and groaned. Hearing Pfeffer plead for a bullet.

He'd stopped, half facing Pfeffer, unable to pull his eyes from the gore where once had been pants and a belt and a man. Dietrich's body had felt like it was still running, but his eyes and his heart were pinned. On Pfeffer's face, all agony, imploring, lost and hopeless and nothing left. "Oh, Emil, for the love of Christ, put me away. I'm gone up."

The horror gripped and squeezed the breath out of Dietrich. The world spun in chaos around them, a flash of hell, tipping, whirling, but Pfeffer pinned right here in the middle of the storm.

Dietrich had twisted his head away, couldn't look, couldn't meet that deep swallowing gaze. He'd broken then from the little place of shattered trees and run. Hard. As the rebels came on and more men in blue flashing by on all sides. He'd put his head down and run. Left Pfeffer to his agony.

Now the firing stopped, for a time, maybe for the night. Dietrich and Pierach and the men around them were exhausted and on edge. They'd found little bits of shelter—fallen trees, tiny ridges, little mounds of earth they'd scraped up with bayonets and plates—and were hiding behind them, low to the ground, facing west where Jackson's hordes were. Unseen and menacing.

Every sound in the woods ahead of them knifed through their weariness. The shock of the flank attack had blown open their hearts and their souls and their minds, their breath and their thoughts were galloping still. There they had been, Hooker's whole army spread huge and invincible through the woods, just waiting their time to roll over Lee and Jackson and march victorious on to Richmond. And in the flick of a moment it had all turned, ripped open. And here they were, those not shot or captured, quivering like wounded rabbits in the brush. The terror of the flank attack was subsiding as the fear of a night attack—something unseeable tearing out of the dark—grew.

Pierach was scrubbing his face with his hands. He looked into the growing shadows, his shoulders hunched as if for a blow. He ran his hands through his hair, rubbed the back of his neck, rocked back on his haunches and sat hard on the ground.

"Emil, I've never been so scared in my life." His sharp fine nose, his clear blue eyes, his wavy shock of hair, his clear skin and trim little chin beard made him look young, but the fear on his face was ancient. He'd lost his cap, his blouse was open at the neck, and he picked at his chest with his thin fingers.

He'd never been so close to death. The reality of it had hammered all around him as he saw men fall, saw bullets flick at arms, explode cheeks, jerk men to the ground. The threat of it hung like an immense winged presence lurking in the trees above him now. He pulled in his shoulders and his arms, making himself small.

The woods, this place called The Wilderness, seemed to be pulsing like the heartbeat of a monstrous predator poised to leap with claw and teeth. Pierach could hardly keep himself in his place, his body yearned to run again.

He slid through the leaves and twigs on the ground closer to Dietrich. He looked intensely at the older man, searching his eyes. "Emil, what do you think happens. When you die?" He swallowed, bobbed his head. "What has happened to those boys killed back there?"

"Jesus, Karl, I don't know. How can you think about that now? I can hardly breathe, say nothing about think."

"How can you think about anything else, Emil? This is it, this is the final time. Death is chasing us through these godforsaken woods and it almost caught us. Might still catch us, and, and, and I want to know what it is."

"Stop thinking, for Jesus' sake, will you? Just rest and breathe, man."

Pierach shook his head hard, as if a bat had clutched into his hair. "This might be my last chance to think, you know? There could be a Minie ball coming right through those trees there, right at my damned head. What will it do?"

"Split you like a melon, boy. And that's it."

"What do you mean, that's it? Is there nothing after that?" Pierach stopped talking abruptly, but his eyes were burning into the older man.

Dietrich didn't say anything either for a moment. He shook his head slowly, then said, "The Bible says there's resurrection, life for those who are saved."

"Do you believe that, Emil?" More shots cracked in the night, pulling a haunted silence in behind.

Emil turned his head back from searching the woods they'd run through and looked curiously at the thin man kneeling in the dirt in front of him. He didn't want to be having this conversation, but Pierach's pleading questions had caught him. "Are you saved, Karl?" he asked.

"Oh, God, I want to be. I want to be." Pierach dropped his head, his chin on his breast, tears and snot running off his nose. He trembled. "How do you know if you're saved?" he said in a small, quavering voice.

"I don't know. I wish I did, tonight."

Pierach snuffled, pulling breath into his lungs like a parched man sucking and sputtering water. He dug his dirty fists into his eye sockets, pressing at the bony ridges. "Some of the men are so sure, they seem to, they have, a peace about them." Dropping his hands, Pierach dug in the dirt and leaves with his outstretched fingers, grabbing for something, anything. "I just wish I knew." He kept crying, softly, rocking forward and back.

"Well, we may not know until it happens." Dietrich looked up into the brooding mass of branches above them, cocked his head as he heard a distant cannon bark. He thought he could hear a high thin screech of pain. It was awful in this wilderness, this pathless tangle of brush and darkness. "May never know, if there's nothing. God, I don't even know if it matters anymore, I just want to get out of here."

"I don't want it to happen," Pierach whispered. "I'm not ready. I don't know. There's nothing sure. Oh God I can't stand this. Emil, Emil, God, what happens when you die?"

"Karl." Dietrich reached across the space between them and dug his strong right hand into Pierach's thin left shoulder. "Karl, you'll be all right. You're not going to die."

Pierach shrugged Dietrich's hand away, scuttled back a foot away from Dietrich. "That's what we all thought." He looked angrily at Dietrich. "And then those bastards came screaming out of the woods and killed us, blew us into our own campfires." He heaved in another breath. "There are dead men back there, Emil, men I knew and marched with, men I ate with and joked with and slept on the ground with and where are they now, Emil, where in the hell are they now? I need to know." He looked fiercely at Dietrich, dark strands of hair caught in the sweat and tears beside his eyes. "Where?"

"Karl, I don't have enough faith to be certain, and I wish you'd just shut up about this. Grab hold of yourself, you're coming apart." His voice was harsh and low, his eyes now angry too.

Pierach's voice was small. "Where do you go when you die?" He sobbed. "I just want to know."

"I don't intend to find out, not now, so hush." He felt helpless, watching Pierach. He wanted to reach him, to at least quiet him down somehow, but the boy was shooting down a rapids of despair.

They both heard brush move and snap in the dark behind Dietrich. "Emil," Pierach whispered sharply, "there's something there. It's coming for us. Emil, don't leave me."

To their right, someone yelled out, "Who's there? Move once more and I'll blow you to hell, rebel."

It rushed in so fast. Rifle muzzles flared yellow and red in the dark, shots exploded in their ears, tree branches snapped off trunks, shouts erupted.

"Where do we go…" Pierach, slashing his head back and forth, cried to Emil.

Pierach's wild eyes grabbed onto Dietrich's face. Then, just as maybe an answer was coming, saw the older man's eyes widen, his mouth open, a ragged hole tear out of his throat, black liquid spattering forward. On Pierach's face.

Breath guttered out of Dietrich's ripped throat, and he toppled face down into the leaves. Pierach could hear his nose snap as he hit the ground.

Blood and breath sank from Pierach's head and eyes and chest, and he went blank for an instant, shutting down for an eyeblink. Then he sucked in a great rush of air, and screamed.

And ran.

Blindly.

Into the evil night.

Lexington, May 2, 1863, 9 p.m.

Margaret Junkin Preston stood on the porch of her father's house in the little town of Lexington, several blocks from the only home Thomas Jackson had ever owned. Jackson was like a brother to her—he had taken her sister Ellie as his first wife, lived in the Junkin family house, and after Ellie had died in childbirth, Jackson and his sister-in-law had shared sorrow and then a reawakening of life.

She remembered this evening a poem she had written when Ellie had decided to marry Jackson, a union Margaret had at first resisted. The poem ended with these words:

> Forgive these saddened strains Ellie
> Forgive these eyes so dim!
> I must—*must* love whom *you have* loved
> So I will turn to him,—
> And clasping with a silent—touch
> Whose tenderness endears
> *Your hand and his between my own*
> I bless them with my tears.

This evening, in Lexington, 105 miles by birdflight from the woods of Chancellorsville, Margaret had heard the muffled rumble of cannon fire. Had heard it most of the afternoon, and now, at dusk, could hear it no more. She stood still, straining her ears. Nothing.

She was frightened. Her husband, one of the founders of the Virginia Military Institute and a long-time friend of Jackson's, was in the army, but not at Chancellorsville. Her father, a minister and college president, was in Pennsylvania, a Unionist who had fled what he called the erring South when Virginia seceded.

The war had thinned life in Lexington. Earlier in the day she had made two petticoats out of a curtain, and cut drawers for her husband from a sheet. Then, while she sewed, she'd heard the cannon. So far away, but it had stopped her.

She felt alone. She feared for Jackson, who had shown her such a tender side in the years since Ellie's death. Standing now on the deep porch in the town she loved, she remembered for an instant Niagara Falls, where she had gone with Thomas and Ellie on their honeymoon. She could see the water tumbling over the precipice, tumbling and falling into space. Falling.

The silence of the night chilled her as she stood, wrapped in loneliness.

Chancellorsville, May 2, 1863, 9 p.m.—Confederate Army

Two pair of Confederate stretcher bearers met on the Plank Road west of Chancellorsville. Those going away from the battleground carried a boy of 19, bleeding from the neck. Those going toward the soldiers who still crouched in the woods ahead carried boxes of ammunition on their stained red stretcher.

They paused, looked at each other, one said, "More work up there, we'll get 'em." The wounded boy groaned. The men nodded and walked past each other.

Chancellorsville, May 2, 1863, 9 p.m.—Confederate Army

The risen moon illuminated a narrow dirt road that led to Hooker's rear. The Bullock Road. A little to its south, the Orange Plank Road, larger and roughly paved with wooden planks, led directly to the Chancellor mansion that Union General Joseph Hooker had taken as his headquarters. Beside the roads, around everything, trees. The entire right of Hooker's huge army had crumpled under Jackson's flank attack, bending from its original east-west alignment and collapsing back in shocked retreat to a ragged north-south line. Ahead on the Plank Road were batteries of cannon aiming at the Confederates where the Federals had made the stand that had held here finally at the end of the bloody day.

William Sutton, crouched on the ground with winded Tarheels all around him, heard the sharp thwack of axes in the woods ahead.

"They're fortifying," the man next to him said, turning his head to the left to put his right ear to the noise. His left ear was a crusty mess still oozing blood from a shot that had just missed taking his head off an hour earlier.

"It'll be damn hard to get them out of there now," the man said, squatting on his knees and shaking dirt out of his musket barrel. "But they'll send us in there anyway. Old Jack won't stop 'til Hooker's in the river."

Behind Hooker's position curled the Rappahannock River, a trap for his army if his soldiers broke under pressure again and had to try to cross in chaos under fire.

"I wish we hadn't stopped," Sutton said. He spit, as he'd been doing for five minutes, to try to get the fine, bitter grains of powder out of his mouth. In the rapid firing of the attack, he'd bitten open so many of the paper cartridges that held the lead ball and the powder to propel it that his mouth was black and dry. "We should have kept after them. We had them on the run. We could have rolled them right into the river and gotten this thing over with."

"Couldn't," the man said. "That charge mixed us up so bad we'd have been shooting our own men. Can't tell one unit from another out here anymore. Even the officers don't know where anybody is."

"We know where *they* are," Sutton said, jerking his head up to show with his chin where the Federals were. In the thick woods and splintered trees and inky shadows in front of the Southerners.

"Whew, boy, that was a chase, weren't it?" The man sat back on his butt now, held his musket in front of him like a farm implement. He shook his head, whistled until a smile broke the whistle off. "Like a turkey shoot, with a whole lot of turkeys. Fat German boys, but they knew how to run. Damn. I liked seeing them go, didn't you?"

Sutton didn't say anything, just kept looking ahead into a darkness stippled with thin moonlight that fell through the trees. Trees crowded on both sides of him—silent watchers leaning in. The woods and the thick underbrush made it hard for armies to move, hard for anyone to see.

"I think I got me one or two, saw 'em fall. These trees were like a sieve, let the skinny ones through but the fat ones got stuck so we could shoot 'em." The man laughed at the image. "You get any?" he asked Sutton.

"Don't know. Just know they haven't gotten me. Yet."

"I think Old Jack's thinking of a night attack. You wanna do that?"

Sutton had a quick picture flash through his mind of trying to run under fire through that thick dark forest in front of him, and he shuddered. "I don't know. I guess we've got no choice if he thinks we can do it. I just want to get this over."

The sound of thudding axes came out of the darkness again.

Rustling steps came from behind, and a tall officer strode up and knelt beside the two men. Major John Berry, commanding the 18th North Carolina. The 18th was part of the brigade led by Brigadier General James Lane, a student of Professor Jackson's at the VMI 10 years earlier. The regiment had been one of the leading units in the flank attack on Hooker, and it had been marching and shooting and running all day. Everybody, including Berry, was exhausted, but buoyed by the adrenaline surge of seeing the Yankees run and knowing they'd surprised the hell out of Hooker.

"Keep your eyes bright, boys," Berry said. "They're out there, the Yankees, might counterattack. Other regiments have been charged by cavalry, so watch for them. Kneel when you shoot, that will keep you steady."

A whippoorwill called, its soft hooing eerie in the night. Sutton could see Berry grin. He was nerved up.

"How you doing, boys?" Berry asked.

"Tired, hungry," said the man beside Sutton.

"The Yankees are too. We spoiled their dinner and made them run. They're worse off than you are. Didn't you grab any of that food back there?" Many of the Confederate soldiers had paused as they overran Howard's Federals to grab the beef they'd been cooking, then run on, chewing and yelling and firing as they went.

"Naw, we didn't stop, thought it weren't polite to join their dinner uninvited, major," the man said, laughing again.

"Well, you keep awake here. We may be going after them yet tonight, if they don't come after us." Berry slapped Sutton on the shoulder, rose and walked up the ragged line to the left.

Quiet settled in again. Sutton peered ahead, trying to see movement, reflections on metal, stirring branches, anything in the trees in front. In small clearings, the nearly full moon made enough light to see a little, but in the thickets under groups of trees the dark could hide enough men to kill you. The clearings were like stages waiting for a play, the trees were like curtains. Sutton decided he didn't want to see anything begin out there. War in daylight was frightful enough. This was an added depth of terror.

Minutes passed, and Sutton felt a thickening behind his drooping eyes. He rolled his head back on his shoulders, stretched out his arms, clenched his fingers into fists, released them and stretched every finger wide, feeling the thin muscles burn up his wrists. The waiting was building up a tension that almost lifted him off the ground.

Then, off to the right, a shot. Sharp and piercing in the quiet night. Quickly more followed, in ripples and volleys. Shouts flew among the trees, Sutton looked to his right, his nerves zinging, and saw crouching Confederates illuminated for a brief bright flash as flames shot out of rifle muzzles. One man shooting appeared in this ghostly light then disappeared in darkness as another next to that one was lit up for a second by another shot. Little jolts of lightning playing up and down the ranks.

The sound of hooves beating the ground came distinctly through the uproar.

"They're coming, riders!" Berry shouted down the line, and the men of the 18th North Carolina knelt on one knee and raised their rifles, the classic position for infantry trying to repel the speeding shock of a cavalry attack.

Sutton dropped to his knee and felt his right kneecap slam into a stone, sending a bright sharp pain lancing up his leg. He grunted, squeezed his eyes shut and ground his teeth together, then raised his rifle.

He shook his head to clear his eyes, thought he saw shadows coming toward him, heard clopping pounding hooves, and he fired his rifle into the night.

Suddenly more hooves, clattering on stones, muffled thumpings on leaves. Cries everywhere. Sharp. Angry. Frightened. Shots. The night and its shadows whirled around Sutton.

"Hey, who are you?" "Who's out there?" "They're coming!!"

Up and down the line, more strange jack'o'lantern faces were lit by more firing rifles.

Splattering shots. Rips in the air. Close enough to hear the thud into cloth, into bone. A wheeze, "Hnnhhuhh."

Horses whinnying. "Y'all can go to hell." "Give it to 'em." Sutton, hands trembling, gunpowder sticking to his sweathing palm, lifted his rifle, rammed it to his shoulder and fired again.

Then a voice, high and terrified and angry, yelled, "Stop, you're shooting your own men."

A pause, then Berry yelled, "It's a lie, pour it into them," and more shots gushed forth.

Though it might have been a Yankee deception, Sutton instantly knew in his gut it was true. Darkest revelation.

"Stop. They're ours," he heard.

And horror closed around him.

Chancellorsville, May 2, 1863, 9 p.m.—Confederate Army

Thomas Jackson had ridden out just north of the Orange Plank Road ahead of Lane's Carolina troops to see the situation of his own men and Hooker's. To feel the ground, to see for himself what had been done and what might still be done this night. Initiative, once gained, could not be surrendered. "Press them, press them," he'd called out fiercely a hundred times during the rolling flank attack. Don't let up the pressure. Push the destruction to its end.

Jackson was out here looking for Yankees. He and several men of his staff were now in front of their own lines. In the deadliest space between two uncertain armies. The sun gone, it was difficult to see through the woods or down the road in the dying day.

Ahead of him somewhere were Lane's Carolina skirmishers hidden in the brush. Then the Federal army, wounded but deadly. A little ways south, by the Plank Road, General A.P. Hill, Jackson's lieutenant who commanded the division Lane was part of, was also out in front of the lines reconnoitering. To stay in communication, Jackson had sent his staff engineer, Captain J. Keith Boswell, mapmaker Jed Hotchkiss' best friend, to ride with Hill. No one had warned Lane that the generals were going out in front of the lines. Although it was customary to do this, perhaps Hill thought Jackson had, and Jackson thought Hill had as Lane's men were his.

Jackson looked over the moon-splattered terrain between the angled intersection of the Plank Road and the Bullock Road. Most of the trees before him were thin, a few inches around, their branches holding out lacy strands of leaves like offerings. Scattered about were larger trees, their boughs bending down to add higher layers of small darkening shapes. Many trees were wounded by metal from the shooting, torn bark slowly leaking sap.

A third lane, the Mountain Road, ran between the Plank and Bullock roads. It was a murky tunnel through the dense woods this night. Jackson asked a soldier whose home was just up the Bullock Road which way would best take him to Hooker's rear. The private, David Kyle, led him east on the Mountain Road. Into The Wilderness.

Smoke still slid in trailing tatters low to the ground across which Howard's German troops had tumbled through this brush-choked woods chasing their bare salvation as the shadows wove into darkness. A dog that saw his fleeing prey burrow into deep brush at the far end of a field would no more give up the chase than would Jackson.

He had driven the Yankees before him many times. Most famously at Henry Hill above Bull Run, although there he had not been able to follow them much beyond the bottom of the hill. Starting from Winchester he'd driven Banks' men north through towns and across fields until their backs were to the Potomac and his own troops were scattered, heaving for breath, across miles of Virginia. At Port Republic he'd sent Shields torn force limping down the Valley. He'd driven Pope's surprised ranks north again at Second Manassas, having gotten behind them, hidden and pounced like ten thousand lions, then fought for a long bloody day along a ragged line before shoving them again across Bull Run in shreds. He'd only been able to stand his ground in the destroyed cornfield at Sharpsburg, and had stood almost rank to rank slugging with Pope's men at Cedar Mountain with neither side budging until a final collapse of the Federal lines with Jackson's men too exhausted to pursue. At Fredericksburg he'd hammered Burnside's dogged boys back against the Rappahannock, but their retreat was slow and as orderly as beaten men could make it.

He had never been able to pursue them to annihilation. Those people. Wipe their stain away. Shove them home, never to return and invade again. His Virginia.

He had never been able to drive them into the river, to erase, eradicate, destroy them.

This was his chance.

Right here. Tonight. These trees. These woods. These men. These guns. These rifles. This ground.

Tonight's blood, so there will be no more spilled.

Let us push this to the end. Now.

Avid for the final tearing clamp and rip of jaws that would break the neck and still the body, he rode in front of his tired riflemen, Little Sorrel weaving among the tall thin trees. Were the Federals scattered, in frightened pockets of broken units clinging to little dips or rises of ground? Were they still running, stumbling through the brush, muskets dragging? Were they forming again in lines, the remnants digging in, piling logs to shoot behind?

The dark was thickening. Jackson's aide Sandie Pendleton said, "General, don't you think this is the wrong place for you?" Jackson barely shook his head. "We must press them," he said quickly to Pendleton, "we must not let them escape." He jerked his head and cap toward the dark ahead. "They always have more men to fill the lines, they will always keep coming across our land unless we destroy one of their armies so utterly that they stop in horror. The whole nation, the generals, the parents, the people. Stop, because the cost is too high."

He looked through the trees as if he could see the Rappahannock and the blue troops tumbling in.

He reined Sorrel to the left, leaning away from a branch, pushing the leaves away, Sorrel skittering then striding again, forward. Jackson looked back at the riders with him, several behind and to his left, a few spread off to the right. All were peering forward, reaching with their vision through the dark, ears keenly searching for sounds. "We could end this, tonight, if we can press them, drive them," he said, jaw pressing forward, skin tightened around straining eyes.

"If we can find them," Pendleton said, batting at a branch.

Jackson seemed to know all he needed to know. "The enemy is routed," he said. "The danger is over. Go back and tell A. P. Hill to press right on."

A rider departed.

Suddenly scattered firing came from ahead and somewhere to the side, and loud calls. An aide, Richard Wilbourn, cantered up, drew his reins and said over his horse's bobbing mane, "Yankees, ahead and to the right. They've stopped running."

"Have they formed lines? Have they dug in?" Jackson asked, looking toward the road to their right, still searching for a way to hit them.

"I can't tell," Wilbourne said, "they're in clumps, mostly, but there seem to be a good many of them."

"We can't see where anybody is, General," Pendleton said from Jackson's left, his horse sidling nervously. "Our men will get tangled up in here and shoot at anything they can see, or anything they can't see. Keeping order, or formations, or even a common direction would be hard."

Jackson nodded once, his beard a shadow beneath his long face, his eyes roofed in darkness by his cap. No one else spoke—Jackson held no counsels of war, asked for only facts. A moment passed, the horses barely shifting their stances. Jackson leaned toward the shadows, his gaze toward the enemy, toward the night, toward his desire. Night attacks were rare and dangerous, but in this moonlight...

As the seconds passed without his own men coming hollering through the trees again, he could feel in the dark ahead the Federals holding on firmer and firmer, grabbing a log, leaning against a tree, flattening onto the backslope of a tiny rise. Becoming harder and harder to dislodge. To drive into the river.

He yearned forward. Saw ahead only shifting shapes, maybe trees, maybe men. Nothing he could reach and seize and crush.

His right hand clenched. He hit his thigh with it.

He shook his head, turned Little Sorrel with a squeeze of his leg, and looked up into the black canopy. "We'll go back for now," he said. The few near him who heard his low voice waved the others to turn and go back to their own lines. Pendleton and Wilbourne had no idea if they were going back to initiate the night attack or going back to wait for daylight to renew the battle. Jackson shared his plans with no one.

But Jackson looked back over his shoulder to the formless front of the battle, eyes locked on nothing the others could see. Then all the horses turned and the group of tired men rode back toward the 18th North Carolina stretched now in front of them, straining also to see through the gloom.

Then it came.

A spatter and then ripping of rifle fire. Dark, no direction clear. Yelling, from ahead, from beside Jackson. A horse reared, a frightened whuffling neigh. Wood breaking, a branch tipping down fast before his eyes. Sounds, voices, shots, the woods in spin, shreds of leaves and bark on the forest floor burst up as spitting bullets hit.

Twack, Jackson's left forearm was snatched, a burning spot, deep inside a pain both sharp and spreading. The general quickly raised the arm. Touched his lips to the cloth of his sleeve, a hot dribble of blood slid into his beard. Sorrel kicked, snorted, backed then sidled to the right before jerking forward. More shots, fast, coming without order. "Don't shoot," he heard Wilbourn yell, then a javelin was hurled through his upper left arm. His head jerked to the side, eyes dragging down as he tried to look at what had finally happened after years of thousands of shots and shells in the air he'd ridden through. He tried to move the arm, swing it up from the shoulder, and felt tears and splinters inside the meat. A bullet, in and through faster than a thought, the lead dented by the bone as it ricocheted through tissue and skin and out into the dark of the trees. Wet blood ran down the tender inside of Jackson's arm, like drops of sweat but faster, hotter. A wave, as from a large rough stone slung into a small pool, surged through his body from his upper arm, and his stomach dissolved into an acrid slough. A thinning white heat flowed from his temples down his cheeks and the soft hollow of his neck just below the jaw hinge, making the back of his eyes sink and draw in. The trees started to tip around him and he lifted his right hand and in a heartbeat it was pierced by another of the buzzing flock of Minie balls hammering through the leaves. A ragged hole, the bones beneath his palm grating like rusted metal. Sorrel now leaped forward, spun left on stiff forelegs and raced away from the rattling sound of gunfire.

"Pour it into them," Jackson heard from behind, the words barely touching his ebbing mind as he saw the low bough of a tree come swinging toward his head like a leveled sword. He raised his wet right hand and the branch hit his wrist and scratched across his face and he tipped to his left, his right calf slipping up Sorrel's heaving right flank.

Sound started to fade and in the bleeding general's thought was a dimly-shaped riverbank, the water curving through a darkening bend, and he felt a spreading regret that he would not see Hooker's men pushed stumbling and crying into it. Into the river. To end it.

And he fell.

Lane's North Carolina troops south of the Plank Road had seen a perhaps-lost Federal officer wandering in front of the line, and fired at him. One shot caused more up the line, then more, shattering the night, from Federals and Confederates. A fusillade. Then the Confederate riders coming back seemed a threat, and it was done. Riding with A.P. Hill, Keith Boswell's heart was pierced by lead and he fell from his horse, his life suddenly over.

Beside Little Sorrel, Captain Wilbourn reached up to Jackson as he sagged to the ground. Jackson looked for a few seconds at Wilbourn, astonished. He knew where the shots had come from.

The firing slackened. Stonewall Jackson lay bleeding on the soft Virginia earth. And the course of the war and the nation was changed.

Chancellorsville, May 2, 1863, 10 p.m.

In the pale light of the moon, petals glowed on low trees. Dogwoods. The angels of Spring. They'd started in April, opening tiny hands of white that spread like applause through the woods at the waning of winter. Unusually cold, more snow than anyone needed, the winter had been hard. Then the woods had turned soft.

Redbud trees had reached their iridescent lavender flowers up to the height of one man, two men, flashes of fire in the dark forests around Chancellorsville. Then they'd faded, flames blown out by the wind. But the dogwood lingered, beautiful branches of ivory spread like arms giving blessings.

The petals, so thin, like fine china. Drifting now to the ground. They touched the earth, the smaller ones like the delicate fingertips of girls.

Blood sunk in the ground, and the dogwood roots pulled it in.

Chancellorsville, May 3, 1863—Confederate Army

A day later. An eternity later. The woods were so thick. It was hard to tell where anyone was. As Sutton rose slowly into consciousness, he heard firing all around. He could see green and tan things close up against his eyes. Fuzzy, indistinct. He blinked. The shapes became leaves and a branch, lying across his face. He couldn't tell which way he was facing. He rolled his head, and the world tipped and spun, the green whirred in front of him, and he closed his eyes.

Burning. Burning, deep in his thigh. Which one? He couldn't separate out where the pain came from. He blinked, and light leaped into his brain. He raised his right arm to cover his face—it pushed the branch into the skin of his cheek, jabbing and cutting, and he flapped his hand to clear away the twigs and leaves that covered his face. That accomplished, he lay there, sucking in air, keeping his eyes closed.

The ground shook, and he heard clomping and swishing and the heaving breath of men nearby. Boots on the ground, metal fastenings and canteens and straps slapping. Men were running, right by his head.

"Spread, spread to the left, boys, fan out there and keep some separation. Don't let 'em take you all with one damned canister shot, now move." The yelling man—it was Sparrow's voice he heard, he was sure, but he couldn't cry out—ran past Sutton, the end of his order delivered already a few feet beyond Sutton's head. He heard hands and jacket sleeves slapping against branches as they went ahead into the woods.

Sutton opened his eyes again, and saw the trunks of several trees leaning above him, their branches woven together in a thick umbrella keeping out the sky. He felt a wet trickle on his cheek. Blood, a small mound of it, slipping down the stubble. He'd jabbed himself with that branch. He rubbed his knuckle against the wet spot, held it before his eyes, saw slick red on top of the dirt ground into the skin of his hand.

He remembered stabs of flame coming out of the twisted trees and brush in front of him as he ran. And he remembered falling. They were going to slam Hooker back into the river, destroy the Yankee army, finish the job they'd started by rolling up Hooker's flank yesterday. They were going to do it. Lane's North Carolina troops had kept pushing through the tangled woods and overrun a log barricade the Federals had built perpendicular to the Plank Road. Bluecoats were running again, not as fast as yesterday, but they were falling back, those who could move. At the logs piled up, there were crumpled men in butternut on the west side, sprawled dead men in blue on the east. The Confederates had run, shouting while they fired, "Remember Jackson!"

And then Sutton had fallen. Was smashed down.

Now, hours or maybe a day later, he couldn't tell, he tried to straighten his body, and gasped as he felt his spine twist almost out of his hips. He looked down and saw that, while his shoulders were flat against the ground, his right hip was jutting up in the air. His body was twisted and it felt like the small of his back was coming apart. He tried to straighten and flame shot straight into the space above his tailbone. He must have wrenched his back as he fell. He closed his eyes and slowly tried to lower his right hip to the ground. The bad part in the flat of his back eased some as he brought his hips level, and he could breath a few deeper breaths without having the air pulled from his lungs by pain.

Then he noticed the smell. Rich, thick, heavy as gravy. Some of it was burning. Burning brush, it smelled like, and a deeper tone, like charred timbers from a building burning. Those were good aromas, could remind him of home, at least the brush. He didn't want to think about what buildings might be on fire. Then a sharper smell, laced through the burning wood—gunpowder, he decided. That part of it made his nose twitch, almost like pepper. He could taste it on the tip of his tongue, the metallic tang of the powder from the cartridges he'd bitten open, and the airier scent of exploded powder riding on the breeze.

But then, under and around the other things in the air, he became fully aware of a more cloying stink that grew now in the back of his nose and mouth. Rot.

Spoiled blood. Meat going bad. He knew in a second what it was from. Dead horses, and dead men, all around. The smell of a dead mouse under the flooring, or a fish putrifying on the river bank, or kitchen meat kept too long and turned. Those smells were bird song. This foulness was like a scream. He shook his head to get away from it, moved to rise.

And then he felt that burning in the fat front part of his thigh again. Left one, clearly. That's where the trouble was. Same one he'd been shot in at Port Republic. He lifted his head to look down the length of his body, and as he brought his chin toward his chest he clenched muscles all up and down his body and a deep thick echoing pain exploded inside his leg. He saw a wet slick of red on his leg, then his head dropped like a rock onto the hard black earth and he knew he was in a very bad way. He could feel his pants leg, soaked, stuck against the skin of his leg. Sweat flowed, along his forehead and temples, his armpits and crotch, his stomach and his back. Things went white again, and he spun. And then dark.

Wilderness Tavern, west of Chancellorsville, May 3, 1863— Confederate Army

The wind puffed the walls of the tent this Sunday morning. The leaves fluttered in the trees. The thin morning light gave the scene a fragile, fresh green glow. Made it look peaceful.

But there was no peace here. Skirmish fire could be heard from a few miles to the east, where the battle still remained uncertain. Hooker's Federals would either be pushed farther toward the Rappahannock today, perhaps into it, or they would counterattack and roll over the tired Southerners. The fighting—the Minie balls and cannon shells—could tear apart the Wilderness Tavern field hospital in an hour or less, Tucker Lacy knew.

They should move. Lee had asked them to. He should see what was needed. Plan and do. Try to save what was certainly slipping away.

But for a moment he wanted just to stand here. Breathe. Think. Grieve.

Pray.

For Jackson.

The field hospital gave groaning testimony to the agony and filth of war. Here shattered men curled in shock and desperation around torn limbs and ragged holes. Flies buzzed their wonder over the feast spread seeping before them. There was no peace here as men's hope bled through wool and cotton and canvas into the ground.

Jackson was inside the tent, where his left arm had been amputated.

General Jackson wasn't just the most zealous Old Testament fighting force in the Confederacy to Beverly Tucker Lacy. For Lacy was also Reverend Lacy, the chaplain for Jackson's Second Corps, and Thomas Jonathan Jackson was, in a broad sense, his parishioner. Both were Presbyterians, and serious about it. Lacy and Jackson carried their church with them. Two devout men bringing the fire of retribution to the invaders. Two men, both questioning and certain, talking in spare words around campfires about the plans of God. Revealed or still inscrutable. Where was God in this war? What would he have them do? All the killing—was it right? All they could do, they'd conclude, was do what seemed to be just and pray for support—or forgiveness.

This blow to Jackson had shaken Lacy, shaken his faith. It was a calamity, Lacy thought. Jackson was a companion of the soul to Lacy. The general wasn't a man to get close to many people, and Lacy didn't know him well, although he'd known him for several years. But Lacy was drawn to this strange, driven man. He saw that Jackson was capable of joy and playfulness, knew the man of war addressed his wife in letters with Spanish words of love—mi querida, mi corazon. Lacy suspected that Jackson in the dark of night had doubts—perhaps doubts he wouldn't even admit to himself—that made him so very human. And vulnerable. That must be why he prayed so hard and so often, Lacy thought. Lacy never entirely understood what drove Jackson. A man of God had to be confused by the terrible carnage of war, by the way it shattered human values with every trigger pull. Yet Lacy knew Jackson credited God with his troops' victories. "God blessed our arms with victory today," Jackson often wrote in dispatches. How could God have a hand in so much death and suffering? Perhaps to the Presbyterian God, suffering was part of what we all must pass through, Lacy thought. To be tried. He and Jackson had talked about these things in low voices at night. Lacy himself was reluctant to express his war-born doubts. But he talked with Jackson, by the campfires, in the tents, in the comfortable cottage at Moss Neck. Jackson stated his belief in God's will so firmly, so frequently, that Lacy wondered sometimes if the general was trying to convince himself.

Jackson had told Lacy he was certain, from the time he'd stood with his VMI cadets and watched John Brown hanged in Charlestown, Virginia, that there would be war. And he was certain, absolutely certain, that the North was wrong. States had the right to resume the independence they had only temporarily suspended in forming the national government under the Constitution. And the North had no right to interfere with slavery, which was guaranteed by that Constitution. Jackson himself owned slaves, and never apologized for it—slavery was in the Bible, and as long as a master treated his slaves well, it was all right. And Jackson treated his few slaves well—so much so that more than one slave in Lexington had asked that Jackson buy them. Jackson, who'd always been a

Democrat, had looked for a compromise to solve the national differences over slavery. But now, with the war that he'd hoped would never come, there would be no compromise.

The time for talk was over. The issues would be settled at arms. Jackson had said he was certain that God ordered human events, and certain that in defending Virginia he was doing God's will.

And even though Jackson said he was certain that his righteous soldiers would find a reward in heaven, he was deeply troubled that so many were sent on that journey in the battles he led.

"Do you believe that it is God's will that so many die?" Lacy had asked Jackson one night.

"Yes," the general had said, quietly.

"How can God want this?"

"We cannot know what God wants," the general had said.

"Aren't you troubled by so much killing, by being the agent of so much killing?" Lacy had asked.

Jackson had been silent for some time, searching the fire with his deep, blue-grey eyes. "Man does his duty, and is never satisfied if anything can be done better. My duty is defending Virginia." He had paused. "That requires death. Perhaps all our deaths. I cannot question that duty."

Quiet again for awhile, Jackson had then said, more softly, "But the weight of their precious blood is heavy on me. I know the sadness of the orphan, and we are creating so many. I would that God protected more, wrapped more in his arms, shielded more. But we cannot know his plans, and I do not question, Lacy. I do my duty."

Lacy had wanted to ask him how doing that duty made him feel, but he didn't think it was his place, and didn't believe the general would answer. He'd thought he'd heard as much resignation as conviction in Jackson's voice, and that surprised him. That may be as close as he'd come to seeing inside the general, so self-contained except for God.

Jackson wasn't given to questioning God. But he did question men. The misguided, arrogant Northerners were killing so many of his men. Many were his friends. Some had been his students. And it angered him. His feelings toward the Northerners hardened into a hatred that Lacy feared was unhealthy, perhaps unChristian. But that was another subject Lacy kept to himself and to his own thoughts at night.

Jackson was a serious man. He took war seriously, and he took the questions underlying this war seriously. While Jackson took advice on waging war from almost no one—Lee was probably the only person—he had always sought guidance on spiritual matters from men of God. The general would talk endlessly with ministers like Lacy, his former chief of staff Rev. Robert Dabney, Rev. James Graham of Winchester and Rev. Willliam White of Jackson's home church in Lexington, men of abiding faith who were also open to questions about the mysteries of making God's precepts work among fallible human beings.

This was part of what tied Jackson and Lacy together. This was one of so many things that made Lacy's mind veer so sharply away from thoughts of Jackson's death. His wounds were grave. Yet he would recover. Wouldn't he, God?

This edge of the field hospital was quiet. Dr. Hunter McGuire had gone away to sleep a bit, his night's work done, the wounds probed, the muscle and gristle and bone cut. Jackson's brother-in-law Joseph Morrison sat beside the tent on a small folding chair, his head drooping to his chest. Not wanting to go far, staying in earshot but not intruding on the general in his chloroformed sleep. And, Lacy thought, simply not able to be so close to the man struck down. Not wanting to see, not wanting to recognize, what had happened. Morrison served on the general's staff, had been in the woods with him when he was hit, had thrown his body over Jackson's when cannon fire tore through the woods as they were carrying the general back to the Confederate lines. It had been a time of horror for Morrison, and soon he would be sent to bring Jackson's wife Anna, his sister, to the wounded general's side.

A gloom hung here that the morning breeze couldn't blow away. Lacy felt the wind light and cleansing on his stubbled cheek, but the refreshment couldn't penetrate the skin, couldn't touch the soul.

Like an eagle with a broken pinion, Lacy thought, and repeated the phrase to himself. Inside the tent, trapped by its inability to fly, was the grand, brave eagle that was Jackson.

Lacy stood a dozen yards from the tent, his eyes drifting across the bent form of Morrison, over the trampled ground, over to the trees, back to the tent. Then Lacy saw it.

Pale. Torn.

It chilled him. Stopped his breath. His heart.

Discarded. Forgotten. Powerless. The life drained from it.

His friend Thomas Jackson's severed left arm.

In the dirt beside the tent. Half wrapped in a bloody rag.

"Dear God. The poor man. Thomas," he said aloud, to no one.

He walked to the tent, slowly. Trees rustled. The grass was beaten down around the tent, showing patches of raw earth. Near the tent, jumbled in his vision, a fire ring and cook pot, some rifles stacked, a canteen and belt apparently discarded. He heard birds singing, saw a dragonfly dart to the tent peak, then shoot away.

His eyes had to come back to the arm. He could see bone projecting from torn flesh. He kneeled, opened the folds of the rag. The arm was terribly ravaged. There were rips down the forearm, and blackened tissue, where a bullet had traveled beneath the skin. And above the elbow, the bone fragments showing the worst wound, then the squared edge of the bone where it had been sawed.

Lacy didn't want to see this. It was too close, too intimate, too much to know about another person. This destruction of what had once been animated and powerful was obscene.

And, he thought, it was too horrible a symbol. Lacy believed in symbols. Not omens, but pictures that illustrate life, its triumphs and travails. He saw meaning in people's posture, their eyes, the way they handled their children, the condition of their crops and livestock. He saw God's grace or retribution in an easy pregnancy or a lightning-struck tree. He was not so arrogant that he thought he knew what these things meant, but he was certain they had meaning. As with everything about God, figuring out the message was the challenge.

But he knew what other soldiers would make of the broken and discarded arm if they saw it. It was too literal. Strength cut away. A leader, leadership, diminished. A rallying point gone.

He had to take it away from others' eyes.

He went to a commissary wagon and got a towel. He hurried. He didn't want anyone else to see him at his mission. He knelt again by the tent, lifted the arm, so light it felt like nothing, and laid it on the towel. He wrapped it, and stood with it cradled close to his chest. He could feel the individual fingers pressing against his body.

He felt dizzy. The blood sank out of his head, making the world go pale.

Where could he go?

He believed God's spark is in the soul, not the flesh. But still, this refuse, this meat, was a part of his friend, and it should be treated with respect.

He wrapped the arm tightly and walked, unsteadily, away from the tent.

He saw another man standing in a clearing nearby, a metal cup hanging from his hand. The man stared through the woods to the open country beyond. He didn't move. The distant "carrrrump carrrump" of cannon fire could be heard.

The man looked up before Lacy could turn away. It was Lieutenant James Power Smith, Jackson's aide-de-camp, who had helped bring Jackson out of the Chancellorsville woods and had held the light in the tent for the surgeons. Smith had been a divinity student before the war, studying under Robert Dabney. He had enlisted in the Rockbridge Artillery, serving under another fighting preacher, William Pendleton, an Episcopal rector and father of Sandie Pendleton, who now served with Smith on Jackson's staff. Just before the battle of Sharpsburg, Jackson had asked Smith to join his staff, adding another man of God to his fold.

"Reverend Lacy," Smith said in a muted greeting, tipping his head forward, his slight chin beard touching his open shirt collar. He looked exhausted and pale.

"Smith. I, I…" but Lacy couldn't finish.

"That man is the heart of this army. What will the men think now?" Smith said, gesturing aimlessly with his arms, tilting his head a little to the side and looking at Lacy. He saw the lost look on Lacy's face. "What is it, Reverend?"

Lacy closed his eyes, wavered on his feet a little. He pressed the palm of his free hand against his forehead. "Mr. Smith, I need your help."

"We all need help now, Reverend. God's help. How is he? I don't want to disturb him. Dr. McGuire said to leave him be. But how is he?"

"Smith, I have…" Lacy's head sagged.

"I know you're very close to him, Reverend Lacy. My condolences. Is there anything I can do? How can I help you?"

"Smith, this is…" He held the towel now in both hands and lifted it in front of him, as if offering it to Smith. A great talker, in parlors, around campfires, behind the pulpit, Lacy couldn't find words now.

"What is it?" Smith asked.

"It's. Oh, Smith, it's the general's arm," he said, his voice falling to a tortured whisper.

"My Dear God," Smith said. He tilted his head back and closed his eyes. His lips moved. A prayer.

Other men were moving amid tents at the edge of the clearing. They heard voices calling for speed. "Let's get this done," a tall man yelled over his shoulder, "we may have visitors soon." A horseman galloped into the clearing, a messenger looking for someone in authority.

Smith stepped closer to Lacy, helping shield the towel. "What do they do with the arms from the surgery?" Lacy asked.

"There are so many, they're in piles. They must bury them. In some trench. The flies there, they're awful," Smith said, looking toward the hospital tents.

"We can't," Lacy said. "There must be someplace…"

"Should it stay near him?" Smith asked. He didn't want to say that if the general died, the arm should be buried with him.

"No, lieutenant, we must take care of this now," Lacy said. He stood straighter, regaining some of the energy and initiative that his burden had sapped.

"Yes," Smith said, "it's, well, it's a relic, reverend. We must treat it with dignity, with grace." He looked down at the towel and his breath tore. "What will we do?"

A thought came to Lacy, a picture of trees and a hill. "Perhaps Ellwood," he said quietly, then more firmly said, "Yes, Ellwood. My family's place. It's a mile away. We have a graveyard. I can think of nothing else, and this will have to do. Don't you think?" Lacy said. Smith nodded.

Lacy looked up to the rolling hills and woods rising to the south from the field hospital. He had given little thought to where they were when he got word of Jackson's wounding, had only rushed to be with him. Now he saw that, just beyond a curve of hillside and hidden by a narrow patch of woods, the family home where his brother Horace still lived in summers was close by. It was a pretty spot, on a hill, old, heavy trees shading the square two-story house, a long view of the countryside. The armies hadn't yet come near it, he was fairly sure, so it should be safe. He would go there.

"Let's go, lieutenant, let's go now," Lacy said.

"Reverend Lacy, one of us should stay. The general should have a man of God nearby." Unspoken again was the thought that Jackson could die at any time. It was only an amputation, and a wound in his right hand. Many men had lived through worse. But many had died from less.

"Yes, he needs the comfort of God's words," Lacy said.

He looked at Smith. The two men were shrouded in sadness.

"He is a great man," Lacy said.

"And he's willing to go where God sends him," Smith said. He knew Jackson well. Those were almost the words Jackson had said to Lacy to turn aside the minister's protestations of grief, telling him no one could be unhappy with the will of God.

"I'll go," Lacy said. "You stay with him."

"I will." Smith looked at Lacy with a mix of compassion and fear on his face, gripped the preacher's arm. "Thank you," Smith said. "God speed."

And Lacy walked toward Ellwood on the hill.

It was a lovely place, Ellwood. A tall house, two stories atop a raised cellar, the front door and porch reached by half a dozen steps. Square and strong, with a wing off the back. It sat atop a low ridge, facing east to the morning. The ridge sloped down to the east and north, giving a gorgeous prospect of rolling fields and woodlands toward the Chancellorsville crossroads.

Lacy had been here many times before the war, to family gatherings, tables spread on the front lawn beneath the trees, children running to a swing, to the chicken houses out back.

He climbed the stairs to the front porch, cradling his burden in his arms. No one was home, the place was quiet. With the field hospital nearby, the house had not been filled with wounded men, as so many had. It felt like a sanctuary to Lacy. The daylight fluttered through the leaves swayed by the breeze.

The minister sat in a rocking chair while his breathing slowed. He was so far from his church, from the messages of peace and understanding he preached. From the farmers and townspeople, rich and poor, to whom he brought the word of God. Across the shallow valley he could see dirty white puffs of smoke, marking where cannon aimed death and mutilation at his countrymen, his parishioners. Why had God allowed this? What lesson was He teaching with all this blood? Was it the lesson of John Brown, that the sins of the country could only be washed away with the blood of the sinners? He wasn't sure what was a sin anymore, with so much killing around him. How did the words and stories of the Bible connect with what had happened in the thickets around Chancellorsville? What was the lesson in the lead and steel that sought the soft bodies of men, cutting off their dreams, their failings, their promise? Was it the Old Testament lesson, that transgressors must be punished? If so, who were the transgressors? So many around him in the South were certain sure that it was the Northerners, come trampling where they didn't belong. Lacy thought that must be true. Wasn't that why God had given so many victories to the South? Wasn't that why God had raised up this college professor to slay the cold aggressor? But then, why had God taken Jackson now? Surely the man would recover. Yet for so many thousands amputation had been a mortal insult to bodies weakened by bad food and long marches. The general might well die, Lacy knew. Indeed, as he held a fragment of the great man in his lap, he had a stab of intuition that this man could not live so sundered. That Jackson's time had come and passed. The feeling made him shiver. He felt a despair like that he'd seen in the eyes of hundreds of people who'd come to him questioning the tragic turns of life.

He sat and rocked, the arm heavy now in his lap. The meaning of it all, if there was any, was way beyond him.

He'd heard a young lieutenant in the Stonewall Brigade say that day that Jackson was being taken away from them because his troops, and the Southern people, had made almost an idol out of him.

No man was to be raised above God. But Jackson had never done that, had always given the credit for victories to God. Had gently but quickly corrected men who'd said the glory was the army's, or the men's, or the generals'. It was always, in Jackson's mind, that God had granted the victory, and to him should go the credit. When Lee sent a message congratulating Jackson on the Chancellorsville victory, Lacy remembered, the wounded Jackson had said, "General Lee is very kind, but he should give the glory to God." He had no hubris in him; why was he struck down? For our sins? Lacy thought this harsh, but easy lessons are seldom learned.

The view from the porch of Ellwood was deceptively beautiful. There was horror out there still amid the soft, burgeoning green. Too much, yesterday. More today. Lacy had a piece of that horror in his lap.

He inhaled a ragged sniff of air. He bowed his head, clasped his hands before his face, pressed his gathered knuckles to his mouth. He tried to stop thinking.

The fragrance of woodfire drifted up to Lacy. Down the hill, to his left and in front of him, men were cooking breakfast. The pungent, thick smell of burning oak. It called him back to the campfires he'd shared with so many men. With Jackson, on many nights. He remembered those campfires fondly, but how could that be? They'd been surrounded by death, by shattered bodies, by cries of torn men so many of those nights. How could a man of God like himself stand those evenings, much less like them? Did the surge of adrenaline that gripped so many men in battle act on him, too? He didn't fight, although he'd carried a gun now and then. He wasn't there to shoot, he was there to minister to the men who did. To help them deal with the ripping conflict in their guts that came from shooting other men, other creatures of God. Made in God's image, torn asunder by fallible men. How could he participate? His beliefs, that the North had no business invading the South, taking their war of aggression to the homes of his peaceful neighbors, held firm in his intellect. But in his soul, wasn't there a cost?

This land, this hill, these trees and fields, they were so beautiful. This was where men and women made lives, reared children, built homes, grew crops that fed themselves and their animals. The miraculous richness of God's creation was abundant here as in few places on earth.

The lawn of Ellwood, rolling down from the porch, shaded by oaks planted by people who'd come down from Pennsylvania, following the embracing Valley into their dreams, their future. The tumbled grass, the gardens off to his right, the children's rope swing swaying like a playful pendulum in the morning breeze. This ground, its fecund nurturing, was still whole, had not been torn, its stones and roots splattering, by metal heated with anger and thrown across whole fields and borders with murderous intent. It was an oasis in a terrible storm, its peace mocked by the random prowling monster that lurked just beyond. How could he have been part of this dance of death for so long, how could he now sit on this porch and breathe a few moments peace without throwing himself to his knees and...

And what? Asking forgiveness? His people hadn't brought this war to this place. But did that matter, who started the shooting, who first leaped in righteous, misguided anger from words to iron? The South threw its metal against Sumter first, but only because the warships of the North were bearing down on Charleston.

His troubled mind drifted to another Virginia hill, where Thomas Jefferson had sat, tormented, saying, "I tremble for my country when I reflect that God is just."

Throw himself to his knees and keen, in pain, at the destruction, at the path that man had chosen. Throw himself to his knees and simply weep until his tears, and those of all the bereft women and children and parents, washed the blood of this war from the soil God had given them to tend, not to taint.

Lincoln said the country would not be cleansed of its sins until the volume of blood matched the magnitude of pain and wrong inflicted on the slaves through centuries of bondage. Could he possibly be right, this uncouth man who sent the armies flooding into Virginia?

The minister looked over the lawn, the hills, the fields and trees beyond, and thought left him. Sadness lay on him like night thrown by an eclipse across the brilliant day.

He sat, the arm of his friend a talisman in his lap. Saying what? He couldn't read it.

Lacy heard horses, a wagon's wheels. After a time two men, carrying a burden, came around the corner of Ellwood. They walked slowly, and Lacy saw one was Jed Hotchkiss, Jackson's mapmaker and staff officer. The two men were carrying a third. Dead.

"Who is it?" Lacy called as the men passed the porch.

"It's Boswell," Hotchkiss said, his voice caved in with sadness, his face calm but desolate.

Captain J. Keith Boswell. Hotchkiss' close and dear friend. He had been killed that dark haunted night by the same volleys that tore through Jackson. After Jackson had been wounded and taken to safety, Hotchkiss had missed his friend. He went to where the general had been shot, and found Boswell dead on the ground 20 paces in front of the place Jackson fell. Boswell had taken two bullets in the heart, and one in the leg. What a terrible scene for Hotchkiss to come on, Lacy thought. Cruelty to the spirit. How much can men bear, Lord?

Hotchkiss also knew of the Lacy family burying ground, and asked the minister where it was. Lacy pointed toward his right, beyond a little dip in the ground that led past cornfields to a grove of oaks.

The men asked if Lacy would say a word over their friend. Lacy nodded again, saying nothing, and they moved on toward the grove.

Lacy looked out beyond the hills at the edge of the lawn, searching through the growing morning light for something he couldn't name. He saw, beyond the many shades of green of fields and woods, a thin column of men, marching slowly back toward the battlefield of Chancellorsville. Back toward Hooker and the huge army of the North. Back toward more death, more limbs torn from living men, more ground turned slick and muddy with leaking blood.

He stood. He asked God to take over the task of determining what it was all for. He heard no answer, only a bird call mocking his inner emptiness. He stepped heavily across the broad boards of the porch, lowered himself down the steps, walked slowly across the waving grass toward the grove of oaks. He would bury his general's arm next to the body of the young and blameless officer borne from the battlefield. Then he would continue in his place with the army Jackson had led. He would go on without an answer, with only his faith, shot through now like the battle flags of the Stonewall Brigade. He prayed that faith would not fray away to nothing in the tempest still before him.

The thick scratching of a shovel cutting through the earth of the family grave-yard finally chased his thoughts away. Hotchkiss, doing something in the little graveyard he could never have imagined in his youth only heartbeats ago, dug, and dug, and dug into the hard-yielding soil. Cutting Virginia, slicing through the peace of the morning.

The trees on the slope stood sentinel, shading the men beneath, as the sounds of the cannon and the sounds of the shovels mingled in the fresh green leaves.

The battles around Chancellorsville would go on for another three days, ending when Hooker pulled his Federal troops back across the rivers, defeated but not destroyed. The big Chancellor house at the crossroads, where wounded men's arms, legs, hands and feet had been amputated on the piano in the parlor, was pounded by cannon shells and set on fire. Bursting shells had set some of the thick woods on fire also, burning to death wounded men who could not crawl away. Charred corpses were found after the battle with a little space of ground around them frantically cleared of leaves and branches by dying hands or feet. To try to stop the fire.

Death was everywhere, the second-worst butcher's bill of the war, after the Seven Days Battles to save Richmond, where Jackson and his men had also fought. Here, more than 22,000 men had been shot in the week of fighting around Chancellorsville, 3,418 of them killed.

This time, William Sutton's wound was too bad for the exhausted, blood-spattered surgeons to save the leg. It was sawed off, and Sutton was set on the ground in another storeyard, with hundreds of other wounded, to recover or die. He lived.

The most grievous casualty was Thomas Jackson.

Captain Richard Wilbourn had carried the details of Jackson's wounding to Robert E. Lee at his headquarters on the Plank Road east of Chancellorsville. The Confederate commander had been deeply shaken. "Captain, any victory is dearly bought that deprives us of the services of Jackson even temporarily," Lee said. Lee had heard earlier by dispatch from Jackson about his being shot, and had sent back a message to his most aggressive and resourceful lieutenant: "I cannot express my regret at the occurrence. Could I have directed events, I should have chosen for the good of the country to have been disabled in your stead."

In churches and parlors and public squares across the South, people prayed that Jackson would recover. Their hopes lay with him on his cot. Nobody fought like Jackson, and they knew he couldn't be spared.

Chancellorsville, May 4, 1863—Confederate Army

Sutton woke again to pain, dull and thick.

Around him he heard groaning. One high voice calling for Mother. Two others laughing about the "Flying Dutchmen," the Germans of Howard's Federal corps that Jackson's flank attack had routed. "They weren't worth shit," a husky voice said.

"Some of 'em fought, enough to shoot us."

"Bad luck."

Sutton, on his back, could see the blue sky through green leaves. He smelled sour sweat around him, vomit, urine, excrement. Blood. Dust. Damp wool. Smoke. The sweet, rich, cloying scent of decaying flesh, some of it still attached to men, some in piles on the ground. He was lying in the dirt near a small store that was now a field hospital.

"Any food coming?" a voice asked.

"Nothin' you'd want to eat," another said.

"I got some of Billy Yank's food when we kicked 'em out of their camps, by that big log breastwork. Pretty good beef."

"They always eat better'n us."

"Makes 'em slow."

A scream from the other side of Sutton. "Don't move me! OOO-ooow, don't move me. Oh, Christ." Grumbling then, as somebody moved away.

"That boy's a little touchy."

"What he's got left to touch."

"Ain't that so."

Sutton closed his eyes, scratched at his filthy head.

The husky voice again. "God, my shoulder hurts. Ripped all to hell. I think they dug in there with a mattock."

"They were entrenching, Bobby."

The two voices laughed.

Cannon boomed from miles away.

Sutton lifted his left leg a little. A hot ring of pain. A strange feeling. Light. No weight.

His leg was gone.

Two men walked by, towering tall from Sutton's perspective on the ground. They went to a man laid out below Sutton's foot. "This one's gone, Joshua, let's get him out of here."

"We got enough shovels for all this?"

"Yeah, shovels we got. Not enough of anything else, but shovels we got."

Sutton, marooned on his back, felt the world spin out of his control.

Farther away, the tall man's voice again. "Josh, another one over here. We're falling behind."

La Vista Plantation, May 4, 1863—Confederate Army

A knot of wounded, exhausted men sat by the side of a little country lane, to the south and far behind the lines of the battle around Chancellorsville.

Behind them, through trees and shrubs, could be seen set back from the road a two-story house, made taller in its aspect by two great pillars on either side of the front door. Stately, proud, gracious. In peaceful times, this was a gorgeous prospect over clearings and woodlands in fertile Virginia. But now, the thump of distant cannons rolled over the land, making the songs of the fluttering birds seem out of place.

The humidity of the day made the men leaning against fence rails seem even more miserable, their faces a sheen of sweat. But as they saw a wagon coming down the dusty road, they stood, those who could, and moved close to the edge of the wagon ruts.

Two horses pulled the wagon, which was covered by a rounded canvas top. A few men on horseback road before and behind the wagon. An ambulance.

"Is it Old Jack?" a man with a bloody rag around his neck asked, leaning forward to see.

"Dunno," said another, leaning on his rifle to ease his foot, which no longer had a heel.

The horses strained into their traces, pacing evenly, their heads bobbing up and down in rhythm, their shoulder muscles rippling as they pulled. Metal clattered, wet leather creaked. The ambulance pulled even with the cluster of men, all standing now, hats off.

"Who you got? Is it the general?" the man with the neck wound called to an officer riding in front.

The rider nodded, solemn, leaned over and said, "And Crutchfield. We're taking them to Guiney's Station." Stapleton Crutchfield was Jackson's artillery chief, also painfully wounded at Chancellorsville.

When Jackson was being withdrawn from the battlefield at Chancellorsville to Wilderness Tavern where he was initially treated, he hadn't wanted the men to know it was he being carried by stretcher and ambulance, afraid that fear would spread and sap their fighting spirit. But now everyone knew Jackson had been wounded, and all along the winding road, 27 miles from Wilderness Tavern to Guiney's Station, men seemed to know that it was Jackson passing in the ambulance.

These men at La Vista had seen many wagons go by bearing wounded men, blood dripping off the tailboards of some to mix with the dirt of the road. This wagon, so still, the cloth drawn tight at the back, pulled their eyes to it.

A man who'd just come up from the main house with fresh water stopped by the little group, gestured a question with his head, heard the word "Jackson" in reply, let the canteen fall in his hand against his thigh and let his head hang for a moment.

Then he lifted his face and called out, "General, I'd trade places with you if I could, I honest would."

The rider, now past them, turned in his saddle, his boyish face showing above his shoulder, and raised his gloved hand in a small upright wave. The silent closed wagon rolled on.

Chancellorsville, May 5, 1863—Confederate Army

General Fitzhugh Lee was walking his horse through the camp when Patterson Neff saw him.

"General Lee, how are you, sir?" Neff said, standing and walking over to where Lee now stopped. Lee put his hand on his horse's muzzle, stroking it from between the eyes to the animal's soft nose.

"I'm tired, Neff, very tired, like everybody here," Lee said. He reached his left hand up into his horse's mane, kneading it with his fingers. Lee's uniform was rumpled and dirty, showing the many days of riding and fighting he and the rest of Jeb Stuart's troopers had been doing during the Chancellorsville campaign.

"Have you heard anything about General Jackson?"

Fitzhugh Lee, the nephew of Robert E. Lee and one of Stuart's best cavalry commanders, lowered his head. "They've had to amputate his arm, you knew that?" Neff nodded. "His left arm," Lee continued. "It was so badly damaged by several shots it couldn't be saved. He's resting. They've taken him away from the battlefield, I believe, Dr. McGuire and others on the general's staff."

Neff shook his head. It was hard to believe. Everyone had hoped Jackson was only lightly wounded, but clearly that wasn't the case. There was a foreboding in the camp. Until the troops saw Jackson mounted on Little Sorrel and riding among them in his ungainly shamble again, they would worry about how the army would fare. Hooker had been pushed back across the river, but the elation at the victory was subdued by concern for Jackson.

"How is he, will he recover? He will, won't he?" Neff asked.

"No one can say, Neff. We've lost so many, and we surely can't afford to lose General Jackson. I suppose all we can do is pray, now." He leaned against his horse's tall strong shoulder and rubbed his own forehead with the back of his hand, chasing away bugs and trying to wipe away weariness.

"I have some biscuits and coffee here, sir, if you'd like some."

"I would, yes, thank you," Lee said, and looped the reins of his horse over a branch and walked with Neff to a log next to a small fire.

Lee drank from the cup Neff handed him. "Many men have recovered from worse wounds. We have so many who've come back into service after having a limb cut off. Dick Ewell says he's coming back, without the leg he lost at Second Manassas. That's courage."

"Nobody wants to give up, sir, especially now when we've hurt the Yankees so badly," Neff said.

"But what a cost, if we lose Jackson."

Neff let a few moments of silence pass, crossed his legs under his thighs. He could hardly let himself think of Jackson dying, or being so incapacitated that he couldn't return to the army. He changed the subject. "General Stuart did very well handling the troops in Jackson's place," Neff said. "Do you think he'll stay in command of the infantry?" Stuart, because A.P Hill had also been wounded, took over command of Jackson's corps to finish the battle against Hooker.

"Oh, Stuart's a horseman. He likes to fly free. I can't see him commanding infantry very long, things would move too slow for him. Even Jackson's foot cavalry would seem too plodding for Jeb," Lee said, with a faint smile. "He'll do whatever General Lee asks of him, but I don't think he'll stay with the infantry."

The two men took small bites of hardtack, and Neff pulled at a piece of chaff stuck in his teeth. Conversation seemed hard, even though a hundred thoughts were swirling through Neff's mind. There was a listlessness, a weight on Neff and most of the men around him. He could feel it on Lee as well. Lee was handsome, tall, a gentleman cavalier, as well-bred as royalty. But by this campfire, on this uncertain afternoon, he looked diminished.

"How is your uncle taking the news of Jackson's wounding?" Neff asked.

Lee didn't answer right away. He no longer worried about having to prove himself apart from his lineage—his ability had been so clearly shown in the years of war. But he spoke very little about his uncle. Although the men always wanted to hear stories about their famous commander, Fitz Lee seldom indulged them.

Now he said, "The General doesn't like bad tidings or conflict. Doesn't want to take time or energy for them. He's a very positive man, only wants to find solutions to problems, only wants to get 'those people' as he calls them out of Virginia and get the fighting over with so we can build a country. He focuses very much on what can be done and doesn't spend much time on what can't be. I expect he's praying for General Jackson and trying to keep the frightening possibility that Jackson won't return out of his mind. It's probably best for us all to refrain from speculation about what might be. We have plenty to do." Lee stretched his legs in front of him, looked over his shoulder to make sure his horse was all right.

"I haven't talked to General Lee, but I would say he's disappointed that we didn't crush Hooker. He's like Lincoln that way. I read that after Antietam all Lincoln wanted to know was why McClellan hadn't pursued us and finished us. He wasn't satisfied that we'd been chased out of Maryland and that Washington had been secured." Lee looked over at Neff, his voice was tired but his words, though quiet, were firm. "This war isn't about territory, and Lincoln knows that, and so does General Lee. So just pushing Hooker north of the Rappahannock again isn't enough. We had a shot at him. Jackson was pushing for the fords of the river. If he'd made it, we could have smashed Hooker between Jackson, General Lee from the southeast and Jubal Early coming up from Fredericksburg. That's the chance we lost. We could have ended it right here." His face showed the yearning for the end, and despair from the knowledge that the war would go on, with whoever was left to fight it.

"Yes, sir, I think we could have done it," Neff said. "Might still."

"We'll have to, Neff. We have no choice. There's talk that we'll go north now, take the war to the Yankees. Maybe Pennsylvania this time."

"That's what Jackson would want," Neff said.

"Yes, that's right. And with luck he'll be with us. It's hard to imagine going without him. He provides so much..." Lee paused to find a word. "Drive. Fire. Quiet, banked, powerful fire."

"The firebox in the locomotive," Neff said.

Lee smiled. "Something like that, yes."

Neff straightened himself up, leaned back and forth to loosen the muscles tightened by days of riding. "What was Jackson like on the flank march? You led him, I heard."

"No," Lee said, "I didn't lead him. I'd been out to the west, seeing what was happening on Hooker's far right. Stuart and I found that his flank was unprotected, and Stuart rode to tell Lee and Jackson, and I stayed out there. Watching. Hoping to God Hooker wouldn't realize his mistake. Jackson could have taken that long march and at the end found Hooker's right fortified and all the flank move would have done would be to have split our army down the middle, where a real fighting general could have taken us apart in pieces." Lee could see again in his mind the trees, so thick, the underbrush so dense, The Wilderness aptly named. He'd ridden nervously all around Hooker's flank, watching for signs that the Federals knew Jackson was coming. Time had gone so slowly. He rode and kept watching for Jackson's troops to appear, quick before the chance was gone. He'd seen the Federals watching, pickets and outposts seeing the movement of the Confederate troops. He knew they must have warned their officers in Howard's corps. Thank God Howard apparently didn't listen to the reports, or didn't take them seriously. Jackson was fortunate to be going against a general so thoroughly unlike him. Jackson always knew what was going on around him, was always thinking ahead to what his adversary might do. Not so Howard; he'd seemed asleep.

"When Jackson came up to the Plank Road at the head of his troops, I did go to meet him and take him up on a knoll to show him the Federals' disposition," Lee said. "He'd thought he'd go up the Plank Road to hit Howard, but I suggested the Orange Turnpike, a couple of miles farther to the north, would give him a better angle. On the Plank Road he'd have come up against Howard on an oblique, but from the Orange Turnpike he could hit his rear. Jackson saw it immediately."

"What did he say?"

Lee smiled and let out a little laugh. "Not a thing. That man doesn't waste words." Lee took off his hat and scratched at his thick hair, then flipped the brim of the hat against his left hand. "I'd have said something, in his place, I think. I'd have let out a whoop and then realized too late we could be heard. But Jackson doesn't let anything out. He's tight as a cork in a bottle. That's why, I expect, he can always appear where the Yankees don't think he could be."

"Yes, sir, that's Jackson. Did he show any emotion, any excitement?" Neff asked.

"Not really. But his eyes, they just bored in, swept over the scene, captured everything in an instant. There were the Federals, their rifles stacked, sitting. We could see some of them slaughtering beef behind the line. They could have been on guard duty back on the Potomac. They must have had no idea we were there, despite those sightings by some of their pickets. They must have thought it was just cavalry roaming the flank. The poor fools."

Others coming into the camp nearby saw Lee and called hello. Lee waved his hat, nodded his head at them, said a word or two to several. Then he continued, leaning a little toward Neff. "Jackson's eyes seemed to light up. That's a cliché, I know, but his face was so intense, his eyes were like a predator's locked on his prey. It was eerie. And exciting, I must say. I thought we had them, and he knew we did.

"Then he turned to the one courier who'd come up on the knoll with us and told him to tell General Rodes to move his men across the Plank Road and up to the Orange Turnpike, and Jackson would join him there. He was eager, taut, absolutely focused and ready. I remember thinking Howard was in deep trouble because this old blue-light Presbyterian was after him. God have mercy on those Federal boys, because Jackson would have none. That's what I thought." Neff could hear the excitement in Lee's voice as the cavalry general pictured the scene again. "I think that was the most thrilling moment I've had in the war," Lee said. "Jackson had done it, or almost. He had marched clear around Hooker's flank, and victory was spread out there right before us, so close we could reach out and grab it. I hardly wanted to breathe, I didn't want my horse to wiggle and set the leather creaking because I didn't want the Federals to hear us and raise the alarm. We could see them clearly, so I know they could see us. If they'd been aware enough to look. It was all right there in the balance, a few more miles, another half-hour, and we'd be on them. I was just charged."

He looked up into the trees, watching the leaves turn dark in the waning day. "That's when it's best, just before. The scouting is done, you've gotten everything in place, if you try for any better disposition you'll lose the moment so you go with what you have. And you lean forward in the saddle and it's all right before you, whatever happens now is in the hands of the fates. And you go in." The pitch of his voice rose at the end, making the statement seem so simple, so matter-of-fact.

Quietly now he said, "And after that, it's awful. It's just the killing. The excitement, the intensity, the fear all rush through you, but while it's what you've trained for, it's not...satisfying. It's the horror of war then, especially once it's done and you see what's around you." He paused, then his voice became more firm. "I don't mean to be melancholy, it's what we're here to do. We're soldiers, you've felt it all, Neff."

Neff nodded, and Lee stood up. "After Jackson gave that order to the courier, he just left." Lee chuckled. "He just left, didn't say anything to me. Didn't wish us luck, didn't say thank you, didn't say carry on, just turned his mount and left." He looked down at Neff, smiling. "Seemed like he didn't want to waste a moment or a single spark of energy. Actually, I suspect he was already on the Orange Turnpike in his mind, positioning his troops.

"He rode away and I never saw him again." Lee put on his hat, brushed off his sleeves, and said, "Thanks for the little repast, Neff. I think we all need some rest now." Neff rose too, saluted, and said, "Thank you for stopping, general. I appreciate what you told me. I very much wish us all luck."

Lee returned the salute, and said, "Yes, we'll all need it if Jackson stays down very long. But we'll do all right. Be careful. Keep these men alert. This fight may not be over."

"Oh, I suspect Hooker's already making his excuses to Washington, telling them he's executed a strategic change of base or something, like Little Mac. I think there will only be talking for a few days, anyway."

"May be. But there will be more fighting coming. I'll see you up the road."

Lee gathered his horse's reins, swung up in the saddle, and Neff thought he heard both the man and the horse groan.

Neff watched Lee as his horse's thick hindquarters switched along, stepping high over the thick brush. He liked this man, hoped no Federal bullet would find him. So many in the Lee clan were on the front lines. Hell, everybody was on the front lines, Neff thought.

Still standing, he looked down at the fire. And he drifted back to the porch in Port Republic, where he'd seen Jackson go inside the house where Turner Ashby's body was laid out. That evening had touched him, frightened him. It was the first time he'd seen that such a dynamic leader could fall. And even though he'd only exchanged a few words with Jackson then, he'd felt close to the man. And now Jackson seemed so far removed from them. Now the quiet, the heavy realization of mortality, was about Jackson.

Reaching across his breast with his right arm, Neff grabbed his left arm around the bicep. It was strong and firm, from pulling his horse's reins, from the work he'd done on his family's farm at the north end of the Shenandoah Valley. He stretched the arm out in front of him, felt all the muscles tense along the length of it. Flexed the fingers, opened them, closed them into a fist. Opened them again. Looked at the hand. Brought it close to his face. Such a complex mechanism, so many muscles moving to allow the hand to do so many tasks. Amazing. And so fragile. All the flying metal around him so many times. The tender flesh would have no chance against it.

What would it be like with the arm gone? As Lee said, many men had lost arms, hands, legs, jaws even. Their lives would be different forever. Maimed. Crippled. Lame. The terms chilled him. All the things that your body can do that you just take for granted—when it's all there. Pulling your cheek taut with your left hand as you shave it with your right. Scratching yourself. Gesturing while you talk. Keeping your balance as a horse prances and turns. Embracing a woman. Pulling on your boots. He couldn't conceive of it. But that would be life for thousands of men for decades to come. Every day, reminded a hundred times what they can no longer do.

He stretched his left arm straight out to the side. Felt the weariness in the muscles as he held the arm out, felt the beginning of trembles as it held up its own weight. The feeling—just feeling—was wonderful to him now.

Amid the sadness that hung like fog all around him, he felt a guilty thrill that he was still unhurt.

He lowered the arm. And lowered his head.

Neff hadn't prayed much in the war. It had seemed wrong to pray for victory that would mean death to so many people who were probably also praying to the same God. But now he breathed a short prayer as the embers of the little fire turned grey. For Jackson's life. And for his own.

Chancellorsville, May 7, 1863—Confederate Army

Sparrow's unit, the Stonewall Brigade, hadn't been in the fighting at first. They'd been placed south of the Orange Plank Road when the main thrust of the flank attack against Howard had hit to the north, along the Orange Turnpike. But on the second day, the day after Jackson was shot, the Stonewall Brigade had been in the midst of it. Pressing the Federals, charging against the log-and-earth barricade, breaking stand after stand, inflicting and taking heavy damage.

After two more days of fighting, Hooker had withdrawn across the Rappahannock to where he started the campaign. He hadn't been able to get his troops at Fredericksburg, under General John Sedgwick, to come up and attack Lee from the rear while Hooker fought him around Chancellorsville. And his cavalry was gone—Hooker had sent them looping south at the beginning of the campaign to cut the railroad from Richmond behind Lee, which they accomplished too late. Not having cavalry made Hooker blind during the battle, never knowing where he'd be hit next. Hooker himself had been knocked flat by a cannonball that hit a column he was leaning against on the front porch of the Chancellor house. His head was battered, he suffered a concussion, and in a semi-stupor he left the army rudderless while Lee and Jeb Stuart pounded away at his army. Beaten, he'd retreated.

No ground gained on either side. The Federals were pushed back, but Lee was bitterly disappointed. He wanted more. Always. More than just dead men.

The South had a great victory, if you measured it in stopping the huge Federal army. But victory wouldn't come until "those people" as Lee called them were destroyed or back at the North for good.

And the South again had a hero—again Stonewall Jackson. The greatest flank attack of the war had nearly annihilated Hooker. Nearly. Then the shots from the North Carolina brigade, and the South had a bleeding hero, a wounded hero.

Now, while both armies sank to the ground and panted, burying the dead, easing their wounded, eating cooked food, Sparrow stood at the small store and shed that served as one of many field hospitals around the battlefield. He'd been looking for Sutton, and now he'd found him.

Asleep.

Sparrow looked at the lean form of his friend lying on the ground, covered by a muddy blanket. Sutton's stubbled face was turned to the side, fallen, weak. His mouth was open, a little crust on the lips. His hat was tipped over his eyes to keep the sun out. His shirt and jacket were dirty. The blanket covered him from the belly down. At the fork in his legs, where the long ridges of Sutton's legs should be running down under the blanket, Sparrow's eyes stopped. On the right, the leg stretched, covered. On the left, only a mound a few inches from the crotch. And then there was nothing there.

"Oh, Will," he whispered.

He sat, his own legs giving out.

A katydid chirred. Sparrow heard snuffling. Realized it was his own.

So long, this war. He'd seen so many go under. He hoped Will would last.

Sparrow's side ached. Had since the flank march past Catharine Furnace. When Sutton had found him, halfway up the spout.

Now, he was as weary as rock.

Sutton's chest rose and fell slowly, steadily. Sparrow watched. Thought of the rainy marches in the Valley. The flickering campfires, boiling pork. Laughs. Talks together. Bucking each other up. Just being there, quiet company. Hard questions. Obedience. Following someone who wouldn't tell you anything, but in whom you had blind faith. Mountains. Marching over mountains. Jackson, stern, tireless, a force like a mountain moving, speed of a tumbling river.

What a long march. Was it over? For Sutton.

Virginia? A ways to go.

Sutton's right hand was out, open toward Sparrow. Long fingers, broken nails, dirt ground in. Strong hand. But delicate. Sparrow reached, touched the fingertips with his, couldn't see because his eyes were swimming.

Will. He needed the sleep. It would heal him.

Sutton got out a pencil stub. Wrote. Curled the paper into Sutton's hand. Held it.

Stood. Looked down for a long moment. And walked away.

> *You're going home. Wherever that is for you.*
> *I'll see you after the war.*
> *You carried me. Thank you, brother.*
> *James*

Fairfield Plantation, Guiney's Station, May 7, 1863

Thomas Chandler stood on the porch of his house, Fairfield Plantation, just up the road from Guiney's Station. He was thinking about Stonewall Jackson, who lay wounded in the little outbuilding that had served as the farm office. Jackson's doctor, Hunter McGuire, had said the main house was too crowded with wounded, and Chandler had let the general's staff clear out the office. Chandler had greeted Jackson three days before when the general arrived at Fairfield by ambulance. Jackson, tired but ever polite, had said, "I am sorry I cannot shake hands with you, but one arm is gone and my right hand is wounded."

One more macabre touch in a time when his house and grounds had been turned into a hospital full of bleeding and dying men.

Now, he watched men digging in the tree-shaded yard. It looked like they were digging a grave. But as he watched, he saw with a shock of horror that they were exhuming a body, buried just a few days earlier. General Frank Paxton, the commander of the Stonewall Brigade, would be sent home to the Shenandoah Valley.

Chandler groaned. The war was taking over the world.

When Frank Paxton had been a major in the Stonewall Brigade, he wrote his wife after a 26-mile march one day during the Valley campaign, "Verily, it is a moving life we lead." Now he would be moving one last time.

Before the war, Paxton had been a bank president and attorney in Lexington and had become a friend of Thomas Jackson. Called "Bull" in the army, Paxton was a big man and had a big voice, which he used roughly on the men he commanded in the 27th Virginia. He was so gruff with the men that they refused to reelect him to his position, and Jackson took his friend onto his own staff.

In the fall, Jackson had named Paxton to command the Stonewall Brigade, a choice that was not popular at first. But Paxton fought well at Fredericksburg, and took good care of the brigade during the cold and difficult winter. Previously an agnostic, he became a Christian that winter, as did many men in the brigade. He exempted from military duty any man who would help build the chapel at Camp Winder, where the brigade moved after Moss Neck. When the battle at Chancellorsville came, his men followed him eagerly into the woods. There, he was shot down leading a charge against Hooker's right flank.

He had written his wife that winter, "I feel that life to many of us hangs upon a slender thread."

The night before his last battle, he asked Henry Kyd Douglas of Jackson's staff to make sure his body and his letters would be sent to his wife. He wasn't maudlin or morbid, Douglas thought, just resigned. When the order came to begin the attack, he was reading his Bible.

Staff member James Power Smith had the duty of telling the wounded Jackson that Paxton had been killed. The general had said, "Paxton, Paxton," then turned his head to the tent wall and struggled to control himself, the only time anyone on his staff saw him lose the iron hold he'd kept on his emotions since he'd been shot.

Chandler hadn't known Frank Paxton, but he knew he had a wife and children back in Lexington. Another widow, more orphans, another leader of a community cut down. This war left so much in ruins.

As Chandler watched the soldiers struggle to pull the coffin out of the dirt, he saw a figure walking in the yard. It was a woman, and as Chandler looked, she turned toward the men with the coffin. She stopped in mid-stride. She stared, then raised her left hand to her head as her body bent and she bowed with the weight of what she was seeing.

It was Anna Jackson, the general's wife. And a friend of Paxton's wife. She had arrived a short time ago, and the doctors hadn't let her see her husband yet, as they were changing the dressings on his wounds.

What a terrible, chilling introduction to his home, Chandler thought, as he stepped wearily off the porch to go to her.

Fairfield Plantation, Guiney's Station, May 9, 1863

In the fading afternoon, rich light made the spindle of the bed glow. Cut and turned from a four-by-four post, the spindle was square where the bed's frame was held by the post, curved above in flowing lines rising to an acorn-shaped knob at the top.

The light fell also on the scuffed wood floor, the grain visible in a soft luster. Dust motes floated.

From the bed, only a whisp-slight rising and falling of hesitant breath trickling through fluid-filled lungs.

Anna Jackson sat in a curved, plush chair at the foot of the bed where her husband lay.

The shutters were mostly closed, because so many people had come up from the little railroad station just southeast of the plantation to see Jackson if they could. He was, right now, the most famous man in North America, bold victor, wounded hero.

But the strong light of the falling sun flowed into the room through the opening in the shutters, highlighting white rolls of bandage on the table by the fireplace, and catching a corner of the fabric of the chair, kindling it to a rich, warm brown.

Outside the window, through the trees, silver sparkles on water. The Po and the Ni rivers came together here, just west of Fairfield, and flooded low spots in the thick woods. Sleek water flowing, cleansing the land.

The room was pierced with the sound of the clock on the mantel above the fireplace. Its regular pulse built a silence around it, wrapped each click of the mechanism in a thick still quiet. Click-clock, click-clock, click-clock. The first note high and thin, the second lower and full. Click-clock, click-clock, click-clock. Between each pair of ticks a tiny rest of absolute stillness. The small sharp sound made the following absence of sound total and wide as a flat calm river.

The sound and the no-sound paired and beat and stopped and flowed and coalesced the air of the room into a single living thing. A place, a state, a world, wrapped only around this man, this woman, this moment.

The whole room, chambered in wood and flowing with light, beat like a heart.

Anna sat, her eyes closed, and listened, adrift, as the whole room beat like a heart.

Fairfield Plantation, Guiney's Station, May 9, 1863

In the small room above where Jackson lay, James Power Smith stared out the window. In the yard were wounded men being carried to the cars at Guiney's Station just down the road. Wagons with supplies coming up from the trains to the tent camp of wounded beyond the main house of Fairfield. People standing, staring at the office building where he sat. Standing vigil, he and they.

His breathing was hard, fast, shallow, his thoughts a storm. He hadn't moved his head, neck, arms for many long minutes. Although his gaze was aimed through the window, he saw nothing of what happened outside the house. He was, rather, seeing tumbling scenes from the immediate and more distant past.

Inside a tent, the light of a lantern bright against canvas, three surgeons working, bent over Jackson. Hunter McGuire first cutting out the bullet stuck in the skin on the back of Jackson's right hand. Then beginning the circular cut through the slack flesh of Jackson's left arm, just inches below the shoulder. Skin so pale, the stricken man so frail. Smith was holding the light for the doctors.

Then, the image in the trees as he helped carry Jackson on a litter, only minutes after the general had been shot. On Jackson's staff, Smith had been there when the bullets flew in the dark. As they carried him, frightened faces emerged from the dark and asked who it was. "Say it is a Confederate officer," Jackson had whispered. Later, when McGuire had come to them in the trees, he asked if the general was badly hurt. "I'm afraid I am dying," Jackson had said. But he hadn't been, then. The pain was so bad, though, that you could see the imprint of

Jackson's teeth through his drawn-taut lips. Still, the man had been calm, his emotions held on a tight rein.

Then an image of a tall thin man on a bench. At a wedding, in Rockbridge County, just outside of Lexington. 1859. They were on the porch of Bellevue, a lovely mansion overlooking a peaceful valley. Smith hadn't known the man, who was dressed in the uniform of a major of artillery in the United States Army. The man had large hands and feet, was neat in appearance, with serious but gentle eyes. His conversation was awkward as they chatted of country life, but his manner was courteous. Smith asked a friend, when he had a chance, who this was, and was told Thomas Jackson, a professor at the Virginia Military Institute who had won renown in the Mexican War. They talked several times that day, walking the road, standing on the porch, sitting in the parlor. Jackson was grace-less, unlike his wife, who was small and refined and moved easily in the social setting. The major was terse and abrupt, fixed in his convictions, but bright, good-humored, and clearly happy with his life of school, church and wife. They talked of books, Europe, faith, gardening, the Valley. Jackson said he'd never seen a more beautiful place in the world than Lexington. Smith found Jackson kind and—through his very awkwardness at social intercourse—strangely intriguing. That attraction, hard to define, had lasted and strengthened to this day for Smith.

Gardening. Hard to picture this man's big strong hands in the garden, touching fragile flower stems, tamping wet earth around young plants. Did he kneel, as others do, in front of the rows, damp black dirt pressing into his knees? Did he go out in the morning, when the leaves were wet with dew, to survey the rich green growth, to raise his face and thank God for the peace and the glory of the morning? Did he smile then?

Sounds. The stairs creaked. Jim Lewis, Jackson's servant, a slave hired out from a Lexington neighbor, coming upstairs from the sickroom, going to lie down for a few moments in the little room across from where Smith sat. Lewis sighed as he sagged onto a pallet. What must he be thinking? How horrible a life in bondage must be—far beyond horrible. Hopeless. Now his master was dying. Would Lewis see this as divine retribution? A bill come due? Jackson was fighting to retain slavery, no matter the patriotic language that flew around the cause. So was this now justice? Or would Lewis see this as a loss, of a man decent within an indecent institution? Lewis, of course, would say nothing of this to a white man—perhaps not even to himself.

A scene from the battlefield. Kernstown, the first fight in the Valley Campaign. The Confederate lines were coming apart under relentless fire, and Jackson called to a drummer boy. Calm, unruffled, his resolve completely focused on this action, he said to the boy, "Beat the rally." The boy did. Cannon shells blasted the air, musketry racketed on all sides, grim men yelled and fell and

Jackson kept his hand on the boy's shoulder, holding him to his task while the line reformed to the beat of the drum. That strong hand on that slim shoulder— Jackson pumped his conviction like electricity into the boy and through the drumbeats to his men. Holding the boy against his natural instinct to run and be saved. Death could have found them both in one quick exploding heartbeat, but he held them both there, sure that death would only come if God meant it to, and sure that what was needed at that exact moment was this rallying point. Cruel, murderous, to hold the boy so. But it was what was needed.

On the field at Winchester, Banks' Federals routed, running. Jackson almost exploding with drive, never a pause, crying to his weary troops as he waved his hand forward, "Press right on to the Potomac!" Pushing with his will to destroy the Yankee army, pushing with a thunderhead of righteous keening desire that his exhausted men could simply not obey.

Smith looked at his hands in his lap before him. In training to be a minister, Smith thought his hands should be instruments of blessing. Now they were worn, callused, strong from pulling on horses' reins, nicked and scraped from packing gear and tightening straps and buckles.

He had felt blood with these hands. Slick on his fingers when fresh, holding the back of a soldier's head when a piece of shrapnel had ripped through his skull. Warm, alive, streaming through his grasp. Tackier when the wound was old, Smith's hand on a boy's breast, shirt and breast torn by grapeshot, the blood cooler, more thick. One shouldn't be feeling blood. Touching blood.

Jackson's blood. On his sleeve, dripping from his hand. A shirttail someone had torn off and pressed against the general's wound, the cloth heavy and soaked.

Are you washed in the blood of the lamb?

Inundated.

Smith sucked air through his teeth. All the wounded outside. All the blood.

Remembered words came to Smith, here in this darkening room. Earnest, searching, awed words from John Esten Cooke, an officer on Jeb Stuart's staff, who recently told Smith he found Jackson's will gigantic, almost beyond human. Cooke said—the words were so powerful Smith could hear them still—Jackson had "a tenacity of purpose so unbending, a resolution so stern and obdurate that he seemed to possess the power of overwhelming all human opposition and compelling destiny to crouch before him, and obey him." Smith heard those words intoned in his head now, and found them true and terrifying. "Compelling destiny to crouch before him." This man Jackson, so gentle he would, unbidden, dry a stranger's sleet-soaked coat at his own fireside in winter camp, was on the field a barely contained inferno of power like a star. Smith shuddered. Did Jackson reach too far? Did he want beyond bounds? Did he call heaven down, try to bend its power to his will—and reap now the whirlwind on his own frail fading body?

Outside, a train whistled, driving north. Smith looked out, saw molten red sparks shooting from the firebox into the violet sky.

Lee's Headquarters, Chancellorsville, May 10, 1863

Rev. Beverly Tucker Lacy found Robert E. Lee standing outside, waiting for him. Lacy had left Jackson's bedside at the Chandler place near Guiney's Station to preach to the troops this clear, sunny Sunday morning. He would lead them in prayer for Jackson's health. Lacy hadn't wanted to leave, but Jackson told him to go, to lead the service as he normally would. To the deacon, keeping the church going was paramount.

Lee had sent for Lacy, so the minister stopped by the general's headquarters before going to the service. Lee asked about Jackson's condition, and Lacy told him Jackson was failing, that there was little hope. Even that, Lacy knew, was an exaggeration, a politeness. Pneumonia had settled in Jackson's lungs, which had been damaged, perhaps, in the fall from the litter as he was carried from the woods, and he was exhausted. Lee, ever so solid, rocked a little as he heard.

"Surely General Jackson must recover." Lee's graceful voice was low, yearning, pained. "God will not take him from us, now that we need him so much. Surely he will be spared to us, in answer to the many prayers which are offered for him."

Lacy didn't know what to say. Lee knew it was not a case of bargaining with God, offer so many prayers and you get what you want. Children thought this when they tried to understand what their parents were saying about religion, trying to squeeze their childish wonder into the narrow aisles of church behavior and ideas. Maybe Lee felt like a child today, lost and hurting. Lacy could only tell the aching general that it was in God's hands. Lee nodded. He had grown used to letting go, to giving Jackson, as a battle offered, only a general direction and leaving the how of it to him. He trusted Jackson, and the trust was more than repaid. Now Lee had to let go again; his hands couldn't hold this either. He wanted to trust, but he was afraid.

Lacy went, led the service, said the prayers, but felt an emptiness inside. Today it all felt like motions, like a drill. God forgive him, he still wanted to believe in the power of prayer, but he believed more today in the wasted form of that good man at Chandlers'. He wanted to believe that God had somewhere else for Jackson to be, but all he could feel was the leaving.

The soldiers sang, they prayed, but it was all strangely quiet. There was a great sadness, a tentative fear, a waiting. What would happen to Jackson? What would Hooker do? What would Lee do? What would they do?

As he left to return to Chandlers', Lee called him again. The grey beard, the soft hair, the almost feminine gentleness of his eyes, the calm that was always about this man all wrapped Lacy in a sliding sadness. Lee was strong, but this was hurting him. Lee, on whose shoulders the country weighed, seemed to find this too heavy.

"When you return, I trust you will find him better," Lee said, a forced hope in his voice. His eyes searched Lacy's. He continued, softly. "When a suitable occasion offers, give him my love," the general said, the word perfectly but strangely right from this man of war, "and tell him that I wrestled in prayer for him last night as I never prayed, I believe, for myself."

Lee turned quickly away, his narrow chest moving quickly up and down, his eyes on the trees beyond.

Lacy went to his horse, went to find Jackson, fearing for the future and his faith.

Chancellorsville, May 10, 1863—Confederate Army

On the ground of the field hospital, Sutton stirred in fever. Someone had come by and ladled a little water into his mouth. His forehead, neck and chest were damp with sweat.

His leg burned, where it ended.

He came partly awake, felt pain in almost every muscle from when he'd been running, when he'd been hit, when he'd fallen and clenched around his wound.

His eyes rolling beneath his eyelids, he saw the woods again. His head lolled slowly from side to side as the images flowed in half light across his mind. As consciousness faded, the memory of that night rose like a curtain.

The trees were scattered columns holding up a low canopy of darkness. Below was ragged underbrush with occasional clearings, lighter than the ground or leaves. Sounds, as if very distant—small muffled shots, thin voices. Shapes moved through the clearings, crouching. Some carried long rifles. Off to the right, maybe 20 yards ahead, several carried a man.

There was a fragment of road on the right. The men were carrying their burden that way. Erratic shots still popped in the night.

Louder, a cannon blast erupted. The flash could be seen, farther away than the struggling men, and the shot hit way to the right. Grapeshot. He couldn't hear the eerie whuffling of the balls flying, but he knew their heft and the strength of their hit by memory. Several had ripped apart the chest of a man beside him, twirling the man sideways and cascading blood in an arc that bathed him and several others. The man was dead in mid-air.

Sutton could barely see the men lay down their burden on the road. Several bent over the wounded man, arranging his arms it looked like, being tender of one. It looked like the left. Then they lifted him again and walked, ungainly, rushing, toward the rear.

"It's Old Blue Light," said a man beside him.

"How do you know? It can't be," Sutton whispered, afraid of the sound and afraid of the answer.

"It just is. That was him up front."

"What was he doing there?"

"Chasing Yankees. What he always done."

They stopped talking. Then the man said, "He won't do it no more."

"Don't say that," he said. "It's not true."

"Stonewall was never carried away from no fight before."

"It can't be."

They watched the men to the right carry the wounded man—only wounded, he hoped. Then more shots came from up the road, where the Federals were. The men carrying Jackson—if that was him—dropped him. They heard sharp words. Sutton thought he heard a groan. But he couldn't, from this far away, with all the other tumbled noise.

Sutton had shot, earlier, at the men on horseback, he knew that. The agony of it pierced his haze. Several times, as fast as he could tear the cartridges and load, spitting the powder off his dry lips. Fired at the horses coming toward them. From the Yankee lines. Lines? There were no lines. They'd all rushed ahead in the thickets, joyful and terrified, chasing the invaders. Just groups of men, twos and threes, running, stooping, shooting ahead at no targets, just at the thought of the Federals running.

Then those horses coming at them.

He fired at the men.

He knew. Although he couldn't know.

He'd hit one.

Sutton groaned in his tattered sleep.

The men carrying the wounded officer had him up again, each holding part of him, fashioning a stretcher out of coats or a blanket and rifles, it looked like. They were moving beyond his sight. A few muzzle flashes still blinked ahead in the woods. Fatal fireflies. Looked like the Yankees weren't going anywhere either. There would be more killing tomorrow, plenty.

From off to the right came a low muttering as one man passed word to the next, and the next.

"It's General Jackson. He was shot."

"Old Jack."

"Shot by our boys."

"He's dying."

"It's Jackson they carried away."

Sutton' gut flipped. It was hard to breathe. There was nothing under his lungs—where his diaphragm was supposed to be was now just a hole, falling.

It couldn't happen.

Many men had fired at the group of horsemen, it might not have been him who hit Jackson. But it might have been. How could it be? How could Jackson be shot, and by us?

"We had Hooker on the run," the man said now. "We coulda pushed him into the Rappahannock, drowned the bastard. It was a glory, watchin' them run.

"And now Old Blue Light gets out in front of us and doesn't tell nobody and now we've killed him when he was comin' home.

"Now we're lost."

Sutton couldn't say anything, couldn't answer. Jackson could not be dead, and the battle surely wasn't lost, wasn't over. But without Jackson…

The heart would go out of us.

"We shot out our own heart," Sutton said to the man.

"That's God's truth, and sad as hell," the man said back. "As if we don't got enough sadness already in this goddam war."

Sutton's eyes came open. Trees above him, sunlight, clouds drifting. A surgeon calling for more bandages.

"As if we don't got enough," Sutton said out loud, lying on his pallet, tears leaking down his temples into his filthy hair.

Fairfield Plantation, Guiney's Station, May 10, 1863

Dr. Hunter McGuire stepped out of the darkened room where Jackson lay, scratched his fingers through his dirty hair, bent down a little to see beyond the roof of the porch to the sky between the trees. A little blue amid the sail-cloth white of cloud. His eyes rested, drifted around the green and blue and white. His mind drifted.

He said to the guard standing just beyond the porch, "This man played the violin, did you know that, soldier?"

The guard looked shocked, McGuire thought. Was it the incongruous picture of Jackson making sweet music on the small, delicate instrument, or the fact that McGuire had used the past tense?

"Is, is he gone, sir?" the guard asked, quietly, tentatively, hardly wanting an answer.

"No, he lives yet. Pray for him, son."

"I will, sir. And I'm sure he's praying too."

"Yes, he is. But not for himself."

Dr. Hunter McGuire, Jackson's friend and medical director for his corps, walked away from the little porch and leaned against one of the two tall oak trees that shaded the entrance to the small office of the Fairfield Plantation. He stared at the dirt driveway, and thought of how Jed Hotchkiss, Jackson's mapmaker, had smoothed the road all the way to Fairfield by clearing away logs and stones and other obstructions to ease the ambulance's journey.

The plantation office was a small, cozy building, three rooms and a fireplace on the ground floor, two small rooms above. The main first-floor room was now Jackson's sick room. He lay on a rope-trellis bed, facing the fireplace, a window opening to the west. The idea had been for Jackson to recover here, away from the fighting and the field hospitals, surrounded by friends and fresh breezes and his family.

His wife Anna and their daughter Julia had come, three days ago. That same day, pneumonia settled in Jackson's lungs.

McGuire looked back at the little building. So domestic. So ordinary. Wood. Broad plank floors. Windows. Shutters. The outside newly whitewashed. It smelled faintly of farm animals, because tack and feed and other equipment were often stored here. But Mrs. Chandler had just had the place cleaned for spring, and she kept sending out more furniture to make it more comfortable for Jackson, the doctors, his staff and his servant Jim.

A simple place, strong and square on a little rise. Not a place where anything more important than the calculation of crops and accounts happened. Not a place fate would likely visit and turn the flow of history.

Dr. McGuire had just told Jackson's wife that he would die this day. She told her husband. He replied that he had always wished to die on a Sunday. Jackson had called McGuire into his room. "Doctor, Anna informs me that you have told her I am to die today. Is it so?" he'd asked. McGuire had said yes. Jackson's eyes had drifted upward, then he'd said, "Very good, very good, it is all right." Now, thinking of Jackson's acceptance, his composure, McGuire's squared, rough-hewn face twisted with emotion, his thick black moustache trembling.

The little room had been so full of human passion these past days. When Anna had been talking to Jackson on Friday, he'd motioned her to stop, as

McGuire had told him he shouldn't expend energy on conversation. But, to make sure she didn't feel pushed away, he'd said to her, clearly, "My darling, you are very much loved." The next day, to soothe his soul, Jackson had asked his wife to sing to him, spiritual hymns. She and her brother, Joseph Morrison, knelt by the bedside and sang, stumbling over one hymn's lyric, "Show pity, Lord, O Lord forgive; Let a repenting rebel live." Both joy and deep sadness flickered in their voices as they pushed the songs through chests and throats constricted with emotion. And only hours ago, Jackson's little daughter Julia had been brought to see her father for the last time. His eyes and face brightened with a smile and in a strong voice he'd called to her, "Little darling, sweet one!" He'd lifted his remaining hand, tied in a splint, and gently touched her head. "Little comforter, little comforter," he'd said.

With a thick sigh the doctor pushed away from the tree, turned from the small building and walked through the gate in the little fence, away from the house, away from his charge, his friend, the man newspapers called the mightiest warrior in the Confederacy. Little might left now, except that required for the final journey.

Lee had said he wished he could have changed places with Jackson, it would be better for the new nation. Exaggeration, of course. "You have lost your left arm, I have lost my right," Lee had said in a message to Jackson. Closer to the mark, McGuire thought.

And now it was lost indeed. Or would be in hours. McGuire felt he should be worried about the fate of the nation, with Jackson soon gone. What other general had his initiative, his daring, his drive? What other general was so ready to move so fast and so far without waiting for everything to be in place? What other general drew so much from his men?

He couldn't answer these questions, and he let them fade away.

He saw Jackson, the previous December, when he had made his headquarters at this very plantation before the battle of Fredericksburg. Jackson had refused to stay in the main house, or even an outbuilding, and pitched his tents on the grounds. He declined to join Mrs. Chandler in her dining room for meals, even refused the trays of food she sent to his tent, saying he didn't want to fare any better than his men. McGuire remembered tucking into some of those offered and refused meals himself, quite enjoying turkey and biscuits and pie. He and the others on staff didn't tell the general. He also remembered how much Jackson loved hearing the Chandlers' 10-year-old daughter, Lucy, playing and laughing in the yard.

Jackson always loved children, and wouldn't people be surprised by that, McGuire thought. Little Janie Corbin, at Moss Neck, cutting paper dolls on the floor, calling them her Stonewall Brigade. Once she admired a gilt band on a new cap Jackson's wife had sent him, and he cut it off with a penknife and gave it to her. "This shall be your coronet," he'd told her. "It suits a little girl like you better than it does an old soldier."

Later that spring, Jackson got word that little Janie had died of scarlet fever. He wept and wept. When he heard that men of the Stonewall Brigade had made a coffin for her from the wood of a fence at Moss Neck, he wept anew. The man who could watch death rampage across a valley could not stand the death of an innocent child.

The trees formed canopies over the road to the plantation house, shaded the edges of the fields, bobbed their soft leaves, caressing the breeze.

Where were the Chandler sons this moment, McGuire thought to himself as he walked slowly down a little lane between two fields. Gone to war, all three. Were they watching trees wave in the wind somewhere in Virginia? Was one lying wounded, was one lying dead? Could they know that the war was about to turn for the South, with the death of its most successful, most terrible, most Christian soldier?

McGuire looked down at the dust on his boots. Black, frayed in places to a toneless grey, a little mud caked under the arch. Too many miles on these boots. He would never have allowed himself to wear them in his practice back home. But here, they served. He scuffed at a stone, picked up a stick and tossed it away.

McGuire's energy, volition, were ebbing away. Like Jackson's. Perhaps like the nation's. No, he thought, don't equate Thomas Jonathan Jackson with the Confederate States of America. *He* never would. Unlike so many politicians and generals, Jackson never talked himself bigger than he was. McGuire remembered last July, walking into Jackson's tent while the general was bent over a letter. McGuire asked to whom he was writing, and Jackson named a minister, Rev. Francis McFarland, who had written to say he was praying for the general and his army. Jackson read part of his reply: "It cheers my heart to think that many of God's people are praying to our very kind Heavenly Father for the success of the army to which I belong."

The army to which I belong, McGuire recalled, smiling a little to himself on the dusty road. I shall remember that. Forever. That was Stonewall Jackson.

McGuire lifted his face, watched the clouds float over Virginia, watched the time slip away, while behind him dozens and dozens of people—soldiers, neighbors, chaplains, sutlers, mule drivers, children, widows—gathered in the yard, quietly standing vigil.

After a while, the calmest, most peaceful moments the doctor had had in months, he walked back through the crowd, nodding quietly, answering the questions spoken and unspoken with a soft, "It's in God's hands, and so will he be soon. I must go to him." He stepped onto the porch and...faltered.

No.

I cannot, he thought.

General Jackson.

I cannot do this.

This cannot be.

It is irrevocable.

Across McGuire's flagging soul tumbled images.

The uncomfortable young professor pushing himself toward the struggle of his classroom. The smiling man calling his wife esposita. The singing deacon, his voice toneless and loud and lilting. The soldier, contained fire on horseback, quietly ordering more men into hell. The man, weary after battle, anger and sadness and endless determination on his face lit by firelight.

Thomas.

He leaned his trembling hand on the wall.

The guard touched his arm. For support. For closeness.

McGuire looked in the guard's blue eyes, saw tears on the roughened young skin.

No. But yes. I must. I will. Oh my dear sweet awful Lord.

The guard gripped his arm. Nodded.

McGuire went in.

Jackson sensed McGuire's entrance. He couldn't see, but he could feel, a pushing of the air, a flow. All was thin, thinning, stretching.

He heard echoes of song—hymns. No words, but a rising and falling, a pulsing of music, a distant organ resonant and floating away.

Warmth near him. A hand on his. Love near him, present as lightness and fullness. And grace.

Tears, sadness, falling spirits roiling the air. But it would all blow away, pass away. That dark cascade of sadness he felt too by his side would all flow away.

So quiet.

His lungs disappeared.

It had been so hard, dragging them, sodden, along with him. Air crawling as if through mud. Now, all gone. All ease.

No breathing. Time. Gone. Just now.

That broad spare plane. Endless.

Soft noise, fluttering. Wings? Leaves? Days?

Out of the white before his sightless eyes a shrieking comet of blood hammered past, a howling madness of pain. Screaming straining mouths, wet and stinking, matter spattering down. For less than an instant, for whole tumbling lifetimes. Then nothing.

A feather, floating, dancing on the wind.

A glove, empty.

A man limping.

A glorious little child, alight with laughter that sparkled like water.

Lost. No map. No path. No mountains no forests no roads no rivers. No where. No guide.

The air suddenly thick with bullets flying, cannonballs flying. Bullets, cannonballs, flying.

Limbs snapping off trees, great gouts of earth hurled upward.

A voice from nowhere, his throat convulsing, "Call A.P. Hill to the front." A gasp. "Where's Pendleton? Tell him to push up the columns."

Long lines of ragged men, marching over mountains. Then mountains in flame.

A church, burning, the steeple toppling into red sparks and flaring tongues, the cross crumbling into coals. A dove on fire.

A hurricane wind sweeps it all away.

Absolute quiet.

White movement. Birds? Raiment? Fog by a riverbank?

A drift of consciousness. A face rising, eyes closed.

A sonorous voice from no mouth. Had I enough faith? Did I do right? Should I have turned away from the invaders? Submitted? Was fighting God's will? Was killing God's will? How could it be? How could it ever be? Ever be? But we must defend. How, oh my dear terrible God, how could I presume to know thy will? How could I....

And consciousness slipped.

He felt now, knew now, the questions were over.

Rest.

Time a slow winding stream.

A gown, a curtain, rolling in the breeze. Clean scent of pine and honest earth.

And there, as he lofted across the plain, colors below as of flowers, was beyond, out there, coming now, a riverbank, clear in the light of a day with no end. Across, dancing green.

Boughs of trees spreading like arms.

The voice, calm, throat and mouth barely moving, the words soft but sure—"Let us cross over the river and rest in the shade of the trees."

And he was over.

McGuire heard that soft voice whisper the graceful and haunting last words, folded his hands, found absolutely no words of his own, no sounds, no thoughts in his mind. He reached up and, with a shaking finger, stopped the hands of the clock on the mantel. A quarter past three.

Jackson lay still. His high forehead was smooth now, cares gone, no more plans, no more secrets. Or one last one—that which finally smoothed his brow.

McGuire touched Jackson's forehead, mouthed goodbye with barely a tremor of his lips, walked through the little waiting room, and stepped onto the porch into the waning afternoon light.

The guard looked at him, and McGuire nodded. Tears in his eyes now.

They stood there, side by side, not seeing the small crowd of watchers, the doctor's gaze roaming out beyond the trees.

Behind his clouded eyes McGuire saw banners, and troops marching north, and smoke drifting over luminous green fields, and a great distance of hills and woods cresting to red-glowing sky. And one man riding.

Headquarters, Army of Northern Virginia, May 11, 1863

General Order No. 61

With deep grief the commanding General announces to the army the death of Lieutenant General T. J. Jackson, who expired on the 10th instant, at quarter past 3 p.m. The daring, skill and energy of this great and good soldier, by the decree of an Allwise Providence, are now lost to us.

But while we mourn his death we feel that his spirit still lives, and will inspire the whole army with his indomitable courage and unshaken confidence in God as our hope and strength.

Let his name be a watchword to his corps, who have followed him to victory on so many fields.

Let his officers and soldiers emulate his invincible determination to do everything in the defense of our beloved country.

R. E. Lee, General.

War Department, Washington D.C., May 11, 1863

"Good. Now maybe we can end this thing."

Secretary of War Edwin Stanton rose, turned his square bulky body and strode out of the little telegraph room across from the White House, leaving his gruff voice echoing behind.

Chancellorsville, May 11, 1863—Confederate Army

"I'll remember the whiskey. That man was death on whiskey."

"Yeah, when we got behind Pope up by Manassas and hit his supply depot, I've never seen so much whiskey flowin' in the streets. It was a pure waste. All that marchin' we'd done, got around the Federals' fat backside, and the man wouldn't let us have a little reward, just give us a little soak. No, he had to dump it all. Now that's a tyrant, we shoulda rose up. That's the real Second American Revolution for you, give me whiskey or give me death."

"And he'd have given you death mighty quick."

"Would have at that."

The men laughed a little, and James Sparrow had to smile. He was standing by a tree, looking at the endless stars above Virginia. Two men near him were talking about Jackson. Everyone was talking about Jackson. Some were taking it hard. Some, like these two, were taking it the same way they'd taken everything else that had come at them in the last two years—no shoes, bugs in their food, no pay, letters from home saying everything was falling apart, sleeping under snow, tree lines lit up by fire as cannon filled the air with metal. They were just taking it and moving on.

"And at Harper's Ferry, he asked for an officer who was a teetotaler. Had him be in charge of banging in all the heads of the whiskey kegs and keeping the men away."

"Didn't work. I was there, we was lappin' it up out of the road like dogs. So they took the barrels and poured 'em in the Potomac, and by God we got us pails and lowered them on ropes off the bridge into the river and had us whiskey and water. Kept it from goin' down the river to Old Abe."

"You needed it worse than he did."

"I need some now, don't you. It'd be just perfect, wouldn't it? Wish we hadn't let Hooker's supply trains get away. Hell, in the Navy they get regular tots every day."

"You should have joined the Navy, then, Buck."

"Can't swim. But I can sure as hell walk. And Ol' Jack made us do plenty of that. Maybe now we won't have to march so far in a day."

They paused. Sparrow loved listening to the men. They complained, then they just up and did what needed to be done. Time and time again.

"I'll remember him sleeping, too. He could sleep anywheres, fence corner, his horse. Slept through most of the preachin' at winter camp. I heard he slept in the generals' meetings, even with Uncle Robert there."

"I heard he told somebody that he wasn't much at talking, at persuading the other generals to come around to his way. So he'd say what was on his mind once, then let it be, and drift off."

"Practical man, didn't waste his wind."

"Didn't talk enough to rustle a leaf."

"Better that way. Lot of those one-horse generals, all they do is talk. Ol' Jack he just set out and did things without a by-your-leave. And he got it done."

"He was a rare bird."

"That he was. Crazy smart."

No words for a moment. Then, "There won't be as much cheering now, with him not riding up the line."

"Ol' Jack or a rabbit, one, we'd always say when we heard that cheering. Nope, not so much to cheer about, now. We've eaten up most of the rabbits in this poor countryside."

Sparrow heard one of the men flip his blanket to get the dirt and bugs off, heard them stir as they got ready for sleep. Jackson had told the people tending him in his last days that these men would be proud one day to tell their children they served in the Stonewall Brigade. Said the name was theirs, not his. They'd earned it.

These men would go on. And Sparrow would go with them. But it would be a harder road. And not so much cheering.

Richmond, May 11, 1863

"He always wanted to go North. He pushed for it, every time."

Alexander Boteler stood by the window of his office in Richmond. His hand was on the curtain, which he'd pulled back to see the waning sun. It was a clear evening in the capital; the humidity that made the city so close and steamy later in the summer hadn't settled in yet. A breeze fluttered through, rustling the fringe on the heavy curtains. Boteler's right-hand fingers played up and down the cloth, while the fingers of his left hand fiddled with his moustache and plucked at his bottom lip.

Word of Jackson's death had reached him hours ago, but he was still pale, his eyes drifting, unable to catch on anything for long.

"Take the war north, that was his goal. Make them feel the steel, the pain, the displacement, the fire." He paused, looking out the window, shaking his head slowly. "Make them witness the war in their dooryards, make them mop the blood of the wounded from their churches, rip their ground with graves, line up the dead like sheaves in their farmfields and maybe that would end it."

Boteler drew shallow, jerking breaths. "After Manassas, he told Jefferson Davis, to his face, you understand—give me 5,000 fresh men and I will be in Washington City tomorrow morning." He paused, looked back at his friend and aide, Captain Michael Rathburne. "That was his way. Press on, press on. He wanted to take it north, make them bleed, end it."

Boteler, a sometime member of Jackson's staff, a delegate to the Confederate Congress, a proud man of Virginia who was astounded the war had gone so long and so badly, had understood Jackson intuitively from the start. Had known that in Jackson the Confederacy had a man of such certainty, a man who understood the cost of inaction when others worried about the dangers of action, that if he could be supported by policy and logistics and leadership he could be their best hope in the war.

And Boteler had come to understand that what others saw as Jackson's stiffness and pride was in fact the man's clear understanding that hesitating was literally deadly and only harsh adherence to duty and the willingness to take risks based on solid knowledge of opponents and ground could win for the outnumbered Confederacy.

Now Boteler was playing pieces of the war over in his mind, wondering what would have happened if Jackson's drive had been followed. Wondering about each time Jackson had wanted to push north. After Manassas. After Romney. After the Valley Campaign. After the Seven Days fight around Richmond. After Second Manassas it had happened, but the drive had died in the bloody flow of little Antietem Creek after a lost order let McClellan know—and break up—Lee's plans. And Jackson had looked north again these past days, looking through Hooker's huge army to a North tired of death, knowing he could roll the invader back and bring him to his knees, by pushing north, by pushing north.

But now, he wouldn't be there, as his men splashed once more across the Potomac. For north they would go, as Jackson had seen. But Jackson was coming, in a box, back to Richmond.

Lee was heading into Maryland, perhaps Pennsylvania, following up the defeat of Hooker's huge host. Would he succeed without Jackson? Could he?

What would have happened if the Confederate military leaders had let Jackson go north? Jackson always seemed to see farther than his superiors, Boteler thought, always seemed to keep his eyes on the next steps that he was convinced would end the war. Jefferson Davis was a strategist, or fancied himself so. He had been secretary of war in the U.S. cabinet before this wretched civil war began. But he was so burdened with seeing so many people, fighting with the Confederate Congress and the newspapers, reading petitions and special pleadings. Had he been able to focus on the movements, the commitment of troops, the aligning of forces needed to engineer the final success? Not yet, surely.

The secretaries of war—Judah Benjamin, then George W. Randolph—did they have the vision it took to push this thing to its end? Or were they administrators at heart, creatures of politics and drawing rooms? The latter, he feared.

The other generals, did they have the broad view that would let them see many streams at once moving toward a confluence? Joe Johnston? He mostly retreated, strategically he said, and then he'd been shot. Beauregard? Bragg? Nobody had that intense concentration and drive that Jackson had. Lee did, surely. But he had to look to so many things, so many places where pressures were building or dams were breaking.

Jackson pushed and maneuvered and slammed and kept at it. But he had the advantage of being able to focus on one area, one theater of the war, just Virginia. But wasn't that where this bloody trial would be won or lost?

Rathburne interrupted his thoughts by asking, "Could he have done it, Jackson, gone north and ended the war?"

Boteler turned, looked at Rathburne with a weariness of spirit the captain had not seen on his friend's face before. "Sometimes I don't think this war will ever end, Michael, nothing will stop it." He ran the fingers of one hand through his hair, two times, three times. "I don't know if Jackson could have done it. The North is so strong, has so many men, such force of industry and resources. I don't know. But we should have tried to find out, it seems to me. Before this."

Rathburne walked over to Boteler, put a hand on his shoulder, gripped for a moment.

"He was so bold. No," Boteler paused, "that's not the right word." He looked at Rathburne, held his hands open before him as if trying to feel and hold something. "It never seemed to him like he was taking great chances, from what I could tell of him. What looked like huge risks—passing Banks to hit Milroy in the Valley, getting between Fremont and Shields twice, sweeping to the flank at Chancellorsville—didn't seem so risky to him. It was a greater risk to stand still and let the Federals come to him, he'd say. He disagreed with Longstreet there, although not openly. Action reduced the risk every time, he'd say."

"His actions were surely bold," Rathburne said.

"But he was so sure they were the right actions. Convinced, dead certain, that they could work. 'You may be what you resolve to be,' he always said. He seemed to believe that if it could be done at all, enough firmness and discipline and alacrity would get it done. So it wasn't boldness so much as, as certainty. He had a deep conviction that if he and his men strove as hard as they could and struck at the enemy's weak point, they could sweep the Federals from any field. So to him it didn't seem like a risk, no matter how frightening it might look to any of us."

Boteler stepped again to the window, saw knots of people on the street talking, stopping others walking by, gesturing widely, holding hands to mouths, shaking heads. The smashing victory at Chancellorsville, the death of Jackson, Lee's march north, had people in a stir every minute in the capital.

"He believed," Boteler said, looking down at the street.

"In what?"

"In himself, and his men, and the rightness of our cause."

"He believed God was on his side?"

"No. Not on his side, on the side of right. If God wanted a battle won, it would be won. The man seemed to give himself up to…to a higher vision, to an ordering of things beyond our knowledge. It made him hard to deal with on this plane, sometimes, that's certain."

"Was he a fatalist, then?" Rathburne asked.

"No. Well, not in the sense that he thought everything was preordained. He didn't just sit back passively because everything was already written. It took the concentrated efforts of men to bring results. But he was somehow able to let it go, to be so intense in planning and to push so hard in execution, but then somehow, I don't know, let go and leave whatever would unfold to that God of his."

Rathburne chuckled a little, thinking of those who would disagree. "Dick Garnett wouldn't say he let go. He'd say he was vindictive, obsessive."

"Yes, I know, and maybe he was those things. But that was the other side of his conviction that something undertaken must be done fully and well. I just know I saw him have some unusual ability to hold, oh, something like fire and ice at the same time, conflicting elements. He would push and release at the same time." He looked apologetically at Rathburne. "I can't explain it well at all. He was hard to understand."

Boteler walked to his desk, fidgeted with the papers there, picked some up, tossed them down again without looking. He pulled out his pocket watch, then didn't open it, just let it lie in his half-opened palm.

"He could hold so many things in his head at one time. Details, and broad views. The Valley Campaign. He studied Hotchkiss' maps like a deacon poring over scripture, you'd think he was planning out every step of every man. But all the time he was looking well beyond the day at hand." He came out from behind his desk, putting the watch back in his pocket. "I hadn't understood this before, but he was looking at the day or two ahead, but also seeing where the Federal armies would be in a week or two or three. But he was also looking farther, I'm sure of it, to what he would do after those armies in front of him were moved aside or chased away. He held different amounts of time in his hands at once, a pint of it, a quart, a gallon, a river of it. All at once, he could see it all, balance it, keep it all flowing at different rates."

Rathburne looked at him, nodded.

"He could watch it all swirl, one thing pulling in the next, one force pushing on two more." Boteler's voice had risen in strength and pitch, but now it dropped. "Why didn't we let him go?" He stopped. Looked up. "He wanted 25,000 more men after Port Republic, sent me to Richmond to ask for them, so he could push north into Pennsylvania. He said it would draw McClellan away from Richmond, would have to. The North would be terrified by invasion, by the armies that had defeated Banks and Fremont and Shields all at once descending on the fat farms and coal fields and railroads of Pennsylvania. It would have swept the North into a panic."

Again, his voice dropped, his hands clasped one another to stop their trembling reaching gestures. "But not even Lee was as bold as Jackson. Not even Lee would strip the troops away from Richmond, from in front of that bloated plodding army of McClellan's."

Boteler looked up at Rathburne, the skin around his dark eyes bunched tight with regret. "The tragedy is, Lee would have done it if he'd known Jackson's power as he knows it now. Look what Lee let him do at Chancellorsville. Take most of the army away from Hooker's front, leaving an easy opening for Hooker to blast through Lee's little remaining holding force. But Hooker didn't move, and Jackson did, and Lee let him because he'd learned to trust that unswerving total commitment Jackson had to his own vision, his own view into the future. Lee could have done it then, last June after Port Republic, but he didn't know. Only Jackson knew."

There was silence in the room, the muffled sounds of the people talking outside drifting through the window glass.

Rathburne started to say something, then stopped. He knew Boteler admired Jackson—all the South did, especially today. The man had become a legend even before his wounding and death. Now he was becoming a saint. Rathburne admired Jackson as well, but he also wanted to learn from him. And that meant looking at all sides of a thing. But perhaps today wasn't the day.

Still, he thought he'd push a little. It might help his friend, to talk about the strategy of it all again, keep his mind from the melancholy that the loss had dropped upon him.

"Jackson might have seen more than he could accomplish, isn't that possible?" Rathburne asked. "After Port Republic, his men were broken down. They couldn't even pursue Shields. Even his friend Dabney said he thought Jackson didn't take his troops' condition enough into account, pushed them until they were almost destroyed. He lost thousands of men to straggling and sickness, more than he lost to Federal guns. Winder was ready to quit because he thought Jackson used his men too hard, remember?"

Boteler turned, a flash in his eyes. Then he smiled, understanding that Rathburne was exploring, not criticizing. "I know. General Winder was one of many men who thought Jackson was insane." He smiled more fully. "But with fresh troops, Michael, Jackson's army would have been revived."

"But those troops would have never fought and marched before under Stonewall. Would they have been ready for him? Could he have gotten them into shape to fight his way?"

Boteler nodded. "It's a good point. It would have taken time, surely. And Jackson didn't have much patience, wanted to go whether anyone else was ready or not."

"And time, Colonel. Think how much time it would have taken to get those troops from Richmond to the Valley. Our railroads were a shambles then, almost as bad as now. It would have taken a week or more to get those men to Jackson. And McClellan, slow as he was, was moving."

"I know," Boteler said, lowering his head, shaking it slowly. "So many questions, so many if's. It's pointless, I suppose, to go over it all again. But it is intriguing. So much came so close to happening, both good and bad. Who knows if he could have beaten Banks and Shields again in the lower Valley to get across into the North."

"If Ashby's cavalry had been pulled together and ready at Winchester back in May, there might not have been a Banks to worry about," Rathburne said. "Jackson could have annihilated him then and there. There's an if for you."

Boteler was tired. He didn't know if he had the strength of spirit to go on. With this talk of Jackson and the war, or with the war at all any more. The war had pulled the new country's energies together, created a rush of excitement, made people buzz about heroism and gallantry. But it had taken away so much at the same time. So many lives, so many hopes. It was crushing to think of going on, of creating more long lists of casualties, more cripples, more graves, more widows. People talked so much about the war, it was an obsession. Endless talk, endless war. But, Boteler thought, the talk helped stave off despair, in the country, in this room. He straightened, and went on. "Yes, it could have happened that way." He stroked his moustache again, an absent-minded habit. The room was getting darker, and Rathburne lit a lamp. "I suppose," Boteler said, "I'm being unfair to Lee. We've seen what a fighter he is. Perhaps he was right to bring Jackson to Richmond to go after McClellan." He paused, then said more rapidly, "But that rush to the North—invasion—it would have been so dramatic then when the North was off balance. That bold stroke, maybe unexpected and right precisely because it was the less cautious, less prudent choice—it could have hurt them badly. Might have even given England or France reason to recognize us, and help." He looked again at Rathburne to see if he'd made a point.

"But that huge Army of the Potomac in sight of Richmond, it seemed the biggest threat, and the biggest opportunity, didn't it?" Rathburne asked. "If Lee could have destroyed McClellan, taken him apart as he straddled the Chickahominy or pinned him against the James, the war might have ended right there."

"Could have, yes. It was the main Federal army, and Lee came so close to killing it," Boteler said with energy back into his voice.

Rathburne paused before saying, quietly, "And if Jackson hadn't been so exhausted, he might have moved faster and helped Lee more at the Seven Days battles, fighting Little Mac."

Boteler nodded. "Yes, Richmond. So many people said Jackson did poorly at Richmond. A. P. Hill was terribly disappointed, blamed Jackson for not getting there in time, and so many of Hill's men died."

"What do you think happened to him then?" Rathburne asked.

"I don't know. He wouldn't say, at least to me. But I think he simply misjudged what he and his men could do, thought they could do whatever was needed. They had just beaten so many Federals in the Valley, done things that seemed impossible. So when Lee asked him when he could get his men to Richmond, he promised an arrival at least a day, maybe two, earlier than was realistic. Perhaps he succumbed to hubris, was listening too much to what everyone in the South was saying about him. It would have been understandable. But I'm sure he was also indeed exhausted, hadn't slept much."

Boteler thought a minute, putting together in his mind pieces of impressions. "I think in some ways he felt trying was enough. That if he tried his best to get his men to Richmond in time, for example, that was enough. It was in God's hands after that. I don't think his poor performance around Richmond bothered him, because of that. He'd done what he could."

"But a lot of men paid the price for his failures here," Rathburne said.

"That's the horror of war. Officers make judgments, and when they're wrong, men die. It's not like anything else we do, where mistakes cost money, or time, or hurt relationships that can later be mended. What a terrible strain that puts on commanders."

"Maybe Jackson bent under that strain, this one time," Rathburne said.

"Could be. He bore it well enough for three years. Maybe he just couldn't summon his powers one more time, so soon after the Valley fights, all those chances he took, all those near escapes."

"Some people say if he'd been up against better Federal generals in the Valley, he'd have been beaten taking some of those long shots."

"That could be too, Michael. But he took the chances knowing well the strengths and weaknesses of his adversary, and that's a crucial part of what looks like genius."

"I don't mean to tear him down, God knows," Rathburne said, with kindness in his voice. "But you've heard people say Jackson was best when he had an independent command, and didn't do well when he had to fit into other people's orders, coordinate with other forces, as he had to in the Richmond battles. What do you think? Is that right?"

Boteler smiled. "And I don't mean to defend him blindly, Michael. He doesn't need that, from me or anyone. But I don't agree with that view. Look how well he did at Sharpsburg, holding Lee's left against so many attacks, after taking Harper's Ferry and arriving at Antietem Creek just when Lee needed him. And at Second Manassas he was part of Lee's army, making complex movements timed with Longstreet. Ask John Pope how poorly Jackson did there. If you can find Pope." Both men smiled. After being so thoroughly defeated by Jackson and Longstreet, Pope had been exiled to Minnesota to fight starving Sioux Indians rebelling because they weren't getting promised government supplies. "No," Boteler said, "Richmond was an anomaly, a poor performance, but a rare one for Jackson."

Boteler's head drooped, as he realized again that they were talking about Jackson now in the past tense, and not about what he might do next. It was still a shock.

"Well, my good captain, despite what people are saying now out on those sidewalks, Jackson wasn't a god," Boteler said, looking with less intensity now at Rathburne. "He liked glory well enough. He had flaws, plenty. A thousand men will tell you that. Still, he was our best chance, I'm sure of that. He could best grasp what it takes to beat the Federals with all their power and all their soldiers." He crinkled his eyes, raised one corner of a smile. "And he almost reached it. He might have."

The two looked at each other, feeling the weight of the moment, but knowing there was no stopping, not even for grief.

"But we have Lee. And now he's going north," Rathburne said, hoping to hear encouragement in his own voice.

"But without Jackson," Boteler said softly.

Rathburne nodded, acknowledging. "And Lincoln," Rathburne said, "he keeps trying to find a general who will march and hit and clamp on and not let go. A general who will move. When he finds one, to organize and put all that might of his to use, we'll be in trouble. I'll wager he wishes he had a Jackson."

"And we'll wish we still did, every day from now on," Boteler said. He blew out his breath slowly, closed his eyes.

The two men stood still, at the window side by side. "You know, Michael, I can't stop seeing a picture. In my memory, right here behind my eyes," he gestured up toward his face.

"A candle flame, flickering inside a tent. I'm lying on the cot inside Jackson's tent. We've just pushed Burnside back at Fredericksburg. So much carnage." Boteler's voice was soft, deep, his hand out in front of him, gesturing slowly.

"Jackson has given me his cot to sleep on, and he stayed up to write. Dispatches, letters, maybe his first report on the battle. I fell asleep, exhausted, as he must have been. Later I felt him stretch beside me, and he must have slept for a time. Then I awoke, and he was at the little camp desk again, writing by candlelight."

Boteler's long thin fingers fluttered in front of him, mimicking the dance of a candle flame. "The candle was bright in that dark night. I watched it flicker and sway, but I didn't move, or say anything. Then I saw Jackson's strong right hand lift a book, and set it down on edge, between the candle flame and me. To shield me from the light."

A pause again, his hand setting down a remembered book, then Boteler resumed. "To shield me from the light. Like a thoughtful mother with a child. It's those little touches that come to me now." And his hand turned up, open, empty.

Rathburne was quiet, appreciating the image. And they both stared out the window, certain only of what was gone.

The Richmond, Fredericksburg & Potomac Railroad, May 11, 1863

Henry Kyd Douglas felt like a boy who'd lost his father. Oh, his own father was still living in fact, and Douglas loved him. He'd had the terrifying experience of looking across from the south bank of the Potomac and seeing his father in the yard of his Maryland home, held by Federal troops, a cannon in the front yard. His father, weakened by a stay in a Yankee prison, was all right, but beyond reach. And now so was Jackson. Forever.

Douglas had been the youngest member of Jackson's headquarters staff. Twenty-four. He'd been a courier, an inspector general, a rallier of troops under fire, a young, vibrant, impressionable man at the center of the most exciting and terrible storm this country ever knew. And, in the intensity of war, he'd come to know Jackson surprisingly well. As well, perhaps, as anyone could.

Now Douglas was riding the train carrying the still, battered body of his general. Jackson's wife and other members of the staff were on the train, heading for Richmond. The proud beleaguered city that five Union generals had tried to reach, but failed.

Douglas felt his heart, and the country's heart, was broken.

Yet Jackson himself said death was not a tragedy. Seemed at peace with it. One night he'd talked about death. Said he had no desire for it, although he put himself at the front of his troops so often, shells exploding all around him. He said life was bright for him, but he would go happily, without trepidation or regret, when God called him.

This was a man who knew no indecision, a man who lamented no lost opportunities. He embraced it all.

This man so loved life. He loved growing things. He loved walking. He loved early morning. Douglas laughed, a short chuckle out loud. Remembered Stapleton Crutchfield, Jackson's artillery chief, saying there should be a law against marching or fighting before 8 a.m. or after sundown. Crutchfield loved his sleep. Chose the wrong general, that's for sure.

Jackson loved life, liveliness. His whole staff was young men. Me, a kid, and look like one. Hunter McGuire, his medical director, only 25 or 26, I think. Sandie Pendleton, Jed Hotchkiss, James Power Smith, all 10 or 15 years younger than Jackson. He loved listening to us make jokes, talk all night. Didn't join in much, but seldom chased us away. And oh he loved Jeb Stuart. That man could jab him, say things nobody else would even dare think around him, and all Old Jack did was laugh. He loved the aliveness, the flash of Stuart.

He loved the Valley, the glorious Shenandoah. Maybe because it was so open and lush, compared to those pinched, constricted hollows of northwest Virginia where he grew up. I think he needed room for his soul, and that's the Valley. Daughter of the Stars. He wanted to protect it. His home.

He didn't wonder what life was like, he lived it. He did not think, debate, anguish. He seized life. He examined, yes, he thought deeply and peered into the mysteries. He talked, long into the night, with his clergymen friends, about life at its most unreachable. And he held back most of the time, that was his way, he was decorous and proper, not loud and brash. But he took life in; just didn't crow it to the world.

He tried. He reached. With only bits of formal schooling as a boy, he still strode into West Point, knowing he could do it. And by sheer application of will, he did. He strode into war in Mexico, knowing he could do it. And he didn't quail, but stood firm and advanced into the fire. And here, outnumbered and outgunned, he went right at the Federals every time. And he pounded and harassed and confused them to the point that his name became a force of fear.

But when this war came he only wanted the invader to be pushed back, out of his beloved Virginia. All he wanted was to go back to Lexington, his prettiest place in the world, and to teach, even though he was clumsy at it. He loved the books, the schedule regular as a clock, the walks across town among people he knew. All he wanted from the war was its end.

No. That's not entirely true, Douglas thought. The war kindled his ambition, and he always struggled with that. Didn't think it was right to be big in his own eyes or to take glory that really belonged to God. But he did love the taste of glory, like he loved the taste of liquor. And denied it to himself, as he denied himself liquor, or he'd end up a braggart, as he could have ended up a drunkard, he said. Even Robert Dabney, his chief of staff and a minister, said Jackson aspired too much for fame at first. Jackson himself said that his only fear his first time in battle in Mexico was that the "fire would not be hot enough for me to distinguish myself." Richard Taylor called Jackson's ambition vast and all-absorbing. It must have been part of what drove him so hard. Jackson fought that ambition with prayer; he knew how strong a temptation it was. His only vice, ambition, pride pushing inside him like an unspeakable thrill.

Still, at the end he'd said that he'd get far more credit for this brilliant attack at Chancellorsville than he deserved. "I simply took advantage of circumstances, as they were presented to me in the providence of God," he'd said. Simple. It seemed that way only to Jackson, Douglas thought.

It must have been hard to hold himself in, all along. All those women around him when he'd stop in towns sometimes, it made him speechless. All that adulation. The men cheering him. He loved it, but he rode away from it fast as he could. He never seized the stage, remained humble, at least on the outside, would not go into the parlors of Richmond to be celebrated. Maybe afraid he'd drink too deep of it all.

The train lurched, Douglas swayed against the bench's wooden back. These tracks were feeble, had been overloaded for so long, broken recently by Stoneman's Yankee cavalry. Everything in the Confederacy stretched so thin, Douglas thought.

His smile. When it came it was like the sun.

But so few saw it. A man came to him after First Manassas, asked for a leave because his wife was dying. Jackson said no, although he knew the pain of a dying wife—his first had gone in childbirth. But he said no, because duty meant staying with the army. Good God, the man never forgave him, and how could he? His wife died without him.

One of the last nights of Jackson's life, on the field of Chancellorsville, James Power Smith threw his cape over Jackson sleeping on the ground. After a little, Jackson arose and put it back over the sleeping Smith.

Harsh and loving. Tender, steel.

Outside the window. All these people at the stations. Standing, with flowers, with sadness. Just looking at the train as it passed. Staring. Now what?

So many underground. The rivers of blood. The rows of dead.

He had known, Jackson, the cost. He had seen it in Mexico. He had said war was abhorrent. He had warned people that they did not know what they were calling forth. It was a monster he had known. A darkness he had trembled in. And yet he would go there again.

And he became the symbol for this war, this country, he and his troops. Undermanned, barefoot, cheerful and miserable at once, beaten down and irrepressible.

There were others—Stuart, Forrest, Ashby—who were symbols of the speed and impact and decisiveness the Confederacy must have. But they were cavalry, dashing cavaliers. Jackson had no dash. He rode slumped, he walked stiff. He looked like a ragged private who slept on the ground and carried on his clothes the grit of the fields he'd fought over.

But Jackson would not be moved. Like the mighty Massanutten Mountain, when he held his ground he was just there, solid, planted, a barrier of terrain.

And when he chose to move he could not be caught, not be found, not be stopped. Up, go, others ready or no, he pictured where he had to be and projected himself, and those who could keep up, with the force of his will—and there he was, smashing.

With almost enough.

Down the aisle of the rumbling car, men leaning over, talking low. McGuire, that fine, handsome face, so haggard now. He must feel shocked, heartsick. That he couldn't save him.

Stern warrior, Jackson, yet beauty was with him. I think that's why he was most successful in the Valley, the most majestic and intoxicating part of Virginia. The flow of the rivers, the glide of the fields, the swell of the Blue Ridge. They were part of him. He lived in the Valley, and the Valley lived in him. And he had a childlike quality, in that he was what he was and didn't pretend to be anything else. "I have no gift for seeming," he once said. Maybe that's why the lovely little children—at Grahams, at Corbins, at Yerbys, his own little Julia—were so easily attracted to him, would play with him so naturally on the ground and scramble into his lap.

Although his way, his words, his manner, were prosaic, his life as spontaneous as a multiplication table, he felt deeply, Douglas was sure. Jackson could not look upon this Valley that he loved and not hear the music of the wind whispering in the wing of a sailing hawk.

Virginia passing by, Douglas looking. Beyond the glass, trees in scattered thickets, fields with just a touch of tender green, curling waterways, small houses, huts, stately mansions at the ends of long roads. People watching, heads bared.

He wasted not a minute of his life.

He knew life was a gift, a precious, fragile, sacred moment.

That could whisk away.

At any time.

To the next great mystery. For him, the next great joy.

And so he had peace. That peace that cannot be understood from outside, by those who do not feel it. Know it.

He knew. Far beyond his certainty that kept him from asking the advice of his commanders about the small matters of strategy, war, death. It was a certainty about the universe, and what it was, and what it meant, and his place within its many flowing worlds.

He had all the advice he needed, from his God. His Book. That was his knowledge, given to him—and to any who would accept it—as a gift. So clear to him.

Oh, there must have been moments when his faith faltered, but it seemed he always could find it again, embrace it again.

But he didn't preach, he didn't lecture. Even though his faith was so central in his life, he never thrust it out for others to see, didn't push them to believe as he did. He just was. He just held out what he saw, what he believed. And very often, he was right. And you could take what he offered and go with him, on faith. Or he would go alone.

I think this is what pulled people to him, Douglas thought as he rocked with the motion of the train. The magnetism of one who knows the deepest things. And even if he couldn't say them with the grace of a poet or bring them alive with the resonance of a preacher, you could feel it. Feel it inside him. And you wished you had it too. You wished you had what he had.

The men. They truly loved him. He was hard on them, but he put them where they could be effective. Where they could get done what had to be done. Too many generals would wait, and in indecision waste men's lives. All the men wanted was leaders who could get it done. And that was Jackson. He had no show in him. He had no bluster. No false camaraderie. Only duty. And accomplishment. With the warmth of a distant star, he still pulled them to him.

Jackson brought us death. Now, in the end, his own.

Whatever will we do with it?

Whatever will we do without him?

The train rattled and creaked, the lovely land slipped by, and Henry Kyd Douglas felt like a child at night. Alone.

Lexington, May 13, 1863

The letter lay on the writing tray of her desk. To her brother-in-law, Thomas Jackson. It told him of people in the town, people he knew, what they were doing. Of the weather, already warm. Of the flowers. Of the view from her porch, of the calm and quiet one could find sitting there, feeling the evening breeze, talking with friends.

Margaret Junkin Preston had heard that Thomas had been wounded, had lost his arm. It had shocked her—shocked the whole town. People walking up the hills of Lexington, from Washington College to the shops downtown or under the trees lining Main Street, stopped to talk quietly, shaking their heads, asking what each other had heard. Margaret—Maggie—had tried to act like Thomas would, steady, resolved that whatever happened was God's will. She nodded to friends, patted their hands as they took hers to wish her well, tried to smile but her mouth stayed in a thin flat line, what had oftentimes been irrepressible flashes of puckishness gone now as she waited for news, for Jackson to come home.

Her letter told him how pleasant his recovery would be in Lexington. How so many people would be praying for him and visiting him, how eager she was to have him home.

She had written the letter yesterday, lain it on the desk to post today. But now she sat at the desk, its writing surface low to fit her short stature, staring at the small drawers and bookshelves rising above where her hands rested not on the letter but on her diary. One lock of hair had fallen across her forehead; she brushed at it, missing. Her right hand dropped slowly to the diary, her fingers running slowly along the edges of the pages. She did not look down. She did not look anywhere.

She had heard this morning, just leaving her house, letter in hand, that Jackson had died.

The letter took on a horrible weight.

The loss of Jackson was a calamity for the South. Who now would ever be as bold in turning back the aggressors? But for Maggie Preston this death was not as large as a nation or a war. It was a small searing point in her middle, drawing her shoulders and her head in, around a ragged emptiness that was slowly growing and pressing against her chest so that it was hard to breathe.

She couldn't even pray. Her lips formed the name, "Thomas."

Unseen now the words she had written in her diary in her firm clear hand an hour ago. "Everybody is in tears.…The people made an idol of him, and God has rebuked them."

"Thomas," she said.

Richmond, May 13, 1863

Richard Garnett—relieved of command by Jackson in 1862 for pulling the Stonewall Brigade, their ammunition gone, off Sandy Ridge at Kernstown—had been reassigned as a brigadier general in James Longstreet's corps. Nine months ago, he had eagerly fought Jackson at the court martial trying the issues of Kernstown, hotly cross examining his former commander, calling him a liar to friends. The battle of Cedar Mountain, another Jackson victory, had interrupted the court martial, which never reconvened. Garnett's reputation survived the clash with Jackson; many good generals, including A.P. Hill, had been arrested during Jackson's furies. Garnett was leading troops again.

But not today.

General Garnett stood, his head uncovered, by a coffin in the Capitol of Virginia, in the frail heart of his fledgling country. Garnett, with General Richard Ewell, who'd also once called Jackson crazy, was a pallbearer at General Jackson's state funeral.

On the slow march from the Executive Mansion to the Capitol, Garnet had watched the brass band, the infantry, a battery of six cannon, Jefferson Davis in a carriage, his cabinet on foot, and Jackson's horse, led by his servant Jim, as they'd moved solemnly, along with many silent veterans of the Stonewall Brigade and hundreds of plain citizens of Virginia.

Garnett was touched, honored to be there, shocked by the occasion, and a little ashamed at the smoldering anger the fallen general's name could still make glow within him.

Whether he was right or wrong, and no matter the cost, this man had always moved, Garnett thought to himself. He took his own counsel, ignored all of ours. But he moved.

Garnett looked across the coffin, draped in the new Confederate battle flag of crossed bars, and saw Ewell's bald head tipped forward. Ewell, who had cursed Jackson so often with his fluent cascade of profanity. Ewell was shaking his head, very slowly, side to side. A crystal drop of tear fell from Ewell's eye.

In six weeks, near a stone wall at Gettysburg, as the ruins of Pickett's charge slid back down the slant of Cemetery Ridge, Federal bullets would end forever Richard Garnett's conflicting feelings about Thomas Jackson.

Washington, May 13, 1863

"While we are only too glad to be rid, in any way, of so terrible a foe, our sense of relief is not unmingled with emotions of sorrow and sympathy at the death of so brave a man. Every man who possesses the slightest particle of magnanimity must admire the qualities for which Stonewall Jackson was celebrated—his heroism, his bravery, his sublime devotion, his purity of character. He is not the first instance of a good man devoting himself to a bad cause."
—*Daily Morning Chronicle*, Washington

"I wish to lose no time in thanking you for the excellent and manly article in the *Chronicle* on 'Stonewall Jackson.'"
—Abraham Lincoln, in a letter to the *Chronicle's* editor

Lexington, May 15, 1863

Cannon, from a Stonewall Brigade battery, had been booming all morning, and all day yesterday.

Patterson Neff had left his company to stand on this hill in Lexington, just on the edge of the parade ground of the Virginia Military Institute. Trees were all around him, just reaching full leaf. A slow breeze moved through the leaves, sweeping like the blessing hand of a pastor from the VMI hill down the colonnaded slopes of Washington College.

HOOOM!! The sound of the cannon rolled through the trees, grey smoke billowing from the far end of the parade. Every half hour, the cannon had sounded. Neff had heard so many in the war, around him and before him, speaking swiftly of danger. This time they spoke, more roundly, more slowly, of death. How could a cannon shot sound peaceful, he thought, but this did.

Behind him, before him, bells started now. Deep, clear tones, echoing gracefully from homes and stores all over the little Valley town. They heightened the stillness. The waiting.

He couldn't move. The war had been all about motion, about speed, about getting behind or in front of or away from the Federals. But now the motion had stopped. There was a pause. A reckoning.

Thomas Jonathan Jackson would be buried today. In the town where he lived and taught and married twice and walked the streets with his curious blend of purpose and distraction.

Neff heard the familiar sound of jingling and stamping. Horses, starting to move on the far side of the parade, by the barracks where Jackson's body had lain since yesterday. Eleven o'clock, and the funeral procession was starting to move, draped with the sound of church bells.

Young men marching in front. Slowly. The core of cadets. Not much younger than many of the men Neff had seen shot down in battle. Then a company of horsemen. Solemnly reining their horses tight, not difficult as the animals were so tired from years of war. Then the caisson bearing the fallen general.

The riders came abreast of Neff, and he didn't move. He'd ridden here on his cavalry mount, with no permission, because he had to be here. He could have ridden with the cavalry escort, he supposed, but he wanted only to watch. To bear witness.

His practiced eye fell unbidden on the cinches and saddles and blankets of the horses, seeing how trim and taut it all was. The joining of leather to horse hide had been for so long a matter of life and death that he scanned it all like an editor must scan a page someone else has produced. All was secure, he noted without thinking.

The caisson rolled before him. The casket covered in a new Confederate flag, no dust, no holes ripped by metal. The caisson jerked with the steps of the horses, an echo of the painful jolts so many wounded had felt as they were carried from the many battlefields of the war. But there were no cries. Jackson, silenced for the ages, went beyond.

Then Neff saw, behind the casket, men marching in broken, halting step. Not young. Weathered, worn. It took Neff a moment to understand. When he did, his heart filled. The wounded of the Stonewall Brigade, pushing one last mile behind their general. A limp, an empty sleeve, a missing eye. Tears rose in Neff's eyes. He wanted to turn away, but had no strength. A man, with both arms bandaged, walking proudly, nodded at Neff. They didn't know each other, but they knew what each had seen. They were comrades. In travail, in glory, in horror, in this moment of hard-bought peace, when no one knew the future, but when this gaze, this march, this homage was enough.

This procession in this small mountain-cradled town would hold people together for an hour or so. In an illogical way, it would keep them—Neff, the marchers, the townspeople gathered stunned along the streets—from thinking of the loss the rolling casket symbolized. It would put off for a summer hour the frightening question—what would happen now?

Neff raised his right hand slightly to the man with bandaged arms. He'd lost track. He thought he held his hat in his right hand. But the hat was in his left. Up before his face, in a greeting to the marching soldier, came a flower, white, just starting to wilt. He'd forgotten he held it. An old soldier, coming from the barracks, had handed it to him an hour ago. The man had taken it from Jackson's bier, and the honor guard had not stopped him. They knew he had earned it on many roads and fields, following Jackson.

Neff held the flower in the May of Virginia, the most beautiful of times and places. He and the marching wounded soldier looked, and wanted so to smile. But could not.

The South would not recover for a hundred years.

Had Jackson not been shot, had he been spared even one more day, long enough to complete the destruction of Hooker's army, the South might have won the war. Jackson and Lee were that close. With Jackson gone, the long odds became insurmountable. Ewell, his successor, did not have the drive, the will, the righteous certitude. Ewell could not force his way up Cemetery Hill at Gettysburg when that battle was tipping toward Lee—didn't even try. Jackson would surely never have hesitated, and might have shoved Meade back to Washington. And then who knows.

Instead, the war was lost, and an entire generation of educated, cultured, brave if misguided leaders was gutted. By the end of the war, one in four Southern men of military age would be dead of battle wounds or the diseases in the camps. The South became an occupied country, its frail economy destroyed, its social system—fraying before the war—utterly wrecked. A century later the South was still the poverty belt of the richest country on earth. A third world.

Jackson's beautiful Shenandoah Valley was burned. "So a crow flying over it will have to carry its own provender," Phil Sheridan promised. And followed through.

The symbol of the South, at the end of the war, was a scorched chimney standing stark in the rubble of a burned-down house. And homeless people, black and white, wandering. More than displaced. Their place was annihilated.

The war brought blacks a freedom in words on paper, but it took another century, and more battles and blood, for that freedom to begin to be realized.

A new birth of freedom. But at such cost. It was worth paying, but it was hard to see that through the smoke that blew across once-fertile fields now burned and bloody.

PART FOUR

THE RETURN

The Last Bivouac

Outside Raleigh, North Carolina, July 15, 1891

"Old Jack didn't have any idea what would happen up there on Henry Hill. He just went where he was told." James Lewis Sparrow was a big man still, with a heavy speckled beard and a chest that bulged from beneath the beard and rolled full to the tuck where his belt was. He'd added many pounds in the decades since the July morning he was telling about, since the first battle of Bull Run, or Manassas. The front of his head now stood out high and bald. What hair was left around his ears and the back of his head was long and bushy and grey. His face had a reddish cast, his cheeks and the flesh below his chin were full. His eyes had receded as his face had grown, but they were bright, and he smiled constantly when he talked. A big face, so a big smile.

William Sutton, whose porch the two men sat on, had once been as close to Sparrow as war could draw two men. They'd fought up and down the Valley in the same regiment until Sutton was wounded in the leg and left, and then served in different regiments, but still under Jackson, after Sutton came back. Now, Sparrow's work had brought him to Raleigh, where Sutton had lived since his second wounding, and Sparrow had come out in the countryside and found him. He wanted to bring Sutton back with him to a ceremony in Lexington, Virginia, unveiling a statue of General Jackson. Sparrow wanted to go to the ceremony, and he wanted Sutton there with him. He thought it would do Sutton good. Sutton wasn't so sure.

It had been 30 years since the Shenandoah campaign. The two men hadn't seen each other since the war, although they'd sent an occasional letter. Now that they were together on Sutton's porch, and as Sparrow had asked Sutton to come with him back to Lexington, their talk centered on Jackson.

Sparrow was the more ebullient, happy to recall the war. Sutton, as always, was more reserved. But he was fascinated when Sparrow talked of Jackson. For three decades, Sutton had been haunted by General Thomas Jonathan Jackson. Sutton's life and near-death were tied to Jackson, and Jackson's death was tied to Sutton. Like a stone.

Sparrow turned to Sutton, nodding his head. "Joe Johnston put Jackson in there, it wasn't his own idea. But Jackson got all the credit, and he's mostly what people remember from First Manassas.

"Still, when he got up there he did make his mark, and he deserved that name he got. Stopped the Federal advance, his men—us—stubborn and tough across that field like a wall. Turned the battle, and started the Yankee boys running. Stonewall became a hero. Although I don't think he ever liked being called Stonewall. Said the name belonged to us, his brigade, not him."

Sparrow leaned on the rickety porch rail, felt it give, stepped back. "You gotta put yourself in a new railing here, Will," he grinned. "Or get lighter friends."

He looked back at Sutton. "You kept any mementos from the war, Will?"

"No," Sutton said. Only the pictures in my head, he thought. And I can't get rid of those. "I try not to think about it very much. It was a long time ago, Jimmy."

"It was, but it seems fresh sometimes. I've kept my cap, and that rifle I hauled all over Virginia. My uniform wore off me," Sparrow said. Then he gestured down at the bulk of his stomach and laughed. "Course, if I'd have kept it, it wouldn't do me much good now, would it?"

Sutton looked at Sparrow and smiled. "Times have been good to you, looks like. Those clothes of yours are nice, and it looks like you eat better than we did in the Valley."

"Better by a damn sight. Let me take you into town tonight and we'll have a good dinner. You tell me what you've been doing down here in the woods."

Sutton said he'd like that. He was still a slight man, thin like he was in the war. He'd kept his hair, but his face was rutted, like the roads they'd marched. He did all right these days, repairing things people brought him. He didn't lack for much, but he'd like a good meal in a nice restaurant.

Sparrow rubbed his forehead and looked a little sheepishly at Sutton. "Talk about mementos, for a long time I kept a few hairs I'd cut off Little Sorrel's tail, Jackson's horse, you know. Sorrel wasn't too happy about it, but after Second Manassas the man had become such a hero that I wanted to have some token. A lot of people did, especially up in Winchester when he chased the Federals out. Surprised the horse wasn't bald. You know they've got that horse stuffed and on display over at the VMI in Lexington?

"People want to see things from Jackson. Like religious relics. Like pieces of the true cross." Sparrow laughed, at himself as much as the others.

"And probably a lot of that Jackson memorabilia is as authentic as the thousands of pieces of the true cross," Sutton said, smiling at his friend.

"Maybe you can get a piece of the true cross to fix this porch," Sparrow said. "Or some genuine rails from a Jackson campfire." They both laughed.

"There's a woman in Gordonsville who says Jackson stayed at her family's house after the Seven Days battles at Richmond, on his way to beat up Pope," Sparrow started on another story. "She was just a little girl then, she says, and he played with her, bounced her on his lap. She said she wanted one of his buttons, and he told her he'd send her one when the uniform wore out. And you know what he did? A few months later he sent her one. Damnedest thing, right in the middle of the war, remembered this little girl. The woman's had it ever since. Shows it off, treasures it."

"I'll bet that button is the real thing," Sutton said. "That sounds like Jackson. He was crazy for kids. People say they reminded him of his daughter back home. I think they just gave him a little peace, a little pleasure. A shot of the regular world in the middle of all that..." he waved his hand to signify all that was contained in the years of war.

Shaking his head, Sutton said, "That's all Jackson wanted, I guess, was to get that regular world back. All he wanted out of the war was a nation, and we didn't get that."

Sutton stretched his arms above his head, leaned back, and said, "He never saw his own daughter until his wife came to visit him a couple of weeks before he was killed. They baptized her just before Chancellorsville. She was born during the war, and he never went home. Fought all over the Valley, always only a couple of days' ride from Lexington, and he never went home. Until he did in a coffin."

"Well, the man's become a legend," Sparrow said, "he's been lionized. Strange, for someone who killed so many Americans, tried to rip the country apart and fought to preserve slavery." Was that what Jackson had tried to do? Sutton thought as he listened.

"It's partly because he died young when he was at his best," Sparrow continued. "People could fill him up with a lot of 'what-ifs', say we'd have won the war, won at Gettysburg, if Old Jack hadn't been killed. People could see in him what they wanted to see—for themselves, for the South, for the Cause. By dying, he was kept alive, you might say. If he was still around, an old codger like us, people would probably get tired of his stories. Like they are of mine." Sparrow always had a chuckle in him, seemed to enjoy life, clearly enjoyed talk.

Sutton felt an emptiness open below him when anyone talked of Jackson's early death. He'd been there when Jackson was killed, at Chancellorsville. Right there in the North Carolina regiment that shot him by mistake. Fired himself. Fired at Jackson. It flooded him with horror, then and now. He hated thinking about those shots in the night, but he couldn't stop. Still woke up at night hearing the sounds of horses and rifleshots and shouts.

People said the high tide of the Confederacy had been Pickett's charge at Gettysburg. Sutton thought it had been two months earlier, in the thick woods called The Wilderness south of the Rappahannock River, at the end of another of Jackson's surprise flank marches, when the North Carolina bullets caught Jackson in the dark in front of his own lines. A horrible mistake. It changed everything.

And the war, of course, changed Sutton. It changed everybody who passed through its crucible. Had he hated it? He'd been seriously wounded twice. Seen friends killed right beside him. Shot men he didn't hate. Shot men. Good God, he had done that. So hard to picture now, on this porch, daily life just going by. It had burned some hope out of him, everything he saw and did in the war. Aged him, worn him. Yet it had put him close to things that mattered. To friends, to loyalty, to finding what you can endure and achieve. And to a wild aliveness. Primitive, uncomplicated.

Still, he thought, it probably wasn't worth the cost. But he had never been asked. Had never had a choice to make, really. He'd enlisted, because the Northerners were coming after his country, marching into the parlors and kitchens of people who had done them no harm.

Sutton was tired of the arguments about the war. Its causes, its contradictions. He'd never fully understood why it happened, or even why he'd gone to fight in it. But he had. There was a call, an alarm, and he responded. To stop an invasion. And he lost his leg, and he lost his country, and he lost not only some hope in the future but a sense of belonging to the present. He lost his place. He lost his way.

"He's even a hero in the North, ain't that amazing," Sparrow continued, not noticing Sutton's silence. "They claim Old Jack now as one of America's greatest generals, along with Lee. Hell, during the war, even the Federal troops cheered him. Federal prisoners always wanted to get a look at him, and they'd holler when he rode by. After Cedar Mountain, I remember we were out on the field burying the dead under a flag of truce. We talked to the Northern boys who were working out there, and they said if they had generals like Jackson they could win some battles. Said their generals were all for show, riding with big color guards, talking big, then folding when the fighting started. They envied us Jackson. The man would fight."

Sparrow kept talking as the sun lowered its rich afternoon light into the trees. He asked Sutton if his leg hurt, and Sutton said it did sometimes. He wore an artificial leg, and got around pretty well, although he couldn't farm anymore. His left leg had been shot twice in the war, and the second time it had to come off. Like hundreds of thousands of men, he carried the war with him every day.

The talk came back to Manassas.

"He wouldn't give up any ground," Sparrow said. "He was damned ornery, from what I knew. So it didn't surprise me, although I wished he'd had a little give in him when those Yankee bastards came over the rise right at us.

"But Old Jack was fixed. Wouldn't budge. That ran in his family."

"You knew him before the war? I'd forgotten that," Sutton said, looking up from the beers he was pouring.

"Knew his family. His father was cantankerous, argued with anything that moved. He died when Jackson was a little boy. Old Jack grew up with his uncle, another man who sued anybody who crossed him. Always thought he was right. Held grudges like they were heirlooms. And Jackson himself knew only one way to do things, and you'd better agree with him or he'd have you court-martialed. Very single-minded. Got his orders direct from God," Sparrow said. "That made him a good fighter, but a bear to be around."

Sparrow's memory flashed back to that day above Bull Run.

"I walked through those trees with Jackson, from Lewis Ford up to Henry Hill. Was never so scared again in my life," Sparrow said. "After 'while you got used to walking into gunfire, but that first time…. I damn near soiled my pants. The noise. I didn't see how a man could choose to walk into it. But being with Jackson, you couldn't choose otherwise. Didn't seem a sane choice, either way."

"What does it say about us that we could get used to such a thing, Jimmy?" Sutton asked.

"If we hadn't gotten used to it, there wouldn't have been a war. The Union boys would have finished us at Manassas, if they could have stood up to the fire. Nobody'd know Jackson's name."

"Maybe that would have been all right," Sutton said. "Could have gotten it over with earlier, without so many dead. Jackson could have gone back to teaching school."

Sparrow laughed, his body bumping up and down. "But what stories would we have to tell each other? What would we do at the bar with a beer in our hand?"

"Could tell lies. Enough do that now."

And Sparrow laughed again, saluting Sutton with his mug of beer. "True, it surely is true. They can stretch it."

"And you too?"

"Oh, but much of what I say actually happened. I was there. And I've only decorated it some since then. A little more each year, don't you know?" He smiled again, shaking his head, scratching the side of his belly, shifting in his chair, a rocker he could barely squeeze into.

He stared then over the porch rail, tilted his head, shook it again very slowly side to side.

"But this one I remember clearly," Sparrow said more softly. "Least, that's what I think. On Henry Hill, the first time, that part where your stomach jams up against your lungs and you can only breathe about an inch deep. Looking out there, where they were fighting, it was completely bewildering. It was just godawful crazy. But, you know how it was, Will, it was exciting too. God help us, it was exciting."

"I guess," Sutton replied. "Where's that come from, the excitement? I'd have thought we'd have just been, been, oh, wanting to dig into the ground and never get up."

He leaned forward from his chair and looked at Sparrow intently. "What's the draw, Jimmy," and he pulled the short word long, loading it with question and pain. "What's the draaaawww?"

Sparrow was quiet, looking again over the porch rail.

"To walk out of those woods, you had to believe in something, that's one," he answered.

"What was it?"

"Oh, maybe it was country. Patriotism, even if it was in the wrong direction, we might say now. But mostly, I think, it was….the belief that those people didn't belong there."

He looked at Sutton, both now leaning forward in their chairs. "You lived in that Valley once, just like I did, Will. We couldn't let them have it."

That beautiful Valley. Ravaged. Sutton's fields trampled by both armies. His wife dead of some kind of fever. He hadn't gone back there to live after the war. Only to see, to hobble over the beaten land, take a few things, and go away.

Sutton spoke. "No. No, we surely couldn't. But wanting to keep them away from our homes, it didn't give us that excitement you said."

"That's true. It was more than believing. That part came from the head, maybe the heart. This, this came from the guts, the balls. Something you don't think about. Thought's blanked out. Just electric sparks rushing up and down the cord of your spine." Sparrow paused. He was looking into the woods as if he saw something.

"An animal thing. You know the way a mountain lion chases a deer?" He turned his eyes to Sutton. "Tracks right on it, tears up the ground making turns, focuses right on that neck. Won't stop, not 'til he has it. I saw it once, a few years back, in the mountains in West Virginia. I recognized it." He nodded his head, saying yes to himself. "I recognized it.

"That lion smashed into trees as it ran and didn't even notice, it wouldn't have heard a train coming. All it was was the chase, and the end. He wanted his teeth in that neck, but I think he wanted more...just the moment when he leapt.

"That's it, the second when you commit, when you go at it. The awful sailing rush of it."

Sparrow blinked, lifted his head. Neither said anything. Both could feel it. Distant, but remembered in their flesh, their breath.

"We used to say about Jackson his blood was up. It was true of us, too, wasn't it?" Sparrow said.

Sutton remembered blood. Way too much. Others'. And his own, at Port Republic, and at Chancellorsville. He said, "What's it mean? Did we want to kill people?"

"Maybe that was part of it. I don't think we thought that. Although, when they were shooting at me I damn straight wanted to stop them, knock them down with everything I had, for sure. But it was something more." He paused. "It was freedom. It was no thought. Everything was taken off. No rules. Not just...rules of law, but rules like gravity. Nothing you knew applied. It was all different, knocked sideways by this impossible thing that couldn't be happening. But was.

"It was physically different, don't you remember? Almost your body wasn't held inside your skin. You could feel things up and down the line, your senses were stretched so when somebody got hit a few men away it seemed you felt it too. You could have flown from one end of the line to the other. Like you were floating, a balloon full of gas. Your emotions were all over that field. Alive, alive."

Sparrow paused again.

"And there was the speed of it. You've seen kids run sometimes just to run, Will. They turn, twist, tumble and get up again, full speed. They don't care, they don't think, have no idea they could get hurt. It's just to run."

He thought for a moment.

"It was like, off a cliff, with no care, only just to do it.

"And there was nothing but the single instant. Just right now. It was all on the line, no past, nothing coming later, just now. Everything rushing into now.

"And you could die.

"And while that was right there, you didn't care."

Sparrow hadn't been looking at anything, his eyes just stared into a corner of the porch floor. He was hunched over, hands pressed together between his thighs, rocking forward from his hips. There was something inside him that wanted to get out, if only he could find it.

"It was all...so...bright."

He stopped rocking.

"The excitement was to try it all and not to give a good god-damn what happened."

Sparrow fell quiet, and Sutton looked at him. Nodded. It was something like that. He did remember. But he also remembered the horror. That, mostly. He tried to get past it, and sometimes he could.

Sparrow stood. His black boots thumped on the wood.

"For Jackson now, I think it was different. It might have been all that, but it was also divine retribution. He was a righteous son of a bitch, and I'll bet his excitement came from carrying the spear of God."

"Jackson," Sutton said, pronouncing the name slowly. "Do you think he ever got tired of it? Of the killing?"

"No, I don't think he ever got tired of the killing."

"But he was a religious man. Had preachers around his headquarters, always had services in the camps."

"Yes," Sparrow said, "and he prayed for God to help him kill just enough Yankees to make *them* tired of it, so they'd go home."

"So he understood, do you think, maybe like Sherman and Grant, that it would take a lot of killing to end it?"

"I don't think in the same way, Will. It wasn't like that with Jackson. Not something he thought. Or felt. It was conviction."

The light slipped away from the porch. The two men sat.

"The Yankees were wrong and they should be punished. Hard," Sparrow said. "And he was happy to be riding in the chariot God sent to do it."

Both men were still, turning over thoughts and images of this man, Jackson. He had been an immense force in the war, in their daily lives of march and sleep and wait and fight. Not just their commander, but a symbol for the Southern cause. The skill and daring, the righteous certainty that were the only things that could overcome the fearsome odds against the new Confederacy. His name made Northern troops duck down and Northern generals quake. Jackson. Unlikely hero, professor, halting talker, stiff as iron, he stood then and now for absolute courage and commitment.

And he was a puzzle to Sutton. A mystery with the key just out of reach, always.

"He was a hard one to figure, Jimmy," Sutton finally said. "I heard young men from the VMI and Washington College say he talked and laughed and sang with them one night when they were guarding a house where he was staying during the Valley battles. He was a friend of Jeb Stuart, a braggart and a joker, so unlike Jackson, but Stuart could always make him laugh. But you'd see his face most times and it would be grim as a stone. Arrested officers who wouldn't fight. Wouldn't give men passes to go home to dying wives, had deserters shot without a flinch. A man who prayed on the battlefield and then brought hell down on the Yankees. Soft with kids, hard as a cannonball with his enemies.

"I wonder what the man was really like," Sutton said softly.

"He caused so much killing."

It wasn't what he wanted, the killing, Sutton thought. It was a means to an end for Jackson. Wasn't it? Wouldn't a religious man pass through the killing to the lesson it made, to the change it was aimed at, to the values it was meant to protect? Wouldn't he have to?

He'd seen Jackson a few times. Not very close. He'd talked endlessly about him around campfires, on long marches. When men's lives—their *lives*—depend on the skills and moods and character of their generals, those generals are endlessly pulled apart and hashed over by their men.

No one had seemed to know him. Not really know him. Some had taken classes from him before the war. Some had lived in his town and passed him on the street. They said he kept his eyes down, mostly, while he walked, wrapped up in some talk with himself inside. Some had been near him on the march, seen him napping in a fence corner, been under his piercing eye as he watched them trudge past. All had heard stories about him, some accurate, some stretched with endless telling.

Sutton had never talked to Jackson. This man with whom he'd intertwined lives and gambled death. Never exchanged a word. But Jackson was in his mind. Even now. And so were all the deaths.

Sparrow looked across the porch at Sutton. "So much killing, yes."

Sparrow put his hand to his mouth, cupped his chin with it. He shook his head slowly in his hand. There were scenes in there, stirring. All the veterans had them. "What I remember most from that field at Manassas…one old boy from South Carolina. Dead on his face, a patch of red on the back of his blouse where a bullet had come through. His fingers…" Sparrow stopped, and breathed deeply. "His fingers had dug through the sod to the second knuckle."

He looked up, taking more breaths. He turned his eyes to Sutton. "It was one hell of an experience, Will. I'm glad nothing like it ever happened again.

"I couldn't stand any more."

The darkness slipped in on them, they rose and went into the city for dinner. Their talk drifted away from the war, and Sutton enjoyed renewing his friendship with Sparrow. The war had woven tight bonds, narrow but strong. Sparrow renewed his plea for Sutton to accompany him to the Jackson ceremony in Lexington, and Sparrow said he'd think about it.

The next evening, his porch thick with twilight, Sutton sat alone. Sparrow was at work in Raleigh. They'd take the train north the next afternoon, if Sutton would go with him.

Vines from the woods climbed over the end of the porch where Sutton sat in a straight-back chair. It was dark enough that the worn wood of the porch floor and the splintered ends of the boards didn't show so harshly. The porch railings were anchored only loosely to the rough square posts; anyone leaning against that railing would quickly be in the weedy remnants of the flower garden below.

Tonight his left leg pained him. What's left of it. It was not the phantom feeling some people say they have of the lost limb. Sutton could hardly remember the feel of his left shinbone beneath his skin, of dirt between the toes of the foot long gone.

This pain wrapped around the end of the stump of his leg. It was the pain of the border between two worlds; the world when he was whole, the world when he is not. This pain was a pressure ache. The grainy, crumpled skin that was pulled over his flesh when the leg was severed by a saw dirty with the bone-and-blood-slush from the men before him on the table felt tight tonight. As if the leg were trying to grow back out, push to the floor.

Deep in the meat of his leg, the bone burned. It had been sawed through a few inches above where it was shattered by a slug that twisted its shape as it hit into a tearing pinwheel of lead. Sutton could still feel the saw vibrating in his bone.

And he could still hear the shrill cries, the words as shattered as the bones, the confusion taking all sense out of the night and replacing it with horror.

War was awful enough. But then this.

The old haunting came back so easily.

Had he really fired the shot? Was it him?

"God save me if I did. I didn't know," he said now, almost out loud to the darkening evening.

What were they doing out there, why didn't they sing out? Why didn't we wait? Just another heartbeat?

Cuz we were scared as rabbits. Excited, primed, we'd raced through those woods tumbling the Yanks into their cookfires as we rolled up their line. The damned Dutchmen. We shoved them down the roads back toward the fords, slammed them against trees with our muskets and canister, shredded their organization, mixed up their units in the brush and muzzleflash.

But we were mixed up just as bad. Had run so fast, so thrilled to see those bastards skedaddle, that we didn't much know where we were or who was near us. Didn't know where the Yankees were, didn't know where our friends were. Couldn't see much as it got dark in those thickets. But we could still hear shots, ripping ahead to the left, a few to the right.

We were scared. A little drunk with almost-victory, and afraid it could turn around on us in an instant. The snout of a cannon might poke through the brush with bright flashes of infantry fire on both sides and we'd be the ones running.

Sutton could still feel the trip-wire terror, 30 years later. In the shred of a second the world could turn.

And it did.

He couldn't even shake his head. The air felt too thick, time too clotted. The darkness wrapped him in his thoughts.

He didn't dwell on this. Didn't want to go back to those dark woods in Virginia. It didn't paralyze him, like it had some. He knew a few whose gaze was still so long and deep and lost that they'd never get away from it. It didn't have him like that.

But it did come back to him sometimes, with a power that shook him, then hollowed him out. Tonight. He could feel a thickness in his chest, his spine and shoulders caved forward, the everyday voices and thoughts inside his head scattered like birds at a shot, leaving silence.

"Cease firing, you're firing at your own men."

The panicked, baleful voice, always there.

His North Carolina porch felt like a cocoon, although nothing new would come out of it.

Friends who had been there told him he wasn't responsible for Jackson's death. "A lot of us fired, Will. You can't know it was you. How likely is that? There were bullets everywhere. It was a damnable mess."

One friend told him, "And even if it was you, look what you did. You sent him into the ages. That's how heroes are made."

It was no comfort.

He hadn't wanted a hero. He'd wanted a live general. And a victory. Independence for the South. Mostly, he'd wanted the Yankees to go home, and General Jackson was the best hope to make that happen. Far above any politics or statecraft, Sutton had simply wanted the war to be over. Jackson was the best hope for that, too. To push through it as hard and fierce and mercilessly as a bayonet through a belly, and get it over with.

But that hadn't happened. Jackson had died, and the war had gone on for two more terrible years. Virginia had been shattered, the South bled to death. And then the Yankee occupation; homeless people wandering the wasted land like lost tribes.

Homeless people, and homes without people. So many had not returned. Hands not steering the plow handles, not guiding the saws, not gentling the horses, not thanking the wives with a touch.

Sutton kept a list in the drawer by his reading chair inside. But he didn't have to limp in there to go over it. He had read it, stared at it, so many times it was in his head forever. Men he knew personally who had died in the war. A few he'd known before the war, most he'd gotten to know on the march, in the camps, under fire.

Matthew Barclay, 22, shot at the stone fence at Kernstown.

J.B. Johnston, 47, shot off his horse at the battle of McDowell, dead in midair.

Watson Switzer, 19, shot through the face at Winchester.

Bernard Carroll, 33, dead of dysentery outside of Harper's Ferry.

Andrew White, 19, his leg run over by a cannon wheel near Middle Town. Gangrene came and couldn't be stopped.

Peter Paxton, 25 or so, shot by a sharpshooter while urinating next to an oak tree near Cedar Creek. Lingered in the hospital for two months, and died.

Charles Anderson Preston, 20, most of his upper body blown away by a cannon ball at Front Royal.

Harris White, 20, Andrew's brother, died in his sleep camped at Woodstock, cause unknown. Maybe loneliness.

John Lightner, 22, dead of typhoid near Strasburg.

Brick Burgess, upwards of 50, shot through the knee near Strasburg, leg amputated, dead three days later.

Frank Preston, 31, head shot at New Market.

Sandy Whitmore, 20, dead of a burst bowel outside of Harrisonburg.

Patton Lyle, 30ish, broken neck from a fall while rollicking on the river bank near Luray.

George Chapin, 14, shot in his narrow chest while drumming at Cross Keys.

Piper Eads, 27, shot in the stomach at Cross Keys, died being lifted to a stretcher.

Little Pete, a slave, porter and cook, quite old, shot in the throat outside of Port Republic.

James Chapin, 21, his privates and belly ripped away by an exploding shell at Port Republic.

Sutton stopped. He could feel again the pressure of bluecoats coming through the fields in the Valley, lead flying before them. He could feel in his hands the searing heat of his gun barrel. For a second the sound, the bedlam, surged out of his head and he heard it on the inside of his eardrums. He shivered, stood, squared his shoulders, inhaled deeply. The sound of the woods came faintly back, a twitter, a rustle, a chirrup of insects.

Baxter Mott, 19, drowned in the Chickahominy after being shot in both legs.

Calvin Moore, claimed to be 16, cut in two by a shell at White Oak Swamp.

John McKee, 29, shot 15 times on Malvern Hill.

Samuel Jordan, 45, dead of camp fever at Richmond.

Peter Hoge, 33, wounded in the stomach at Cedar Mountain, died three weeks later in a nearby farmhouse.

Daniel Jackson, 17, dead of infection after his hand was amputated at Second Manassas.

Wallace Day, 56, dead of a fever of unknown origin at Bristoe.

Joe Chester, 19, head shot at Second Manassas.

Edward Moffett, 40 or so, blown to pieces at Sharpsburg.

Alexander Cockrell, 32, dead of stomach poisoning after surviving Sharpsburg.

Brady Woods, 29, shot once in the heart at Fredericksburg; could hardly see the wound, and there was no blood on his shirt.

Hugh Watson, 23 but he looked 15, shot sideways through his stomach at night at Chancellorsville, the worst pain we'd ever seen. It didn't last long.

Samuel Godwin, 52, died on the operating table at Chancellorsville with the saw still in his leg.

Ted Compton, 28, endless bloody flux in southern Pennsylvania.

John Myer Morrison, 34, his head, I'm told, turned to mist by a cannonball on his birthday at the foot of Cemetery Ridge at Gettysburg.

Briscoe Browne, 18, lost without a trace in the burning woods of the Wilderness.

Griffin Fraser, 19, both arms ripped off when the cannon he was tending exploded....

Sutton's mind stopped. His list had 43 names on it. But he couldn't go on. He tolled over this list several times a year, painfully, reluctantly, but thinking somehow it did his friends honor. Kept their memory alive. Sometimes he rolled through it like a prayer, the words coming fast, end-to-end, without lifting up the specter of the scenes he'd witnessed. But this twilit evening the words were too sharp and cut through his emotional calluses. His breath came fast. It was so long ago, but it seemed all around him. He stared, trying to focus on the trees in front of his cabin, the chittering of a squirrel.

One name he hadn't put on his list. Thomas Jonathan Jackson. Lost. A haunt more than a legend. A question more than an answer. A challenge. And an enigma, always, to the end.

The others on Sutton's list had been at rest for decades. But with this last name in his head, aching in his heart, Sutton could never be.

Standing on his wooden leg, watching shapes change in the dark woods, he decided he'd go back to Virginia with Sparrow. See what was there. What shapes in the dark.

Lexington, Virginia, July 21, 1891

Sutton had come back to the Valley. Back to what had once been his home, for the first time since…since so many lives had been broken in this heartwrenchingly beautiful place.

On the way to Lexington, he'd stopped near the south end of Massanutten Mountain, to see what had once been his farm near Cross Keys. He had stood for a long time in a light mist, looking at the fields that had once been his, at the ground among trees where his house had once stood, where his wife had once helped him with every bit of the hard and wonderful work of the little farm. He'd cried quietly.

He hadn't seen these fields since they'd run dark with blood. In 1862. Now he'd let the green and gold of the renewing life here flow into his eyes, hoping the image of the bright healed land would replace the horrors still dimly lurking in his memory.

He'd turned to the peak of the Massanutten just to the north, where lookouts in grey had kept watch on armies in blue. He'd always loved how the looming solidity of the mountain seemed almost to lift and sail on days when the blue sky behind it filled with fleets of tall white clouds.

He could hardly believe now, after almost 30 years, looking at the patches of woods, the fields, the silver rivers in the distance, what had happened here. It seemed a foreign country, although once it had been home. The war had jarred it into another world, even when it was his home. Time had returned this land to peace, but it still hadn't returned him to home. Or to his own peace.

Then this day, in Lexington, at the cemetery where their general was buried, they dedicated amid ceremony and short speeches a tall proud statue of Thomas Jackson. Anna Jackson, the general's widow, was there, and his two grandchildren pulled the cord that unveiled the statue. Almost 25,000 people crowded into Lexington to honor Stonewall Jackson and remember the time of glory and fear. Many of the men had wept at the dedication, but Sutton had done his weeping at his homesite, in the arms of the rivers, where he'd felt so violated that June in 1862.

There had been a walk through the Virginia Military Institute, a visit to Washington College, now Washington and Lee, and respectful aching silence before the stately tomb of Robert E. Lee in the college chapel. A grand dinner had followed, with talk and food and wine. Then, in the growing darkness of the small-town summer evening, the men had walked under the trees in pairs and groups, tobacco smoke flowing back from whiskered heads as they went. Their camaraderie, diluted by years as bankers, bakers, farmers, lamed former soldiers, returned as they felt again the draw of the stern professor, the righteous warrior, who rested now so near.

With little planning, they gathered to sleep once more on the ground of the Valley. They chatted as they settled, ready in their souls if not their bodies. This was their truest tribute.

"How're your bones?" Sparrow said, with a small, quiet laugh as they spread their blankets on the ground.

"They hurt," Sutton said, wriggling to find a soft spot, if there was one.

"When's the last time you slept on the ground?"

"Hunting, a lot of years ago," Sutton said.

"Me, it was when I was drunk at my daughter's wedding seven years ago. Didn't mean to do it, and the missus dragged me in once she woke up and realized I wasn't there." Sparrow laughed again, his eyebrows waggling. "Want a snort? I've got a flask here. Might help us live through this."

"Sure," Sutton said. "One would be good." As Sutton tilted his head and drank, Sparrow asked if he remembered raiding the whiskey supply of a neighboring Kentucky outfit during the Valley Campaign. "Right out the back of their tent, it was a pretty piece of thievery, I must admit," Sparrow said.

"You were a hound for foraging, and didn't much care where it came from," Sutton said.

"Did you?"

"Not once you'd gotten it, no." They both chuckled, and Sutton handed back Sparrow's leather-and-silver flask. "Thank you. You're still good at it."

They stretched out, quiet growing around them.

"How old are you again, Sutton?"

"Sixty-two, if I figure it right, which I don't do too regular. You?"

"I got a couple of years on you. Feel older tonight, on the ground?"

Sutton thought, quiet for a few moments. "You know, I feel a lot of ages at once, here." Sparrow looked at him thoughtfully, not saying anything himself for a change, waiting for Sutton to say more.

"I feel young, like I was once in this Valley, a young man trying to make a farm pay and cocky-sure I could do it." He flipped the blanket over his feet, nodding his head as if hearing himself. "And I feel all the ages I felt in the war here. Young, little, like a kid with a scare, with excitement. And old, with a weight that seemed like it would never come off."

Sutton looked up at the first faint stars shining amid the leaves. "It's all kind of floating here. Drifting. The times. I feel…connected to this place, and then I feel I'm drifting away. I'd been in this Valley for so much, and then not for so long."

Sparrow, head resting in his hand, elbow on the ground, his other arm across his ample belly, hmmmed his understanding.

"It's like I, I had to come farther up the Valley now. Crawl up it to find some shelter, maybe," Sutton said quietly. "The head of the Valley, up near Kernstown, that was my first battle. Then Cross Keys and Port Republic, deeper into the Valley. We fought, right there on my own land, and then I got shot at the battle at the Port."

The busy silence of the night filled in. Sparrow rolled on his back, he and Sutton both staring up, next to each other.

"I left then, seems like I had to. And I never came back to the Valley. Came back to fight at Chancellorsville..." Silence for a time. "And that was that."

"Yes," Sparrow said, "that was more than enough, for you. Left part of yourself there."

They both paused, breathed, thinking, feeling the place.

"But here," Sutton said, "farther up the Valley. We never fought here. They did later, but I wasn't with them. This place." The night calm, wrapping around them, rich and deep. "There's some peace here. It's a comfort."

Sparrow shifted a little under his blanket, his bulk a little hill.

"I'm glad you're here," Sparrow said to Sutton. "It means something. To me, to all of us. To be here. It's good, you know."

Sutton just nodded. It was good, and it was bad, but it was touching something in him, strong.

Around them, a score of other men were talking quietly, rustling blankets, laughing a little at their awkwardness on the ground, looking at the sky, at each other, at the statue.

From up the street they heard voices. Several people came, somewhat breathless, looking shocked at what they saw.

"But, gentlemen, we have places for you to sleep, of course. You're our guests, people are opening their homes to you, and, the hotels, won't you please..." one woman who had been at the dedication dinner said, her voice falling off. "We've been looking for you."

"We're where we belong, ma'am," came a Louisiana voice from the dark beyond Sutton.

The townspeople couldn't say any more. They looked again, beginning to understand. A squad of old men, some bent, most grey or bald, strewn on the ground in blankets and greatcoats. In the cemetery. Around the statue they had helped to consecrate. Of Jackson.

"We've slept around him many a night on the battlefield," Sparrow said in his voice rich as the earth, quiet but firm. "We want to bivouac one more time with Old Jack."

The people turned, nodded, and slowly left, and the soldiers laid down their heads. Their talk faded, drifted away.

After a little while Sparrow said, "Will, I brought you something."

"What is it?"

Sparrow sat up, reached in his coat pocket, and brought out a small book. Printed without cloth covers, it was a bit tattered. On the front, a drawing of Jackson.

"It's John Esten Cooke's book about Jackson. 'The Life of Stonewall Jackson.' I found it in an old book store. Have you read it?"

"I looked at it once, at a neighbor's. Meant to borrow it, but never did. How is it?"

Sparrow chuckled. "Well, it's a little bit of a fantasy. Makes our friend here out to be a saint, of course." He held the book, and Sutton could tell his friend thought there was something in there that was important. Something that Sutton should know.

"But you should read it," Sparrow said. "That's why I brought it for you. Cooke wrote it while the war was still on. In his tent. Said he could hear cannons roaring sometimes while he was writing it. He was on Jeb Stuart's staff, you know. A novelist before the war, so he knew how to make things pretty, and dramatic. But he talked to a lot of people who were there with Jackson, and read a lot of what was published right away. And he'd met Jackson, several times, and knew a lot of his staff. Studied the man. Got it pretty good, I'd say."

He handed the book to Sutton. It was a fragile thing. "Printed in 1863," Sparrow said. "Held up pretty well."

Sutton held it, looking at the drawing of Jackson in the faint light. It felt like a relic. Almost alive in his hands.

"Cooke says Jackson loved danger for its own sake. Courted it, thirsted for battle," Sparrow said, lying back on the ground again. "Now I don't know if that's true, but Cooke says Old Jack told one of the cavalry boys he wished he could go out on a raid with them, for the excitement of it. Sounds like him."

Sparrow was trying to say something, but didn't know how. Almost like Jackson found what he was looking for. Maybe the North Carolina men in the woods that night where the Plank Road and the Bullock Road and the Mountain Road all came together near Chancellorsville shouldn't feel so, so responsible for what happened. It was too delicate a thing to say directly, though, for a man of Sparrow's limited skill with saying things delicate.

"That book says Jackson believed absolutely that things happened for a purpose. That God determined what was right," Sparrow said. "There's a part in there you should read. After he's shot, and his arm has come off, his chaplain, Tucker Lacy, comes in and talks to him. And another place, when he talks to his wife. You should read those, Will."

"Too dark now, Jimmy," Sutton said quietly, holding the slender book out in front of him. "You tell me."

Sparrow hesitated, looked over at his friend, then started in. "Lacy tells the general his wound is a calamity, and Old Jack says he doesn't think so at all. He calls it a blessing. Can you imagine that?" Sparrow shook his big head. "He was more religious right then than the preacher. He said the shooting had been a blessing because he was brought face to face with death and found that all was well. Now that's a kind of courage, I think more than I've got."

Sutton remained quiet. Sparrow wasn't sure what more to say. Decided not to embellish it. Went on by saying, "Then, a few days later, when he's with his wife, at the Chandler place down by Guiney's Station, and he's fading. His wife tells him he's going to die that day."

Now it's very quiet around the two old soldiers, nobody else is talking, and Sparrow's voice is very low.

"His wife tells him that and in the book Jackson says, 'Very good, very good, it is all right.'" Sparrow wasn't sure that Sutton was getting his meaning. "That's how much faith he had, Will." But it wasn't just the faith Sparrow was talking about. He wanted Sutton to know, to hear what Jackson had said. The words. What they said. To Sutton.

"It is all right," Sparrow said. And then he gave up. He'd put it out as best he could.

Night deepened. The locusts and whippoorwills fell silent. Leaves trembled in the wind.

Sutton looked deep into the sky. Didn't say a word. Nodded.

Sutton thought for a long time. Slowly, like the old soldiers today, a few things came into line.

When I first tried to figure why I followed this man, lying there legshot by the river at Port Republic, I thought it was because he was certain he was right. About the war, and how to run it. Then when I came back from North Carolina, it was because I wanted to see it finished, and I thought he was the best to see it through. Now, I don't think it was because he was certain he was right. Something more. Something beyond what I can really understand. But something he had. A gift that gave him peace in a time when peace was always out of reach. And a peace that we around him could feel without knowing. Maybe it's that he knew that whatever was, was all right. Whether it was a good horse or a fence corner to curl up in for a few minutes' sleep or a little girl's smile or a flank attack where you shoot people you once sat with by a campfire.

It doesn't make any sense. None at all. But maybe that's what God's all about.

Sutton looked above his head at the statue of Jackson, standing firm against the night, holding binoculars, a sword at his side, his face raised to the wind.

Jackson carried a peace with him. And it was here. It drifted like the cleansing fragrance of flowers around Sutton, and he breathed it in.

The night passed, the sky darkened until Sutton's eyes fell closed.

There were still shards of hell in Sutton's soul, but it was a little quieter here, by this statue, by this strange man underground.

"It is all right."

ACKNOWLEDGEMENTS AND THANKS

Warmest thanks to Lawrence Hewitt, David Benidt, Michael Benidt, Brad Brown and Albert Eisele for reading all or part of this manuscript and giving smart suggestions, and to Lisa Dewey Joycechild for her careful listening to many sections as I wrote them.

Thanks to Celeste Gervais and Steve Thayer for their help in connecting me with my agent, Barbara Gislason, and to Barbara for her wonderful belief in this book. Thanks to Jorg Pierach, Angie Revier, Scott Meyer, Jeremy Duerson, David Stillman, Sharon Stillman, Fran Hitchcock and Lisa Dewey Joycechild of the Core Discovery Group for their support, to Daniel Pitlik for his support and patience, to Tony Carideo for pushing me inside Jackson's death, and to Jorg for the trip to find Stonewall Jackson's arm.

And especially to my partner Lisa, who became a war widow while I wrote for so many nights, for her sustaining faith in me and this book.

Thanks to Alan Willis of CartoGraphics for fast, clear work on the maps. I greatly appreciate the help and dedication of the staff and volunteers at the Stonewall Jackson House in Lexington, Virginia, the Virginia Military Institute Museum and Archives in Lexington, the Virginia Historical Society in Richmond, the Frank Kemper House in Port Republic, Virginia, and the Stonewall Jackson Shrine near Guiney's Station, Virginia, where Frank O'Reilly was extremely helpful. And I appreciate everyone at the National Park Service's National Battlefield sites and monuments whose work and commitment preserve our history.

I have walked many battlefields and wandered many back roads in Virginia while writing this book, to get the feel. And I have drawn information from many books in an effort to hew as close to the facts of Jackson's story and the war as possible. These books include:

Allen, Randale & Bohannon, Keith S., Editors, *Campaigning with "Old Stonewall" Confederate Captain Ujanirtus Allen's Letters to His Wife*, Louisiana State University Press, Baton Rouge, 1998

Anderson, Paul Christopher, *Blood Image, Turner Ashby in the Civil War and the Southern Mind*, Louisiana State University Press, Baton Rouge, 2002

Bean, W.G., *Stonewall's Man, Sandie Pendleton*, University of North Carolina Press, Chapel Hill, 1959

Chambers, Lenoir, *Stonewall Jackson and the Virginia Military Institute, The Lexington Years*, Historic Lexington Foundation, Lexington, Virginia, 1959

Colt, Margaretta Barton, *Defend the Valley, A Shenandoah Family in the Civil War*, Crown Publishers, Inc., New York, 1994

Cooke, John Esten, *The Life of Stonewall Jackson*, Charles B. Richardson, New York, 1864

Coulling, Mary Price, *Margaret Junkin Preston, a Biography*, John F. Blair, Winston-Salem, 1993

Dabney, R.L., *Life and Campaigns of Lieut. Gen. T.J. (Stonewall) Jackson*, Sprinkle Publications, Harrisonburg, Virginia, 1983, first published 1865

Douglas, Henry Kyd, *I Rode With Stonewall*, University of North Carolina Press, Chapel Hill, 1968, first published 1899

Ecelbarger, Gary L., *"We Are In For It!" The First Battle of Kernstown*, White Mane Publishing Company, Inc., Shippensburg, Pennsylvania, 1997

Foote, Shelby, *The Civil War, A Narrative*, Random House, New York, 1958

Furgurson, Ernest B., *Chancellorsville 1863, The Souls of the Brave*, Alfred A. Knopf, New York, 1992

Gallagher, Gary W., Editor, *Chancellorsville, The Battle and Its Aftermath*, University of North Carolina Press, Chapel Hill, 1996

Greene, A. Wilson, *Whatever You Resolve To Be, Essays on Stonewall Jackson*, Butternut and Blue, Baltimore, 1992

Happel, Ralph, *The Last Days of Jackson*, Eastern National Park and Monument Association, Richmond, 1971

Hassler, William Woods, *A.P. Hill, Lee's Forgotten General*, University of North Carolina Press, Chapel Hill, 1962

Henderson, Col. G.F.R., *Stonewall Jackson and the American Civil War*, The Blue and Grey Press, Seacaucus, New Jersey, 1987

Hotchkiss, Jedediah, *Make Me A Map of the Valley, The Civil War Journal of Stonewall Jackson's Topographer*, Southern Methodist University Press, Dallas, 1973

Jackson, Mary Anna, *Memoirs of "Stonewall Jackson, By His Widow*, Morningside, Dayton, Ohio, 1993, first published 1892

Kegel, James A., *North with Lee and Jackson*, Stackpole Books, Mechanicsburg, Pennsylvania, 1996

Krick, Robert K., *Conquering the Valley, Stonewall Jackson at Port Republic*, William Morrow and Company, Inc., New York, 1996

Mahon, Michael G., *The Shenandoah Valley 1861-1865*, Stackpole Books, Mechanicsburg, Pennsylvania, 1999

Martin, David G., *Jackson's Valley Campaign*, Combined Books, Pennsylvania, 1988

Novak, Marian and David, Editors, *Stonewall, Memories From the Ranks*, Signal Tree Publications, Livermore, Maine and Rockbridge Baths, Virginia, 1998

Opie, John N., *A Rebel Cavalryman*, Morningside, Dayton, Ohio, 1997, first published 1899.

Parrish, T. Michael, *Richard Taylor, Soldier Prince of Dixie*, University of North Carolina Press, Chapel Hill, 1992

Pfanz, Donald C., *Richard S. Ewell, A Soldier's Life,* University of North Carolina Press, Chapel Hill, 1998

Poague, William Thomas, *Gunner with Stonewall,* University of Nebraska Press, Lincoln, 1998, first published 1957

Robertson, James I. Jr., Editor, *John O. Casler's Four Years in the Stonewall Brigade,* Morningside, Dayton, Ohio, 1971, first published 1893

Robertson, James I. Jr., *The Stonewall Brigade,* Louisiana State University Press, Baton Rouge, 1963

Robertson, James I. Jr., *Stonewall Jackson, The Man, The Soldier, The Legend,* MacMillan Publishing, USA, New York, 1997

Schildt, John W., *Stonewall Jackson and the Preachers,* McClain Printing Company, Parson, West Virginia, 1982

Schildt, John W., *Stonewall Jackson Day by Day,* Antietam Publications, Chewsville, Maryland, 1980

Sears, Stephen W., *Chancellorsville,* Houghton Mifflin Company, New York, 1996

Shaw, Maurice F., *Stonewall Jackson's Surgeon, Hunter Holmes McGuire, a Biography,* H. E. Howard, Inc., Lynchburg, Virginia, 1993

Sutherland, Daniel E., *Fredericksburg & Chancellorsville, The Dare Mark Campaign,* University of Nebraska Press, 1998

Tanner, Robert G., *Stonewall in the Valley,* Doubleday & Company, Inc., Garden City, New York, 1976

Tate, Allen, *Stonewall Jackson, the Good Soldier,* J. S. Sanders & Company, Nashville, 1991, originally published in 1928

Turner, Charles W., Editor, *Ted Barclay, Liberty Hall Volunteers, Letters From the Stonewall Brigade,* Rockbridge Publishing Company, Berryville, Virginia, 1992

I have also drawn information from many articles in the Southern Historical Society Papers both in manuscript and CD-ROM, from the *Confederate Veteran*, and from the Official Records of the Union and Confederate Armies on CD-ROM.

0-595-31756-1